David Brin is the acclaimed Hugo and Nebula award-winning author of eight novels and two collections of short stories. He has a doctorate in astrophysics, and has been a consultant to NASA and a graduate-level physics professor. He lives in California.

Otherness

DAVID BRIN

ORBIT

An *Orbit* Book

First published in Great Britain by Orbit in 1994
This edition published by Orbit in 1995

A CIP catalogue record for this book
is available from the British Library.

ISBN 1 85723 310 7

Printed in England by Clays Ltd, St Ives plc

Orbit
A Division of
Little, Brown and Company (UK)
Brettenham House
Lancaster Place
London WC2E 7EN

To Ben, our twenty-first-century hero

Contents

COSMOS

OTHERNESS

TRANSITIONS

The Giving Plague

1

You think you're going to get me, don't you? Well, you've got another think coming, 'cause I'm ready for you.

That's why there's a forged card in my wallet saying my blood group is AB Negative, and a MedicAlert tag warning that I'm allergic to penicillin, aspirin, and phenylalanine. Another one states that I'm a practising, devout Christian Scientist. All these tricks ought to slow you down when the time comes, as it's sure to, sometime soon.

Even if it makes the difference between living and dying, there's just no way I'll let anyone stick a transfusion needle into my arm. Never. Not with the blood supply in the state it's in.

And anyway, I've got antibodies. So you just stay the hell away from me, ALAS. I won't be your patsy. I won't be your vector.

I know your weaknesses, you see. You're a fragile, if subtle, devil. Unlike TARP, you can't bear exposure to air or heat or cold or acid or alkali. Blood-to-blood,

that's your only route. And what need had you of
any other? You thought you'd evolved the perfect
technique, didn't you?

What was it Leslie Adgeson called you? The perfect
master? The paragon of viruses?

I remember long ago when HIV, the AIDS virus,
had everyone so impressed with its subtlety and effec-
tiveness of design. But compared with you, HIV is just
a crude butcher, isn't it? A maniac with a chainsaw, a
blunderer that kills its hosts and relies for transmission
on habits humans can, with some effort, get under
control. Oh, old HIV had its tricks, but compared
with you? An amateur!

Rhinoviruses and flu are clever, too. They're profligate, and they mutate rapidly. Long ago they learnt
how to make their hosts drip and wheeze and sneeze,
so the victims spread the misery in all directions. Flu
viruses are also a lot smarter than AIDS 'cause they
don't generally kill their hosts, just make 'em miserable
while they hack and spray and inflict fresh infections
on their neighbours.

Oh, Les Adgeson was always accusing me of
anthropomorphising our subjects. Whenever he came
into my part of the lab, and found me cursing some
damned intransigent leucophage in rich, Tex-Mex
invective, he'd react predictably. I can just picture
him now, raising one eyebrow, commenting dryly in
his Winchester accent.

'The virus cannot hear you, Forry. It isn't sentient,
nor even alive, strictly speaking. It's little more than
a packet of genes in a protein case, after all.'

'Yeah, Les,' I'd answer. 'But *selfish* genes! Given
half a chance, they'll take over a human cell, force it
to make armies of new viruses, then burst it apart as
they escape to attack other cells. They may not think.
All that behaviour may have evolved by blind chance.

But doesn't it all *feel* as if it was planned? As if the nasty little things were *guided*, somehow, by somebody out to make us miserable . . . ? Out to make us die?'

'Oh, come now, Forry,' he would smile at my New World ingenuousness. 'You wouldn't be in this field if you didn't find phages beautiful in their own way.'

Good old, smug, sanctimonious Les. He never did figure out that viruses fascinated me for quite another reason. In their rapacious insatiability I saw a simple, distilled purity of ambition that exceeded even my own. The fact that it was mindless did little to ease my mind. I've always imagined we humans overrated brains, anyway.

We'd first met when Les visited Austin on sabbatical, some years before. He'd had the Boy Genius rep even then, and naturally I played up to him. He invited me to join him back in Oxford, so there I was, having regular amiable arguments over the meaning of disease while the English rain dripped desultorily on the rhododendrons outside.

Les Adgeson. Him with his artsy friends and his pretensions at philosophy – Les was all the time talking about the elegance and beauty of our nasty little subjects. But he didn't fool me. I knew he was just as crazy Nobel-mad as the rest of us. Just as obsessed with the chase, searching for that piece of the Life Puzzle, that bit leading to more grants, more lab space, more techs, more prestige . . . leading to money, status and, maybe eventually, Stockholm.

He claimed not to be interested in such things. But he was a smoothy, all right. How else, in the midst of the Thatcher massacre of British science, did his lab keep expanding? And yet, he kept up the pretence.

'Viruses have their good side,' Les kept saying. 'Sure, they often kill, in the beginning. All new pathogens start that way. But eventually, one of two things happens.

Either humanity evolves defences to eliminate the
threat or . . .'

Oh, he loved those dramatic pauses.

'*Or?*' I'd prompt him, as required.

'Or we come to an accommodation, a compromise
. . . even an alliance.'

That's what Les always talked about. *Symbiosis*.
He loved to quote Margulis and Thomas, and even
Lovelock, for pity's sake! His respect even for vicious,
sneaky brutes like the HIV was downright scary.

'See how it actually incorporates itself right into the
DNA of its victims?' he would muse. 'Then it waits,
until the victim is later attacked by some *other* disease
pathogen. Then the host's T-Cells prepare to replicate,
to drive off the invader, only now some cells' chemical
machinery is taken over by the new DNA, and instead
of two new T-Cells, a plethora of new AIDS viruses
results.'

'So?' I answered. 'Except that it's a retrovirus, that's
the way nearly all viruses work.'

'Yes, but think ahead, Forry. Imagine what's going
to happen when, inevitably, the AIDS virus infects
someone whose genetic make-up makes him invulnerable!'

'What, you mean his antibody reactions are fast
enough to stop it? Or his T-Cells repel invasion?'

Oh, Les used to sound so damn patronising when
he got excited. 'No, no, think!' he urged. 'I mean
invulnerable *after* infection. *After* the viral genes have
incorporated into his chromosomes. Only in this individual, certain *other* genes *prevent* the new DNA from
triggering viral synthesis. No new viruses are made.
No cellular disruption. The person *is* invulnerable. But
now he has all this new DNA . . .'

'In just a few cells—'

'Yes. But suppose one of these is a sex cell. Then

suppose he fathers a child with that gamete. Now *every* one of that child's cells may contain both the trait of invulnerability *and* the new viral genes! Think about it, Forry. You now have a new type of human being! One who cannot be killed by AIDS. And yet he has all the AIDS genes, can make all those strange, marvellous proteins . . . Oh, most of them will be unexpressed or useless, of course. But now this child's genome, and his descendants', contain more *variety* . . .'

I often wondered, when he got carried away, this way. Did he actually believe he was explaining this to me for the first time? Much as the Brits respect American science, they do tend to assume we're slackers when it comes to the philosophical side. But I'd seen his interest heading in this direction weeks back, and had carefully done some extra reading.

'You mean like the genes responsible for some types of inheritable cancers?' I asked, sarcastically. 'There's evidence some oncogenes were originally inserted into the human genome by viruses, just as you suggest. Those who inherit the trait for rheumatoid arthritis may also have gotten their gene that way.'

'Exactly. Those viruses themselves may be extinct, but their DNA lives on, in ours!'

'Right. And boy have human beings benefited!'

Oh, how I hated that smug expression he'd get. (It got wiped off his face eventually, didn't it?)

Les picked up a piece of chalk and drew a figure on the blackboard.

HARMLESS→KILLER!→SURVIVABLE
ILLNESS→INCONVENIENCE→HARMLESS

'Here's the classic way of looking at how a host species interacts with a new pathogen, especially a

virus. Each arrow, of course, represents a stage of
mutation and adaptation selection.

'First, a new form of some previously harmless
micro-organism leaps from its prior host, say a monkey
species, over to a new one, say us. Of course, at the
beginning we have no adequate defences. It cuts
through us like syphilis did in Europe in the sixteenth
century, killing in days rather than years . . . in an orgy
of cell feeding that's really not a very efficient *modus* for
a pathogen. After all, only a gluttonous parasite kills
off its host so quickly.

'What follows, then, is a rough period for both host
and parasite as each struggles to adapt to the other.
It can be likened to warfare. Or, on the other hand,
it might be thought of as a sort of drawn-out process
of *negotiation*.'

I snorted in disgust. 'Mystical crap, Les. I'll concede
your chart; but the war analogy is the right one. That's
why they fund labs like this one. To come up with better
weapons for our side.'

'Hmm. Possibly. But sometimes the process does
look different, Forry.' He turned and drew another
chart.

HARMLESS→KILLER!→SURVIVABLE ILLNESS→INCONVENIENCE→CLUMSY INCORPORATION→BENEFICIAL INCORPORATION

'You can see that this chart is the same as the
other, right up to the point where the original disease
disappears.'

'Or goes into hiding.'

'Surely. As e coli took refuge in our innards. Doubt-
less long ago the ancestors of e coli killed a great
many of our ancestors before eventually becoming the

beneficial symbionts they are now, helping us digest our food.

'The same applies to viruses, I'd wager. Heritable cancers and rheumatoid arthritis are just temporary awkwardnesses. Eventually, those genes will be comfortably incorporated. They'll be part of the genetic diversity that prepares us to meet challenges ahead.

'Why, I'd wager a large portion of our present genes came about in such a way, entering our cells first as invaders . . .'

Crazy sonovabitch. Fortunately he didn't try to lead the lab's research effort too far to the right on his magic diagram. Our Boy Genius was plenty savvy about the funding agencies. He knew they weren't interested in paying us to prove we're all partly descended from viruses. They wanted, and wanted *badly*, progress on ways to fight viral infections themselves.

So Les concentrated his team on vectors.

Yeah, you viruses need vectors, don't you. I mean, if you kill a guy, you've got to have a liferaft, so you can desert the ship you've sunk, so you can cross over to some *new* hapless victim. Same applies if the host proves tough, and fights you off – gotta move on. Always movin' on.

Hell, even if you've made peace with a human body, like Les suggested, you still want to spread, don't you? Bigtime colonisers, you tiny beasties.

Oh, I know. It's just natural selection. Those bugs that accidentally find a good vector spread. Those that don't, don't. But it's so eerie. Sometimes it sure *feels* purposeful . . .

So the flu makes us sneeze. Salmonella gives us diarrhoea. Smallpox causes pustules which dry, flake off and blow away to be inhaled by the patient's loved ones. All good ways to jump ship. To colonise.

Who knows? Did some past virus cause a swelling of

the lips that made us want to kiss? Heh. Maybe that's
a case of Les's 'benign incorporation' . . . we retain the
trait, long after the causative pathogen went extinct!
What a concept.

So our lab got this big grant to study vectors. Which
is how Les found you, ALAS. He drew this big chart
covering all the possible ways an infection might leap
from person to person, and set us about checking all
of them, one by one.

For himself he reserved straight blood-to-blood infection. There were reasons for that.

First off, Les was an altruist, see. He was concerned
about all the panic and unfounded rumours spreading
about Britain's blood supply. Some people were putting
off necessary surgery. There was talk of starting over
here what some rich folk in the States had begun doing
– stockpiling their own blood in silly, expensive efforts
to avoid having to use the blood banks if they ever
needed hospitalisation.

All that bothered Les. But even worse was the fact
that lots of potential donors were shying away from
giving blood because of some stupid rumours that you
could get infected that way.

Hell, nobody ever caught anything from *giving* blood
. . . nothing except maybe a little dizziness and perhaps
a zit or spot from all the biscuits and sweet tea they
feed you afterwards. And as for contracting HIV from
receiving blood, well, the new antibodies tests soon had
that problem under control. Still, the stupid rumours
spread.

A nation has to have confidence in its blood supply.
Les wanted to eliminate all those silly fears once and
for all, with one definitive study. But that wasn't the
only reason he wanted the blood-to-blood vector for
himself.

'Sure, there are some nasty things like AIDS that use

that vector. But that's also where I might find the older ones,' he said, excitedly. 'The viruses that have *almost* finished the process of becoming benign. The ones that have been so well selected that they keep a low profile, and hardly inconvenience their hosts at all. Maybe I can even find one that's commensal! One that actually *helps* the human body.'

'An undiscovered human commensal,' I sniffed doubtfully.

'And why not? If there's no visible disease, why would anyone have ever looked for it! This could open up a whole new field, Forry!'

In spite of myself, I was impressed. It was how he got to be known as a Boy Genius, after all, this flash of half-crazy insight. How he managed not to have it snuffed out of him at Oxbridge, I'll never know, but it was one reason why I'd attached myself to him and his lab, and wrangled mighty hard to get my name attached to his papers.

So I kept watch over his work. It sounded so dubious, so damn stupid. And I knew it just might bear fruit, in the end.

That's why I was ready when Les invited me along to a conference down in Bloomsbury, one day. The colloquium itself was routine, but I could tell he was near to bursting with news. Afterwards we walked down Charing Cross Road to a pizza place, one far enough from the University area to be sure there'd be no colleagues anywhere within earshot – just the pre-theatre crowd, waiting till opening time down at Leicester Square.

Les breathlessly swore me to secrecy. He needed a confidant, you see, and I was only too happy to comply.

'I've been interviewing a lot of blood donors lately,' he told me after we'd ordered. 'It seems that while some people have been scared off from donating, that has been largely made up by increased contributions by a central core of regulars.'

'Sounds good,' I said. And I meant it. I had no objection to there being an adequate blood supply. Back in Austin I was pleased to see others go to the Red Cross van, just so long as nobody asked me to contribute. I had neither the time nor the interest, so I got out of it by telling everybody I'd had malaria.

'I found one interesting fellow, Forry. Seems he started donating back when he was twenty-five, during the Blitz. Must have contributed thirty-five, forty gallons by now.'

I did a quick mental calculation. 'Wait a minute. He's got to be past the age limit by now.'

'Exactly right! He admitted the truth, when he was assured of confidentiality. Seems he didn't want to stop donating when he reached sixty-five. He's a hardy old fellow . . . had a spot of surgery a few years back, but he's in quite decent shape, overall. So, right after his local Gallon Club threw a big retirement party for him, he actually moved across the country and registered at a new blood bank, giving a false name and a younger age!'

'Kinky. But it sounds harmless enough. I'd guess he just likes to feel needed. Bet he flirts with the nurses and enjoys the free food . . . sort of a bi-monthly party he can always count on, with friendly, appreciative people.'

Hey, just because I'm a selfish bastard doesn't mean I can't extrapolate the behaviour of altruists. Like most other user-types, I've got a good instinct for the sort of motivations that drive suckers. People like me need to know such things.

'That's what I thought too, at first,' Les said, nodding. 'I found a few more like him, and decided to call them "addicts". At first I never connected them with the other group, the one I named "converts".'

'Converts?'

'Yes, converts. People who suddenly become blood donors – get this – very soon after they've recovered from surgery themselves!'

'Maybe they're paying off part of their hospital bills that way?'

'Mmm, not really. We have nationalised health, remember? And even for private patients, that might account for the first few donations only.'

'Gratitude, then?' An alien emotion to me, but I understood it, in principle.

'Perhaps. Some people might have their consciousness raised after a close brush with death, and decide to become better citizens. After all, half an hour at a blood bank, a few times a year, is a small inconvenience in exchange for . . .'

Sanctimonious twit. Of course he was a donor. Les went on and on about civic duty and such until the waitress arrived with our pizza and two fresh beers. That shut him up for a moment. But when she left, he leaned forward, eyes shining.

'But no, Forry. It wasn't bill-paying, or even gratitude. Not for some of them, at least. More had happened to these people than having their consciousness raised. They were converts, Forry. They began joining Gallon Clubs, and more! It seems almost as if, in each case, a personality change had taken place.'

'What do you mean?'

'I mean that a significant percentage of those who have had major surgery during the last five years seem to have changed their entire set of social attitudes! Beyond becoming blood donors, they've increased their contributions to charity, joined the Parent–Teacher organisations and Boy Scout troops, become active in Greenpeace and Save the Children . . .'

'The point, Les. What's your point?'

'My point?' He shook his head. 'Frankly, some of these people were behaving like addicts . . . like converted addicts to altruism. That's when it occurred to me, Forry, that what we might have here was a new vector.'

He said it as simply as that. Naturally I looked at him, blankly.

'A vector!' he whispered, urgently. 'Forget about typhus, or smallpox, or flu. They're rank amateurs! Wallies who give the show away with all their sneezing and flaking and shitting. To be sure, AIDS uses blood and sex, but it's so damned savage, it forced us to become aware of it, to develop tests, to begin the long, slow process of isolating it. But ALAS—'

'Alas?'

'A-L-A-S.' He grinned. 'It's what I've named the new virus I've isolated, Forry. It stands for "Acquired Lavish Altruism Syndrome". How do you like it?'

'Hate it. Are you trying to tell me that there's a virus that affects the human mind? And in such a complicated way?' I was incredulous and, at the same time, scared spitless. I've always had this superstitious feeling about viruses and vectors. Les really had me spooked now.

'No, of course not,' he laughed. 'But consider a simpler possibility. What if some virus one day stumbled on a way to make people enjoy giving blood?'

I guess I only blinked then, unable to give him any other reaction.

'Think, Forry! Think about that old man I spoke of earlier. He told me that every two months or so, just before he'd be allowed to donate again, he tends to feel "all thick inside". The discomfort only goes away after the next donation!'

I blinked again. 'And you're saying that each time he gives blood, he's actually serving his parasite, providing it with a vector into new hosts . . .'

'The new hosts being those who survive surgery because the hospital gave them fresh blood, all because our old man was so generous, yes! They're infected! Only this is a subtle virus, not a greedy bastard, like AIDS, or even the flu. It keeps a low profile. Who knows, maybe it's even reached a level of commensalism with its hosts – attacking invading organisms for them, or . . .'

He saw the look on my face and waved his hands. 'All right, far-fetched, I know. But think about it! Because there are no disease symptoms, nobody has ever looked for this virus, until now.'

He's isolated it, I realised suddenly. And, knowing instantly what this thing could mean, career-wise, I was already scheming, wondering how to get my name on to his paper when he published this. So absorbed was I that, for a few moments, I lost track of his words.

'. . . And so now we get to the interesting part. You see, what's a normal, selfish Tory-voter going to think when he finds himself suddenly wanting to go down to the blood bank as often as they'll let him?'

'Um,' I shook my head. 'That he's been bewitched? Hypnotised?'

'Nonsense!' Les snorted. 'That's not how human psychology works. No, we tend to do lots of things without knowing why. We need excuses, though, so we rationalise! If an obvious reason for our behaviour isn't readily available, we invent one, preferably one that helps us think better of ourselves. Ego is powerful stuff, my friend.'

Hey, I thought. Don't teach your grandmother to suck eggs.

'Altruism,' I said aloud. 'They find themselves rushing regularly to the blood bank. So they rationalise that it's because they're good people . . . They become proud of it. Brag about it . . .'

'You've got it,' Les said. 'And because they're proud, even sanctimonious, about their new-found generosity, they tend to extend it, to bring it into other parts of their lives!'

I whispered in hushed awe. 'An altruism virus! Jesus, Les, when we announce this . . .'

I stopped when I saw his sudden frown, and instantly thought it was because I'd used that word, 'we'. I should have known better, of course. For Les was always more than willing to share the credit. No, his reservation was far more serious than that.

'Not yet, Forry. We can't publish this yet.'

I shook my head. 'Why not! This is big, Les! It proves much of what you've been saying all along, about symbiosis and all that. There could even be a Nobel in it!'

I'd been gauche, and spoken aloud of The Ultimate. But he did not even seem to notice. Damn. If only Les had been like most biologists, driven more than anything else by the lure of Stockholm. But no. You see, Les was a natural. A natural altruist.

It was his fault, you see. Him and his damn virtue, they drove me to first contemplate what I next decided to do.

'Don't you see, Forry? If we publish, they'll develop an antibody test for the ALAS virus. Donors carrying it will be barred from the blood banks, just like those carrying AIDS and syphilis and hepatitis. And that would be incredibly cruel torture to those poor addicts and carriers.'

'Screw the carriers!' I almost shouted. Several pizza patrons glanced my way. With a desperate effort I brought my voice down. 'Look, Les, the carriers will be classified as diseased, won't they? So they'll go under doctor's care. And if all it takes to make them feel better is to bleed them regularly, well, then we'll give them pet leeches!'

Les smiled. 'Clever. But that's not the only, or even my main, reason, Forry. No, I'm not going to publish yet, and that is final. I just can't allow anybody to stop this disease. It's got to spread, to become an epidemic. A pandemic.'

I stared, and upon seeing that look in his eyes, I knew that Les was more than an altruist. He had caught that specially insidious of all human ailments, the Messiah Complex. Les wanted to save the world.

'Don't you see?' he said urgently, with the fervour of a proselyte. 'Selfishness and greed are destroying the planet, Forry! But nature always finds a way, and this time symbiosis may be giving us our last chance, a final opportunity to become better people, to learn to cooperate before it's too late!

'The things we're most proud of, our prefrontal lobes, those bits of grey matter above the eyes which make us so much smarter than beasts, what good have they done us, Forry? Not a hell of a lot. We aren't going to think our way out of the crises of the twentieth century. Or, at least, thought alone won't do it. We need something else, as well.

'And Forry, I'm convinced that something else is ALAS. We've got to keep this secret, at least until it's so well established in the population that there's no turning back!'

I swallowed. 'How long? How long do you want to wait? Until it starts affecting voting patterns? Until after the next election?'

He shrugged. 'Oh, at least that long. Five years. Possibly seven. You see, the virus tends to only get into people who've recently had surgery, and they're generally older. Fortunately, they also are often influential. Just the sort who now vote Tory . . .'

He went on. And on. I listened with half an ear, but already I had come to that fateful realisation. A seven-year wait for a goddamn co-authorship would make this discovery next to useless to my career, to my ambitions.

Of course I could blow the secret on Les, now that I knew of it. But that would only embitter him, and he'd easily take all the credit for the discovery anyway. People tend to remember innovators, not whistle-blowers.

We paid our bill and walked towards Charing Cross Station, where we could catch the tube to Paddington, and from there the train to Oxford. Along the way we ducked out of a sudden downpour at a streetside ice-cream vendor. While we waited, I bought us both cones. I remember quite clearly that he had strawberry. I had a raspberry ice.

While Les absent-mindedly talked on about his research plans, a small pink smudge coloured the corner of his mouth. I pretended to listen, but already my mind had turned to other things, nascent plans and earnest scenarios for committing murder.

2

It would be the perfect crime, of course.

Those movie detectives are always going on about 'motive, means and opportunity'. Well, motive I had in plenty, but it was one so far-fetched, so obscure, that it would surely never occur to anybody.

Means? Hell, I worked in a business rife with means. There were poisons and pathogens galore. We're a very careful profession, but, well, accidents do happen . . . The same holds for opportunity.

There was a rub, of course. Such was Boy Genius's reputation that, even if I did succeed in knobbling him, I didn't dare come out immediately with my own announcement. Damn him, everyone would just assume it was his work anyway, or his 'leadership' here at the lab, at least, that led to the discovery of ALAS. And besides, too much fame for me right after his demise might lead someone to suspect a motive.

So, I realised, Les was going to get his delay, after all. Maybe not seven years, but three or four perhaps, during which I'd move back to the States, start a separate line of work, then subtly guide my own research to cover methodically all the bases Les had so recently flown over in flashes of inspiration. I wasn't happy about the delay, but at the end of that time, it would look entirely like my own work. No co-authorship for Forry on this one, nossir!

The beauty of it was that nobody would ever think of connecting me with the tragic death of my colleague and friend, years before. After all, did not his demise set me back in my career, temporarily? 'Ah, if only poor Les had lived to see your success!' my competitors would say, suppressing jealous bile as they watched me pack for Stockholm.

Of course none of this appeared on my face or in my words. We both had our normal work to do. But almost every day I also put in long extra hours helping Les in 'our' secret project. In its own way it was an exhilarating time, and Les was lavish in his praise of the slow, dull, but methodical way I fleshed out some of his ideas.

I made my arrangements slowly, knowing Les was

in no hurry. Together we gathered data. We isolated, and even crystallised, the virus, got X-ray diffractions, did epidemiological studies, all in strictest secrecy.

'Amazing!' Les would cry out, as he uncovered the way the ALAS virus forced its hosts to feel their need to 'give'. He'd wax eloquent, effusive over elegant mechanisms which he ascribed to random selection but which I could not help superstitiously attributing to some incredibly insidious form of intelligence. The more subtle and effective we found its techniques to be, the more admiring Les became, and the more I found myself loathing those little packets of RNA and protein.

The fact that the virus seemed so harmless – Les thought even commensal – only made me hate it more. It made me glad of what I had planned. Glad that I was going to stymie Les in his scheme to give ALAS free rein.

I was going to save humanity from this would-be puppet master. True, I'd delay my warning to suit my own purposes, but the warning would come, none-theless, and sooner than my unsuspecting compatriot planned.

Little did Les know that he was doing background for work I'd take credit for. Every flash of insight, his every 'Eureka!', was stored away in my private notebook, beside my own columns of boring data. Meanwhile, I sorted through all the means at my disposal.

Finally, I selected for my agent a particularly viru-lent strain of Dengue Fever.

3

There's an old saying we have in Texas. 'A chicken is just an egg's way of makin' more eggs.'

To a biologist, familiar with all those Latinised-Graecificated words, this saying has a much more 'posh' version. Humans are 'zygotes', made up of diploid cells containing forty-six paired chromosomes . . . except for our haploid sex cells, or 'gametes'. Males' gametes are sperm and females' are eggs, each containing only twenty-three chromosomes.

So biologists say, 'A zygote is only a gamete's way of making more gametes.'

Clever, eh? But it does point out just how hard it is, in nature, to pin down a Primal Cause . . . some centre to the puzzle, against which everything else can be calibrated. I mean, which *does* come first, the chicken or the egg?

'Man is the measure of all things,' goes another wise old saying. Oh yeah? Tell that to a modern feminist.

A guy I once knew, who used to read science fiction, told me about this story he'd seen, in which it turned out that the whole and entire purpose of humanity, brains and all, was to be the organism that built starships so that *house flies* could migrate out and colonise the galaxy.

But that idea's nothing compared with what Les Adgeson believed. He spoke of the human animal as if he were describing a veritable United Nations. From the e coli in our guts, to tiny commensal mites that clean our eyelashes for us, to the mitochondria that energise our cells, all the way to the contents of our very DNA . . . Les saw it all as a great big hive of compromise, negotiation, *symbiosis*. Most of the contents of our chromosomes came from past invaders, he contended.

Symbiosis? The picture he created in my mind was one of minuscule puppeteers, all yanking and jerking at us with their protein strings, making us marionettes dance to their own tunes, to their own nasty, selfish little agendas.

And you, *you* were the worst! Like most cynics, I had always maintained a secret faith in human nature. Yes, most people are pigs. I've always known that. And while I may be a user, at least I'm honest enough to admit it.

But deep down, we users count on the sappy, astonishing generosity, the mysterious, puzzling altruism of those others, the kind, inexplicably decent folk ... those we superficially sneer at in contempt, but secretly hold in awe.

Then you came along, damn you. You *make* people behave that way. There is no mystery left, after you get finished. No corner remaining impenetrable to cynicism. Damn, how I came to hate you!

As I came to hate Leslie Adgeson. I made my plans, schemed my brilliant campaign against both of you. In those last days of innocence I felt oh, so savagely determined. So deliciously decisive and in control of my own destiny.

In the end it was anticlimactic. I didn't have time to finish my preparations, to arrange that little trap, that sharp bit of glass dipped in just the right mixture of deadly micro-organisms. For CAPUC arrived then, just before I could exercise my option as a murderer.

CAPUC changed everything.

Catastrophic Auto-immune PUlmonary Collapse ... acronym for the horror that made AIDS look like a minor irritant. And in the beginning it appeared unstoppable. Its vectors were completely unknown and the causative agent defied isolation for so long.

This time it was no easily identifiable group that came down with the new plague, though it concentrated upon the industrialised world. Schoolchildren in some areas seemed particularly vulnerable. In other places it was secretaries and postal workers.

Naturally, all the major epidemiology labs got

involved. Les predicted the pathogen would turn out
to be something akin to the prions which cause shingles
in sheep, and certain plant diseases . . . a pseudo life
form even simpler than a virus and even harder to track
down. It was an heretical, minority view, until the CDC
in Atlanta decided out of desperation to try his theories
out, and found the very dominant viroids Les predicted
– mixed in with the *glue* used to seal paper milk cartons,
envelopes, postage stamps.

Les was a hero, of course. Most of us in the labs
were. After all, we'd been the first line of defence. Our
own casualty rate had been ghastly.

For a while, funerals and other public gatherings
were discouraged. But an exception was made for Les.
The procession behind his cortege was a mile long. I
was asked to deliver the eulogy. And when they pleaded
with me to take over at the lab, I agreed.

So naturally I tended to forget all about ALAS. The
war against CAPUC took everything society had. And
while I may be selfish, even a rat can tell when it makes
more sense to join in the fight to save a sinking ship . . .
especially when there's no other port in sight.

We learned how to combat CAPUC, eventually.
It involved drugs, and a vaccine based on reversed
antibodies force-grown in the patient's own marrow
after he's given a dangerous overdose of a Vanadium
compound I found by trial and error. It worked, most of
the time, but the victims suffered great stress and often
required a special regime of whole blood transfusions
to get across the most dangerous phase.

Blood banks were stretched even thinner than before.
Only now the public responded generously, as in time
of war. I should not have been surprised when
survivors, after their recovery, volunteered by their
thousands. But, of course, I'd forgotten about ALAS
by then, hadn't I?

We beat back CAPUC. Its vector proved too unreliable, too easily interrupted once we'd figured it out. The poor little viroid never had a chance to get to Les's 'negotiation' stage. Oh well, those are the breaks.

I got all sorts of citations I didn't deserve. The King gave me a KBE for personally saving the Prince of Wales. I had dinner at the White House.

Big deal.

The world had a respite, after that. CAPUC had scared people, it seemed, into a new spirit of cooperation. I should have been suspicious, of course. But soon I'd moved over to WHO, and had all sorts of administrative responsibilities in the Final Campaign on Malnutrition.

By that time, I had almost entirely forgotten about ALAS.

I forgot about you, didn't I? Oh, the years passed, my star rose, I became famous, respected, revered. I didn't get my Nobel in Stockholm. Ironically, I picked it up in Oslo. Fancy that. Just shows you can fool anybody.

And yet, I don't think I ever *really* forgot about you, ALAS, not at the back of my mind.

Peace treaties were signed. Citizens of the industrial nations voted temporary cuts in their standards of living in order to fight poverty and save the environment. Suddenly, it seemed, we'd all grown up. Other cynics, guys I'd gotten drunk with in the past – and shared dark premonitions about the inevitable fate of filthy, miserable humanity – all gradually deserted the faith, as pessimists seem wont to do when the world turns bright – too bright for even the cynical to dismiss as a mere passing phase on the road to Hell.

And yet, my own brooding remained unblemished. For subconsciously I *knew* it wasn't real.

Then, the third Mars expedition returned to worldwide adulation, and brought home with them TARP.

And that was when we found out just how friendly our home-grown pathogens really had been, all along.

4

Late at night, stumbling in exhaustion from overwork, I would stop at Les's portrait where I'd ordered it hung in the hall opposite my office door, and stand there cursing him and his damned theories of *symbiosis*.

Picture mankind ever reaching a symbiotic association with TARP! That really would be something. Imagine, Les, all those *alien* genes, added to our heritage, to our rich human diversity!

Only TARP did not seem to be much interested in 'negotiation'. Its wooing was rough, deadly. And its vector was the wind.

The world looked to me, and to my peers, for salvation. In spite of all my successes and high renown, though, I knew myself for a second-best fraud. I would always know – no matter how much they thanked and praised me – who had been better than me by light years.

Again and again, deep into the night, I would pore through the notes Leslie Adgeson had left behind, seeking inspiration, seeking hope. That's when I stumbled across ALAS, once more.

I found *you* again.

Oh, you made us behave better, all right. At least a quarter of the human race must contain your DNA by now, ALAS. And in their new-found, inexplicable, rationalised altruism, they set the tone followed by all the others.

Everybody behaves so damned *well* in the present calamity. They help each other, they succour the sick, they all *give* so.

Funny thing, though. If you hadn't made us all so bloody cooperative, we'd probably never have made it to bloody Mars, would we? Or if we had, there'd have still been enough paranoia around so we'd have maintained a decent quarantine.

But then, I remind myself, you don't *plan*, do you? You're just a bundle of RNA, packed inside a protein coat, with an incidentally, accidentally acquired trait of making humans want to donate blood. That's all you are, right? So you had no way of knowing that by making us 'better' you were also setting us up for TARP, did you? Did you?

5

We've got some palliatives, now. A few new techniques seem to be doing some good. The latest news is great, in fact. Apparently, we'll be able to save maybe fifteen per cent or so of the children. Up to half of those may even be fertile. If our luck holds.

That's for nations who've had a lot of racial mixing. Heterozygosity and genetic diversity seem to breed better resistance. Those people with 'pure', narrow bloodlines will be harder to save, but then, racism has its inevitable price.

Too bad about the great apes and horses, but then, at least all this will give the rain forests a chance to grow back.

Meanwhile, everybody perseveres. There is no panic, as one reads about happening in past plagues. We've grown up at last, it seems. We help each other.

But I carry a card in my wallet saying I'm a Christian

Scientist, and that my blood group is AB Negative, and that I'm allergic to nearly everything. Transfusions are one of the treatments commonly used now, and I'm an important man. But I won't take blood.

I won't.

I *donate*, but I'll never take it. Not even when I drop.

You won't have me, ALAS. You won't.

I am a bad man. I suppose, all told, I've done more good than evil in my life, but that's incidental, a product of happenstance and the bizarre caprices of the world.

I have no control over the world, but I can make my own decisions, at least. As I make this one, now.

Down, out of my high research tower I've gone. Into the streets, where the teeming clinics fester and broil. That is where I work now. And it doesn't matter to me that I'm behaving no differently than anyone else today. They are all marionettes. They think they're acting altruistically, but I know they are your puppets, ALAS.

But I am a *man*, do you hear me? I make my own decisions.

Fever wracks my body now, as I drag myself from bed to bed, holding their hands when they stretch them out to me for comfort, doing what I can to ease their suffering, to save a few.

You'll not have me, ALAS.

This is what *I* choose to do.

Myth Number 21

Elvis roams the interstates in a big white cadillac.

It has to be him. Flywheel-bus and commuter-zep riders see plumes of dust trailing like rocket exhaust behind something too fast and glittery for the naked eye.

Squint though, and you might glimpse him from behind the wheel, steering with one wrist, fiddling the radio dial, then reaching for that always frosty can of beer. 'Thank you, honey,' he tells the blonde next to him as he steps on the accelerator.

Roar of V-8 power. Freedom-smell of gasoline. Clean wind blowing back his hair . . . Elvis hoots and lifts one arm to wave at all true Americans who still believe in him.

Chatty bit-zines run blurry pictures of him. 'Fakes!' claim those snooty tech types, ignored by the faithful who collect grand old TwenCen automobiles and polish them, saving ration coupons for that once-a-year spin, meeting at the nearest Graceland Shrine for a day of chrome and music and speed and glory.

They stop at ghostly, abandoned filling stations, checking for signs that he's been by. Some claim to find pumps freshly used, reading empty yet somehow reeking of high octane. Others point to black, bold tyre tracks, or claim his music can be heard in the coyotes' midnight serenade.

Elvis roams the open interstates in a big white cadillac. How else to explain the traces some have found, sparkling like faery dust across the fading yellow lines?

A pollen of happier days ... the glitter of rhinestones.

Story Notes

The preceding little fable, cribbed from my novel *Earth*, is an example of the super-short story, which some call a 'drabble'. Collections have been published in the 100- and 750-word categories, but my favourite length is precisely 250.

'The Giving Plague' was a reflection on the times, written as the first deadly pandemic of post-industrial society shattered our brief, blithe illusion that the old dangers were behind us. AIDS has transformed the way people look upon each other, the world, and life itself. The cruel ironies of disease and death were poignant for most of human history, when illness was a dark mystery. Now, as we unravel the genetic codes and begin looking our enemies in the face, so to speak, the paradoxes seem only to multiply. Symbiosis and genetic 'negotiation' are also contemplated as themes in a novel I wrote with Gregory Benford, *Heart of the Comet*.

One editor rejected 'The Giving Plague' because he thought it 'irresponsible to undermine confidence in the blood supply'. I leave it to the reader to compare that unique proposition to the tale itself, and decide which is more far-fetched. Fortunately, weighty matters of public policy remain unaffected by scary SF tales . . . even Hugo nominees.

Coming up next, 'Dr Pak's Preschool' seems a natural extrapolation of the *enrichment parenting* craze that's sweeping not only Japan, but yuppie America and elsewhere, as well. Having recently embarked on fatherhood, I know the temptations all too well.

'Detritus Affected' is about exploring vintages from ages past, and was inspired by news accounts concerning a new breed of archeologist.

This collection also features several of my published essays, gathered and reworked to express a theme which has fascinated me for some time, that of 'otherness'. The first appeared as a guest editorial in *Analog* magazine, some years back, and was reprinted in *Whole Earth Review*. To be taken in a spirit of humour, it deals with a quirky way to look at this bizarre culture we live in. A culture too strange to have been thought up in a science fiction story.

Dr Pak's Preschool

Hands, those strong hands holding her down upon the tabletop . . . in her pain and confusion, they reminded her of those tentacled sea creatures of fabled days which ola-chan *had described when she was little, whose habit it was to drag unfortunate mariners down to a watery doom.*

Those hands, clasping, restraining – she cried for mercy, knowing all the while that those hands would ignore her protests, along with any pretence at modesty.

Needles pricked her skin, hot localised distractions from her futile struggles. Soon the drugs took effect. A soporific coolness spread along her limbs, and she lost the will to resist any longer. The hands loosened their grip, and turned to perform yet other violations.

Stormy images battered her wavering sense of self. Moiré patterns and Moebius chains – somehow she knew these things and their names without ever having learned them. And there was something else – something that hurt even to contemplate – a container with two openings, and none at all . . . a bottle whose interior was on the outside . . .

It was a problem to be solved. A desperate quandary. A life-or-death puzzle in higher level geometry.

The words and images whirled, hands groped about her, but at that moment all she could do was moan.

'Wakarimasen!' she cried aloud. 'Wakarimasen!'

1

Reiko should have been more suspicious the night her
husband came home earlier than usual, and announced
that she would accompany him on his next business trip
to Seoul. That evening, however, when Tetsuo showed
her the white paper folder containing two red and green
airline boarding passes, Reiko could think only in the
heady language of joy.

He remembers.

Her elation did not show, of course. She bowed to her
husband and spoke words of submissive acceptance,
maintaining decorous reticence. Tetsuo, in his turn,
was admirably restrained. He grunted and turned his
attention back to his supper, as if the matter had really
been of little consequence after all.

Nevertheless, Reiko was certain his gruffness over-
laid a well of true feeling.

Why else, she thought, would he do such an
unheard-of thing? And so near the anniversary of their
marriage? That second ticket in the envelope surely
meant there was still a bit of the rebel under Tetsuo's
now so-conventional exterior – still a remnant of the
free spirit she had given her heart to, years ago.

He remembers, she thought jubilantly.

And it was not yet nine in the evening. For Tetsuo
to return so early for supper at home, instead of having
it with business colleagues at some city bar, was
exceptional in itself. Reiko bowed again and suggested
awakening their daughter. Yukiko so seldom got to
spend time with her father.

'*Iye*,' Tetsuo said curtly, vetoing the idea. 'Let the
child sleep. I wish to retire early tonight, anyway.'

Reiko's heart seemed to flutter within her ribcage at
his implication. After clearing away dinner she made
the required preparations, just in case.

And indeed, later that night he joined with her in their bed – for the first time in months without beer or tobacco or the scent of other women commingling in his breath. Tetsuo made love to her with an intensity she recalled, but which, of late, she had begun to think she had imagined all along.

Almost exactly six years ago they had been newly-weds, trapped joyously in each other's eyes as they honeymooned in Fiji, hardly noticing the mountains or the reefs or the exotic native dancers for the resonant happiness, the amplified autarchia of their union. And for the following year, also, it had remained that way for the two of them, as if they were characters from a happy romantic tale, brought into the real world. In those days even the intense pressure of Tetsuo's career had seemed to take second place to their love.

It had lasted, in fact, up to the time when Reiko became pregnant. Until then she hadn't believed they would ever stop being lovers, and begin the long tedium of life as a married couple. But they did.

Tetsuo closed his eyes tightly and shuddered, then collapsed in a lassitude of spent coitus. His breath was sweet, his weight a pleasure for her to bear, and with her fingertips Reiko lightly traced the familiar patterns of his back. The boy she had known was filling out, gaining the looser fleshiness of a grown man. Tonight however she felt a slight relaxing of the tension that had slowly mounted along his spine over the grinding months and years.

Tetsuo seldom spoke of his work, although she knew it was stressful and hard. His supervisors seemed still to hold him under suspicion over an incident a few years ago, when he had tried unsuccessfully to introduce un-Japanese business practices into the firm. This, she imagined, was one reason why he had grown so distant, allowing the flame of their passion to bank back in favour of more important matters. That was, of course, as it would have to be.

But now all seemed restored. Tetsuo had remembered; all was well in the world.

When, instead of simply rolling over and going to sleep, Tetsuo stroked her hair briefly and spoke to her softly in unintelligible mumblings of fondness, Reiko felt a glow like the sunrise within her.

2

It was her first trip to the airport since the honeymoon, so long ago. Reiko could not help feeling disappointed, for the experience was not at all the same this time.

How could it be? She chided herself for making comparisons. After all, different destinations attracted different classes of people. The occupants of this departure lounge could hardly be expected to be like those down the hall a ways, bound from Tokyo to Fiji, Hawaii, or Saipan – young couples close-orbiting on trajectories of bliss.

Sometimes on such honeymoon flights groups of newly-weds would have singing contests to help pass the time, clapping with courteous enthusiasm however terrible the voice. After all, there were harmonies that went beyond music, and much holding of hands.

Travellers not bound for the resorts dressed differently, spoke and behaved differently. It was as if the departure terminal were a series of slices of modern life – each distinct, representing a separate phase or moulting.

Jets destined for Europe or America generally carried tour groups of prosperous older couples, or gaggles of students, all dressed alike and hanging together as if their periphery was patrolled by dangerous animals, ready at any moment to snap up the unwary straggler.

And, of course, there were the intense businessmen, who spent their transit time earnestly studying their presentation materials . . . modern samurai . . . warriors for Japan on the new battlefields of commerce.

Finally, there were the gates nearest Reiko, from which departed flights for Bangkok, Manilla, Seoul. These, too, carried businessmen, but bound instead for the rewards of success. Women told each other rumours about what went on during these . . . *kairaku* expeditions. Reiko had never really been sure what to believe, but she sensed the anticipation of the ticket holders in this particular lounge. Most of the passengers wore suits, but their mood did not strike her as businesslike. They carried briefcases, but nobody seemed much interested in working.

Reiko had few illusions about the 'commerce' that went on during such trips. Still, the Koreans were industrialising rapidly. Certainly there were many bona fide dealings, as well as junkets. Tetsuo's company had to be sending him for real business reasons, or why would he have invited her along? Reiko wondered if all those stories had been exaggerated after all.

A contingent of foreigners awaited the opening of the gate with typical *gaijin* impatience, speaking loudly, staring impertinently. An orderly queue of Japanese formed behind the jostling Europeans and Americans.

Reiko's sister, Yumi, held Yukiko up to wave goodbye to her parents. The little girl seemed confused and unhappy, but determined to behave well. Already Yukiko exhibited a sense of public propriety, and she did not shame them by crying. As Tetsuo led her down the crowded ramp Reiko felt a pang of separation, but she knew Yukiko would be all right for a few days with her aunt. At worst their daughter would be spoiled by too much attention.

On board, Reiko saw there were a few other married couples beside themselves, all seated towards the rear of the aeroplane. The women seemed less at ease than their husbands, and listened attentively as the stewardess went over emergency procedures. Finally, the great machine hurtled down the runway and propelled itself into the sky.

When the safety lights turned off, the cabin began to fill with drifts of cigarette smoke. Men got up and drifted forward towards the lounge. Soon there was heard, beyond the partition, the clinking of glasses and harsh laughter.

Reiko discreetly observed the other women, sitting quietly with empty seats between them. Some gazed out upon the green mountains of Honshu as the plane gradually gained altitude. Others conversed together in low tones. A few just looked down at their hands.

Reiko pondered. So many husbands could not be bringing their wives if their business in Seoul were only concupiscent pleasure. Could they?

She realised she was staring and quickly lowered her eyes. Still, Reiko had noticed something; all the other wives aboard were young, like herself. She turned, intending to whisper this interesting observation to her husband, and blinked quickly when she found herself facing an empty seat.

While she had been looking around, Tetsuo had quietly slipped away. Soon Reiko heard his familiar laughter coming from just beyond the partition.

She looked down then, and found fascinating the texture and fine lines that traced the backs of her own hands.

3

That evening, in their hotel room, Tetsuo told her why he had brought her along with him to Seoul. 'It is time for us to have a son,' he said, matter of factly.

Reiko nodded dutifully. 'A son is to be hoped for.'

Tetsuo loved his daughter, of course, but he clearly wanted to have a boy in the family, and Reiko could hope for nothing better than to please him. And yet, had he not been the one insisting she buy birth-control devices weekly from the neighbourhood Skin Lady, and use them so carefully?

'We can afford to have only one more child,' he went on, telling her what she already knew. 'So we shall want to make certain the second is a boy.'

Only half seriously, she suggested, '*Shujin*, I shall go to Mizuko Jizo Temple daily, and burn incense.'

If she had hoped to draw a smile from him, Reiko was disappointed. Once upon a time, he had been witty in his mockery of the ancient superstitions, and they had shared this delicious cynicism between them – she the daughter of a scientist and he the bright young businessman who had been to university in America. Now, though, Tetsuo nodded and seemed to accept her promise at face value.

'Good. However, we shall supplement prayer with technology.' From his jacket pocket he withdrew a slim brochure which he handed to her. He left Reiko then to read the pamphlet in their small room while he went down to the bar to drink with friends.

Reiko stared down at the bold type, glittering in stark romanji script.

Pak Jong Clinic
Gender Selection Service
Seoul, Hong Kong, Singapore, Bangkok,
Taipei, Mexico City, Cairo, Bombay
Satisfaction is Guaranteed

A little while later she got undressed and went to
bed. But lying there alone in the darkness, she found
she could not sleep.

4

They were actually quite kind at the clinic. Nicer, at
least, than Reiko had anticipated. In her mind she
had pictured a stark, sterile-white hospital setting. It
was reassuring, then, to sit in the pastel waiting room,
with cranes and other symbols of good fortune traced
out delicately upon the wall reliefs. Tetsuo remained
behind when her name was called, but he did smile and
offer her a nod of encouragement as the nurse bowed
and ushered her into the examination room.

The doctors were distant and professional, for which
Reiko was grateful. They tapped and thumped and
measured her temperature. When it came time to take
various samples there was only a little pain, and her
modesty was protected by a screen across the middle
of her body.

Then she was returned to the waiting room. One of
the doctors accompanying her bowed and told Tetsuo
that she would be ready to conceive in three days' time.
Tetsuo replied with a polite hiss of satisfaction, and
exchanged further bows with the doctor before they
turned to leave together.

During the next few days Reiko saw little of Tetsuo.

He really did, it seemed, have business to do in Seoul
– meetings and sales analyses. The clinic provided
a guide to show Reiko and a few other prospective
mothers the sights, such as they were. They saw the
Olympic Village, the war memorials, the great public
museums. Only occasionally did some passer-by glance
sourly at them on hearing spoken Japanese. All in all,
Reiko found the Koreans much nicer than she had
been led to expect from the stories she had heard since
childhood. But then, perhaps the Koreans she met felt
the same way about her.

Still, this was no second honeymoon. Not the
resumption of bliss she had hoped for. When Tetsuo
returned late to their hotel room the following two
nights, she could tell that he had spent part of his day
in close proximity to other women.

Even the explanation offered by one of the other
wives did not much ease Reiko's disappointment.
'The clinic prefers to have some fresh semen to
supplement the frozen samples they stored during
our husbands' past visits,' Mrs Nakamura confided
while they waited together on the third day. Reiko's
head spun in confusion.

'You – you mean he has been . . . donating for
some time?'

Mrs Nakamura nodded, confirming that Tetsuo had
had this in mind for months. On at least his last
two trips to Seoul, he must have visited the clinic to
collect his seed for freezing. Or, more likely, he had
used the *kairaku* house next door, which Reiko was now
certain maintained a business relationship with the Pak
Jong doctors.

'I am sure the place is licensed and regularly
inspected,' Mrs Nakamura added. And Reiko knew
which establishment she meant. Reiko nearly bristled
at the presumption, that Tetsuo would ever *think* of

patronising an unlicensed house, and so risk his family's health with some filthy *gaijin* disease.

She restrained herself, knowing that part of her passion arose out of a sense of bitter disappointment. Somehow, Reiko managed to see a bright side to it all. *The donated material probably has to be prepared quickly. That is why he continued to use the pleasure house, even when I was* here.

She was well aware that she was rationalising. But right at that moment rationalisation was all that stood between Reiko and despair. When, a little while later, she had to endure intromission by cold glass and plastic, Reiko lay back and clasped her arms tightly across her breasts, dreaming of her first conception, which had come the natural way, with her hands and legs wrapped around a living, breathing, sighing man, her loving husband.

5

Three weeks after they returned to Tokyo it became apparent they had succeeded – at least so far as impregnation was concerned. Queasiness and vomiting confirmed the joyous news as surely as the stained blotter of the little home-test kit. As for whether the child-to-be was male, several more weeks would pass before anyone could tell. But Tetsuo was full of confidence and that made Reiko happy.

Little Yukiko had reached the age where she attended preschool half of every day. Reiko would deliver her daughter to the playground entrance and watch all the children line up in their little uniforms, attentive to every phase of the carefully choreographed exercise activity. They seemed to be enjoying school, clapping

together in time as the instructors led them through
teaching rhymes. But who could actually tell what was
best for a child?

Reiko often wondered if they were doing the right
thing, starting Yukiko's education so early, a full two
years before the law required.

'*Doozo ohairi, kidasai!*' the headmistress called to her
little charges. The neat rows of four-year-olds filed
indoors under an arched doorway decorated with
origami flowers. It all felt so alien and remote from
Reiko's own childhood.

Modern times are very hard, she knew. And Tetsuo
was determined to provide their children with the
very best advantages to face such a competitive
world. Yukiko was one of only ten little girls in her
juku preschool class, all the rest being boys. It was
commonly said to be a waste to bother much on a
female's education. But Tetsuo believed their daughter
should also have a headstart, at least compared with
other girls.

Piping sounds of earnest recitation . . . Reiko remembered that examinations in only four more weeks
would determine what kindergarten would accept little
Yukiko for admission. And for boys the cycle of *juku*, of
compressed learning and scrutiny, began even earlier,
with some parents spending small fortunes on special
'baby universities'.

A month ago there had been a news story about
a six-year-old who took his own life in shame when
he did not do well in an exam . . . Reiko shuddered
and turned away. She straightened her *obi* and looked
downwards as she hurried to the nearby station to catch
the next train.

It seemed there was no escaping rush hour anymore.
Staggered work schedules only spread the chaos over
the entire day. Reiko endured being packed into the

car by white-gloved station proctors. Automatically, she raised invisible curtains of privacy around her body and self, ignoring the close pressure of strangers – women with shopping bags at their feet, many of the men hiding their eyes within lurid, animated magazines – until the train at last reached her stop and spilled her out on to a platform near Kaygo University.

Smog and soot and noisy traffic had erased the semi-rural ambience she recalled from long ago. Reiko's earliest memories – from when she had been Yukiko's age – were of this ancient campus where she had grown up as a professor's daughter, playing quietly on the floor of a dusty study stacked high with aromatic books, the walls lined with fine works of *makimono* calligraphy. Unknown to her father, she used to concentrate and try to listen to his conversations with students and faculty and even *gaijin* visitors from foreign lands, certain in her childish belief that, over time, she would absorb it all and one day come into that world of his, to share his work, his pride, his accomplishments.

When did I change my dreams? Reiko wondered.

Usually, memories of such childish fantasies made her smile. But today, for some reason, the recollection only made her feel sad.

I changed very early, she knew. And how can I be regretful, when I have everything?

Still, it was ironic that her sister Yumi, so reticent as a child, had grown to become assertive and adept, while she, Reiko, could imagine no higher role, no greater honour, than to do her duty as a wife and mother.

It would have been nice to stop to visit her father. But today there would not be time. Anyway Yumi should be the first one told the news. Reiko hurried across the street to the great row of commercial establishments facing the university – the phalanx of industrial giants whose benign partnership had helped Kaygo to thrive.

The guard at the side gate of Fugisuku Enterprises recognised her as a former employee and frequent visitor. He smiled and bowed, asking her merely to impress her chop upon a clipboard before she passed through.

Reiko took the quickest route towards the Company Garden of Contemplation, a path taking her along a great glass wall. Beyond that barrier she could view one of the laboratories where Fugisuku manufactured the bio-engineered products it was famous for worldwide.

Thousands of white cages lined the walls of the vast chamber, each containing three or four tiny, pale hamsters, all cloned to be exactly alike. Automatic machines picked up cages and delivered them at precise intervals to long benches, where masked technicians in white coats worked with needles and flashing scalpels, all to an unheard but insistent tempo.

Even through the glass, Reiko caught the familiar, musty, rodent aroma. She had worked here for some years, up until the time of her first pregnancy. *Gaijin* 'liberalism' had penetrated that far, at least. Women no longer had to retire upon getting married. Frankly, though, Reiko did not miss the job all that much.

The rear doors opened upon a walled setting of peace and serenity in the middle of sprawling Tokyo. Out in the garden, beside carefully tended dwarf trees and neatly raked beds of sand, a ceremony was nearing completion under a delicately carved Tori spirit gate. Reiko folded her hands and waited politely as the priest chanted and many of the women of Fugisuku bowed to an altar swathed in incense. Unconsciously, she joined in the prayer.

Oh *kami* of little mammals, forgive us. Do not take revenge upon our children for what we do to you.

The monthly ritual was intended to appease the spirits of the slaughtered hamsters, who gave their lives in such numbers for the good of the company and their common prosperity. Once upon a time the prayer gatherings had amused Reiko, but now she did not feel so sure. Did not all life strike a balance? The *gaijin* argued endlessly about the morality of mankind's exploitation of animals. 'Save the whales!' they cried. 'Save the krill!' But why would the Westerners be so obsessed with preserving inferior animals unless they, too, feared the implacable retribution of karma?

If animals did indeed possess *kami*, Fugisuku would certainly be haunted without the right protections. Barely after their eyes opened, the young hamsters were injected with viruses to stimulate production of antibodies and interferons. They were sacrificed by their thousands in order to produce just a few milligrams of precious refined molecules.

With new life now taking form within her, Reiko was not of a mind to ignore any possible danger. She fervently added her own voice to the chant of propitiation.

Oh angry spirits, stay away from my child.

6

Later, Reiko sat with Yumi in the garden, sharing lunch from the lacquered box she had brought along. Yumi reacted to her news with enthusiasm, speaking excitedly of all the preparations that must be made in order to welcome a new child into a home. At the same time, though, Reiko thought she felt an undercurrent of misgiving from her sister.

Of course Yumi had suspected early on the true reason for the journey to Seoul. In many ways Reiko's younger sister was much more worldly. Still, Yumi would never rebuke her, or ever say anything to

bring down her hopes. About Tetsuo she had only
this to say:

'When our family first met him, Father and the rest
of us thought you might face problems from Tetsuo's
unconventionality, his Western, liberal ideas. He has
certainly been a surprise, then. Who ever would have
expected, so few years later, that your husband would
try so very hard to be perfectly Japanese?'

Reiko blinked. Is that what Tetsuo is trying to do?
she wondered. But no encouragement would force
Yumi to say anything more.

7

The next trip to Seoul was even briefer than the first,
and taken on even shorter notice. Reiko barely had
time to pack a satchel for Yukiko and deliver her to
Yumi before they had to rush to the airport to catch
the flight Tetsuo had arranged.

Again, the Pak Jong Clinic doctors took samples just
beyond the curtain of modesty. Reiko was well enough
educated to understand much of what she overheard
them saying.

They spoke of tests ... tests for potential genetic
defects, for recessive colour blindness, for the insidious
trait of near-sightedness, for the correct sex chromosomes. When the implication of their discussions sank
in, Reiko's knees shook.

They were holding court on whether the foetus – still
so small that Reiko wasn't even showing yet – was to
live or die.

She'd heard that in parts of rural China they were
drowning girl babies. Here though, they were tested,
discovered, and taken from the *womb* before their first
cry. Before their spirits could even form.

Reiko was terrified they were about to tell her the foetus carried some unpalatable defect, such as femininity. So when they returned and bowed, smiling, with the good news, Reiko nearly fainted with relief. The very real attentiveness Tetsuo showed her afterwards caused her to feel as if she had achieved some fine accomplishment, and had made him very proud of her.

They held hands during the flight home. And for the following four wonderful months Reiko thought her trials were at an end.

Now Tetsuo came home early often, spurning all but the most important business-and-dinner parties with colleagues. He played with Yukiko and laughed with his family. He and Reiko spoke together of plans for their son, how he would get the finest of everything, the best attention, the best schooling, everything required to arm him for success in a competitive, judgmental world.

His son's fate, Tetsuo swore, would not be to face an endless subservience to subtle hierarchies and status. He would not be one of those who were bullied in school, in cruel rituals of *kumi* group solidarity, by children and teachers alike. His son would *head* hierarchies. When his son toasted *kampai*, it was *his* glass that would be highest.

Touching her swelling belly, Tetsuo's eyes seemed to shine, making Reiko feel it all had been worthwhile, after all.

Then, in her fourth month, Tetsuo came home with yet another slim white folder containing two red and green airline boarding passes.

8

She gasped in surprise when she saw the image on the

screen. The Pak Jong Clinic doctors focused beams of ultrasound into her womb and computers sorted the muddled reflections into a stunning image of the life growing within her.

'It looks like a monkey!' she cried in dismay. Her thoughts whirled, for surely this was something the doctors would never allow!

One of the men laughed harshly. The other doctor was kinder. He explained. 'At this stage of development, the foetus has many of the attributes of our distant ancestors, who lived in the sea long ago. Only recently, for instance, it had gills and a tail. But these were re-absorbed. And in time he will look like later forefathers, until he at last appears quite human.'

Reiko sighed in relief. Someone mentioned the *gaijin*-sounding technical term, 'recapitulation', and suddenly she did remember having heard or read something about it sometime. She blushed, shamefaced, certain her outburst had made them think her a hysterical woman.

'The important thing we have determined,' the doctor went on, 'is that the acoustic nerves are already in place, and soon the eyes will be functional.'

'So all is well now?' she asked. 'My baby is healthy?'

'A fine, strong little boy, your Minoru will be.'

'Then I can go home now?'

The second doctor shook his head. 'First we will be fulfilling the next phase of our contract. We must install a very special device. Do not be alarmed. We are very skilled at this. It will not cause much discomfort. You will only have to stay for two nights.'

Dazed, Reiko did not even think of complaining as they gave her an injection. With sudden drowsiness swarming over her she watched the world swim as they wheeled her into an operating room.

There was hushed, professional talk. Nobody spoke to her.

'*S'karaimas. Gomen nasai*,' she said as the anaesthetist's mask came down and a sweet, cloying odour filled her mouth and throat. 'Forgive me, I am very tired.'

Reiko's shattered thoughts orbited a burning core of shame. She seemed to have forgotten the reason she was apologising, but whatever she had done, Reiko knew it had to have been terrible.

9

Dreams began disturbing her sleep soon after her third homecoming. They started out as muddy, uncertain feelings of depression and fear, which did not rouse her but left her tired in the morning when it came time to prepare Tetsuo for work and Yukiko for preschool. Often she would collapse back upon the *tatami* after they were gone. She had no energy. This pregnancy seemed to be taking much more out of her than the first one.

Then there was the music. There was no escaping the music.

At first it had been rather pleasant. The tiny machine that had been implanted into her womb could barely be traced with her fingertips. Nothing extruded. It drew power from small batteries that would easily last another five months.

And at this stage in the foetus's development, all the device ever did was play it music. Endlessly, over and over again, music.

'*Minoru wa, gakusei desu*,' Tetsuo said. 'Little Minoru is now a student. Of course his brain is not yet advanced enough to accept more complex lessons, but he can learn music even this early. He will emerge with perfect pitch, knowing his scales already, as if by instinct.'

Tetsuo smiled. '*Minoru kun wa on'gaku ga suki deshoo.*'

So the harmonies repeated, over and over again, throbbing like sonar within the confined sea of her insides, diffracting around and through her organs, resonating at last with the beating of her heart.

Yumi no longer visited when she thought Tetsuo might be at home. Their father had voiced his disgusted disapproval of Tetsuo and this invasion against the ways of nature. Reiko had been forced to answer loyally in Tetsuo's defence.

'You are too Westernised,' she told them, borrowing her husband's own words. 'You too blindly accept the *gaijin* and their alien concepts about nature and guilt. There is no shame in this thing we are doing.'

'A dubious distinction,' her father had replied, irritably. Yumi then interjected, 'Guilt consists in doing the right thing, even when nobody is watching, Reiko. *Shame* is making sure you don't get caught doing what others disapprove.'

'Well?' Reiko had answered. 'You two are the only ones expressing disapproval. All of Tetsuo's associates and friends admire him for this! My neighbours come by to listen to the music!'

Her sister and father had looked at each other at that moment, as if she had just proven their point. But Reiko did not understand. All she knew for certain was that she must side with her husband. No other choice was even conceivable. Yumi might be able to have a more 'modern' marriage, but to Reiko, such ways seemed to promise only chaos.

'We plan to give our son the best advantages,' she concluded in the end. And to that, of course, there was very little the others could reply. 'We shall see,' her

father had concluded. Then he changed the subject to
the colour of the autumn leaves.

10

At the end of Reiko's sixth month the thing in her
womb spoke its first words.

She sat up quickly in the dark, clutching the covers.
In a brief moment of terror Reiko thought that it had
been a ghost, or the baby himself, mumbling dire
premonitions from deep inside her. The words were
indistinct, but she could feel them vibrating under her
trembling fingertips.

It took a few moments to realise that it was the
machine once again, now moving into a new phase of
foetal education. Reiko sank back against the pillows
with a sigh. Next to her Tetsuo snored quietly, contentedly, unaware of this milestone.

Reiko lay listening. She couldn't make out what the
machine was enunciating slowly, repetitiously. But the
baby *responded* with faint movements. She wondered if
he were reaching out towards the tiny speaker. Or
perhaps, instead, he was trying to get away. If so,
then he was trapped, trapped in the closest, most
secure prison of them all.

The doctors were certain it was safe, Reiko reminded
herself. Surely those wise men would not do anything
to hurt her child. Anyway, though it was a pioneering
method, she and Tetsuo were not the very first. There
had been a few before them, to prove it was all right.

Consoled, but convinced that sleep would not return,
she rose to begin yet another day before the sun turned
the eastern sky a dull and smoggy grey. Reiko bent
her attention to daily life, to chores and preparations,

to doing what she could to make life pleasant for her family.

One evening soon thereafter they sat together, watching a television programme about genetic engineering. The reporters spoke glowingly of how, in future years, scientists would be able to cut and splice and redesign the very code of life itself. Human beings would specify everything about their plants, their animals, even their offspring, making them stronger, brighter, better than ever.

She heard Tetsuo sigh in envy, so Reiko said nothing. She only laid her head on his shoulder and concealed her own relieved thoughts.

By that time, I will have finished my own childbearing years. Those wonders will be for other women to deal with.

Reiko knew what was coming next. She tried and tried to prepare herself, but still it came as a shock when, a week or so later, her belly began to glow. At night, with the houselights extinguished, faint shimmerings of colour could be seen emerging through her flesh from one corner of her burgeoning belly. It flickered like a tiny flame, but there was no added warmth. Rather, it was a cold light.

Soon the neighbour women were back, curious and insistent on seeing for themselves. They murmured admiringly at the luminance given her skin by the tiny crystal display, and treated Reiko with such respect that she dared not chase them away, as she might have preferred.

A few of Tetsuo's envious comrades even persuaded him to bring them home to see, as well. One day Reiko had to rush about preparing a very special meal for Tetsuo's supervisor's supervisor. The great man complimented her cooking and spoke highly of Tetsuo's drive and forward thinking.

Reiko did not much mind showing a small patch of skin in a dim room, nor the cold touch of the stethoscope as others listened in on Minoru's lessons. Modesty was nothing against the pride she felt in helping Tetsuo.

Still, she did wonder about the baby. What was the machine showing him, deep inside her? Was he already learning about faraway lands Reiko herself had never seen? Was it describing the biological facts of life to him? Where he was and what was happening to him?

Or was it imprinting upon him the cool, graceful forms of mathematics, fashioning genius while the brain was still as malleable as new bread dough?

Her father explained some of it to her during Reiko's next-to-final visit to her parents' home. While Yumi and their mother cleared the dinner bowls, Professor Sato looked over some of the titles of the programmes listed on the Pak Jong Clinic brochure.

'Abstract Geometry and Topology, Musical Tone Recognition, Basic Linguistic Grammar ... *Hon ga nan'satsu arimas'ka*? Hmmm.' Her father put aside the brochure and tried to explain to her.

'Of course the foetus cannot learn things that an infant could not. It cannot really understand speech, for instance. It doesn't know yet about people or the world. The technicians apparently know better than to try to cram facts into the poor little thing.

'No, what they appear to be after is the laying down of tracks, pathways, *essences* ... to set up the foundations for talents the child will later fill with knowledge during his schooling.' Reluctantly, her father admitted that the doctors seemed to have thought these things out. 'They are very clever,' he said.

With a sigh he added: 'That does not necessarily mean, of course, that they really know what they are doing. They may be too clever by half.'

A warning glare from Yumi shut him up, then.

But not before Reiko shivered at the tone in his voice.

Soon she started avoiding her father, and even Yumi. The days dragged on as the weight she carried grew ever heavier. The foetus stirred much less, now. She had a feeling he was paying very close attention to his lessons.

11

Pak Jong Clinic technicians visited their house. They examined her with instruments, some familiar and others very strange. At one point they pressed a unit to her skin very near the embedded machine and read its memory. They consulted excitedly, then packed up their tools. Only as an afterthought, one of them told Reiko her son was developing nicely. In fact, he was quite a fine specimen.

Tetsuo came home and told her that there was something new and exciting the Pak Jong people wanted to try.

'A few foetuses, such as our son, have responded very well indeed to the lessons. Now there is something which may make all he has accomplished so far seem as nothing!'

Reiko touched his arm. 'Tetsuo, it is so very near the time he will be born. Only another month or so. Why push little Minoru every minute?' She smiled tentatively, making an unusual effort to contact his eyes. 'After all,' she pleaded, 'students on the outside get occasional vacations. Can he not, as well?'

Tetsuo did not seem to hear her. His excitement was fiercely intense. 'They have discovered something truly fantastic recently, Mother. Some babies actually seem to be *telepathic* during the final weeks before birth!'

'*Te . . . te-re-paturu?*' Reiko mouthed the *gairaigo* word.

'But it is extremely close range in effect. Even mothers usually detect it only as a vague strengthening of their mother–child bonds. And anyway, the trauma of being born always ends it. Even the most gentle of Caesarian deliveries . . .'

He was rambling. Reiko lowered her eyes in defeat, knowing how impossible it would be to penetrate past the heat of his enthusiasm. Tetsuo has not changed, she realised at last. He was still the impetuous boy she had married. Still as reckless as a *zoku*. Only now he knew better than to express it in unpopular Western eccentricities. He would choose acceptable Eastern ones, instead.

When the technicians came the next day she let them work without asking any questions. They gave her a girdle of finely woven mesh to wear over her womb. After they left, she simply lay there and turned her head to the wall.

Yumi telephoned, but Reiko would not see her. Her parents she put off, claiming fatigue. Little Yukiko, sensitive as always, was told that ladies got moody late in pregnancy. She did her homework quietly and played with her computer tutor alone in her tiny room.

Tetsuo was promoted. The celebration with his comrades went on late. When he returned home, smelling of fish, sake, and bar girls, Reiko pretended to be asleep. Actually, though, she was listening. The machine scarcely lit up anymore. It hardly made a sound. Still, she felt she could almost follow its conversations with her son.

Shapes filled her half-dreams . . . impossible shapes, bottles with two openings, and none. Again and again there came one particular word, 'topology'.

Over the following days she tried to regain some enthusiasm. There were times when she felt as she had when she had carried Yukiko ... a communion with her child that ran deeper, stronger than anything the machines could tap. During such moments Reiko almost felt happy.

Year End came, and most of the husbands were out all week, weaving and bobbing in *bonenkai* celebrations, when so many tried to obliterate the old year in a wash of alcohol. The sake-dispensing vending machines at the train stations emptied faster than the drinks companies could restock them. Wise women and children kept off the streets.

One night Tetsuo returned home drunk and ranted long about her father, knowing full well that by tradition he would not be held accountable for anything he said in this state. Nevertheless, Reiko moved her *tatami* into Yukiko's room. She lay there quietly, thinking about something her father had said to her once.

'Both Tetsuo and I believe in a melding of East and West,' he had told Reiko. 'Many people on both sides of the Pacific want to see this co-joining of strengths. But there is disagreement over how strength should be defined, Reiko.

'Tetsuo's kind sees only the power of Western scientific reductionism. They wish to combine it with our discipline, our traditional methods of competitive conformity. With this I fundamentally disagree.

'What the West really has to offer – the only thing it has to offer, my child – is honesty. Somehow, in the midst of their horrid history, the best among the *gaijin* learned a wonderful lesson. They learned to distrust themselves, to doubt even what they were taught to believe or what their egos make them yearn to see. To know that even truth must be scrutinised. It was a great discovery, almost as great as the treasure we of the East have to offer them in return, the gift of harmony.'

Reiko had not understood, either then or now. But Yumi had seemed to comprehend. 'It is not a question then, of whether East or West shall win, is it, Father?'

'No,' he had said. 'There will definitely be a synthesis. The only question remaining is what type of synthesis it shall be. Will it be one of power? Or one of wisdom?'

The next day, Tetsuo apologised without words. Reiko forgave him and moved back into their bedroom.

Technicians visited them twice a week, now. Reiko wondered how they would ever pay for such attention, until Tetsuo told her that the Clinic was refunding all costs. They were special. They would make this process famous throughout the world.

At times Reiko worried that the baby would not even be recognisable when he emerged. Would he wear an expression of sage wisdom from the very start, and stare into space thinking great thoughts? Would he spill from the womb already fully forged into that intimidating, imperious creature, an adult male? Would he even need her love?

Hope also came and went in tempo with those waves of feeling deep within her. Every peak and trough of emotion left her confused and drained. She was glad that it would all be over soon.

Reiko met the other wives in the special group. Some of them were knowledgeable, more confident than her. Mrs Sukimura, in particular, seemed so relaxed and assured. She was the farthest along. Already the Pak Jong techs were ecstatic with the results from her child. They spoke of data transfer rates, of frequency and phase filtering, of Fourier transforms and pattern recognition.

At one point all of the women were picked up by limousines and taken downtown to MITI, the all-powerful Ministry of Trade and Industry, on Sakurada-Dor Avenue. In a great hall, technicians attached mesh girdles and gently, tenderly, wheeled them close to mammoth, chilled machines.

Computers, Reiko thought. They were using powerful computers to *talk* to the foetuses!

When the Minister himself appeared Reiko blinked in astonishment. His eminence shook Tetsuo's hand. Reiko felt faint.

12

They were pledged to secrecy, of course. If the *gaijin* newspapers got hold of this too soon, there would be hell to pay. Worldwide media attention before the right preparations had been made would shame the nation, even though it was really none of the business of outsiders.

Others were already jealous of Japan in so many ways. And Westerners tended to insist that theirs was the only morality. So Tetsuo and Reiko signed their chops to a document. There was talk of a leave of absence from Tetsuo's company, and an important post when he returned. He spoke to her of buying a larger house in a better neighbourhood.

'One of our problems has been in the field of *software*,' he explained one evening, though Reiko knew he was talking mostly to himself. 'Our engineers have been very clever in practical technology, leaving most of the world far behind in many areas. But computer programming has turned out to be very hard. There seems to be no conventional way of catching up with the Americans there. Your father used to claim that it had to do with our system of education.'

Tetsuo laughed derisively. 'Japanese education is the finest in all the world. The toughest. The most demanding!'

'What . . . ?' she asked. 'What does this have to do with the babies?'

'They are geniuses at programming!' Tetsuo cried. 'Already they have cracked problems that had stymied hundreds of our best software designers. Of course they do not understand what they are doing, but that does not seem to matter. It is all a matter of asking questions in just the right ways, and letting them innovate.

'For instance, the unborn have yet no concept of distance or motion. But that turns out to be an advantage, you see, for they have no preconceptions. They bring fresh insight, without being burdened by our worldly assumptions.

'So one of our young engineers solved a vexing problem for the Ministry of Trade, while another has developed an entirely new model of traffic control that should reduce downtown congestion by five per cent!'

Tetsuo's eyes held a glow, a wild flicker that gave Reiko a chill. '*Zuibun joozo desu, ne?*' he said, in admiration of that accomplishment by an unborn child. 'As for our son,' Tetsuo went on, 'he is being asked even more challenging questions about transportation systems. And I am certain he will make us proud.'

So, Reiko thought. It was even worse than she had imagined. This was more than *juku*, more than just another form of cram-education. Her child was being put to work before he was born. And there was nothing at all she could do about it.

Guiltily, Reiko wasn't even sure she should try.

13

A Klein Bottle . . . she knew the name in a dream.

It was what one called that bizarre thing – a container with two openings and none at all . . . whose inside was its outside.

14

When Mrs Sukimura's time came they only knew of it by the fact that the woman did not join the others at the computer centre. Ah, well, Reiko thought. At least the respite was coming soon.

Traditionally, childbirth in Japan was done by appointment, during business hours. A woman scheduled a day with her obstetrician, when she would check into the hospital and receive the drugs to induce labour. It was all very civilised and much more predictable than the way it apparently was done in the West.

But for the women of the test group, matters were different. So important was the work the foetuses were doing that it was decided to wait as long as possible, to let the babies come as late as they wanted.

The reason given was 'birth trauma'. Apparently, emerging into the outer world robbed even the most talented foetuses of their small but potent psychic powers. After that, they would lapse to being babies again. Talented, well-tutored babies, but babies nonetheless.

The MITI technicians regretted this, but it would certainly be no 'trauma' to her. To Reiko, this coming return to ignorance would be a gift from the blessed Buddha himself.

Oh, it would be strange to have a genius son. But they had promised her that he would still be a little boy. She would tickle him and make him laugh. She would hold him when he tripped and cried. She would bathe in his sweet smile and he would love her. She would see to that.

Genius did not have to mean soullessness. She knew that from having met a few of her father's students over the years. There had been one boy . . . her father had wanted Reiko to go out with him instead of Tetsuo, years ago. Everyone said he was brilliant, and he had a nice smile and personality.

If only he had not also had the habit of eating red meat too often. It made him smell bad, like an American.

And anyway, by then she had already fallen in love with Tetsuo.

One by one the other women dropped out of their group, to be replaced by newcomers who looked to Reiko now for advice and reassurance. Her own time would be very soon, of course. In fact, she was already more than a week overdue when she went to the hospital for another examination, and one of the doctors left his clipboard on the counter when he went to answer a telephone call.

Reiko suddenly felt daring. She reached out and turned the clipboard, hoping to see her own chart. But it was only a list of patients on the doctor's other ward.

Then she frowned. Mrs Sukimura's name was on the list! Three weeks after her delivery, which they'd been told had been uneventful.

Reiko recognised other names. In fact, nearly all of the women who had gone into labour before her were under care on the next floor.

The baby churned in response to her racing heart. Footsteps told of the doctor's return, so Reiko put back the clipboard and sat down again with an effort to remain outwardly calm.

'If you don't begin labour by the end of the month, we will induce it,' he told her upon completing his tests. 'The delay was approved by your husband, of course. There is nothing to worry about.'

Reiko barely heard his words. What concerned her was the plan beginning to form in her mind. For her, it would call for daring to the point of recklessness.

Fortunately, she had worn Western dress for her visit to the hospital. A kimono would have been too conspicuous. At first she had considered trying to borrow a doctor's white coat to wear over her street clothes. After all, there were some female physicians here. She had seen a few.

But her protruding belly and slow waddle would have made the imposture absurd, even if she did encounter a white coat just lying around to be taken.

She did still have the grey gown they had given her to wear during the examination. This she kept balled inside her purse. In the ladies room she put the loose garment on over her street clothes. People tended to look right past patients on a ward. The uniform was a partial cloak of invisibility.

First she tried the lifts. But the elevator operator looked at her when she asked to be taken to floor eight. 'May I please see your pass?' the young woman asked Reiko politely.

'I mis-spoke, forgive me,' Reiko said, bowing to hide her fluster. 'I meant to say floor nine.'

On exiting the lift she rested against the wall for a while to catch her breath. The extra weight she carried every moment of every hour was a burden on her overstrained back, sheer torture if she did not maintain just the right erect posture. Soon it would be time to spill her child into the world. And yet, she was beginning to dread the idea with a sick, mortal fear.

A nurse asked if she needed help.

'*Iie, Kekko desu,*' Reiko answered quickly. '*Gomen nasai. Ikimashoo.*'

Giving her a doubtful glance, the nurse turned away. Reiko waddled slowly towards the clearly marked fire exit, looked around to make sure she wasn't being observed, and pushed her way into the stairwell.

Her shoes made soft scraping sounds on the rough, high-traction surface of the steps. Under her left hand, her womb was a centre of furious activity as the baby kicked and turned. By the time she reached the eighth-floor landing, the guard stationed there had already risen from his little stool.

'May I help you?' he asked, perplexedly.

Certainly, honourable sir, Reiko thought sarcastically. Please be so kind as to open the door for me, and then forget that I ever came this way.

The guard frowned. Twice he began to speak then stopped. His confused expression was soon matched by Reiko's own amazement as he blinked several times, then reached back to turn the knob and pull the portal aside for her.

'*Doozo . . . ohairi kudasai . . .*'

'*Ee, itachakimasu,*' Reiko answered breathlessly. She rocked through the opening in a daze until the door was closed behind her again. Then she sagged back and sighed.

For a few moments, there in the stairwell, she had felt something fey radiating from her womb. Her child had reached out in her time of need, and *helped* Reiko . . . probably without having any idea exactly what he was doing. He had helped her because of her deeply felt need.

Love. She had always believed it had power transcending all the cold metal tools men were so proud of. All the more so the love between a mother and her child.

I must find out what is going on here, she knew.
I must.

Fortunately, security in the hospital seemed to have
only one layer, as if the owners of this place expected a
mere ribbon of courtesy to suffice. And under normal
circumstances it would have been more than enough.

Reiko did not have to show great agility, or dodge
quickly from room to room. The halls were nearly
empty, and the few people on duty at the nurses'
station were turned away in a technical discussion as
she hurried out of sight.

She came to a large window, facing the hallway.
Within were the familiar shapes of a neonatal unit
– rows of tiny white cots, monitoring instruments, a
bored male nurse reading a newspaper.

Babies.

They look healthy enough, she thought, nurturing
a slender shoot of a smile. There appeared to be no
monsters here, just pink newborn little boys, each of
them looking very much like a tiny, chubby Buddha
. . . or that English Prime Minister, Churchill.

Reiko's nascent smile faded, however, when she
realised that the children were moving hardly at all.
And then she saw that every one of them was connected
by taped electrodes to a cluster of cables. The cables led
to a bank of tall machines by the far wall.

Computers. And the babies, staring with open eyes,
hardly moved at all.

'*Wakarimasen*,' Reiko moaned, shaking her head. 'I
don't understand!'

15

The plate by the door read 'Sukimura'. Reiko listened,
and hearing no voices, slipped inside.

'Reiko-*san*!'

The woman in the chair looked healthy, fully recovered. She stood up and hurried over to take Reiko's hand. 'Reiko-*san*, what are you doing here? They told us—'

'Us? They have all of the others? Will they keep me here, too, when my time comes?'

Mrs Sukimura nodded and looked away. 'They are kind. We . . . are allowed to nurse our babies while they work.'

'*Work*,' Reiko measured the word. 'But the birth trauma . . . it should return the children to innocence! They promised . . .'

'They found a technique to *prevent* it, Reiko-*san*. Our babies were all born wise. They are *engineers*, doing great work for the good of the realm. It is even said that the palace may take notice, it is so important.'

Reiko was aghast. 'Do they plan to leave them hooked up to wires forever?'

'Oh no, no. The doctors say this will not harm our sons. They say they will still be all right.' And yet a hollow tone in her voice betrayed Mrs Sukimura's true feelings.

'But then, Izumi-*san*,' Reiko said, 'what is wrong?'

'They are mistaken!' The older woman cried. 'The men say we are silly, superstitious women. They say that the babies are all well, healthy . . . that they will lead normal lives. But, oh Reiko-*san*, they have no *kami*! They have no souls!'

Reiko blinked, and the spirit within her writhed in tempo to her sudden breath. No, it cannot be true, she thought. I feel my baby's *kami*. For all he has been through, he is still human!

Footsteps echoed in the hallway. Voices approached the door.

'At birth,' Mrs Sukimura said in a husky voice filled

with horrible resignation, 'at birth they . . . their souls
were sucked away into . . . into *software*.'

The door opened. Reiko heard rough masculine
tones. Felt hands upon her shoulders. She cried out.
'*Iye. Iye!*' But she could not shrug them off. The hands
pulled her from the room.

'Reiko-*san*!' She heard her friend call just before the
door shut with a final click. A gurney waited. Strong
hands. A needle.

Reiko wailed, but no physical resistance could overcome the insistence of those hands.

16

The flutterings caused by inducement drugs soon
became tremors, which turned into fierce contractions.
Reiko cried out for Tetsuo, knowing full well that
tradition would have kept him away, even if frowning
officials from the Ministry did not. Spasms came with
increasing rapidity now, sending the small life within
her kicking and swimming in agitation.

New drugs were injected. Machines focused upon her
womb, and she knew that these were the clever devices
designed to prevent the cleansing fall of innocence
which the doctors hatefully called 'birth trauma'.
They were adamant about preventing it, now. They
were insisting that her baby enter the world wise.

Oh, how they would discover, to their regret, what
they had really done, what they had unleashed. But
even were she able to speak, she knew they would not
listen. They would have to find out for themselves.

In her delirium Reiko's head turned left and right,
trying to track voices nobody else in the operating
room seemed to hear. They came at her from all sides,

whispering through the hissing aspirators, humming from the lamps, murmuring from the electric sockets.

Spirits leered and taunted her from the machines, some mere patternings of light and static, others more complex – coursing in involute electronic dissonance within the microprocessors. Ghosts floated around her – whispering *kami*, dressed up in raiments of software.

How foolish of men to think they can banish the world of spirits. Reiko knew with sudden certainty that the very idea was arrogant. Of course the *kami* would simply adapt to whatever forms the times demanded. The spirits would find a way.

They were loose in the grid, now, biding their time. And they would have revenge.

Ghosts of baby hamsters . . . of baby human beings . . . She sensed her own son, thinking now, desperately, harder than any foetus had ever been forced to think before.

Soporific numbness spread over her as the tentacle-like hands turned to other violations. The shuddering contractions made vision blur. Superimposed upon her diffracting tears were dazzling Moiré patterns and Moebius chains. How she knew the names of these things, without ever having learned them, Reiko did not bother to wonder. From her mouth came words . . . 'Transportation . . . locational translation of coordinates . . .' she whispered, licking her dry lips. '. . . non-linear transformations . . .'

And then there was the bottle that had not one opening but two . . . or none at all . . . the container whose inside was *outside*.

Now Reiko found herself wondering what the word 'outside' really meant.

The hands did not seem to notice or care about the ghostly forms glaring down at her from the harsh fluorescents. Those angry spirits mocked her agony, as they mocked the other one, the one struggling with a problem in geometry.

Another spasm of savage pressure struck Reiko, almost doubling her over. And she felt overwhelmed by a sudden swimming sensation within her . . . an intensifying sense of dread . . . desperate concentration on a single task, to turn theoretical knowledge into practical skill.

The *kami* in the walls and in the machines chittered derisively. The problem was too difficult. It would never be solved in time!

A container whose inside is outside . . .

'*Desu ka ne?*' one of the technicians said, shaking and tapping his monitoring headphones. He shouted again, this time in alarm.

Suddenly white coats flapped on all sides. There was no time for full anaesthesia, so they sprayed on locals that numbed with bone-chilling rapidity. Nobody even bothered to set up a modesty screen as the obstetric surgeons began an emergency Caesarian section.

Reiko felt it happen then, suddenly, as a burst of pure light seemed to explode within her! For that moment she shared an overwhelming sense of wonder and elation – the joy and beauty of pure mathematics. It was the only language possible in that narrow instant of triumph. And yet it also carried love.

The surgeon cut. There came a loud pop, as if a balloon had suddenly burst. Her distended belly collapsed abruptly, like a tent all at once deprived of its supports.

The technicians stared, blinking. Trembling, the stunned surgeon reached in. Reiko felt him grope under the flaccid layers of her empty womb, seeking in bewilderment what was no longer there.

Applied Topology. She remembered the name of a text,

one of the courses they had given her son, and Reiko knew it stood for shapes and their relationships. It had to do with *space* and *time*, and it could be applied to problems in transportation.

The hands did more things to her, but they could not harm her anymore. Reiko ignored them.

'He has escaped you,' she told them softly, and the angry, envious, mad *kami* as well. 'He learned his lessons well, and has made his mother proud.'

Frustrated voices filled the room, rebounding off the walls. But Reiko had already followed her heart, beyond the constraints of any chamber or any nation, far beyond the knowledge of living men, where there were no obstacles to love.

Detritus Affected

Physicians swear a Hippocratic Oath whose central vow is 'do no harm'. I wonder – how many other professions might do well to set that goal above all others?

Schliemann, uncovering Troy, gave birth to modern archeology, begetting it in sin. His clumsy pits tore through the gates and temples of forty levels – three thousand years – callously scattering what might have been sifted, deciphered, all to prove a fact that wasn't going anywhere. Patience would have revealed the same truth, in time.

The next wave of diggers learned from Schliemann's wrongs. They went about 'restoring' ancient sites, sweeping dust from Disney-prim aisles of artfully restacked columns. Such conceit.

Today, we *save* dust, sampling pollen grains to tell what blossoms once grew on the hills surrounding Karakourom, or Harrapa, or fabled Nineveh.

In truth, we have conceits all our own.

Friday

Look, see this broken plastic wheel? Part of a cheap

toy, circa 1970. Giveaway prize in some fast food outlet's promotional kiddie meal. Seventy grams of carboniferous petroleum cooked under limestone sediments for two hundred million years, only to be sucked up, refined, press-moulded, passed across a counter, squealed over, and then tossed in next week's trash.

And here's a flattened cardboard box bearing the logo of a long-defunct stereo store, stained on one side by a mass of nondescript organic matter which we'll analyse later in lab, sampling and correlating what garbage once flew between these hills. Hills overlooking fabulous L.A.

Science, and especially archeology, is never ideal, Professor Paul used to tell us. *In the present, as well as the past, real life is all about compromises.* Not as lofty a slogan as a Hippocratic Oath, I'll admit, but what do you expect from a profession based on rooting through the cellars, garbage heaps, and vanities of bygone days?

We managed to dig down past the thirty-metre level this week, into rich veins of profligacy from a time that knew no limits. It is a smorgasbord feast of information and I want to analyse everything. Each gum wrapper. Each crushed styrofoam peanut and brown ketchup stain. I fantasise computers potent enough to work backward from the positions I find each of these wonders in, tracing how they came to be jammed next to each other under this great pile. I dream of reversing their tumble from grunting, stinking dumptrucks, re-enveloping them in wrappers of shiny black plastic and following each bundle back to its source – the effluent of a single twentieth-century home.

It can't be done. Not today. It would be like asking Schliemann to sift for pollen instead of ripping through ancestral walls in search of gold. Perhaps future researchers will dissolve ancient cities, atom by atom, recording the location and orientation of each *molecule* so that the dust of pharaoh, slave, and temple cat might be tagged, trajectoried, and finally re-assembled on a chip like God's own jigsaw puzzle, resurrecting the dead in simulated splendour, if not the hoped-for afterlife.

My techniques are crude in comparison to what may come. Only a minuscule portion of the raw data we dig up is captured on photos, slides, and these journal entries. 'Slash and burn archeology', Keoki called it last week, in black humour.

Yet, each evening when the day's work is done, I climb out of our trench to look across the vast expanse that is Hyperion, and am consoled. Our trench is just fifty metres by fourteen, while the landfill stretches in all directions.

Mile after mile of garbage. The largest midden – the largest single *thing* – ever built by human civilisation. Bigger, by volume, than even China's Great Wall.

There'll be plenty left over, after we are through digging here. Plenty of data for others to plumb through later, with fine future sieves.

I'm no Schliemann. I do little harm.

Monday

Sometimes an object strikes me in a certain way, and I wonder – could this have once been *mine*?

I am bemused by how different that makes this research from any other I've done. My own father or mother might have thrown out this box, that sofa or old turntable, back when I was very young. The thought makes me sensitive to toys. Pathetic, broken bits of plastic and metal. They grow less electronic and more sturdy with each metre we descend into the past, affecting me with something between *déjà vu* and a poignant sense of lost innocence.

Then my beeping pager interrupts, and I must climb back to the present world, dealing with the latest crisis.

Never have I faced so much political aggravation on a dig! Each day some old fart bureaucrat comes on-site, scratching his head and muttering confused objections. Even the infamous red tape of India pales in comparison. There, or in Egypt, you could smooth things over with a little honest baksheesh. Here, a bribe would just land me in jail without ever discovering what it is these people want!

One learns to be resourceful. Always, in every government department, one can find some bright youngster who is off the formal chain of command. The idea boy. Trouble-shooter gal. This techie plays no office games, but simply makes things run. Boss is usually terrified of Wunder-Kid, so I invite them up together. All moon-wrapped in full breathing gear against the occasional methane blurp, they get a full cook's tour. Nearly always, the young guy goes crazy over something we've found, leaves with an armload of gamma-sanitised 'memorabilia' . . . and makes damn sure we get our permit, licence, whatever.

Works every time.

It's been much the same with the press. One curmudgeon city editor had it in for us from the moment our department got this grant. Tried angling stories about disease germs, festering in the dump along with five billion ancient, disposable diapers. Radio DJs and Net Jockeys came to our rescue . . . so effectively the cops had to cordon off Sanitation Road, keeping out hordes of young amateurs who flocked up to 'help out'.

Los Angeles. Who can figure? Some old-time rocker

once said – 'No place is ever weirder than your own native land.' Maybe that's why, after years exploring the past far away, I finally came back home to dig.

Wednesday

Inch by inch we descend, uncovering mundane wonders. For example, we keep finding newspapers so well-preserved they could even be read by moonlight. So much for biodegradability. No archeologist ever had better help dating strata.

Household mail is a rich font of information. Charge slips and bank records found their way into the trash, along with old tax files and all kinds of revealing junk mail. When my student, Joyce Barnes, released some wonderful stats on TwenCen credit-slavery, a retiree group in Laguna filed suit under some old privacy laws, in an effort to stop the dig. That storm blew over for lack of public support. Today's kids hardly know what an envelope is. If it's not in the Net, what do they care?

Meanwhile, Leslie surveys dietary patterns of Angelenos past. When we penetrated beyond the era of microwave ovens, he found a sudden shift in the packaging poisons found in ready-to-heat food residue. The Department of Urban Pathology at UCLA has expressed keen interest in this work.

Zola chose to study the 'replacement threshold' . . . at which point it used to be more price effective to throw out a machine than repair it. Nothing better typifies the subject era than the sight of countless appliances – from TVs to dishwashers to stereos – all tossed because newer, better models cost less than a technician might charge to find a burnt transistor.

Keoki pays the freight, testing rich veins of complex organics and heavy metals for our industrial sponsor.

It's a long shot, but if the assay proves out, Fabrique Chang may bid to come mine Hyperion. One generation's junk can be the next's mother lode.

So much for all that talk, earlier, about setting fields aside for future archeologists. Maybe it's human nature to spoil what we strive to comprehend. Maybe we're all Schliemann, under the skin.

Oh, don't be so cynical, Joe-boy. It's late. Put away the journal and go to bed. Tomorrow is another day.

Friday

By now I thought we'd wrestled every county, state and federal agency, from public health to Indian Affairs, but I never expected to be stopped dead by the Coroner's Office!

Zola found the bones down at South-22, a neat row of ribs sticking through a pile of dingy rags. At first we thought it was a pet, some large dog. On realising they were human, we had no choice but to report it. We're digging in strata from AD 1958, after all. It might be somebody's long-missing great uncle.

What a mess! Reporters and detectives trampling through the pit. Hot lights reviving dormant aromatics, making the place stink to Sheol. Yellow police tape stretching back and forth in a confusing maze. Fortunately, some of the cops seemed competent and sympathetic. I watched as one young homicide investigator worked delicately with a brush and evidence kit. I couldn't help kibitzing about the effects of time and anaerobic chemistry on fingerprints. Finally – perhaps to shut me up – Lieutenant Starling invited me through the cordon to help.

Turns out our jobs have interesting overlaps, and even more interesting, quirky differences. Afterwards,

we cleaned up and talked shop until late. Her profession
seems narrowly focused from my point of view. But
I can relate. We're both in the business of piecing
together clues, reading hidden stories.

This morning, the lieutenant overruled her gruff
sergeant to let us resume work at the north end,
while her crew keeps fussing down south. It's hard
not to be bothered by all the commotion nearby, but
I exhibit calm concentration for the sake of the team.
We are professional time travellers, after all, privileged
to visit the past. No distraction should make us forget
our jobs.

Sunday

At a pace that makes glaciers seem juggernauts,
the Earth's Pacific Plate grinds alongside the North
American Plate. Unlike the head-on collision shoving
up the Himalayas, this glancing blow makes modest
mountains. Where Hyperion now squats once lay a
gentle valley where mule deer grazed and condors
soared. Quite recently, in geologic time, the Shoshone
discovered a rough paradise here. Then, in an eyeblink,
Spaniards came to graze their cattle. Hopalong Cassidy
filmed exploits where I stand each day, or rather, many
metres lower down, where moulder the smothered roots
of ancient oaks.

When burgeoning Los Angeles engulfed these hills,
little upland valleys like these seemed ideal sites for
dumping refuse. Regiments of trucks came and went,
day in, day out, their way lit by torches burning off
methane gas as buried garbage fermented. More matter
moved here in just one year than Rome put into its
roads. More than was shifted for canals at Suez or
Panama. Then, sooner than anyone predicted, a flat

plain stretched between former peaks and the trucks
had to move on.

Nowadays, the gas gets piped away. You can't build
on this kind of unsteady fill, so no one expected visitors
to this abandoned place, despite its poetical name. Not
until slow processes turned detritus into a new kind
of stone.

Then we arrived to dig and pry.

No human trait ever stirred up such trouble as
curiosity.

Monday

Detective Starling finished her investigation. Her
report – inconclusive, except to say the bones date
from the time of the surrounding stratum.

Net tabloids are rife with speculation about gangland
executions. Artists' renderings show mobsters ceremo-
niously interring their victim beneath a sea of waste.
Getting the dates all wrong, someone nicknamed the
skeleton 'Jimmy H'.

Unfortunately for sensationalists, there were no
obvious signs of foul play. That didn't keep some
of the police brass from trying to shut us down. But
Helen Starling saw no legal cause and refused to sign
the order, so we're back in business! After a decent
interval, I must find a good way to thank her.

Tuesday

The day after work resumed, I found a strange note in
my mailbox. Scrawled on real paper in a thin, cramped
style, it simply read – LEAVE IT BE!

Some kook, I guess. Why should anyone care about
a half dozen eggheads, scratching around in garbage?

Wednesday

Europeans laugh when Americans speak of 'history'. As for Los Angeles, you can find every nationality on Earth within ten minutes of downtown, but each draws its heritage from somewhere else. Here in the 'World City', everyone is rootless, and often *glad* to be cut loose from the past.

Besides, who needs to dig in order to know this place? L.A.'s story is well-documented in newspaper files, ledgers, videotape. Was any culture ever so self-involved? Books on current slang and pop culture come out every year. As they say about pornography – nothing is left to the imagination.

Still, there is something special about the layers we visit. They represent a time and place unlike any other, when people remade reality in new, garish colours, unrestrained by precedent. Towering creativity mixed with profound stupor. Rock bands and symphony orchestras. Stench and stainless steel. Nothing compares save Renaissance Florence, also the object of scorn, hatred, and ultimately envy. Some day, people may romanticise TwenCen L.A. as they do the time of Michelangelo.

And pigs might fly?

They do. One Angeleno took his pet porker hang-gliding. I have the newspaper in front of me, circa 1978.

What a place.

Thursday

No time for a personal entry tonight.

Today's big discovery – this time at South-31 – four more sets of bones.

Friday

My, what a fuss. They're still hollering downtown, but the upshot is obvious. They need expert help and the only place to find skilled hands quickly is right here on-site. I'm sitting quietly, twiddling my thumbs till they ask.

Saturday

They asked. Helen gave us a one-day cram course on how to be Junior Crime Scene Investigators, then deputised and put us to work. Since then it's been slow going, but we're used to that. Only big difference is we don't have to watch our budget, agonising over what to put in labelled plastic bags and what to discard. Near the bodies, we save everything.

Everybody in the world wants to come to Hyperion. The crowd control cordon stretches miles. Helicopters buzz, along with scores of whirring autocams, sent over by newsie-mags and hobbyists. Police drones snap up those straying too close. Still it's quite a din.

The press is calling it 'Jimmy's Pit'. Reporters scan old missing person files like bloodhounds, eager to break the story of the year – who the victims were, why they were dumped here, and who might've dunnit. The city is having a wonderful time.

Well, not everybody. I found another note last night, on coming home.

STOP IT NOW, the scrawled piece of paper read. BEFORE YOU REGRET IT.

Too late, whoever you are. Events now have their own momentum. Tomorrow we start lateral holes, expanding the trench in case one or two more bodies might lie buried nearby.

Funny what bothers you at a time like this. Amid all this furore, what bugs me is the coincidence . . . how unlikely it was that we should have randomly chosen a site directly over Jimmy and company. To a scientist – and a detective, I suppose – coincidence is an awfully suspicious thing.

Monday

Zola was in tears when she reported finding the child. A five-year-old, judging from the little bones. This time the clothing was well-preserved. A pink and blue print dress. We all stared as Keoki and a police pathologist worked. That was when we realised, this was no gangland dumping ground.

Half an hour later, Leslie gave a shout. He had found another pair of skeletons. Then, suddenly, it seemed diggers were yelling from all sides. Autocams began colliding overhead as newsies dove in for pix and we scurried from one set of remains to the next. In minutes, word flashed across the Net to every continent.

Massacre in L.A.!

Tomorrow, over my protests, Helen brings in bulldozers.

Ah, Schliemann.

Tuesday

For a time, during the Second World War, the city of Los Angeles mandated compulsory recycling. Materials of all kinds were needed for the effort, from glass and metals to paper and baking fat. Nothing is wasted when you pay heed to the true value of things. Very little refuse wound up coming to Hyperion during those years.

Then, with the war fading into memory, a candidate ran for mayor on a crowd-pleasing platform, promising to repeal the inconvenient law. He won handily. Curbside recycling ended and the trucks began rolling as never before. By the ton, by hundreds and thousands of tons. In a few years an average family might throw away a volume of material equal to their home. A new, disposable way of life seemed ordained forever.

Archeologists could have told them. *Nothing* lasts forever. The Golden Age of Athens waxed and passed away again within a single human lifespan. So did the Age of Waste.

The world won't soon forget either.

According to the Indian Bones Act, any remains less than a thousand years old aren't specimens, but someone's ancestor. You need the local tribe's permission before digging near a burial ground, and must re-inter all unearthed bones with honours.

Fair enough, but I never thought I'd see the Act applied to *this* project. Today, while yellow machines peeled away detritus for a bigger trench, lawyers arrived with injunctions to halt the *desecration of graves*! Turns out they were fronting for the same bunch of retirees who tried to stop us earlier. Don't these people have better things to do with their time?

The dozers stopped for just three hours, then the stay was overruled and digging resumed. I stood around watching machines tear through layers it had taken us months to penetrate with brush and trowel. Wonderful items kept popping into view, only to vanish into hoppers and be carried away. I stopped Keoki and Les from chasing between flashing back-hoe blades, plucking enticing tidbits. Without careful photography and provenance, none of it would provide useful data. So I set them to work tarping over the north end of the old trench, preserving it from contamination.

I'm making this entry with my portable. We've set up a pressurised tent and sleeping quarters, partly because work continues round the clock now, and partly because each of us has had anonymous death threats. Zola's house was vandalised and someone fired a shot through Les's window. We voted to stay together on-site till it all blows over.

Friday

Helen called the dozers off as we neared early-fifties strata. An army of muscular cops waded in, under our direction, and soon hit bones.

And more bones! More than we can count by searchlight, all mixed in with old boxes and bedsprings, melon rinds and tea bags, newspapers and candy wrappers.

Ribcages. Vertebrae. Femurs. Grinning skulls.

Lieutenant Starling ordered a halt for coffee, to let people catch their breath. That's when word spread about The Theory. Seems the idea's been criss-crossing the Net all evening, but we hadn't heard till half the world agreed it *must* be the explanation.

When you think about it, none other fits! The 1950s was an era of frantic building in Southern California. Inevitably, greedy developers took shortcuts. If an old graveyard stood in the way, you were supposed to move the bodies and markers with due care, but often the whole mass was just scooped up and dumped in a pit somewhere.

And what better pit than Hyperion Landfill? A few bribes, some turned heads ... within days, layers of new garbage would hide the evidence. Besides, who was harmed?

It's remarkable how calming a good theory can be. What had verged on panic now seems placid as people wander back to work at a slower pace. There is talk of wrapping it all up tomorrow, after all.

I keep my misgivings to myself. Somehow, it all seems too pat.

Saturday

It didn't wash. Not even for a day.

Oh, for a time headlines blared – *Dump of Death Mystery Solved!* Big shots came down and posed next to the bulldozers, anointing the graveyard-dumping theory and announcing that, while this had all been a nice, diverting summertime distraction, it was time to stop wasting taxpayers' money on a minor 'crime' whose statute of limitations ran out before most living citizens were born. Time to let the dead rest in peace.

The old farts seemed in an awful hurry to put all this behind them. Some of the young beat reporters said their editors were hastily re-assigning them. All told, things smelled pretty fishy.

We sat around pondering.

Suppose some greedy bastards did once gather up the bodies in a cemetery, trucking them off to make room for houses or a shopping mall. That's plausible. But think, what shape would the remains be in, after tumbling together in a hole? I could testify to that, having excavated ancient battlegrounds where armies of Xerxes, or Teng Ho, buried their dead in haste before the sun could rise. The skeletons here in Hyperion look nothing like those jumbled boneyards. Each one is coherent, whole, and they come spread across an area far too wide for the convenient dumping theory to explain.

We agreed unanimously. We're going back out tonight, orders or no orders.

Thursday

Helen Starling says her boys found the guys who set fire to my garage. I couldn't have been more surprised to learn it was old Mr Hansen down the block! Here I'd been expecting some cabal of fundamentalist loonies to be behind the threats and vandalism against my people. But in each case it's been *individual* action by someone they knew. No visible connection between the perpetrators, except their advanced age. It's all very, very weird.

Haven't made a diary entry in some time. I always thought it part of being a careful scientist, like keeping good field notes. But what we're doing hasn't been science for a long time.

To recap – the big-wigs were horrified to learn we had resumed digging. While they slept, we managed to double the excavation. They then dithered, went back to their offices, made phone calls and issued orders – and we doubled it again. By the time judges signed restraints and had them delivered, the whole chain of command lay in ruins. No cop on the beat was going to enforce a halt.

There were skeletons everywhere!

Big ones, men in their prime. Smaller ones ... women, children ... little babies ...

None showed discernible traces of violent death. No sign they had ever been moved after burial. The cemetery-dumping scenario evaporated in smoke, never to be raised again.

We kept working shifts, digging, loading trucks, hauling the dross of fifty years away to the far end of Hyperion . . . though some suspect even that step might prove temporary. For the most part, we worked silently, though each of us knows what ferment is crossing the airwaves. A ferment of newer, more imaginative theories.

There is talk of death squads, like they've had from time to time in South America, with vigilantes scouring the city for 'undesirables' and burying their victims in the dump. Credible, perhaps, if they had killed dozens, even hundreds, but no way in the numbers we are finding. The same goes for satanic or cannibalistic cults. More colourful notions involve everything from extraterrestrial vivisections to a lost underground civilisation. One fellow suggests that something about the specific gravity of bones causes them to migrate through garbage . . . though where they came from in the first place he has no idea.

My favourite idea of the current crop is *spontaneous calcification*. It is based on homeopathy – the notion that all objects carry the imprint of any other object that was ever in contact with them. And what did every single object in Hyperion Landfill have in common? Every one was touched countless times by human beings! Next throw in a crackpot reversal of fossilisation – the process by which groundwater leaches calcium from bones and replaces it with the stuff of rock – and you've got an idea that would have surely made it to the New Age Bestseller List, back in my parents' generation.

Leave trash alone long enough, and it starts precipitating out skeletons.

In other words, garbage recapitulates its makers. We are what we waste.

A fine, maniacal notion. I don't dismiss it lightly.

*   *   *

Or are they metaphors? Perhaps guilt festers and makes tangible a city's crimes.

What, after all, did we do to the homeless, the forgotten? Those spilled out of mental hospitals to fend on their own? In effect, we threw them away. The malnourished, the ill-educated, the drug-wracked and brain-wounded. We threw out all the possibilities they might have brought to light with strong hands and minds, just as surely as those big trucks carried off all else inconvenient and disposable.

I look back on Persia, China, India . . . wherever I dug and found middens of bones, thinking them burial grounds of real people. Perhaps the same thing happened there, as well! In each culture, *shame* may have leaked from the living, seeping underground to wherever lost hopes go, congealing into hideous shape within the ground . . .

No, no! I have *felt* the bones in my hands. They are real, stretching away in all directions. They were once draped in flesh, I know it.

People are welcome to their crackpot theories. But, all metaphysics aside, something happened here. Something terrible.

September

Nobody is bothering with police cordons, anymore. Everyone and anyone is welcome to come up to Hyperion, to help dig. Sometimes it seems half the population under fifty must be here, assisting with the excavation, browsing through the detritus, carting things away. It looks like a scene from some fantastic D.W. Griffiths epic about the construction of the pyramids, only on a vaster scale, Here, under only the loosest of direction, a mob, a horde, a *civilisation* labours

amid dust and stink to undo the greatest single edifice
built by their ancestors, taking it apart by hand and
hauling the bits off in trucks, cars, wheelbarrows.

What our grandparents created here – what they
buried – is fast growing apparent, and they don't
like it. They wander among us, old folks, confused,
distracted, grabbing us by the sleeve and begging us
to stop. When questioned, none of them can explain
why. Tearfully, they just say that it's wrong. That we
must leave it be.

It's the same with officials, politicians, judges. The
eldest issue pronouncements, file writs. We ignore them
and dig on, uncovering layer after layer of the dead.

A million skeletons so far, with no end in sight.

Reports come in from other cities. Of landfill boneyards in New York, Atlanta, Seattle . . . though none as
extensive or dating so far back as Los Angeles. Perhaps
that means it happened first and most profoundly here,
in L.A.

But what? What happened here? Whence came
the dead?

Zola claims the skulls are different from ours. She
points to a slight, statistical difference in the shape
of the occipital lobe.

'They were more like Neanderthals than we are,' she
says, with the eagerness of a proselyte. 'They would
have been more intuitive, more empathic beings . . .'

Les and I think all this must have driven her over the
edge. None of us can see any difference worth getting
excited over.

On the other hand, maybe we don't want to see. Any
difference that held true would support the scariest
theory – that we are *all* murderers.

That we're invaders.

That the true, rightful denizens of L.A. lie buried

where our grandparents put them, after slaying them, one by one. In the course of taking over their city, their lives.

The fact that the idea comes straight out of classic sci-fi doesn't repudiate it. The paranoiac films of those days may reflect an instinctual terror felt by those who *saw* no difference in their friends and family, but somehow knew them for replacements, doppelgängers. Somehow knew their own turn was coming.

It might explain why old folks act the way they do. Deep inside, at some inner core, they are still aliens. Long ago they adopted the memories, behaviour, attitudes, of the Angelenos they replaced – becoming passionate democrats, republicans, junkies and Zen Buddhists – but deep down part of them still knowing what they were.

But we, their descendants, were born thinking ourselves human, if a bit strange for living in this bizarre city. We grew up glorying in quirky ideas – wild individuality, diversity, cool – and most of all the novel notion that 'weird' is no four-letter word.

If someone killed two million Angelenos, our first instinct is pure, ironic.

To avenge them.

October

There is another theory. We might simply have thrown them all away.

The bodies, I mean.

Just the bodies.

They were ours, and we exchanged them. Traded them in. Got new models. Threw out the old.

Why not? It suits our style. Despite all the conservation laws, passed for harder times. Despite draconian recycling. Despite a soaring cost of living caused by wastrel days, we still think basically the same. Like magpies, we'll try whatever's shiny, new.

What if someone once made our grandparents an offer they couldn't refuse?

'Sign here, and I'll show you how to moult and be reborn livelier, more interesting people! Do this and your city will soar heights, explore depths, no other has ever known. Only, in order to trade up, you must forget this pact. Forget the husks you shed. Toss them in the trash along with this week's newspapers, detergent boxes, TV dinner trays! Toss them out, and live!'

I wonder about the fine print. Would Angelenos even stop to read it, in their rush to sign?

I also wonder if I'm going mad.

Winter

Hyperion is deep . . . deeper than we ever imagined. Yet, slowly, inexorable, it empties itself of all we had put there.

Where the detritus is taken, I don't know. Only that it climbs a hundred trails out of this valley, by machine, by human back, sometimes in a floating haze that seems to scale the dusty hills without aid. Like a superfluid – like some entity awakened – the waste departs, spilling from a container unable to hold it any longer.

Our dross, our toys, our broken machine servants, our used wrappers . . . how could we ever think the bonds linking us to our things could be broken simply by throwing them away? Destiny firmly connects the maker and the made. User and used. Creation and creator. So it was in the myths of Ur and Thebes. So it always shall be.

We never really throw our things away. We just put them down for a while. Now they are coming home.

Millennium

Picked clean, it holds a certain sterile beauty. A valley of bare, trampled clay between steep hills. Bare clay covered with four million skeletons, the only man-made things now left behind.

It makes a pretty scene – Hyperion Boneyard. Peaceful.

All the hordes are gone. Just a few of us remain, sitting around, waiting.

Things are happening just over the rim, where Los Angeles can be heard fast turning into something different again. By now, one theory or another must have proven true. Or else no one cares any more about past truths, so involved are they in rapid changes. Merging the reclaimed into what's shiny new. But some of us stay in Hyperion, fed from time to time by kindly visitors. We wait, keeping vigil for others who cannot.

Sometimes it rains. Bones sink slowly into the softening mud.

Full of nutrients, I hear. Bones are. They belong in good earth.

Yesterday, I thought I saw a condor, winging near the sun.

Yes, yes. I know things are going on, elsewhere. I'll go take part again, really. Soon as I've rested. Thought a few things out. Seen events through to their conclusion.

I'll just stay a little while longer . . . and watch the first oaks grow.

The Dogma of Otherness

It all began when my publisher sent me out on what used to be called a Chautauqua circuit – public seminars and panels and rubber-chicken dinners – to promote my books. That's when I began noticing something very strange about the way people have started thinking these days.

Publicity tours can be pretty tedious, at times. Even science fiction conventions start to blur after too long an exposure. Maybe that's why I started seeing things I otherwise would have ignored.

It started innocuously enough: my second novel was about genetically engineered dolphins, and it's no secret that – next to unicorns – those friendly sea mammals are just about everybody's favourite creatures. People at these gatherings seemed mostly to like the way I handled them.

Inevitably, though, someone in the crowd would ask what I think of porpoise intelligence here and now, in the real world.

It's predictable. There is something compelling about a species that so obviously (for Lord knows what reason) *likes us*. People want to know more about them. They ask how much progress has been made in teaching dolphins to speak our language. Or have researchers yet learned to talk to them in theirs?

Such questions are based on so many implicit assumptions . . . I really hate disappointing folks, but there is a duty to tell the truth.

'I'm not a real expert,' I tell them. 'But the data are pretty easy to interpret. I'm afraid real dolphins simply aren't all that smart. Those folk tales about high cetacean intelligence, at or above our levels, are just stories. It's a shame, but they just aren't true.'

This, apparently, is not how a lecturer remains popular. Not once has the reaction varied.

'*But you can't know that!*'

A universal mutter of agreement. Angry, nodding heads.

'*If we can't communicate with them, it must be because we're not smart enough!*'

I reply as best I can. 'Well, Professor Luis Herman of the University of Hawaii has worked for a long time with the deepwater species *Steno bredanensis* – widely recognised as one of the brightest breeds. Dr Herman has, indeed, proved that the higher dolphins are pretty smart animals. They can parse four- and even five-element command "sentence" signals at least as well as those famous "sign-language" chimpanzees. In fact, the evidence for dolphins is more rigorous than it is for chimps.'

This has them smiling. But I make the mistake of going on.

'Nevertheless, the basic problem-solving skills of even the brightest porpoise cannot match those of a human toddler. I'm afraid if we want "other minds" to talk to, we're going to have to look elsewhere . . . or construct them ourselves.'

Again, instant protests.

'*But . . . but there may be other ways of dealing with the world intelligently than those we imagine!*'

'*Right!*' another person agrees. '*Those problems the dolphins had to solve were designed by human beings, and may miss the whole point of cetacean thought! In their environment they're probably as smart as we are in ours!*'

How does one answer statements like those?

I've listened to recorded dolphin 'speech', transposed in frequency. The sounds are repetitive, imprecise . . . clearly filled with emotional, not discursive, information.

Subjective opinion, to be sure. So I'd patiently describe the brilliantly simple experiments of Herman and others, which had forced *me* to abandon my own early optimism that it was only a matter of time until we learned to understand dolphin speech.

But this only seemed to deepen the questioners' sullen insistence that there must be *other varieties of intelligence*.

Finally, I gave up arguing.

'You know,' I said, 'every group of non-scientists I've talked to reacts this way. It's really had me wondering. But now I think I've figured it out.'

They looked puzzled. I explained.

'Anthropologists tell us that every culture has its core of central, commonly shared assumptions – some call them zeitgeists, others call them dogmas. These are beliefs that each individual in the tribe or community will maintain vigorously, almost like a reflex.

'It's a universal of every society. For instance, in the equatorial regions of the globe there's a dogma that could be called machismo, in which revenge is a paramount virtue that runs deeper even than religion. From Asian family centrism to Russian pessimism, there are world views that affect nations' behaviour more basically than superficial things like communism,

or capitalism, or Islam. It all has to do with the way
children are raised.

'We, too, have our zeitgeist. But I am coming to see
that the contemporary West is very, very strange in one
respect. It just may be the first society in which it is a
major reflexive dogma that *there must be no dogmas!*'

The puzzled looks have spread. This is quite a
departure. I hurry on.

'Look how you all leapt up to refute me. Even though
I'm the supposed "dolphin expert" here, that hardly
matters, since you all assume that any expert can still
be wrong! No matter how prestigious his credentials,
no expert can know all the answers.'

This is a bit of a revelation to me, even as I say it.

'Think about it. "There's always another way of
looking at things" is a basic assumption of a great
many Americans.'

'Yeah?' one of the fellows up in front says, perhaps
with a bit of a chip on his shoulder. 'Well, isn't that
true? There *is* always another way!'

'Of course there is . . . or at least I tend to think
so. I *like* to see other viewpoints.' I shrug. 'But you
see I was brought up in the same culture as you were,
so it's no surprise I share your dogma of otherness.'

I roll the phrase over on my tongue, then repeat it,
perhaps a little pontifically. 'The Dogma of Otherness
insists that all voices deserve a hearing, that all points
of view have something of value to offer.

'Your reactions reflect this fundamental assumption.
Having been raised in the same culture, I believe in it as
fully as you do. Recall how reluctant I was to decide,
at last, that dolphins aren't superintelligent. Most of
us here believe in diversity of ideas.

'But think, for a moment, how unique this is . . . how
unusual this cultural mindset has to be! Throughout
history nearly every human society has worked hard to

ingrain its children with the assumption that theirs was the only way to do things. Oh, we still get a lot of that here. It probably comes automatically with flags and nations and all that tribal stuff. But where and when else has the societal dogma included such a powerful indoctrination to *defend* otherness?'

A man in the front row speaks up.

'That's a culturally chauvinistic statement!' There are agreeing nods all around the room. 'I mean, what's so special about our culture? We're no better than, say, Asian civili—'

'You're doing it again!' I cry; I can hardly sit still. (Perhaps from being too impressed with my own cleverness?) Several members of the audience blink for a moment, then smile faintly.

'I don't see—' he tries to continue, but I'm too excited and hurry on.

'Look, it may be true that there's something to be learned from all points of view. *But it might also be true that that's just the bias our heterogeneous, melting-pot culture has imposed on us!*

'Answer truthfully. You all believe that widely diverse points of view have merit, right?'

'Right,' the young man answers firmly, his jaw set.

'And your insistence could be called a declaration of faith in a "Doctrine of Otherness", right?'

'I suppose so. But—'

'And you'll agree that as a truly pervasive set of assumptions, it's pretty much a liberal Western tradition, won't you? Think how strange this Doctrine of Otherness would seem to an ancient Roman, or to the dynastic Chinese who thought the world revolved around Beijing, or to Tudor England, or to most of the peoples of the world today.'

'Well . . .' He doesn't want to admit it, but after a moment's thought the fellow finally nods.

'All right, so that's just our way of looking at things. But you can't say it's actually *better* than any other way. We have this so-called Doctrine of Otherness. Other peoples have their own cultural assumptions, of equal value.'

'Aha!' I smile. 'But by saying that, by stating that those other points of view have merit, you are insisting that *your* cultural dogma – this Doctrine of Otherness – *is* the best! You're a cultural chauvinist!'

He frowns and scratches his head. A woman on the left raises her hand, then slowly lowers it again.

From the back, a voice calls. 'That's a tautology . . . or a paradox . . . I forget which. It's like when I say "This sentence is a lie." You've got him trapped either way he goes!'

I shrug. 'So? Since when are deep-seated cultural assumptions ever fair? They're adaptations a society makes in order to survive . . . in our case, dictated by being a nation of immigrants who had to learn to get along together. Dogmas don't have to be entirely logical, as long as they work.

'Still, perhaps we ought to be proud of America as the prime promoter of a dogma of difference and choice—'

Ooh. They react quickly to that!

'Why proud?' an elderly lady remarks vehemently. 'That doesn't make us better than anybody else! It's no great shakes to measure our own culture by *our* culture's standards, and come out with the answer that we're okay! We worship diversity, so by that token we see our worship of diversity as virtuous—'

'*That* is a tautology,' I point out. Fortunately, she ignores the rude interruption.

'—But that doesn't mean that our culture doesn't come up lacking by some *other* set of standards,' she insists. 'Other cultural dogmas could be just as valid.'

I sigh. 'You're doing it again.'

This time a few in the audience laugh. The woman glares for a moment. 'Okay. So I'm a product of my culture. But that doesn't necessarily mean I'm right. I mean it doesn't necessarily mean I'm wrong. I mean . . .'

When the laughter spreads, she breaks down and smiles. 'I – I think I see what you're getting at now.'

'I only wish *I* did,' I reply. But we're starting to get into the spirit of this, now. More hands rise, and we're off.

Perhaps it began with Copernicus, who exiled Earth permanently from the centre of the Universe.

If this was so, then no one could claim Europe (or China or Arabia) was the navel of creation, either. The hidden implications were profound. People who accepted the new astronomy also had to adjust to the idea that what their senses told them every day was untrue – that the world did not revolve around them alone.

As the centuries passed, this Copernican 'Principle of Mediocrity' was extended. We discovered that the sun is really a rather mundane star, in a not unusual galaxy, among billions of galaxies. Now we find that the Milky Way's spiral arms teem with the very chemicals of life, implying that our Earth, special as it is, is not likely to be unique.

Mankind's brief existence in the four-billion-year history of the planet is a sure lesson in humility.

Meanwhile, relativity tells us that there is no absolute frame of reference. Gödel's Proof and quantum mechanics have refuted forever old Hegel's mad dream of 'derived certainty'. Truth – it has been proven mathematically – is a thing with fuzzy outlines, when you look up close.

So perhaps it was modernity, as well as the socio-
logical needs of a melting-pot nation, that caused us to
develop the Dogma of Otherness. If there's nothing so
unique about our own place and time, maybe there's
nothing particularly central about our own selves, and
the points of view we happen to hold.

Nor is it even necessarily paramount being human.

(Until a hundred years ago, children's stories very
seldom featured sympathetic animal characters. In
1907 the teddy bear was criticised as 'likely to warp
the mothering instincts of young girls'. Now sympathy
with other creatures is inculcated at an early age, by
wise owls, cuddly pandas, and friendly little aliens.)

The Principle of Mediocrity has not only vitalised
science, it's given us the ability to re-examine centuries
of prejudice, and to shake off old tribal taboos with
hardly a wince. In spite of the new horrors that
madmen can perpetrate when their clutches fall upon
modern technology, we have made progress. It's a more
reasoning, more rational world we live in today.

Still, philosophies, even philosophies that do good,
can outlive their vigour. What Copernicus began need
not continue forever.

There is a new principle making the rounds these
days, called the 'Anthropic Imperative'. Its most
vigorous proponents, including Professor Frank Tipler
of Tulane University, seem to be saying that we have
gone too far in claiming that there is nothing special
at all about the time or place in which we live.

Simply stated, the Anthropic Principle says that it's
quite possible for an observer's time and place to be
unique, if the unique factor is necessary in order for
there to be an observer in the first place.

Bucking the popular enthusiasm for the search for
extraterrestrials, Tipler and a few others dare to
propose that it is quite possible that mankind may

be the sole intelligent species in the galaxy, perhaps anywhere, anytime.

I won't go into their arguments here. But I mention the Anthropic Principle as just one edge of what seems to be a new philosophical movement – one that does not seem to threaten the existence of the Dogma of Otherness so much as threaten it with change.

Old Philosophies

Three major views of Man in Nature contended with each other in Western thought a century and a half ago: Traditional Christian, Mechanistic, and Romantic.

The Traditional Christian point of view was that nature was placed here for the use of man, and that the world was meant for short-duration use anyway. The wilderness was a cruel parody of the Garden of Eden, a travesty to be fought and tamed. Other creatures were separate from man in the fundamental sense of lacking souls.

As Matthew Cartmill put it, civilization 'saw nature as sick, and man as inherently above nature – that is, supernatural'.

The mechanistic view, a reaction to the one above, grew out of the eighteenth-century Enlightenment. The Universe, as the emerging sciences and particularly mathematics unfolded its mysteries, was seen as a majestic clockwork, with mankind merely a complicated little subset of parts, spinning in unseen harmony with the rest, under the apparent chaos of daily life.

This was a tremendous step towards sympathy with otherness, a direct outgrowth of the Principle of Mediocrity. But it, too, had its day and then saw the creation of a counter-reaction.

The Romantic movement answered the Age of Reason with emotion, logic with *Sturm und Drang*. With Rousseau's extolling of the natural, and condemnation of civilisation as the essence of corruption, the suite was complete. Humankind can dream of a return to harmony with the natural world. We can best do this by abandoning an arrogant insistence on our own difference.

Each world view contributed to our culture. The traditionalists oriented us towards the future, and towards taking command of our world. The mechanists taught us to appreciate that world's delicate, beautiful balance. And about the Romantic view, Cartmill said that 'a prevalent vision of man as a sick animal estranged from the harmony of nature conditioned new scientific theories and lent them the mythic force and consequence that they needed to be widely accepted.'

Ducks That Rape

But the twenty-first century looms. Taken by themselves, each of the philosophies discussed above appears ludicrous to a modern woman or man. Might it, perhaps, be time to craft a new view of nature and our place in it?

The Doctrine of Otherness has had powerful propaganda over the last several decades. In particular, the animals have been getting awfully good press.

'Man is the only animal that (take your choice)
  . . . murders its own kind
  . . . kills its children
  . . . kills for sport
  . . . commits sexual assault
  . . . wages war

'. . . hurts the environment . . .'

A generation has grown up being told these things over and over. And in having humility and shame pounded into us, we have begun, indeed, to look upon ourselves differently. It isn't just because of teddy bears that we have started to treat the other creatures around us with more respect. It is also because we have had it driven home again and again that we had better shape up if we ever expect to live up to a standard of decency.

But whose standard?

Why, our own, of course. And here's where that paradox comes in again. Species have *always* gone extinct. That is how evolution works. The pity comes in when *we* see nature's creations as beautiful, and when *we* feel shame over wiping out something as unique and irreplaceable as a blue whale, or a manatee, or even a dodo.

No question where I stand in all this. I think environmentalism is *good*. That's with a capital G. Not only am I a thoroughly acculturated member of my generation – fully inoculated with guilt over mankind's crimes – but I'm beginning to see, along with millions of others, that keeping up a complex ecosystem is the best way of ensuring our own long-range survival.

This view of Man the Destroyer – a beast within ourselves that must be constantly watched – may be the very fairy tale needed to frighten us into our senses. Cartmill put it aptly:

'There is no way to tell for sure whether this mythmaking has contributed to our survival thus far. I suspect it has. I doubt that the world would have ended if Muir or Twain or Freud or Jeffers had never lived. Other visionaries would have come up . . . But I think it might perhaps have ended by

now if we hadn't learned to be afraid of ourselves
long before that fear was entirely reasonable.'

The propaganda we grew up with was a Good
Thing, no question about it. It appears to have saved
the otter, the dolphin, the gorilla and, perhaps, the
whales. Maybe even ourselves.

But is it true?

Bad-mouthing mankind has been important drama.
But once we are in the habit of protecting nature for
its own sake, do we have to keep it up?

It's all a big fat lot of hype. Nice hype, but hype
nonetheless. All over the natural world there is an
almost infinite variety of animals that (take your
choice)

    ... murder their own kind
    ... kill their children
    ... kill for sport
    ... commit rape
    ... wage war
    ... harm the environment ...

Et cetera, et cetera. Day by day we are finding that
the line dividing us from the animal world blurs,
becoming one of magnitude, not quality.

Apes use tools in the wild and can be taught sign
language. They are also prone to simpler versions
of every type of human mental illness, including
infanticide and deadly, 'organised' warfare.

Male lions will kill the cubs of their predecessors,
after winning cunning 'wars' of eviction.

Stallions will deliberately kill each other.

Historically, a large part of the deforestation of the
Middle East seems to have been performed not just by
man, but by goats as well. Elephants are a primary
cause of the deforestation of East Africa.

Mallard ducks have been observed to commit gang

rape on mated females. In more and more supposedly 'monogamous' species of birds, we are discovering that males commit philandery.

Even dolphins, almost alone with mankind in being capable of altruism outside of their own species – of helping others no matter how different – have been observed murdering their own kind.

All three of the old world views lie in shambles around us. Only a traditionalist fool would say that man is the 'paragon of animals', and nature our playpen. Only a pollyanna would contend that the clockwork spins majestically on, in harmony whatever we do. And it is also romantic nonsense to say that we are a pimple on Creation . . . that the world would be somehow far better off without us.

Where does that leave us, then?

It leaves us, I hope, uncomfortable and thoughtful.

We should not stop pumping out the nature films. 'Humility propaganda' serves a useful purpose, for there is still a world out there stuck in phases one and two. But for those of us who have passed through the Doctrine of Otherness, it might be time to move on.

Perhaps to the attitude of Elder Brothers and Sisters only a little more knowledgeable than our fellow creatures, but with the power and the duty to be their guardians. In time, if we do well with the garden, we might even have reason to pause and give ourself a little bit of credit . . . to look, as a species, into the mirror and see neither Lord of Creation nor Worldbane, but merely the first of many in the world to rise to the role of caretaker.

CONTINUITY

Piecework

1

It annoyed Io's best friend to give birth to a four-kilo cylinder of tightly wound, medium grade, placental solvent filters.

For five long months Perseph had kept to a diet free of sugar, sniff, or tobac – well, almost free. The final ten weeks she'd spent waddling around in the bedouin drapery fashion decreed for pieceworkers this year. And all that for maybe two thousand dollars' worth of industrial sieves little better than a *fabricow* might produce!

Perseph was really ticked.

Outwardly, Io made all the right sympathetic sounds, though actually she had little use for her friend's anger. It had been Perseph's choice to hire her womb to a freelance codder of dubious pedigree without even vetting him through an agent.

'They're all sperm crazy,' Io had warned months earlier, as the two of them sat together on her narrow con-apt balcony, watching a twilight-flattened sun squeeze berryjuice colour into stained horizon clouds.

Nearer, a warm mist sublimed from the boggy reed
beds of the Mersey estuary, a haze presently fanned
into tattered wisps by homebound flocks of noisy
sea birds.

'There's no profit in placental jobbing, and no hope
for advancement,' Io told Perseph that evening. 'Me,
I'll stick to egg work.'

'But egg jobs cost you to get started,' Perseph complained. 'And a failure can ruin you in non-delivery
charges. *Then* where's your investment?'

As if Perseph knew what the word meant! Like most
pieceworkers, the tall brunette never saved a penny out
of her delivery fees, blowing it all on the move-party
circuit until it was time to return to her dole cheques
and her next surropregnancy. No wonder Perseph
stayed with placental-fab. Some people just had no
ambition.

Io vividly recalled that evening, several months ago,
when the two of them watched silent marsh fog diffuse
raggedly over the muddy river banks into Ellesmere
Port's cattleyards, softening the complacent lowing of
the animals, if not their pungent aroma.

Twenty-four hours a day, lorries pulled out from
the milking sheds and parturition barns, carrying bulk
loads of gene-designed oils, polymers and industrial
membranes. The mass production of specially bred
fabricows dwarfed the output of small-time contrac-
tors like Perseph or Io. Rumour had it ICI housed
their pampered creatures here on the south bank to
intimidate the pieceworkers living in derelict marinas
and towering co-op houseboats nearby.

If so, the cattleyards had an effect on Io opposite
to that intended. They boosted her morale, reminding
her that there were still some things neither animals nor
machines could do as well as a human craftswoman. No
fabricow would ever produce wares as fine as hers!

That evening, months ago, Io's friend had only just begun her latest surropreg and still yearned passionately for the chemical pleasures now denied her by guild rules. Of course, soon Perseph would be substituting a mellow high from her own hormonal flow. Meanwhile though, she made pretty miserable company.

'Nawi, Io. I don't think I could hold out long enough to do egg work. It takes so long, I'd go crazy for a party.'

'But Pers, look what Technique Zaire's paying for a prime cockatrice, these days. Or a shipbrain—'

'A shipbrain! Hah! How'd a piece like me ever get seeded with a shipbrain? If *I* ever signed up for egg work they'd knock me up with . . . with a traffic cop!' Perseph laughed, a sound Io felt had grown more bitter of late.

Io shook her head. 'All I know's I don't want to have to scrimp for another ten years. Two more successful carries and I'll have paid for tuition and a licence, and have enough left over for nestworks. Anyway, eggcraft leaves me needing less retroconversion.'

'Hmm,' her friend had said, dubiously. 'Meanwhile you live like a tweenie, saving all your bonuses, cashing in all your hobby and travel 'lotments. I swear, Io, sometimes some of us think you—' Perseph bit her lip. 'Well, you just don't party enough.'

'I got no time for move-parties, Pers. You know that. There's school . . .' Instantly Io knew it had been a mistake to mention it.

'Argh,' Perseph had twisted away in disgust, a motion that set her visibly gritting her teeth. She grunted, covering her already tender abdomen. 'Io, you make me tired just thinkin' about it. Some ambitions just aren't worth the effort.'

That conversation had distilled the difference in their

views, and from that day forth they had simply avoided the subject.

But now Io recalled the occasion with eidetic detail as she walked alongside a slowly crawling recovery couch, brushing her friend's sweat-damp hair while postpartum enzymes dripped into Perseph's veins, gradually displacing her cheeks' chalky pallor with a healthy colour one could hardly tell from natural. Over one armrest, a glowing monitor measured Perseph's recovery from the strains of labour, pacing the slow forward progress of her couch to the strengthening of her vital signs.

Pieceworkers in the sperm trade hardly ever got visitors on delivery day. What would be the point? So these moving couches weren't equipped with side-cars, only tiny, spring-mounted jump stools. Io preferred to walk, eyes ever alert for the maintenance carts and cleaner beasts scurrying about on pre-assigned courses. Normally, she'd simply have called after Perseph got home. But Io had been in the neighbourhood, so she dropped by to surprise her friend.

Now she was starting to wish she hadn't. Though Io knew her reaction was old-fashioned, these wholesale decanting centres tended to give her nausea.

She brushed Perseph's black ringlets while rows of other recovery couches periodically emerged from unloading bays like new vans off assembly lines, each conveying a tired, limp, freshly emptied pieceworker. Occasionally, as the doors opened, cries spilled into the vast recovery hall – from the panicky ululations of an ill-trained first-timer all the way to the rhythmic karate-shouts of a skilled veteran – the melodies of modern industrial labour.

No, Io vowed within her thoughts. I'll stick to egg work.

The brush caught on a knot of Perseph's hair. The woman cursed. 'Wrigglers!'

'Sorry, Pers, I—'

'No, dammit, look at that! I knew it!' She bit her thumb at a shimmering holoribbon traversing the vaulted ceiling, carrying late quotes from the Bio-Bourse.

'Meconium! I knew I should've delivered three days ago. Look what's happened to solvent filter prices since then! But no, I just *had* to try to put on those last few grams.'

Disgusted, Perseph shifted on the bed, causing a large lump to jiggle beneath the sheets, like a hunchback dwarf under a tent propped up by her shrouded legs. 'Hey! Watch what you're doin' down there!' Perseph slapped the squirming bulge.

Snuffled grunts, a phlegmatic fart, were her only answer.

'Damn, cheap model cleaners,' she muttered. 'I'd do better without 'em.'

Embarrassed, Io looked around. But none of the other recovering workers riding nearby trolleys seemed to notice. Some slept complacently. A few spoke on hush phones, only their expressions hinting whether they were talking to agents or loved ones. Others watched soaps on tiny armrest TV sets while tailored enzymes dripped into their arms, cutting the time the Company had to maintain this service on overhead. The couch amenities were required under the Piecework Labour Act. There, at least, the guild had actually done some good.

A few of the ladies on nearby carts looked high already, probably on smuggled-in drugs, taking advantage of their very first moments free of surropreg discipline.

'Look, Pers, I'm glad I caught you coming out. But

my lunch break's almost over, and I need a protein fix
before going back to work.'

'Work?' Perseph had a dark glitter in her eye. 'You
got a *job* now, too?'

'Uh, yeah.' Io instantly regretted the slip. 'It's – it's
only quarter time, Pers. One of my teachers noticed my
reading level was up to . . . well, I been filing records
at a psycher's office. It's no big deal . . .'

'School *and* a job. Crapadoodle.' Perseph shrugged.
'All right. Go squeeze in lunch.' She jabbed idly
towards Io's abdomen. 'Can't let th' little toaster
starve, can we?'

Perseph punched a button activating the Soap
Channel on her armrest TV – no doubt to annoy Io,
who quickly averted her eyes from the seductive,
flickering images. Io avoided *all* addictions.

'Um, yeah. I'll – I'll come and see you after you're
back on your feet.' But Perseph had already focused
on the detergent drama. 'Ymmm,' her friend said.

Stepping away, Io had to move nimbly to dodge a
careening service cart. By instinct her hands moved
protectively over her swelling belly. She felt motion
within, responding to her increasing heart-rate – almost
as if the thing inside her were actually alive.

Her tender left breast throbbed.

'Green shit!' Perseph's voice really carried this time,
drawing looks from all sides. 'That does it!'

The sheet flew back. With both hands, the dark-
haired pieceworker dislodged a small furry creature from between her thighs. 'Get out! Women
have sealed their own capillaries for hundreds of
years without pissface little lickers like you. Beat
it!'

A plaintive cry. Service uncompleted. Meal unfin-
ished. The artificial beast dodged Perseph's kicking
feet and crouched at the end of the chaise, mewing for

a handler to come and take it from this unappreciative woman.

Io turned quickly and hurried away.

The usual crowd loitered by the exit, eyeing each weary pieceworker as she emerged blinking into the sunlight.

Pedicabbies offered rides home on government vouchers. Codders passed out their cards and offered to show off their licence tattoos. The inevitable scraggly pair of Madrid Catholic protesters walked their well-worn tracks, placards drooping disconsolately.

The codders were the worst. Of course you had to have codders to run the sperm trade. Placental filter makers like Perseph could never afford to have their own genetic programming done. Even a bundle of high quality platinum-sieves only paid off in five figures, and a woman was limited by law to twenty-five surropregs over a lifetime. So it was men who underwent the expensive treatments to have their reproductive cells modified, amortising the cost against the commissions they received from each pieceworker who carried their wares.

The codders who haunted the exits of decanting centres were generally of a pretty low order – either desperate to grab their percentages on the spot, before their tired clients could blow their fees, or so hard up for customers they'd hawk their patterns to women coming straight off decanting.

The idea made Io feel queasy. Imagine even thinking about another knockup within two hours of labour!

And yet, she saw several pieceworkers of her acquaintance emerge from the recovery bay and stroll gingerly over to the crowd of strutting males – all dressed in bright, tight-fitting tanktops, their multicoloured leggings converging on codpieces tied with laced bows. The codders treated their prospective clients with exaggerated courtliness, offering folding stools, drinks, and sprays of flowers to any fem willing to sit and hear about their exciting, latest-model designs.

And they say romance is dead, Io thought ironically.

'Hey Io, milady. You are the fair one, ain't yo?'

Hair processed flat, parted down the middle in the latest style, his leggings were yellow and bright pink, and the padded codpiece a polkadot combination of the two. He was lacing up one side, as if he had just finished showing off his licence to a client.

'Um. Hello, Colin,' she nodded. The codder was part of Perseph's party circle and so, by convention, a friend of Io's as well. Though there were many types of friends.

'You're here furly early, no Io?' He eyed her surropreg garb, barely yet filled out with the fruits of her own production.

'I came down to see Perseph.' She nodded towards the recovery bay. Colin's eyes widened.

'Fave babe! Thanksyo, Io. I'll station this ever-welcome selfsame to whip out my card just as she re-enters th' hurly world.'

'Just make sure that's all you whip out, Colin. There's ladies present.'

Colin guffawed. As Io intended, he took her remark as a sarcastic, off-colour jibe – unit coin in the strange protocol of jest-bonding. He couldn't know that on another level Io had meant every word, literally.

'So when's your time to give over an' do your work the natchway, Io?'

'By natural, I assume you mean by grunt and shove? Letting a codder like you take ten per cent of my fees and all the credit? No thanks, Colin. Egg work may be harder, but it's between me an' the designers—'

'Between you an' cold glass an' rubber, you mean!' Colin's stiff grin said this was still repartee, but his voice was chill. 'An' you actually *like* it like that? Are you *sure* your profile reads hetero correctly, Io? None of us boys see it that way.'

Io felt a wave of anger. Who had told this cretin about her profile? Had Perseph? Was it possible to trust *nobody*?

Colin loomed over her, showing teeth. 'Y'know, Io, sometimes we get an idea you think you're better than the rest of us. Just because you stayed in tweenie-school, and prefer popping off toasters instead of honest filters, like your friends, that doesn't make you a watch-fobber. You were born down here, babe. Grunt 'n' shove is how *you* got started.'

Io's gut churned. In her Immature Interactions class she had begun learning how to parse exchanges like this – the way Colin was trying to intimidate her with words, body stance, and vague, intimated threats of friendship-withdrawal. Funny how one took this sort of behaviour for granted, until the day somebody finally gave you a model. Showed you that it was a *process* like any other in the world. Then it all seemed to pop into focus, and suddenly look so very silly and primitive.

Ah, theory was fine. But practical applications weren't in her curriculum until next term, and that wouldn't help Io now. She didn't know how to disarm this fellow's aggression, not without leaving him angry.

Oh, what the hell. Io decided she really didn't care what this tissue-stuffer thought of her, anyway.

'Read my lips, Colin.' Io leaned forward and mouthed words in street talk. 'Wrigglers . . . count zero; joppy turnin' floppy.'

Colin rocked back, paling visibly as his hands began a zigzag motion to avert bad luck. Too late, he caught himself. 'Heh. Ha-ho, Io.' He grinned, blinking away sudden perspiration as he glanced to see if anyone else had noticed. 'Very funny.'

He wouldn't forgive her soon for making him show his superstition openly like that. Io winked. 'Didn't mean it, Colin. Keep 'em high, boy. Both the count and the jopper.'

She turned and left before he could reply, making off through the ranks of pedicabs, past the limp, resigned pickets, across the bus lanes and out into the streets of Liverpool proper.

The crowds were as she'd always known them, teeming, bustling. All her life, Io had been awash in a sea of people. It was the way of the world, and would be until the population control measures finally took effect.

At least this century frowned on ostentatious class distinction, and coloured synthetic fabrics were cheap. So nobody dressed shabby unless they wanted to. It took a sharp eye to pick out the types – the dole-fed majority, who spent their days seeking distraction at state-subsidised entertainments – then those with service jobs and some status – and finally the elite, the proud ones, the ones with real work to do.

Mostly the difference could be found in the eyes. Workers had a *look* . . . as if they *belonged* in the world, and weren't just marking time. Every time she noticed that look, Io felt more determined than ever to stay in school. To fight for not just any certificate, but the very highest. Nothing less would do for the survival of her soul.

A sudden wet touch behind her right knee sent panic flashes up her spine. She whirled, heart pounding, her right hand at her breast. Io looked down and sighed.

Bright brown eyes briefly looked into hers. A wet nose snuffled. Its fur was shaded in the blue and yellow bee-striping of official authority . . . the colours of a traffic cop.

The doglike creature, programmed with perfect knowledge of the vehicle code, dismissed Io with a snort and moved on. Traffic cops never forgot a face or odour, never forgave an infraction until the fine was paid. Watching it wander off through the crowd, Io found it hard to believe highly skilled pieceworkers once manufactured such creatures, back when they were experimental, before a final model was certified to reproduce itself.

Still sniffing, hunting violators, the traffic cop turned and disappeared into the crowd.

Io rested her back against a cool display window as people surged by. She looked down the street, seeking distraction as her heart-rate slowly settled again.

Apparently it was rubbish day today. Open-lidded green bins showed that the first set of lorries had already been by. But the red, yellow and silver dust-bins still stood tightly sealed on the kerbs, awaiting pickup. Not far away Io saw a Recycle-Authority policeman ticketing a local merchant for failing to sort all the non-ferric metals out of his organic mulch. As the dispirited proprietor looked on he got no sympathy from the passers-by. Certainly not from Io.

At last, calm again, she felt able to plot a route through the crowds towards a place where she could sit down to a palatable meal

At least there's less rationing than there used to be, she thought, though they say it can come back, anytime.

Io wasn't really hungry, but that didn't matter. She ate more for the thing within her than for herself, anyway.

The 'toaster', Perseph and Colin had called it.

'I don't do home appliances,' she said, under her breath.

Still, the street slang struck Io with its wry aptness. Again, the product throbbed within her.

Yeah. Time to go feed her toaster.

2

. . . By the year 2000 overpopulation had brought on three ominous consequences. The first of these had been foreseen by thoughtful people long before . . . that the needs of over six billion human beings simply exceeded the carrying capacity of the planet. Topsoil, mineral ores, fresh water, and the genetic pool of natural species were among the non-renewable resources rapidly being depleted. Alternative, sustainable practices had to be found, and quickly.

A second effect of overpopulation, however, went almost unnoticed until quite late, and that was the matter of creative unemployment.

Most of the interim solutions enabling society to feed and house the billions arose out of productive technologies controlled by a small, elite labour force. The rest of humanity was utterly dependent, unable to make any noticeable difference. Some countries masked this by providing 'jobs' in a 'service economy', but in the long run serious alienation grew out of the frustrated human need to do work, work that is appreciated, work that is of real value to society.

Then there was the third great problem – that of misapplication of education. For while mammoth literacy campaigns had elevated the general level of culture, a great many people spent years learning to do things that actually required little, if any, real facility. Meanwhile, the most delicate, most demanding job in history was being performed almost universally by unskilled labour . . .

*   *   *

Io closed the book when twinges in her left breast surged again – prolactin-powered hot flashes that were made worse by a basic lateral imbalance.

The clash was fundamental. On one side an organ had been modified by premier industrial technicians and was now setting up to execute complex designer chemistry. At the same time, however, out from under her other arm protruded its conservative twin. Responding to pregnancy hormones, that breast was happily creating archaic precursors to next-to-useless fluids, fucking with her brain, making her imagine impossible things.

Though she tried to hide her discomfort, Io's agent noticed as he performed her weekly check-up.

'I warned you against leaving one tit in natch-state,' Joey reminded her while taking colour readings and sonograms of each gland. 'Here I get you a bid to produce a really choice secondary product, Mobil's latest lubricant for high-torque tools, and you insist on only setting up at half capacity! You know what that does to your rep, Io? It *advertises* that you aren't serious about going full-time pro. What am I to do with you, hm?'

Io put her textbook aside. 'You'll let me do it my way, Joey. That's what you're gonna to do. Anyway, I'll be producing with my left breast, also.'

'Producing what? Colostrum and homosap milk? What'll we do with that stuff, make cheese? Have you see the latest futures? With the birthrate down again, they're a glut on the market!'

'They won't be when I deliver,' she assured him. 'Trust me.'

Nearby, the General Diagnostics surropreg monitor buzzed smugly, a reassuring, complacent sound where it would have blared for bad news. Pushing back a wisp of thinning blond hair, Io's agent tore free a printout of her check-up results, while still muttering irritably. 'Trust me, she says! What are you doing, Io, reciting my lines? I'm the one supposed to say "trust me". You? You're supposed to say, "Oh, Joey, I don't know what I'd ever do without you." '

'That's what I like about you, Joey. You're even more old-fashioned than I am.'

As if to confirm it, and apparently unaware of the irony, Joey put on archaic eye-spectacles to scan the test results. 'You call it old-fashioned to retire on me, just when we've got that body of yours tuned to real premium capacity? What ever happened to the work ethic?'

'I *want* to work,' Io affirmed as she craned to read the chart for herself. Nowadays she knew what the data meant, probably as well as Joey did. 'I just want to move up to a more demanding job.'

As she'd expected, everything was nominal. Io took care of her body. She picked up her blouse. 'So can I button up, now? Or are you getting turned on by preggirls, these days?'

'Sarcastic too. Just for that, I won't tell you what I think you're carrying. You can find out on delivery day. Get dressed and get out of here, Io.'

One of Io's classes had recently covered status bluffing, so she knew better than to let herself be drawn in by Joey's bait. Obviously he had no more idea what Technique Zaire had planted in her womb than she did. 'You probably let them hire me to make a traffic cop,' she sallied, reaching for her book and jacket.

'Smartass. Just be on time for your next check-up. And stay out of trouble. And if your left tit makes you think any more weird thoughts, just remind yourself that toasters don't suckle; neither do traffic cops. And human milk fetches less than three pence a gram.'

'Five,' she said as she turned the antique door knob. 'You'll see, Joey. Five cents a gram, or I go back to knitting.'

'Hah. That'll be the day.'

But Io knew the price had to go up. It was just one reason for letting her left mammary gland alone, no matter what unlikely illusions its archaic secretions sent churning through her head.

3

Some of her courses were clearly relevant to her chosen future profession. In other cases, however, the applicability seemed much less clear. For instance, Io had to fight off ennui as her Industrial Reproduction lecturer droned on and on, covering stuff Io had learned way back during her apprenticeship in the egg trade.

'. . . Until the nineteen eighties,' the elderly woman academic said at the front of the hall, 'some still imagined that cloning human beings would be as simple as cloning, say, frogs. In theory, all you had to do was replace the twenty-three chromosomes in the nucleus of a woman's ovum with a complete set of forty-six from, say, one of her skin cells. Implant this "autofertilised egg" and nine months later you get a baby genetically identical to the donor. Voilà.

'Then we found out just how different mammals really are from frogs. For it seems that, during conception, human sperm does more than just deliver twenty-three chromosomes to match the mother's contribution. It actually *preconditions* certain of those genes to leap into action during the critical moments after fertilisation. These genes are only activated if delivered in a sperm. Similarly, other genes only express working enzymes if they originated in an egg . . .'

A sudden throbbing from Io's bracelet told her of a message coming in. Normally, she would store it for later. But with lecturer Jackone going on repetitively about ancient history, she felt safe to take a look. Carefully tuning down the brightness of her old communicator, so as not to disturb the students around her, she pressed the Read button and aimed the tiny holographic image on to her lap.

HAMPSTEAD TRAVEL AGENCY SPECIAL-ISES IN TOURS SPESHALLY SET UP FOR PIECEWORKERS. <MORE>

The glowing letters were not an advertisement. Obviously, they were part of a message from Perseph. And Io knew it amounted to something of an ultimatum.

Io pressed the button again; another row of letters replaced the first.

TRIP ALL SET UP FOR YOUR TERM BREAK, SO SCHOOLS NO EXCUSE. NOR YOUR 'JOB'. YOU CAN'T CASH MORE VOUCHERS, SO COME ON! <MORE>

Perseph was right, of course. The term would be over soon, and her own piecework delivery wasn't due for another six weeks or so. Also, the law limited how many travel vouchers one could exchange for cash, so her most recent one would go to waste if she didn't use it.

Of course, Io's abdominal distension was already greater than most placental freelancers like Perseph ever reached, so walking long distances was out of the question. But Perseph had covered that excuse, also.

I really could do with a trip, Io told herself.

And yet the idea left her uneasy. Her friendship with

Perseph had begun in the back alleys of Liverpool
when they were only girls, taking turns guarding each
other's ration books, teaming up killing rats for bounty
money. Nevertheless, their drift apart had really been
foreordained from the beginning.

Once, she had hoped to draw her best friend into
sharing her own enthusiasms – her ambitions for
higher things. But such wistful attempts had only
served to anger Perseph. She inevitably misunderstood,
assuming Io was putting on airs.

For her part, Perseph seemed as anxious in her own
way to salvage something between them. That meant
getting Io involved in the activities of her guildmates
and her born social class.

Well, Io thought, if she can't or won't join me, I can
still join her. At least this time.

Suddenly, the lights in the lecture hall dimmed as
lecturer Jackone began showing slides. Io hurriedly
tuned down the brightness of her wrist projector
even more.

'. . . As you can see,' the lecturer enunciated as
a holographic image took shape at the front of the
auditorium, 'if we try to clone a mouse *without* any
sperm-preconditioned genes, what we get is a queerly
warped embryo, one which dies quite soon in the womb
because the *placenta* never gets started.

'Alternatively, when an egg is prepared using *only*
genes taken from sperm nuclei, something radically
different happens.' The image in the tank shifted again.
This time, there was no embryo at all, only a tangled,
exaggerated mass of folded fibres easily recognisable
to anyone familiar with the modern filter trade.

'. . . so while the mother's and father's genes are
equal in the final make-up of any infant mammal,
at the beginning it is genes from the mother's egg
which control how the embryo starts development,

while genes from the sperm take charge of setting up the placenta, that organ lacking in fish or reptiles, whose complex organic filtration chemistry nourishes the mammalian foetus to term . . .'

The same old stuff . . . Io pressed again to read the rest of Perseph's message.

COME, IO. JUST FOR THE FIRST WEEK. THAT'S ALL. YOU NEED THIS. PERS KNOWS WHAT YOU NEED. <END>

The letters seemed to blur for a moment, and Io knew no flaw in her aged watchcom was at fault. She wiped her eyes while the lecturer's voice reverberated on all sides.

'At first this news, while astonishing, was of little interest outside the halls of science. Certain fanatical feminists were disappointed to learn that men weren't quite as non-essential as they'd hoped, but to most of the rest of humanity it seemed just another interesting fact of nature.

'Scarcely anyone guessed the long-range importance of this discovery, or its potential industrial applications . . .'

Io touched the face of her watch. In rapid Morse pulses she silently tapped out Perseph's private access number, and a reply to her friend's offer.

OKAY, I'LL COME. AT LEAST PARTWAY. AND THANKS, PERS. I THINK I REALLY DO NEED A BREAK. YOU'RE A TRUE FRIEND. – IO.

4

True to its reputation, the travel agency set them up on a tour requiring no walking at all. It was a party train bound over the Arctic, from Oslo via upper Norway and across the great faery bridges spanning from the Faröes to Iceland to Greenland to Labrador. It was a December journey into the heart of winter, a trek across a desert as romantic and empty as anything to be found anymore on the surface of overcrowded Earth.

Twin superconducting rails, hanging parallel two hundred metres above the frozen waves of tundra, looked like beaded strings of drawn dew that began in nothingness behind them and speared ahead to a parallax union in the pure blackness ahead. Only the rhythmically reappearing pylons – lonely, slender stalks planted kilometres apart – reminded the passengers that there was any link at all with the death-grey ground.

Io, to be frank, preferred sunshine. But when Perseph showed her the tickets Io had forced a smile and outward show of enthusiasm. After all, she could debark at Iceland or Greenland and still have enough vouchers left for a week in the Canaries.

Anyway, someone had once told her that aesthetic appreciation, while not exactly required for the certificate she sought, couldn't really hurt an applicant. So it was that Io found herself spending hours in the train's observation dome, watching and slowly learning to admire the daunting desolation.

Overhead, the aurorae shaped ever-changing draperies of shimmering blue and yellow gauze, or – if one preferred – rippling currents of diffuse oxygen atoms, ionised by the sun's electric wind, sheeting along lines of magnetic force.

Now and again those gaudy curtains would part unpredictably and reveal a slowly wheeling tableau of bitter-bright constellations, familiar, and yet filled with eerie portent in this chilly, alien setting.

The caribou herds had long departed south for the season, along with the more mundane breed of

tourist. During wintertime, completely different tribes
of itinerants moved in to share these rails with the
freight-heavy transports. For instance, those relying –
like Perseph and Io – on state travel allotments to
exercise their citizen's privilege to see the world – on
off-peak hours.

And then there were others, folk whose manners told
in ways more subtle than clothing or fashion that they
were employed, that they had real jobs, that they had
chosen this strange journey not for budgetary reasons
but out of a taste for moody expanses, or perhaps a
cherishing of the night.

By unstated courtesy, the partiers kept the raucous
stuff to the other cars, though the observation dome
was a favourite trysting spot for lovers. At times the
closeness of such intertwined pairs made Io feel wistful
and poignantly alone.

Unfortunately, such feelings weren't alleviated by
Perseph's incessant attempts to match her up. Finally,
one evening in the bistro car, Io's companion snapped
at her irritably.

'Sometimes you just confuse the bloody hell out of
me, Io! What does it take to turn you on, eh? We showed
each other our charts. Yours was straight hetero, and
I kept that in mind. I've introduced you to your type
of guy.'

My type? But Io bit back her initial response.
Perseph's facial expression was friable. Exasperated.
Irises and flesh tones both showed clear signs of a
hashtite high well past its peak and entering depressive
phase. Perseph's once straight antenna-braids were
drooping now as hairspray slowly gave way under
assault from perspiration and a party running at
desultory medium-broil.

'But you saw my profile also includes things like high
selectivity an' strong bonding, Pers. I can't help bein'

made that way. I sometimes envy you your chart, the freedom your personality gives you to come an' go as you like. Tease, squeeze, thank you please. But I've got no choice, Pers. I've got to hold out till the time's right for me.'

'Hold out for Mr Watch Fob Job, you mean,' Perseph said bitingly.

'For when I've got a job of my own, Pers. An' for the sort of man who'll respect that in me. A codder would never understand what it is I'm after. You know that.'

A tick manifested at the corner of Perseph's left eye. 'And what's wrong with codders?' she asked. 'Some of my best friends are codders!'

Io looked around nervously. The party crowd at nearby tables were watching an act on stage at the front of the car, performing an amiably vulgar dance to the tempo of the gently thrumming rails. Once, Io would have found the show, the tight, acrid atmosphere, the frenetic party odours attractively distracting. But no more. Artificial highs had begun to pall on her years ago.

Smoke and garish lights made black sinkholes of the window behind Io's shoulder, and yet she envied the quiet beyond those perspex panes.

'Hey.' Io forced a grin, trying to cut through the bad mood. 'Don't get me wrong, Pers. Codders are fine. It's just I can't ever get to know one for ten minutes before he offers to strip down and show me his specialty.'

For an instant Perseph's eyes were as deep and untelling as the nightview behind Io. Then she seemed to come to a decision. Her laughter would have made a good dissertation topic in one of Io's classes.

'Yeah, they're like that, aren't they? Even when I'm halfway in the middle of a surropreg, waddling around like a Blackpool publican, half th' codders I know are always tryin' to talk me into tryin' out their wares in advance. I keep tellin' the ones I introduce to you that you're in the egg trade and not interested in their merchandise. But I guess habit's hard to break.'

'Hey, now.' Io laughed. 'I'd like to think they weren't comin' on to me just because they thought of me as a fallow belly t'plant. Ever occur to you they might've found me appealing?'

'You? You skinny-arm charity case? With that out-o'-date yellow hair?'

Io feigned an insulted look.

Now Perseph's laughter was heartier. 'Gotcha! First you're offended when they come on to you. Then you'd be hurt if they didn't, right?'

'No, I just wish they'd . . .'

'I'll tell you this though, Io. I *like* codders. Some of 'em have gone far into debt to finance their conversions. Th' freelance trade would be impossible without them. We'd have to take as many risks as you and your egg—'

'Pers, I never said—'

'And something else, Io. They put a lot more *enthusiasm* into their work than Joey and his hoity-toity ovum designers do. Ever thought there could be pleasure involved in this business, Io? Nawi, I didn't think so. But I tell you it's a helluva lot more natural with codders than with Joey's lot and all their tubes and wires . . .'

Perseph had that gleam in her eye again, a seething sexual energy. She was talking herself into it. Io knew it would culminate quite soon in her friend grabbing the nearest tumescent codpiece, without even asking to see the owner's prospectus, let alone his tattoo.

'Pers, are you remembering to take your pills? You don't want to get knocked at a *party*, for the love of—'

'You mind your own damn business!' Perseph stood up and her chair fell over. 'I don't give you advice on your blasted eggs. Don't *you* tell me where I oughta shop for seed!'

All at once Io knew. This wasn't the first time for Perseph. That unsatisfactory load of commercial grade solvent filters she'd delivered some months back – she hadn't taken the job through a city agent, or even negotiated the surropreg herself. She'd gone and let some random codder inseminate her – probably just somebody who pleased her sexually – as if that said anything at all about the quality of his wares!

Mixing business and pleasure, letting your professional standards lapse, these were the beginning of the end for a craftswoman, especially a pieceworker. Io had an instant fey vision of Perseph in a few years – too far gone to win decent contracts, physically too shabby to draw a codder into making a deposit on spec. She'd wind up taking bulk grade semen and producing goods no better than a fabricow's. Finally, she'd lose her guild standing, and it would be the dole for her, full-time.

The dole would kill Perseph. Without the focus of work, *some* kind of work, the lure of drugs and soaps would soon take her out of the world.

It was only a narrow precognitive instant, but at that moment Io's eyes locked with the other woman's in momentary complete communion. Io's cheeks felt aflame with how, in that moment, she involuntarily betrayed her friend, not only by seeing, but by *showing* on her face that she had seen. From Io, Perseph had not received the lies that were a comrade's duty to tell, but a severe mirror, laying bare a fate she already knew, deep inside.

'I – I gotta make a phone call.' Perseph started to turn, unsteadily.

'Pers, I'm sor—'

'Oh, go abort a hydrocephalic traffic cop!' Perseph
snarled. She whirled, knocking over their drinks, and
made her way unevenly among the tables, leaving Io
alone in the middle of a crowded room suddenly too
filled with truth.

5

*. . . It can be hard for a modern citizen to realise just how
inefficient our ancestors were, even in the bustling industrial
centres of the fabulous Twentieth. But what enabled the people
of those times to build the first globe-spanning culture, to tame
nature, to educate the masses and begin the conquest of space,
was a system that depended essentially upon profligate waste.*

*For instance, a single gram of gold – vital for modern
electronics – could be acquired only by tearing out of the Earth,
pulverising, and washing several tons of ore. Beyond the now
obvious environmental effects, this also required prodigious use
of energy, which was already growing scarce even by the turn
of the century.*

*From high-tech consumer goods to simple breakfast cereals,
far more resources had to be put into each item the consumer
bought than ever came out as product. With seven billion people
to feed – and clothe and educate and entertain – there was only
one option, to switch to renewable processes that used resources
more efficiently. The alternative was to face a culling such as
had not been seen since the Black Death.*

Biotechnology offered a way.

*Today, gene-tailored microbes refine gold and other vital
elements directly from sea water. Organic solvents, once
unbelievably dumped into sensitive watersheds by shortsighted
businessmen, are now recycled through filters grown specially
for the purpose by pampered, well-fed fabricows. And these*

*same animals' modified milk glands produce lubricants to
replace long-vanished petroleum oil in our vehicles. In this
way we make use of efficient fabrication methods evolved over
billions of years by Nature herself.*

*As for products at the very cutting edge of technology, whose
quality standards exceed what can be accomplished with animals,
these are today put into production by a labour force dedicated to
high craftsmanship. And yet, these jobs are not restricted, as
in the past, to the skilled or the privileged. Rather, they are
attainable even on a part-time basis by men and women of good
health from any social . . .*

from ARE YOU INTERESTED IN BIOFAB?,
London, 2043.

6

She met him in the Reykjavik airport lounge.

His manner was courteous, his stance and bearing
unself-consciously athletic.

The clothes he wore showed tasteful reticence, not
the bright excess that over-compensating dole clients
so often mistook for fashion.

And, although he was obviously Eastern European
in origin, he had the good grace not to wear leather here
in the West, where sensibilities now rejected products
made from the death of animals.

For a while they talked about the books she had been
studying, while awaiting her flight. But soon they were
in one of those exciting, open-topic conversations which
touch lightly on the fascination of the world itself. Io
made no effort to suppress the sudden feelings coursing
through her. The methods of emotional control she had
learned in school were still too new, too abstract to her.
And anyway, who wanted to damp down anything as
pleasant as hope?

In his rich, cosmopolitan accent, Wiktor offered to buy her dinner. There was plenty of time, and no hint that he wanted or expected anything in return but her companionship. She accepted demurely, then hurriedly added a smile, lest he take her shyness for reluctance.

As she had secretly hoped, he passed his credit card across the face of the robot maître d' at the first-class dining room, and took her arm as a pink ribbon of light guided them through a maze of candlelit tables to a window setting overlooking the lights of the city.

He also made mistakes . . . smelling the wine cork instead of feeling it, for instance. Obviously he had dined in class before, but neither was he so accustomed to this lifestyle as to be blasé or patronising.

Io only knew about wine corks from having read an obscure magazine in Joey's waiting room. It actually pleased her that Wiktor showed such minor lapses, an almost imperceptible trace of latent, slight awkwardness. She had no ambition to stake a place in the circles of the rich and renowned. But his nodding acquaintance with the finer things spoke of the relaxed eclecticism, the comfortable worldliness of a professional . . . a man with a real job. Someone who *did* something.

Would she, in three years' time, be able to walk into a place such as this without feeling heart palpitations? Would she wear such a relaxed smile? Or order from a menu with such confidence?

Would she meet the sort of men who made the world move and grow better with their skill? Perhaps one who cared about the same craft as she was studying so long and hard for now?

Naturally, the subject of his actual profession never came up on this, an initial encounter. Her present trade was obvious from her attire, and from her tumescence, but they never mentioned it. He spoke instead about the aurorae, visible even from here, so near the urban lights. A hint indicated that he might once have seen them from *above* – from space – but he did not follow up on that, nor did Io pursue it.

It was perfectly all right to speak of Earthly travels though, since all classes were encouraged tourism. The superconducting rails made it cheaper than many other entertainments people might have demanded, and social planners considered it helpful. Tourists waged few wars.

Io felt ashamed of how little she had seen, how little she had to tell. But Wiktor made up for her lack. He had been to Merseyside many times, for instance – both Liverpool and Ellesmere Port – and he spoke with fondness of the Lake District, her own favourite place in all the world.

Against her usual habit when in production, Io allowed herself a single glass of wine. Of course she had memorised the tolerance tables long ago, and knew no harm would come to . . . to her toaster.

Sudden memory of that colourful euphemism triggered a nervous giggle. But then it also caused her to think of Perseph, and that made her suddenly sad. Their parting had been cool. Io had no idea what the future would bring, but the note of finality between them made her vision film as she thought about it.

Gyrating emotions. Damn. An occupational hazard. But what a time to have an attack of surropreg blues!

'I – I don't know what's got over me,' she said as she wiped her eyes. 'Would you excuse me while I—' she gestured in the direction of the lavatories. His smile was bemused, understanding.

'Of course,' he said. 'I will order you that especial dessert I mentioned earlier. And,' his grin broadened, 'a glass of fruit juice.'

'Thanks. That might be best.' She laughed, and departed with a smile.

He didn't even try to pressure me into having another glass of wine, she mused as she negotiated her abdomen towards the ladies room. Many men would have taken it as a challenge to try to get her drunk, even knowing she would be leaving within the hour. It was a rite of machismo she'd never understood, however many times it was explained to her. Wiktor, though, seemed a gentleman.

A low wall topped by a decorative hedge separated the dining room proper from the gilt wall-papered passage to the toilets. On her way out again, Io paused to check her composure. She wanted to maintain a friendly openness that would invite him to ask her watchcom number. After all, he said he passed through Liverpool on occasion. Perhaps he might call.

Io took a momentary guilty peek through the shrubbery, feeling like a little girl spying covertly on an older boy, the object of a delicious secret desire. A waiter had just turned away from their table. Walking towards her, he occulted her view for a moment. Then Wiktor could be seen moving a freshly filled glass of orange liquid to her setting, beside a plate containing something reddish and gold – the promised dessert.

His quick glance in her direction almost made her duck down. His facial expression puzzled Io briefly as he fussed with his jacket pocket. For an instant he looked relieved. Then Wiktor turned to his left – her right – and seemed to nod to somebody seated among the dim booths and shadowed dining cubbies.

Had he recognised someone he knew? Hardly surprising, considering the circles he kept.

Composing her features, Io emerged from behind the wall and smiled as she approached the table. *He is old-fashioned,* she thought as he rose to hold her chair for her. 'What's this?' She dabbed her fork at the creamy eruption on her place.

'A surprise. You'll like it.'

A forkful hesitated near her nose. 'It smells spicy.'

'It is.' He smiled. 'That's why I ordered you something to drink. But I'm sure you'll love it.' With that he winked, and took a portion from his own serving into his mouth. The goggle-eyed pantomime of pleasure which followed made Io laugh.

The dessert was delicious. It also made her eyes water. 'Well!' She coughed. 'I certainly won't have any trouble with my sinuses during the flight!'

'It always makes me thirsty,' he said, taking a sip of wine. Watching his eyes, she reached for the brimming glass of orange juice.

Would she have suspected anything if she had not gone to school? Had she never studied the hardwon wisdom of a century's research, she likely would never have known about those subtle cues given off by child and man, in eye and face and voice, that betray the inner unease.

But then, Io's knowledge was still abstract. So maybe it was instinct – unreliable but desperately useful when it strikes – which made her notice the intense way Wiktor watched her hand.

She put the glass down before it was more than an inch high. His gaze immediately flicked to her face. 'Is something wrong?' he asked.

Please. No. She prayed.

'No, nothing's wrong.' She lifted another forkful of the pungent sweet. 'I was just savouring the taste.'

He seemed to notice the speculation in her eyes, and averted his gaze. That was a mistake. Now he *avoided* looking at the juice glass.

The second spicy taste added power to the first. Io's throat burned, her nostrils felt singed. Still she kept her hand on the table, and concentrated on remembering her lessons.

Speaking with a measured voice, she said, 'Actually, I think I will have another glass of wine, after all.'

Rapid impressions she read almost instantly – brief panic-contraction in the pupils . . . a faint, barely noticeable flush wave, crossing his cheeks at an unsatisfactory angle . . . that involuntary frown, quickly compressed into a slightly asymmetrical smile with the practice of an accomplished poseur . . .

An experienced liar, then. But not a trained one.

The man Io would someday marry would not lie. But he would have taken schooling in what lying *does*. How it is seen, detected, known.

This man, for all his money and worldliness, had never been to school.

'More wine? In your condition?' He laughed teasingly. A little patronisingly. 'Now, Io. Don't try to prove how tough you are. Be a good girl and drink your vitamins.'

My vitamins? Io thought. She reached for the glass. *Here are my vitamins, you son of a fabricow.*

'Jism!' he cried, leaping to his feet as she spilled the drink across the tablecloth.

Two confirmations in one action. An innocent man would not have shouted so over only a silly puddle. Nor would a real professional use a curseword specific to a certain type of freelance artist.

'You bitch, how did you kn—' He stepped forward, and so came within Io's seated reach. With one hand she grabbed the loose folds of his stylish cotton trousers. With the other she stabbed down hard with her dessert fork. There was a loud tearing of fabric. Shouting for strength she had never used before outside the decanting room, Io yanked.

The resulting tableau held for a long moment.

Staring patrons. Aghast waiters. Io, panting with upraised fork, ready to strike again, this time at a loathsome sight.

Under the torn trousers, hanging like a broken flag, lay Wiktor's codpiece, the emblem of his calling. His tattooed licence told of a costly modification – placental platinum extraction filters of the very latest design.

No wonder Wiktor knew his way around style. Just one of the altered wrigglers he produced in millions could set a pieceworker on course towards her best bonus ever. And for him a healthy commission.

'Why?' she whispered.

Motion resumed. Hurried footsteps approached behind her.

'Officers!' Wiktor pronounced loudly, for all to hear. 'I want to press charges against this madwoman, for assault with intent to injure me!'

Hands pressed upon her shoulders. The fork was ungently pried from her fingers. Io shook her hair back and looked him in the eyes, defiantly.

'Shall we take the tablecloth along to the police station, then?' She gestured towards the orange stain.

A quick blinking of the eyes, a bobbing of the Adam's Apple as he suddenly swallowed. 'Wait!' Wiktor said as the guards began pulling her away. His sour expression was her bitter reward. 'I – I have changed my mind. I will forget the incident . . . so long as she boards her flight and gets the hell out of here.'

Oh, I'm sure, she thought, watching him squirm. Men who would poison women – such men had personalities based on contempt for others. Probably until this very moment he had never even considered what might happen if he were caught. Now it was just dawning on him, too late.

'Who?' Io asked, simply, demanding a price.

As if it were costing him his gall bladder, he spat the word. 'Perseph.'

Io knew from the look in his eyes that she would have no need for revenge on her former friend. Far from the type of man he had tried to appear to be, this was a cowardly, predatory creature, the sort who preyed exclusively on those weaker than himself. Io felt certain he would never come near her again. *Perseph*, though – perhaps watching even now from some shadowy corner of the room – had real cause to worry about Wiktor.

'*What* was it?' she asked.

Sweat beaded on his lip and brow. There was an implicit arrangement here, truth in exchange for escape. But in fulfilling his part first, Wiktor knew he was giving himself over fully into her hands.

'Para – Parapyridine 4,' he whispered rapidly, trying to make the words for her alone.

Io felt suddenly dizzy. The hand that had touched the juice glass trembled as if defiled. The substance named would not have affected her own health in the slightest. But it would have ruined the product she carried, and made her own eggs utterly useless for anything in the future. She'd be lucky to be able to make solvent filters if she had taken any of that stuff.

'*Why?*' She repeated her first question.

His face was now utterly resigned. 'You were getting too damned high-almighty. Wanted to climb out and leave your friends, your guild. We . . . they . . . figured it'd do you good to be brought down a peg.

'It was for – for your own good . . .' he finished lamely. His handsome confidence was now so completely gone that Io felt stunned that she had ever been fooled at all.

'Excuse me, Madam, is this fellow admitting to having done you some harm?'

Io turned, noticing the blond Icelandic policeman

for the first time. Obviously, he had followed bits of their low, clipped exchange, picking up on hints with obvious skill. His eyes flicked from her surropreg garments to Wiktor's tattoo, to the stained tablecloth, narrowing with dawning suspicion.

He spoke English as educated Icelanders do, better than the English. 'Perhaps you'd like to file charges of your own, Madam?' he asked.

For an instant, Io stared at the policeman's face in sudden revelation. There she saw compassion and more . . . a *confidence* completely unrelated to arrogance . . . a serenity that only came of skill and the sure knowledge of one's own usefulness. Face to face with the real thing, Io wondered how she had ever been fooled by Wiktor's sham.

Inexperience and wishful thinking, I suppose. She would have to talk this over with her teachers.

'No,' Io said softly. 'I will not press charges. But would you please walk with me to my boarding gate? I think I could use a hand.'

Her last word to Wiktor was to thank him over her shoulder for dinner. The evenness of her tone must have been more unnerving than anything else she might have said. She left him standing there, pale and exposed.

The officer's gentle strong grip on her arm helped Io walk head high. Somewhere in the restaurant's gloom, she knew she was being watched by one more person – someone lacking the guts to show herself. Io didn't bother searching the shadows for those familiar eyes. She would never see them again.

7

. . . *Earlier we have seen excerpts by writers extolling the*

*benefits of an industrial order based on efficient biological
assembly processes. And there is no doubt that these techniques
are in large measure responsible for the relative comfort of
today's nine billion human beings, not least the fact that they
have not starved.*

*The mysticism of the Madrid Catholics, their religious
revulsion towards even completely voluntary use of human
reproductive systems for industry, is not shared by many others
these days. Rather, the right of the poor to use their bodies'
talents for their own benefit is enshrined in law, so long as
volunteers are qualified and restrict themselves to licensed,
non-human, embryonic material.*

*Nevertheless, some dissenting voices have spoken critically of
this system from more rational grounds – scientific, biological,
economic and cultural. Some fear that our fundamental attitude
towards life itself is changing, subtly but profoundly, as each
day passes. And these changes are taking place without adequate
thought to the possible long-range consequences. These are doubts
that must, in all fairness, be taken seriously . . .*

– from A SURVEY OF MODERN PROBLEMS,
New York, 2049.

*. . . The time may come when these peculiarly severe licensing
laws may be relaxed. But for now, the intrinsic value of this
particular product to society – by far the most valuable item
produced by any society – has convinced lawmakers and voters
alike that one particular career calls for schooling, qualification,
and respect above any and all others . . .*

– from THE CERTIFICATION ACT, 2039.

8

Another penalty of egg work was the lengthy, all too
realistic, process of labour. Io took the doctors' word

for it that it was still a bit easier than the 'real thing'. But that was small comfort.

Not that difficulty or exertion held any great fears for her. Io knew what she was doing.

Still, Joey held her hand through the agony of transition. And afterwards he wiped the perspiration from her brow. It was all just part of the agency's service, he told her. Just one more reason why so few of his clients ever left him.

Io knew better, of course. Joey actually cared, bless him.

'Did I remember to curse you for getting me into this?' she asked when the worst was over.

'You forgot.' Joey smiled. 'Missed your chance. The tradition is that nothing said during *transition* can be held against you. Maybe next time.'

'I told you, Joey, there isn't going to be a—'

'Hush. We'll speak of it later. Now, you concentrate. The worst may be over, but you still have hard pushing ahead.'

'Okay, Joey.'

Tremors. Foreshadowings. Io focused on her breathing and was ready when the next contractions came.

'Good, good,' the industrial midwife told her. A technician in the service of Technique Zaire, she commanded her team with crisp precision. 'Now please to be be ready for last effort.'

'Ah.' Io replied in a sharp exhalation. 'Ah!' Then she lost track of time. Lost track of consciousness. Moment by moment she did as she was told by those whose job it was to help her. Several times she cried out in the ways she had been taught, conserving her strength for the final moment.

When it came, it was almost anticlimactic. Passage, release, evacuation. A parting of that familiar connection.

Emptiness.

The scurrying techs had no attention to spare for her. Even Joey rushed forward, eager to see. When he returned, his eyes beamed. 'I – I thought it would be a shipbrain, Io, but I was wrong. It's a *starbrain*!'

'S – starbrain?'

'Yes! It's a fine, big, healthy starbrain. The only bio-manufactured product licensed to use true human genes! The only one capable of sentience!'

Io's lower lip trembled. Tears welled in her eyes. She began to sob.

Joey, mistaking her tears for joy, kept on exulting, obliviously.

'Jeez, Io, it will *think*. It'll pilot starships. Why, they're even talking about a bill to give starbrains *citizenship*, for heaven's sake! Do you know what they're *paying* for a healthy . . .'

Joey's voice droned on, a low ululation of misplaced enthusiasm. Io shut it out. She flung an arm over her eyes so she could not see when they came forward with a swaddled something to show her.

They did not know. They could not know how she felt.

Her breasts throbbed as they attached machines for her first milking, to release the straining pressure. To begin harvesting secondary product from the right. Tertiary from the left.

Tertiary product. Colostrum and homo milk, at five pence a gram.

Her left breast sent unwanted signals to her brain.

'Io, I've just been told they're so happy with you they want to renew—'

'Oh, Joey,' she cried. 'Go away, please!' Io's head rocked. 'Just go away.'

And so they left her then, to listen to the rhythms,

to the machines, to the beating of her heart. To the singing in her veins.

It has to be worth it, she thought. She prayed.

It has to be!

9

To: *Ms Iolanthe Livingstone*
93 Marina Drive
Ellesmere Port, Merseyside

From: *British Division*
Department of Certification and Accreditation

Dear Ms Livingstone,
It is our great pleasure to inform you that your test scores, your record of experience, and the recommendations of your instructors have, in totality, persuaded the Board that you are indeed qualified for the certification you requested. By your assiduous efforts you have acquired skills of great importance to humanity. Skills which may lead, at last, to a generation of people no longer plagued by the age-old evils of cruelty and fear and neurosis and unfulfilled potential – evils which so nearly destroyed our world, and hard beset us still to this day.

Towards that brighter future, you and your professional enthusiasm will surely add new strength and purpose.

Therefore, from this date forward, you are hereby licensed to engage in the most demanding and important occupation of them all.

Congratulations. We are certain you will be a very fine (mother/~~father~~).

For the sake of the children . . .

NatuLife ®

I know, things taste better fresh, not packaged.

They say hamburgers clog your arteries and hurt the rain forests.

We should eat like our Stone Age ancestors, who dug roots, got plenty of exercise, and always stayed a little hungry. So they say.

Still, I balked when my wife served me termites.

'Come on honey, try one. They're delicious.'

Gaia had the hive uncrated and warmed up by the time I got home. Putting down my briefcase, I stared at hundreds of the pasty-scaled critters scrabbling under a plastic cover, tending their fat queen, devouring kitchen trimmings, making themselves right at home in my home.

Gaia offered me a probe made of fine-grained pseudowood. 'See? You use this stick to fish after some nice plump ones, just like chimpanzees do in the wild!'

I gaped at the insect habitat, filling the last free space between our veggie-hydrator and the meat-sublimate racks. 'But . . . we agreed. Our apartment's too small . . .'

'Oh, sweetheart, I know you'll just love them.

Anyway, don't I need protein and vitamins for the baby?'

She put my hand over her swelling belly, which normally softened any objections. Only this time my *own* stomach was in rebellion. 'I thought you already got all that stuff from the Yeast-Beast machine.' I pointed to the vat occupying half of our guest bathroom, venting nutritious vapours from racks of tissue-grown cutlets.

'*That* stuff's not *natural*,' Gaia complained with a moue. 'Come on, try the real thing. It's just like they show on the NatuLife Channel!'

'I . . . don't think . . .'

'Watch, I'll show you!'

Gaia's tongue popped out as she concentrated, quivering with excitement from her red ponytail down to her rounded belly, passing the stick-probe through a sealed hatch to delve after six-legged prey. 'Got one!' she cried, drawing a twitching insect to her lips.

'You're not seriously . . .' My throat stopped as the termite vanished, head first. Bliss crossed Gaia's face. 'M-m-m, crunchy!' She smacked, revealing two legs and a twitching tail.

I found enough manly dignity to raggedly chastise her.

'Don't . . . talk with your mouth full.'

Turning away, I added, 'If you need me, I'll be in my workout room.'

Gaia had rearranged our sleep quarters again. Now the cramped chamber merged seamlessly with a tropical paradise, including raucous bird calls and mist from a roaring waterfall. The impressive effects made it hard navigating past the bed, so I ordered the hologram blanked. Silence fell as the vid-wall turned grey, leaving just the real-life portion of her pocket jungle to contend with – a tangle of potted plants warranted to give off purer oxygen than a pregnant woman could sniff from bottles.

Wading through creepers and mutant ficuses, I finally found the moss-lined laundry hamper and threw in my work clothes. The fragrant Clean-U-Lichen had already sani-scavenged and folded my exercise togs, which felt warm and skin-supple when I drew them on. The organo-electric garment rippled across my skin as if alive, seeming just as eager for a workout as I was.

I'd been through hell at the office. Traffic was miserable and the smog index had been red-lining all week. Termites were only the last straw.

'Let's go,' I muttered. 'I haven't killed anything in a week.'

Long Stick spotted a big old buck gazelle.

'It limps,' my hunting partner said, rising from his haunches to point across a hundred yards of dry savannah. 'Earlier, it met a lion.'

I rose from my stretching exercises to peer past a screen of sheltering boulders, following Long Stick's gnarly arm. One animal stood apart from the herd. Sniffing an unsteady breeze, the buck turned to show livid claw marks along one flank. Clearly, this prey was a pushover compared to last Sunday's pissed-off rhino. The virtual reality machine must have sensed I'd had a rough day.

My hands stroked the spear, tracing its familiar nicks and knots. An illusion of raw, archetypal power.

'The beaters are ready, Chief.'

I nodded. 'Let's get on with it.'

Long Stick pursed his lips and mimicked the call of a bee-catcher. Moments later, the animals snorted as a shift in the heavy air brought insinuations of human scent. Another hundred yards beyond the herd, where

the sparse pampas faded into a hazy stand of acacia
trees, I glimpsed the rest of our hunting party, creeping
forward.

My hunters. My tribe.

I was tempted to reach up and adjust the virtu-reality
helmet, which fed this artificial world to my eyes and
ears . . . to zoom in on those distant human images.
Alas, except for Long Stick, I had never met any of the
other hunters, up close. Good persona programs aren't
cheap, and with a baby coming, there were other things
for Gaia and me to spend money on.

Yeah, like a crummy termite hive! Resentment fed on
surging adrenalin. *Never trust a gatherer.* That was the
hunters' creed. *Love 'em, protect 'em, die for them, but always
remember, their priorities are different.*

The beaters stood as one, shouting. The gazelles
reared, wheeling the other way. Long Stick hissed.
'Here they come!'

The Accu-Terrain floor thrummed beneath my feet
to the charge of a hundred hooves. Sensu-Surround
earphones brought the stampede roar of panicky
beasts thundering towards us, wild-eyed with ardour
to survive. Clutching my spear in sweaty palms,
I crouched as graceful animals vaulted overhead,
ribcages heaving.

Meanwhile, a faint, subsonic mantra recited, *I am
part of nature . . . one with nature . . .*

The young, and breeding females, we let flash by
without harm. But then, trailing and already foaming
with fatigue, came the old buck, its leap unsteady,
and I knew the program really was taking it easy on
me today.

Long Stick howled. I sprinted from cover, swiftly
taking the lead. The auto-treadmill's bumps and gullies
matched whatever terrain the goggles showed me, so
my feet knew how to land and thrust off again. The

body suit brushed my skin with synthetic wind. Flared nostrils inhaled sweat, exhilaration, and for a time I forgot I was in a tiny room on the eightieth floor of a suburban Chitown con-apt.

I *was* deep in the past of my forebears, back in a time when men were few, and therefore precious, magical.

Back when nature thrived . . . and included us.

Easy workout or no, I got up a good sweat before the beast was cornered against a stand of jagged saw grass. The panting gazelle's black eye met mine with more than resignation. In it I saw tales of past battles and matings. Of countless struggles won, and finally lost. I couldn't have felt more sympathy if he'd been real.

My throwing arm cranked and I thought, *Long ago, I'd have done this to feed my wife and child.*

As for here and now?

Well . . . this sure beats the hell out of racquetball.

Mass-produced con-apt housing lets twelve billion Earthlings live in minim decency, at the cost of dwelling all our lives in stacked boxes. No wonder so many await drawings to visit mountains, the seashore, the remaining forests. Between times, Virtual Reality keeps us sane within our hi-rise caves.

On my way to shower after working out, I saw that Gaia's private VR room was in use. Impulsively, I tiptoed into the closet next door, feeling for the crack between stacked room units, and pressed my eye close. Gaia squatted on her treadmill floor, shaped to mimic a patch of uneven ground. Her body suit fitted her pregnant form like a second skin, while helmet and goggles made her resemble some bug, or star alien. But I knew her scenario, like mine, lay in the distant past. She made digging motions with a phantom tool, invisible to me, held in her cupped hands, then reached down to pluck another ghost item, her gloves simulating touch to match whatever root or tuber she saw through the goggles. Gaia pantomimed brushing dirt away from her find, then dropping it into a bag at her side.

Sometimes, eavesdropping like this, I'd feel a chill wondering how odd *I* must look during workouts, leaping about, brandishing invisible spears and shouting at my 'hunters'. No wonder most people keep VR so private.

Gaia tilted her head as if listening to somebody, then laughed aloud. 'I know! Didn't the two of them look funny? Coming home all proud with that skinny little squirrel on a stick? Such great hunters! That didn't stop them from gobbling half our carrots!'

Naturally, I could not see or hear Gaia's companions – presumably other women gatherers in her own, simulated tribe, which she had been visiting since before we ever met. She stopped again, listened, then turned around. 'It's your baby, Flower. That's okay, I'll take care of him.' She laughed. 'I need the practice.'

A warm feeling spread as I watched her gently pick up an invisible child. Her body suit tugged and contracted, mimicking a wriggly weight in her arms. Awkwardly, but with clear enjoyment, Gaia cooed at an infant who dwelled only in a world of software, and her mind.

I crept away to take a shower, at once ashamed of spying and glad that I had.

We had met at a campus Earth Day festival, soon after the price of full body suits fell to a level students could afford. By then, she and I each had our own Pleistocene worlds, the same ones we maintained five years later, with upgrades and improvements. If I had known on that day of our shared interest in the simulated past, it might have made approaching her much easier. As it was, I followed her strolling by booths and exhibits proclaiming this or that planet-saving endeavour, single-mindedly entranced by the graceful way she moved. Since she wore a smog mask and sunglasses against the UV, I couldn't see much of her face. But Gaia laughed a rich contralto, clapping as contestants jousted with padded lances from the backs of flapping skycycles. When the undefeated champion called in vain for fresh challengers, I stepped forward impulsively, eager to impress her . . .

When I came to, later, it was in the air-conditioned first-aid tent. An angel cradled my head on her lap, speaking my name. I didn't even recognise her till she laughed at my confusion. 'You're okay,' she said. 'It's just a bump on the head.'

I recall sagging back, aching and content. It turned out Gaia had already noticed me, days before in the library, asked friends about me, accessed my open postings on the Net . . . As usual, she was one step ahead of me, and I didn't mind a bit. I never had any cause to, until the day of the termites.

Emerging from a long shower, I found the wall screen in the bedroom had been tuned to Mother Earth Channel Fifty-Three. A green-robed priestess recited a sermon.

'. . . *Some radicals say science and nature are foes. That we should get rid of all machines, farms, cities, returning to more natural ways of life . . .*'

Gaia emerged from her closet wearing a bright cotton shift over her blossoming figure, sorting through a cloth bag slung over one shoulder. 'Where are you going?' I tried asking, but the life-size matron on the wall was doubly loud.

'. . . *As we learn about healthy diets, it seems we should eat like our ancestors, back when meat was caught but twice a week or so, and all other food was gathered by skilled women . . .*'

I tugged Gaia's elbow, repeating my question. She startled, then smiled at me. 'NatuBirth class, sweetheart. Lots to learn before I'm ready. Just two months left, you know.'

'But I thought . . .'

'. . . *Fats and sweets were rare back then, hence our cravings. But now forests topple for cattle ranches and sugar farms, producing far too much of a good thi—*'

I shouted, 'Computer! Shut off that noise!'

Welcome silence fell. The priestess's mouth moved silently while Gaia looked reproving.

'You said I might come along, next time,' I complained.

Gaia stroked my face. 'Now dear, we're just going over nest and birthing procedures. You'd only be bored.'

How could I answer that? My dad used to proudly describe the day I entered the world. He was present the whole time, even cut the cord, back when old-fashioned *feminism* touted sharing all life's duties. Unlike today's *femismo*, which says there are some things men just aren't meant to take part in.

Undaunted, I changed tacks. Snaking arms around Gaia's waist, I drew her close. 'Actually, I was hoping this evening . . .'

Her laughter was indulgent. 'You had a good hunt, yes? I can tell. It always leaves you frisky.'

In a decent marriage, you learn to read each other. Clearly, it was futile trying to get her in the mood tonight. We used to have great sex before her pregnancy, and presumably would again. Despite urgent hormones, a grown man learns to be patient.

A grown man *also* has a perfect right to be grumpy, now and then.

'Mph. Go to the damn class, then. I'll be okay.'

'Aw, sweetie.' She tiptoed to kiss my chin. 'Look

by the console for a present . . . something to show I haven't forgotten you.' Gaia blew another kiss from the front door, and was gone.

I wandered to the master house controller and picked up a brightly coloured program chip, still tacky where Gaia must have peeled off a discount sticker from the NatuLife Store. *Something for the Hunter*, the title read, and I snorted. *Right*. In other words, something to keep the man of the house distracted beating drums with a bunch of make-believe comrades, while a wife's attention turns to *serious* matters – nesting and the continuity of life. It might have been meant as a loving gesture, but right then it made me feel superfluous, even more left out than before.

Sliding the chip into the console, I accidentally brushed the volume knob and the booming voice of the priestess returned.

'. . . *must face the fact that Earth's billions won't accept returning to nature by scratching mud and sleeping on dirt floors. We must learn* new *ways, both more natural and smarter . . .*'

I snickered at that. Funny how each generation thinks *it* knows what 'smarter' means.

Long Stick greeted me with a sweeping bow, at once sardonic and respectful. 'Welcome back, oh Great Chief.'

'Yeah, yeah,' I muttered at my simulated sidekick. 'Okay, I'll bite. What's different, this time?'

Everything seemed less real without my virtuality helmet and body suit. Here in the living room, primeval forest cut off sharply where the vid-wall met the couch. Yet, I could have sworn my ersatz companion seemed friendlier, *warmer*, somehow.

'The flint-smiths are ready to show their wares, Chief,' Long Stick said.

'The who . . . ?' I began. But Long Stick had already turned to begin striding down a path. From past adventures in this simulated world, I knew the trail led to a stone-lined gully. The living room had no treadmill-floor, so I stood still, watching the image of Long Stick's fur-draped back plough past trees and boulders down a series of switchbacks. A rhythmic sound grew steadily louder – a tinny clatter of brittle objects colliding and breaking. Finally, we reached a sandy streambed where several figures could be seen sitting on logs, hammering stones together.

Oh, yes. Flint-smiths. NatuLife stocked countless 'You-Are-There' programs in all the ancient arts, from bronze casting to automobile design. With our shared interest in the Neolithic, Gaia had cleverly bought a Stone Age simulation the computer could fit right into my private world, to help pass an evening while she trained for motherhood.

Okay, I sighed. *Let's get on with it.*

A youngster with a wispy beard noticed us, stopped hammering, and nudged the others – a weathered old man and a sturdy-looking fellow with one leg much shorter than the other. Made sense. Tool-making was good work for the prehistoric handicapped.

The smiths rose and bowed respectfully. These wouldn't be full-scale sim-personas, like Long Stick, but animated actors in a limited scenario.

'We have worked those chert cores you traded from Seacliff Tribe, oh Chief,' the oldest one said, lisping through gaps in his teeth. 'Would you like to see?'

I shrugged. 'Why not?'

He spread a fur and began laying out an assortment of Neolithic cutlery, glinting under simulated sunshine. There were spearheads, axes, burins and scrapers – plus other tools I couldn't identify offhand – each item the product of at least a hundred strokes, skilfully cleaving native rock into shapes useful for daily life. A prehistoric combined kitchen, armoury and machine shop. The smiths offered to let me feel an edge, but it was disturbing to watch the computer manifest an image of my own hand, holding an object I couldn't feel. I resolved to try again later, replaying the scenario with body gloves on.

'Well, it's interesting,' I said after a while, feeling fatigued. 'But I think that's enough for n—'

A high shout broke in. Everyone looked past my shoulder, but the scene remained obstinately riveted until a new figure entered view from the left. Shorter, slimmer than the others, this one strode with a springy, elfin gait, clothed in the tunic and leggings of a hunter. The newcomer carried a bundle of slender wooden saplings the right size for fashioning spears. Only when these were dumped with a clatter did I note in surprise that the hunter was female.

'Ho, Chief,' she greeted me, acknowledging Long Stick with a nod.

My companion leaned over and muttered. 'This is Ankle-of-a-Giraffe, daughter of Antler and Pear Blossom. She is one of the beaters in the hunt.'

'That's what I want to talk to you about,' the young Stone-Ager said, planting fists on her hips. She was lithe and a trifle lean for my tastes – as well as being smudged from head to toe – but she made eye contact in a bold, provocative way. 'I'm sick of just beating, Great Chief. I want to be in on the kill. I want to learn from you two.'

The flint-smiths hissed surprise. Long Stick rumbled, 'Ankle! You forget yourself!'

The girl bowed submissively, yet her eyes held fierce determination. She seemed ready to speak again when I shouted.

'Freeze frame!'

All action halted, leaving the 'tribesmen' locked in time. A blue jay halted in flight across the gully while I wrestled with confusion. It wasn't the *idea* of a female hunter ... plenty of tribes had them, according to tradition. But why complicate matters with such a player right now, just as the simulation seemed about to end? What did it have to do with prehistoric tool-making?

'Computer. This isn't just a packaged adventure, is it?'

'*No. These are autonomous persona programs, operating in your private sim-world.*'

So, Gaia had been generous after all! Long Stick was no longer my only, full-scale companion.

'*Core memory has been enhanced to allow up to five flexible personae at any one time.*'

'Oh, I get it.'

Gaia must have needed more memory for her own programs, the midwives and doulahs and other helpers she'd need when the baby came. The expense was already budgeted. No wonder she could afford a few extra playmates for me, thrown in at discount. After wondering whether to feel hurt, pleased, or amused ... I finally decided it didn't matter.

'Computer, hold simulation for transfer to my rec room.'

Minutes later, fully suited for virtuality, I held a flint knife in my hands, each curve and serrated edge conveyed by subtle, electrochem gloves. The flint-smiths seemed pleased by my admiration. It was a good knife, of the finest obsidian, bound to an ivory handle carved with figures of running horses. Despite not being real, it was the most splendid thing I ever owned.

The treadmill worked beneath my feet, mimicking movement as Long Stick and I departed the Neolithic factory, heading towards Lookout Point to observe migratory herds of wildebeest and zebra crossing the plain. Along the way, we passed the young beater, Ankle, squatting by the river bank where she'd been banished by Long Stick for impertinence. Tying stone points to spear-shafts, tightening the leather thongs with her teeth, she looked up as we passed by, unrepentant, a light of challenge in her eyes.

I paused, then turned to Long Stick. 'We could use a scout to carry messages. Next hunt, bring this one along.'

My simulated friend returned one of his sharp-eyed looks, but nodded. Ankle turned away, wisely hiding a jubilant grin.

Amid these distractions, I emerged from my primeval world to find Gaia already home from her class, nestled in our small, darkened bedroom. I slipped between the sheets quietly, but soon felt her hand upon my thigh.

'I've been thinking about you,' my wife whispered, her breath warm on my ear.

Pregnancy doesn't mean *no* sex. Doctors say it's all right if you're careful.

In fact, it can be much better than all right. Gaia was very skilled.

The buffalo groaned, mired in muddy shallows with five spears in its flank. I commanded no more thrown.

Ankle protested, waving her javelin. 'Why not finish it off?'

'Because the Chief said no!' Long Stick snapped. But I gestured for patience. With Ankle for an apprentice, I now appreciated the adage, *You never really know something till you teach it.*

'Think. What happens if he falls where he stands?'

She eyed the panting beast. 'He'll fall into the

riv . . . Oh! We'd lose half the carcass.' Ankle nodded
soberly. 'So we try getting him ashore first?'

'Right. And quickly! We don't want him suffering
needlessly.'

Several tribesmen made pious gestures in agreement.
Through ritual, hunters like these used to appease the
spirits of beasts they killed, which made me wonder
– would modern folk eat so much meat if *they* had to
placate the ghost of each steer or chicken? My time in
a simulated Stone Age hasn't made me a vegetarian,
but I better appreciate the fact that meat once lived.

Long Stick called for rope. Bearing coils of braided
leather, we worked towards the bull from three sides.
The treadmill imitated slippery mud beneath my feet,
while the body suit tickled nerves so that I felt hip-deep
in slimy water. Electronically stirred receptors in my
nose 'smelled' the creature's blood and defiance, above
the rank swamp stench. It was hard work, floundering
towards our prey. Harder and more varied than lifting
weights in a gym, and more terrifying. The buffalo
shifted left and right, bellowing and threatening with
its horns.

Ever since Gaia bought that extra memory, everything had seemed more vivid, including this beast's
hot zeal to survive. 'Watch out!' Ankle cried out as
it lunged. I swerved and felt a wall of fur and muscle
glance off my shoulder, rushing through space I'd just
occupied. Teetering in the mud, I glimpsed a snaking
lasso chase the old bull, landing round its neck. 'Got
him!' Long Stick cried.

'My turn!' called a higher voice. Ankle cast her lariat
– only to fall short as the angry beast thrashed aside.

'Wait!' I cried when she plunged after it. Too late,
I watched the girl vanish beneath the frothy, scummy
surface.

'Ankle!'

Suddenly, I was too busy dodging to worry about my young aide. Sharp horns flashed viciously. While I knew the computer wouldn't kill me, other slip-ups in the gym had left me bruised for weeks.

She's only a program, I told myself, back-pedalling from a roaring, shaggy face the size of a small pickup. *Programs can take care of themselves*.

'Yip-yi-i-yip!'

The cry coincided with a sudden change in the creature's bellows. It whirled and I blinked in astonishment. The young hunter, Ankle, had clambered on its back! Dripping water and marsh reeds, she held tightly to its mane while the bull snorted, wild-eyed and convulsing, and slipped her noose over its shaggy head. Others joined her exultant shout as ropes suddenly pulled taut from three directions.

Resignation seemed to settle over the animal. Slumping in defeat, it let itself be drawn several yards towards dry land. Then, in one last, desperate heave, it reared on its hind legs. Ankle flew off, arms whirling, to splash near the bull's stomping hooves.

With a shout I dived towards her.

Or tried to. Swimming is one thing today's virtuality tech can't handle. No way to fake *buoyancy*, so the machine won't let you try. The body suit stiffened, keeping me on my feet. It did let me flounder forward, though, evading the thrashing horns while flailing underwater in search of my apprentice. Frantic seconds passed . . . and finally I felt the touch of a slim arm! A small hand closed vice-like round my wrist as I yanked back hard . . . just as the buffalo pitched over, toppling with a mighty splash where Ankle had lain.

We made it ashore downstream from where the tribe quickly commenced the frenetic ritual of butchery. In olden times, a kill like this came at best once a month, so the hunters sang their joy to the spirits of water,

earth and sky. But the artful ceremony was wasted
on me as I slogged uphill, feeling pressure leave my
cramping legs exactly like water slipping aside. The
weight in my arms seemed all too real as I lowered
Ankle to a patch of grass.

This was an awful lot of trouble to go to, just for
a piece of software. I might have rationalised that
good persona programs are expensive, but the thought
didn't cross my mind as I hurriedly checked Ankle's
breathing. Pale, mud-grimed from crown to toe, she
gave two sudden, wheezing coughs, then revealed twin
flashes of abalone blue as her eyes popped open. Ankle
gasped a sudden, stricken sob and threw both arms
around my neck.

'Urk!' I answered. Never before had my togs yanked
me down so, into such a flood of sensations. Pain lanced
my palms from impacting pebbles. Sunlight spread
heat across my mud-splattered back. Then there was
the press of her warm body, clinging beneath mine,
much more cushiony, in places, than I had imagined.

Soon, I realised, Ankle no longer clung to me for
comfort. She was moving, breathing in ways having
little to do with reassurance. I grunted surprise for a
second time, and reached up to pry loose her arms.
'Stop simulation!' I shouted.

My last glimpse, before yanking off the helmet, was
of Ankle lying there, muddy all over, wiry-strong and
hunter-attired, yet suddenly utterly female, gazing at
me both worshipful and willing.

She was only software – bits of illusion on a silicon
chip. Besides, I barely knew her.

She was already the second most desirable woman
I had ever known.

Now get this, I love my wife. I always figured myself
one of those lucky bastards whose woman understands

him, inside and out, and *despite* that thinks the world of him.

So I figured, there's got to be a mistake here!

Trembling, I peeled off my sweaty body suit and stumbled into the shower, wondering. *How am I going to explain this to Gaia?*

Then, while soaping myself, I thought. *What's to explain? I didn't do anything!*

Rinsing, I pondered. *And if I had? Would it've been adultery? Or an exotic form of masturbation?*

I recall how Mom tacitly approved of Dad's collection of erotic magazines. She wasn't threatened by a good man's private fantasies. Nor did Gaia ever seem to consider my right hand a rival. Sometimes *she* would dial up my electronic Penthouse subscription . . . 'for the articles'.

Still, if a certain amount of healthy, visually stimulated autoeroticism was okay, I also knew it would hurt her terribly if I had a real-life affair.

So . . . what had nearly taken place in my VR gym? The experience seemed to fall somewhere between boffing a co-ed and an encounter with an inflatable doll.

Too bad they never produced that sci-fi gimmick, a direct computer–mind interface. Then I might have dismissed any sim-adventure as purely mental. But so much of what we are and do is tied up in our bodies . . . the nerves, hormones and muscles. For a vivid experience, you must take your meat along.

With flesh taking part, virtuality can mimic any surface. I've crawled across grass and tide pools and steaming sands while stalking prey.

But simulating a *woman* . . . ?

'Hi-tech marches on, but this is ridiculous!' I laughed, drying under a blast of warm air, then put on a terry cloth robe and went out to tell Gaia everything. I had last seen my wife in the nursery, where she had been humming while sorting things for the baby, and cheerfully wished me a 'good hunt'.

Gaia wasn't there, but I felt a warm glow just looking around the little room, its walls decorated with hologram mobiles and floating planets. I had installed most of the nursery equipment myself, including the bottom-baster, with its simmering vat of Liquid Diaper. The flotation crib would be programmed to mimic my wife's heartbeat and other rhythms, comforting baby's first weeks with sensations familiar from the womb.

This was where my life was anchored, I thought. Not in some make-believe hunting band that femismo psychologists thought every modern man required. My *family*. For all its pollution, crowds and exhaustion, the *real* world was where you lived real life.

'Gaia?' I asked, searching in the living room. 'You'll never guess what happened . . .'

She wasn't there either. I tried the kitchen, throbbing with busy, scrabbling sounds of captive insects. Still no sign of her.

Funny, I thought. She hadn't said anything about another NatuBirth class tonight.

'Computer, did my wife leave a message where she was going?' The control voice answered. '*Your wife hasn't left the apartment. She is in her Virtuality Room.*'

'Ah . . . of course. Her turn. Must have gone in while I showered.'

I sat on the couch gingerly, still feeling tremors from this evening's hi-stress workout. I picked up the remote control and scanned tonight's cable listings. Besides the normal thousand channels of infotainment, there were amateur-vids, pubforums, hobby and spec-interest lines, two-way chatshows, and 'Uncle Fred' showing slides of his blimp-ride to Everest. The usual stuff. I

fell back on dialling a good book from the library,
and actually stared at the first page of *Robinson Crusoe*
for about ten minutes before pounding the cushion
beside me.

'Hell.'

I told myself I was getting up to fetch a drink . . .
then to go to the can . . . then to look in the closet
for my tennis shoes . . . Maybe I'd go outside for an
old-fashioned walk . . .

I found the sneakers where I'd left them, near the
crack in the closet wall. Leaning close, I heard soft
sounds coming from the room next door – my wife's
private sanctum.

They weren't sounds of conversation, but exertion,
heavy breathing.

*Well, gatherers also used to work hard, netting fish, cutting
wild grain . . .*

I knew I was rationalising as I brought my eye to
the crack.

Wearing helmet and body suit, Gaia squatted much
as the last time I had seen her in this place, hands
outstretched and down before her, as if grasping
something. Underneath, the treadmill-floor mimicked
an oblong hummock which she straddled while strenu-
ously rocking back and forth. Whatever she was doing
in her private world, it apparently involved a lot of
effort, for her head rocked back and I heard her
moan aloud.

I knew that sound. I looked again at the shape
beneath her, and saw that it recreated no patch of
ground, no fallen log. Even without goggles for seeing,
earphones for hearing, or gloves for touching, I could
tell the outline of a man.

I needed those sneakers, after all. I left at once, and
took a walk along the sky bridges lacing the grey

metropolis at the forty storey level, overlooking the maze of transport tubes and vibrating machinery which keeps the city alive. Looking up past the towering canyon walls of Chitown, I could see no stars, just a hazy glow diffused by pollutant haze. Late at night I should have been grateful for the countless Public Safety cameras, peering from each lamp post. But they only made me feel conspicuous, *supervised*. On the veldt, you don't fear being victimised by a million strangers. Twenty thousand years ago there *were* no strangers. All you needed was your tribe.

I ducked into a bar. The beer was excellent, the atmosphere depressing. Other men sat nursing drinks, scrupulously avoiding eye contact with those around them. A wire-o in the corner kept dropping quarters into a stim-zap machine, then sticking his head under the hood for direct jolts of electric pleasure. His sighs were sterile, emotionless.

Gaia's had been throaty, lusty.

Now I knew where she had learned that provocative, swaying motion – the one she'd used the last few times we made love. Apparently, she had a tutor, a good one. One I would never meet, let alone get to punch in the face.

Fair is fair, I thought. Hadn't I already rationalised my own encounter with sex-by-simulation, before finding out that Gaia was doing it first? If it fell into the category of masturbation for me, and not infidelity, then why not her?

That's different! part of me replied. But hard as I tried, I couldn't see how. My 'rival' was a phantom, no threat in real terms. He could never impregnate Gaia, or give her a disease, or boast of cuckolding me to my business partners, or ever take her away from me.

What it really came down to was the mental image provoking jealousy at a deep, gut level. Jealousy based on ancient drives a *civilised* man should be able to overcome.

I was no longer sure I wanted to be a civilised man.

No, I didn't get roaring drunk, or provoke a fight with the big guy two stools down. I thought about it, but what the hell? By now I was much too skilled at killing to trust myself in a friendly brawl, out in the real world. Anyway, my neighbour also looked like he worked out. Maybe for exercise, *he* took scalps with Cochise, or rode with a VR Genghis Khan. Under our grey urban disguises, we can all be dangerous mysteries.

I paid up and left.

Gaia was dozing on the couch when I got back, or pretending to be. She seemed relieved to have me home, and I tried not to show my inner turmoil. I turned on the TV wall and she, sensing it wiser, went to bed.

Half an hour later, I slipped into my body suit and re-entered my private world.

Weeks passed. Gaia grew larger. We spoke little.

My consulting firm finally won the Taiko Tech account, worth millions. I rushed home and celebrated with Ankle by first killing a lion, then making love by a cool bend in the river. We lay together, listening to locusts and the wind in the swaying branches, while a dry heat seemed to suck all the dank, foetid odours of the office out of my skin. Tension at work had left knots up and down my spine, which Ankle worked out with her strong hands.

She listened quietly to my recitation of setbacks and victories in the corporate world, clearly understanding none of it. That didn't matter. My VR people knew and accepted that their Chief spent most of his time far away, in the Land of Gods.

In a way, Ankle was the perfect, uncritical sounding board.

If only it had been that simple dealing with the hanging, unspoken tension between me and Gaia. Ankle would have listened to that, too, but what was there to say?

The whole thing was preposterous and my fault. Why should it bother me what my wife did in fantasy play?

It did bother me. It was starting to split us apart.

'I want to show you something,' Ankle announced, picking up her clothes and evading my grasp. 'Come,' she urged. 'Long Stick can send some boys for the lion. There is something nearby you must see.'

I shrugged into my tunic. 'What is it?'

She only smiled and motioned for me to follow. Still wrestling to lace my moccasins, I tried to keep up as she led me towards a forested rise. It lay in the direction of 'Camp', the fictitious home base I had never seen during all of my workouts with small groups of hunters. It would have taken so much computing power to process a full tribe that it simply never occurred to me to journey in this direction.

We reached the top of the rise and soon picked up faint sounds . . . human voices, talking and laughing. We approached stealthily, crawling the last few metres to peer over a steep bluff. There we saw, a couple of hundred metres downslope, a small gathering of people clustered around an oak tree. They were using tall poles to bat away at an object high in the branches. Occasionally, one of them dropped her pole and hopped about, swatting at the air while others laughed.

Gatherers, I realised. *Going after a beehive*. This was my first glimpse of the other half of my 'tribe'. Calmly, I noted that many were accompanied by children . . .

and that one of the unaccompanied ones was decidedly pregnant . . .

My breath suddenly caught as I recognised the rotund, laughing figure.

All this time, Gaia and I had played in our own pretend Neolithic worlds, and never guessed they were different parts of the same tribe!

It hadn't started out that way. We had bought our original programs separately. But in retrospect it seemed an obvious thing for the computer to do . . . to save memory space by pooling our adventures in the same metaphorical landscape.

'It affects us,' Ankle said.

'Who?'

'Your folk.' She motioned towards the gatherers, slapped her own chest, and waved towards the east, where the hunting parties roamed. 'It hurts us.'

'What hurts you?' I asked, perplexed, distracted.

'The break . . . the pain between you two.'

I was too confused, too curious about this new turn of events to follow what she was saying. I peered at the figures below, and saw two *men* among the women down there, helping to steal honey. Just as some women could be hunters, certain males might choose the rites and rhythms of gathering. Probably, one of them was my rival, Gaia's synthetic paramour.

Suddenly it seemed important to get closer. But as I made ready, Ankle stopped me.

'You cannot,' she said.

'What do you mean?'

'Certain charms are needed. To unite us. Unite the tribe.'

'Charms?'

She nodded. 'From the Land of Gods.'

After a pause. '. . . . Oh, I get it.'

She meant more memory, much more. Until recently,

I had hunted with just one companion, then ten or so. Joining the two simulated worlds, depicting several score personified characters, would take more power than our house console possessed.

But that was no problem! I had a big raise coming. I could go right out and buy the chips on credit! My fist clenched in anticipation. By this time tomorrow, I'd get a much closer look at the bastard who . . .

Suddenly, the laughter below broke under a single, warbling cry. One of the women dropped her pole and doubled over in agony, clutching her swollen abdomen.

I didn't stop to think. With a bellow I came to my feet, running downhill towards the petite form, writhing amid a cluster of anxious women. 'Gaia!' I cried, frustrated that the ground grew tarry with each step. The gatherers, too, seemed to blur around the edges as I neared, one heavy step at a time. The earth trembled and Ankle clutched my arm.

'Not that way!' she screamed, cringing as I whirled in anger. 'Oh Chief, you must go!' She slapped the side of her head, then pointed to mine. 'Go *back*!'

Damn the realism of it all!

Cursing, I tore off the helmet, gashing my cheek. The body suit still formed a matrix of other-world sensations – hot savannah and gritty moccasins. But abruptly my eyes saw a tiny, off-white chamber, its coarse floor mimicking a steep hillside. Sense-conflict made me sway in confusion as I dived for the door.

'I'm coming, Gaia!' I cried, stumbling into the hallway in haste to reach my wife.

They're making a big deal out of it. I've been interviewed. There is even talk of reviving childbirth classes for husbands. But it's all silly, of course. Any other man would've done the same in a crisis.

I have my wife and son. What else matters?

Tommy thrives as his stim-crib eases him from synthetic womb-sounds into the gaudy, greater world. He will grow up here in Chitown ... and on Mars, and in an Indian village, and in ancient Greece, and a Neolithic clan. He'll run through forests, to know what we've lost. As a teenager, he'll fulfil fantasies lads of my time could but imagine.

And if he gets a big head from being a prince in a dozen virtualities? Well, he can still be spanked here and now. Even his generation will learn to tell what's real. *Reality* is what hurts when you take the suit off.

As for Gaia and me, we found ways to assuage my male pride, once our tribes united. Each of us plays with personas now and then – who could resist? But always we come home to each other.

Virtuality is fun – it's good to be the Chief – but nothing matches the sweetness of her skin, her breath, or the wonderful unpredictability of her real mind.

My blood pressure is low. My arteries are squeaky-clean and muscles wiry, strong. I stay a little hungry, like my ancestors, and may live past a hundred. In a cramped world of twelve billion souls, I can run for hours seeing no one but gazelles or a lonely hawk.

Lions know to give me a wide berth.

Give me time. I'm even learning to like termites.

What follows is another of my published essays revolving around the topic of Otherness . . .

Science versus Magic

In all of history, no organised system of thought has changed humanity as much as science. Its offspring technologies have brought unrivalled power and wealth to our lives, as well as unprecedented danger. Answers to countless questions which mystified our ancestors are now freely available to all. This expansion and democratisation of knowledge has been a major force for change in a species used to strict patterns of inherited hierarchy.

Yet, in the midst of this renaissance, one hears the question, 'Does science provide everything we need?' Often the reply is a resounding, 'No!'

This rejection doesn't come only from religious conservatives. So-called 'New Age' movements – encompassing everything from astrology, to past life regression, to crystal therapy – fixate many citizens of our modern culture, those feeling a need for more than science and reason seem to offer. Most patrons of these new mysticisms acknowledge the positive accomplishments of technology. (They would hate to do without microwave cookers and CD players.) Still, they proclaim faith in realms of wisdom and adventure inaccessible to rational thought.

This attitude may have been best distilled by author Tom Robbins, in his novel *Another Roadside Attraction*, in which a minor character explains sagely that, 'Science gives man what he needs, but *magic* gives man what he *wants*.'

The conflict is an old one. George Washington and other followers of the Enlightenment Movement wrote of their belief in an imminent maturity of humankind. Feudal ways were splitting asunder, therefore how could truth and freedom not prevail? In fact, the Enlightenment changed humanity forever. Yet its followers forgot something important – that each generation is invaded by a new wave of barbarians . . . its children. Just as Washington, Franklin, and their peers, took joy in toppling the tyranny of Church and King, so the youths of the Romantic Movement thrived on jeering the lofty ideals of *their* predecessors.

'What good is reason,' they sneered, 'if it drives out beauty, terror and vivid emotion? Can a thousand facts compare with that single, epiphanic moment, when a poet stands tall in a lightning storm, hurling challenges at God?'

Heady stuff; Shelley, Byron, and their crowd, made quite a splash by appealing to romantic mystical notions of the ineffable, harkening to inner needs left unsatisfied by cool logic.

The debate is one we have inherited today, both in society as a whole and inside the field of science fiction. Those who proclaim that SF is purely a literature of reason forget that its foundations rest on *both* the Erector Set ribwork of 1920s radio magazines and the grisly, sewn-up ribcage of Frankenstein's monster. Meanwhile, many writers of horror or fantasy, as well as so-called cyberpunks, carry on the tradition of

Shelley and Poe, rejecting any sterile tomorrow based solely on analytic thought.

Naturally, this gulf is a caricature. In real life, there are fantasists and artists who subscribe to *Scientific American*, and physicists who paint and study Zen. Still, many romantics continue to call rationalism soul-killing, while latter-day children of the Enlightenment label New Ager enthusiasms mind-melting drivel. It seems clear that we cannot be *both* trained naturalists and devout dryad worshippers, much as both professions love trees.

Is there a *fundamental* conflict between science and the realms one might call magical?

In a later essay, we'll take up one crucial difference, in the *time sense of wisdom* – whether one looks to a *past* golden age as the ultimate source of truth, or to the future. But for now, let's just consider the image of a perfect wizard.

The magician, as portrayed in countless legends, films and novels, is a solitary being of great power, often depicted as dwelling on some craggy, clifftop aerie where he guards the secrets of his craft. His prowess derives not just from deep knowledge, but also some indwelt force of will, a talent which at an early age set him aside from mere mortals. He – and the magician's most powerful manifestations are nearly always male – generally uses his manna sparingly. Even 'good' wizards perform beneficent wonders grudgingly, and only when conditions seem auspicious.

Ever notice how seldom magicians of fantasy cohabit with printing presses, indoor plumbing, alternating current, free public education, bicameral legislatures, or other democratic amenities? Generally, they share power with sword-wielding kings, reigning over great masses of unwashed, barely noticed peasantry.

Naturally, a wizard's power is accessible only to a select few. He may have a talented young apprentice, but he doles out secrets to the neophyte sparingly. His works and ideas are not subject to scrutiny or criticism.

Naturally, Joe magician thinks he's pretty hot stuff.

So does the scientist, at least as she is portrayed in popular media. Yet, think for a moment of the truly great scientists, the ones most admired. Are the very best of them not seen as kindly? Even saintly? In the ideal image, they are depicted as women or men who keep their egos under control. There are reasons for this.

A scientist who makes a discovery does not hoard it, for the greatest credit comes from instantly *sharing* new knowledge, publishing, not scribbling into some locked book of arcana. Indeed, top scientists love nothing better than narrating popular shows for public television! The assumption seems to be, 'The taxpayers financed my research. And anyway, no one really knows a subject unless he or she can explain it to a nine-year-old.'

No scientist can accomplish anything without the cooperation of hundreds of skilled professionals – from filter manufacturers, glass-blowers and electricians to xerox repairmen and *chalk* makers. They must be team players, or fail.

So Why Is There Magic?

So if magic is inferior, why, even now, does it attract us? Why does the appeal of fantasy not wane in the face of technological marvels and the promise of a glittering tomorrow? Why do so many of us still love to scare ourselves half to death, reading horror novels by firelight?

Even within 'science fiction', this urge remains

strong. Many authors who write 'glittering tomorrows' filled with glossy, ultra-tech imagery wind up describing, not engineers, but magicians dressed in white coats. Never mind the dialogue, consisting of pseudo-techish mumbo-jumbo. A dead giveaway can be seen whenever a book or film's resident wonder-worker *behaves* more like a wizard than any realistic scientist – solitary, secretive, obsessed and tyrannical. These are wonderful traits for a romantic hero or villain, even if they are crippling impediments to researchers in the real world.

Perhaps I sound churlish, picking on the underdog at a time when magic seems down for the count. But remember, this underdog has dominated over rational scepticism since long before recorded history, right up to recent times, and its attraction continues drawing us.

Consider a basic premise of magic – that the universe can be *persuaded* into giving what you want. Using incantations, threats, and cajoling propitiations, the mystic or shaman speaks directly to hidden powers of nature – spirits, gods and elementals – urging bad ones to depart the sick and good ones to bring rain or wealth. Using symbols of the one desired, they cast love spells. Making images of a hated one, they fling curses. If others, watching, truly believe a witch's power, sometimes the hex comes true. Today, we call it the power of suggestion.

Can you really make it rain by dancing? Or restore a parched stream by shouting certain phrases? Of course not.

Then why did people believe it?

Because there *are* certain objects in a person's environment which *can* be manipulated that way! These objects are far more important than wheat, or rainclouds, or flowing streams. They are *other people*.

Other people *can* be persuaded by dance and song and incantation. A talented enough persuader can make other people believe anything. That's what subjectivity is all about.

In other words, a witch doctor may not actually be able to end a drought, but if he's any good, he can make sure other people feed *him*!

Wizardry may have been a wild goose chase for thousands of years, but it's easy to see why. Strong-willed persons in every culture reasoned thus: 'If I can persuade *people* to do my will by incantation, why not animals, plants, the sky?' These charismatic types threw themselves into their art, often with the best of intentions, in order to heal disease, or help the tribe. Augmented by a pragmatic, sometimes splendid herbal lore, they won success just often enough to persuade themselves and others.

Scepticism is seldom anywhere near as much fun. It flies in the face of human nature, especially individual pride and egotism, to switch from flamboyant performance art to a system based on criticism and experimentation ... in which the theory you hold dearest may come crashing down, and you must smile, hold out your hand, and congratulate the snot-nosed grad student who demolished it in front of all your peers. A system which makes it harder every day to suppress inconvenient questions with that favourite, ancient mantra of priests, mages and old poops everywhere – 'You wouldn't understand. Just trust me.'

After countless millennia, human nature is awfully hard to overcome. Magic may *seem* the underdog, but that is a very recent change, and maybe illusory. As in the days of the Enlightenment, science is still the true rebel in this play.

*   *   *

Yet, science itself comes up with grounds for magic!

If the latest creation-myth is to be believed, we evolved in tiny bands of hunter-gatherers, numbering a few dozen individuals at a time. Our brains, deep instincts and egotistic drives were formed when existence was simple, straightforward. Today, our battles are complex, our foes seldom purely good or evil. Often, in order to get by, we must compromise and make complex alliances, trusting others we barely know, each with his or her own murky, unreadable agenda.

Even if we have our outer lives under control, what about the inner self? We may spend our days taking part in the great enterprise of building a mature, diverse, complex society. But inside there often remains that tribal warrior, wanting out.

In *fantasy* we are free to be heroes and heroines. Through a protagonist, we can battle unadulterated evil – by ourselves or in the company of a few stalwart, archetype sidekicks numbering no more than the dozen or so our ancestors knew in a tribal hunting party. Imagination vents fizzing thoughts from a brain which, after all, spent far longer peering into forest glooms than sitting safely by electric lamps. In the fantastic we give our egos room to stretch, and our fears simple shapes we can fight. Midway along evolving from bipedal apes to . . . who knows what? . . . we can't just give ourselves over wholly to maturity. In all of us there remains a need for the extravagant, the irrational, the vividly unreasonable.

Some try hard to squelch that need, suppressing one of our oldest wellsprings of joy. Others bring it into the real world, allowing it to master them, and so lose touch with what is solid, what is honest and mature.

But for some, perhaps a fortunate majority, a balance is struck. The ancient want is fulfilled marvellously well through the magic of art and myth.

Is Peace Possible?

Are we doomed to war within ourselves? To perpetual conflict between honesty and romance? Or can forebrain and midbrain find ground for compromise?

A hint at the answer may be found in the venerable institution of the SF *cautionary tale*. Aldous Huxley and George Orwell, in *Brave New World* and *Nineteen Eighty-Four*, portrayed alternate worlds which so frightened people that – ironically – the scenarios they depicted are no longer possible. Countless examples exist where images, drawn from the pit of an author's fears, have been clothed in the raiment of believable extrapolation and used to scare us into exorcising monsters from the real world. That is the synergism of the cautionary tale, the self-preventing prophecy, the plausible horror story, in which fantasy and reason serve on the same team. In which science and a kind of magic collaborate.

But fantasy need not only serve dire warnings. The images and feelings stretch us, provoke us, and sometimes challenge us, with possibilities.

Suppose for a moment that we *are* slowly maturing towards a civilisation guided by wisdom and what I earlier called 'otherness'. If so, that maturity cannot be one of uniform, crystalline logic. Not a future of antiseptic, sterile utopias or stainless-steel smugvilles. These aren't reasonable or desirable human tomorrows, just as any town bereft of shadows would not be a human city. As we grow up, some of the rage and roaring egotism may seep away. People may grow less cantankerously crazy. But we'll probably never lose a hankering to occasionally hoot and holler at the fringes of a campfire, to shout at the night, or shiver when the wings of an owl eclipse the moon.

I have a feeling that a thousand years from now,

when all our dreaded mental ailments have gone the way of gout and smallpox, when war and murder are fading memories, children will still listen, wide-eyed, as their older cousins whisper ghost stories in the dark, and shriek in play terror when the tale-spinner finally shouts – 'Boo!'

Then the kids will plead, 'Tell us another one!'

Magic will never die.

CONTACT

Sshhh . . .

Nobody speaks much about the Talent, anymore – that aspect of our nature we were asked to give up, for the sake of pity. We gave it up, something precious and rare, for the Lentili.

Or did we?

No one doubts the Lentili merited such sacrifice. They have done so much for humankind. Had we never met them, would we, or our Earth, have survived mankind's childish greed and temper for much longer? I know this – I would never have been able to put off writing my memoir so long, procrastinating for two centuries of augmented life span, were it not for the medical technologies donated by our benefactors.

Ah, but Time is inexorable, or so the Lentili philosophers tell us. So now I pour my testimony into Write-only Memory, that bank which takes only deposits, never withdrawals. Someday there will be no men or women still corporeal whose neuronal recollections reach that time of excitement, when our first starprobes brought back word of contact.

Contact – a word so sweet yet chilling, promising an end to loneliness and a beginning of . . . what?

Oh, such fears we had. Such high hopes! Each

pundit had his or her pet theory. This would end
the miserable, solipsistic isolation of mankind, some
proclaimed. Others predicted our end entire.

Initial reports from our contact team sounded so
optimistic, so wonderful. Too wonderful, we thought
to be true!

As it turned out, they understated. In dazed won-
derment we came to realise that the Universe might
actually be sane, after all. How else could there ever
come about beings such as the Lentili?

Oh, there were many ancient, wise races in the
Galactic Commonweal – advanced, philosophical species who had no more interest in swooping down to
seize our grubby little world than a professor might
wish to steal a small boy's ball. All of a sudden, all
our worst fears seemed so silly. Of course we would
remain awkward newcomers for ages, but starfaring
had transformed us overnight and forever from the
status of clever animals into citizens.

Our appointed advisers in this process would be
the kind, gregarious Lentili, so beautiful and gentle
and wise. Could we ask for any better proof that the
Universe was kind?

They were on their way, great Lentili starships,
escorting two crude Earth Survey vessels they could
just as easily have swallowed and brought here in a
fraction of the time. But there was no hurry, and the
Lentili were sensitive to matters of honour.

Honour can be costly. We learned this when the
Margaret Mead, containing half our contact team,
exploded halfway home to Sol. In the midst of this
shock, the widely respected chairman of the Interim
Council of State Leaders came on the air to address the
world. Platitudes and paeans can be clichés, but that is
not lamentable. Originality is not useful to those freshly

numbed with grief. So President Tridden spoke of our lost emissaries in words oft-used to eulogise heroes, yet seldom so aptly.

But then there came an unexpected coda. Then he said something that took the world by surprise.

Officially, no copies of his address exist any longer. And yet, while it is seldom spoken of, has any speech ever had more far-reaching effects? It endures in secret tapes all over the Solar System. Here is how Tridden revealed his shocking news.

'Fellow citizens and people of the world, I must now talk to you about something I learned only hours before hearing about the loss of the *Margaret Mead*. It is my duty to tell you that the Lentili, these gentle beings who will so soon be our guests on this planet, are not quite as perfect as they have seemed. In fact, they have a serious, tragic flaw.

'Just before she died aboard the *Margaret Mead*, the eminent psychologist-sociologist Dr Beth Rishke sent me a most disturbing document. After two days sleeplessly agonising over what to do, I've decided to share this information with the entire human race. For if anything is to be done about Dr Rishke's disturbing conclusions, it must be now, before the Lentili arrive.

'First off, I don't want to disturb you unduly. We are in no danger from our approaching guests. Quite the contrary. Had they wished us harm, resistance would have been useless. But all evidence shows them to be benevolent. Indeed, we are offered all of the secrets of an ancient, wise culture. Solutions to many of the troubles that have vexed us for ages.

'But I must report to you that there is a danger, nevertheless. The danger is not to us, but to our benefactors. You see, for all of their advancement, the Lentili appear to be deficient in an unexpected

way. Before her untimely death, Dr Rishke was quite
concerned.

'Apparently, we humans have a certain talent,
one which seems to be completely absent from the
Lentili. One which they appear barely capable of
even comprehending. At first, when she referred to it,
they did not seem to understand what she was talking
about. When her persistent efforts resulted in a few of
them finally catching on, the reaction astonished her.
Professor Rishke said, and I quote, "I was appalled at
the consequences to those poor Lentili." Unquote.'

How well I remember the expression on President
Tridden's face. His sympathy for the plight of these
poor creatures was apparent. We had all come to
admire the Lentili so, over recent weeks. Tall and
gangling, with faces that seemed almost droopy with
kindness and gentle humour – they looked so harmless,
so *incapable* of doing harm.

They also seemed omnipotent! Terrifically strong
and coordinated, they lived, as corporeal individuals,
for thousands of years before going on to join their
Universal Minds. Skills a man might spend a lifetime
perfecting were the study of a lazy weekend to a
Lentili. Their accomplishments, both as a race and
as individuals, were awesome.

The Lentili spoke kindly of the arts and achievements
of mankind, never qualifying their praise as some of us
would have, allowing for the fact that these were, after
all, the simple works of children. And yet, how could we
avoid inserting those burning qualifiers, ourselves?

Humanity's overweening pride had come near to
wrecking our beloved world. Even by the time we
launched two crude starships, Earth was still a frac-
tious, nervous place. So humility was medicine that
did not taste as bad as feared. Despite some dissenting

voices, people seemed determined to become good students, to be grateful, hard-working pupils.

So imagine our surprise! How could the President be saying this? How could such mighty beings as the Lentili be flawed?

Such was President Tridden's great authority, however, and the renown of famed Professor Rishke, that we had no choice but to take their word! We leaned towards our sets and concentrated as few ever have in times of peace.

'Professor Rishke sent her information directly to me,' the President went on, 'and now I pass the buck to all of you. For it is up to all of humanity now to decide what we are to do.

'At the very start of our long relationship with a kind, decent race – one whose interest in our welfare is indisputable – we find it actually within our power to wreak untold psychic harm upon our benefactors. The Lentili have a mental block, something like an odd inferiority complex, and it concerns something so mundane to us that few human beings ever bother thinking about it, past the age of ten! It certainly isn't our fault. And yet, we can hurt our new friends terribly if we are crass or rudely force them to see what they would rather not. We are duty bound to try to minimise that harm as best we can.

'Therefore, I have decided to ask you all to join me in making a grand sacrifice.

'Over the coming weeks, as we prepare to receive our visitors, our guests and future guides, we must expunge all references to this human talent from our literature, from our language, from our outward lives!

'To begin with, I have already given orders to various governmental agencies, using my emergency powers. Commencing this hour, the indexes to the

UN Data Bank and the Library of Congress are being destroyed.

'Let me emphasise . . . no books will actually be burned! But in the laborious process of reconstruction, the new indexes will exclude all references to this human ability which so disturbs our new friends.

'All of you can do the same, in your towns and villages and homes. We must not, of course, destroy our heritage. But we can at least make an effort to mask this thing, so that when the Lentili arrive we might spare them avoidable pain.'

Oh, the sadness in his eyes. The *human* wisdom of President Tridden as he spoke these words. I can tell you now what so many of us were feeling, then. We felt dread. We felt fear. But most of all, we felt *pride*. Yes, pride that we humans, too, could bring forth nobility and charity to those in need. We were determined, listening to this great man, to follow his example. Yes, we would do this great thing, and begin our relationship with our mentors nobly, in an act of self-sacrifice and pity.

Only a few of us had begun to worry about *how* to do this. But then the President went on.

'Of course we all know human nature. Part of the work we did in becoming civilised enough to be allowed to join the Galactic Commonwealth involved learning to despise secrecy. We've become a race of eccentric individualists, and are proud of that fact. How then can we hide forever the existence of a human talent? It just wouldn't be possible, even if everyone agreed to do so. Even if we found and eradicated every record.

'And there will certainly be those humans who do *not* cooperate in this undertaking, those who, rightly or wrongly, disagree with me that our benefactors are in danger, or that we should care or bother to try sparing them pain.

'Certainly, despite all our efforts, there will be many retained copies of this very broadcast!

'But there is hope. For, according to Dr Rishke's analysis, those exceptions will not matter! Not so long as the majority of us makes a good effort. And so long as we agree in advance upon the right *cover story*. Any clues, evidence, or testimony remaining will then be largely overlooked by the poor Lentili. For subconsciously they will be our collaborators in suppressing this threat to their collective mental equilibrium. So long as the talent is not flaunted too blatantly, Dr Rishke was convinced the Lentili will simply ignore it.'

He paused, then continued with the words I shall never forget.

'*This*, then, will be our cover story, dear people of Earth.

'It shall be recorded that on this day, in this year, Joseph Tridden, President of the Interim Council of Terra, went stark, raving mad.'

Was there a hint of a smile? Just a *flicker* of one, as Tridden said those words? I have debated with myself a thousand times, watching my own secret tape of that broadcast. In truth, I cannot say, nor can anybody, what fleeting thread of whimsy might have woven through the man's earnest appeal.

Certainly the Earth seemed to *wobble* at that moment, with the gravitational torque applied by ten billion human jaws, all dropping open at the same time, in stunned surprise.

'Yes, people of the world. That is the only way. Tonight, millions of you will do as I ask. You will go forth and meddle, alter records, change archives. It won't matter that you will not be entirely successful, for the resulting confusion can be used as an *excuse* when the Lentili wonder why we talk so little about certain things.

'And next month, next year, on into history, tonight's temporary hysteria will all be blamed on me.

'*There is no such talent* . . . no human attribute that makes the Lentili inherently jealous, that makes them feel painful pangs of inferiority.

'*That* will be our cover story! It doesn't exist! It was all a myth perpetrated by a single man, a neurotic human leader driven over the edge by the approaching end to his days of petty power, a man who seized the airwaves in one last, futile spasm and sent a few millions into the streets for a day or two of relatively harmless tape-shredding, index-burning, and other silly, repairable acts of sabotage.

'This is what you *must* do, my fellow citizens and people of the world. You must expunge all official mention of this talent, out of kindness to our approaching mentors. And then you must say that all of this was the product of one deranged mind.

'Me.'

At this point, I know he did smile. By now half the world was convinced that he *was* insane.

The other half would have died for him, then and there.

'I will try to delay my resignation long enough to see the task well underway. Already, at this moment, political battles are being waged, physicians consulted, constitutional procedures set in motion. Perhaps I only have a little longer to talk to you, so I will be succinct.

'It occurs to me that I have been too vague in one respect. The talent I am referring to, about which I cannot be overly specific, is one that is common

to human beings, though apparently incredibly rare
out in the Galactic Commonweal. So far we have
developed it hardly at all. In fact, it has seemed of
so little importance that all but a few of us take it
completely for granted, thinking of it no more than in
passing, throughout our lives.

'And yet, it is something that—'

He stopped speaking quite suddenly, and reflected in
his eyes we could all track the approach of those intent
on bringing an end to his monopoly of the airwaves.
President Tridden had time only to bring one finger
to his lips, in that age-old sign of secrecy and shared
silence. Then, abruptly, the broadcast ended in that
famous burst of static which held an entire world
hypnotised for endless minutes until, at last, the
screens were filled again with the breathless heads
and torsoes of government officials and newscasters,
blinking rapidly as they told us what half of us already
knew – that the President was not well.

The rest of us – the *other* half – did not wait to hear the
diagnoses of learned doctors. We were already tearing
the indexes out of our encyclopedias, or striding out
the door with axes in our hands, heading towards our
local libraries with evil intent upon – not the books –
but the card catalogue.

At the moment it hardly seemed to matter that he
had never gotten around to telling us exactly what it
was we were trying to hide! *Cause a muddle*, we thought.
Make it possible to disguise this thing of ours which
can hurt others.

Do something noble, while we are still in command
of our own destinies.

That night's hysteria came in a surge of passion, a
Dionysian frenzy that did little actual harm in the

long run – little that could not be fixed fairly easily,
that is. It ended as quickly as it began, in embarrassed,
sheepish return to normality.

Yes, the psychiatrists announced. *The President was
mad.*

When the ship, *Gregory Bateson*, arrived, Dr Rishke's
colleagues were interviewed and all of them swore that
she could never have sent such a report. It just wasn't
possible! Rumours were rampant. There was no solid
evidence to support speculation that Tridden himself
ordered the destruction of the *Margaret Mead*, a crime
too horrible to credit even a lunatic. Anyway, it was
decided not to rake those ashes. The man was now
where he could harm no one.

Soon we were into the glorious days of the Arrival.
Lentili were being interviewed on every channel. And
in their charming ways, their humour and their obvious
love for us, we realised what we had really needed, all
along. These wonderful, wise, older brothers and sisters
to help ease away our awkward, adolescent millennia.
The earnest work of growing up had finally begun.

Today people seldom speak of President Tridden,
or of the strange hoax he tried to pull. Oh, there will
always be the Kooks. Artists, writers, innovators of all
kinds are forever coming forth and announcing that
they have 'found the Tridden Talent'. Often these are
silly folk, the half-mad, those at the fringes whom we
all tolerate in much the same way the Lentili must love
and tolerate us.

But then, on other occasions, the discoveries are
bona fide accomplishments. How often has the public
watched some brilliant new performer, or stared at
some startling piece of art, or listened to new music or
some bold concept, and experienced momentary uncertainty, wondering, could *this* be what Tridden spoke of?
Might this prove him to have been right, after all?

Inevitably it is the Lentili who are the test. How they react tells us. As yet, none of the fruits of our new renaissance seem to cause them much discomfort, or any sign of hysterical rejection.

They say they are *surprised* by our behaviour. It seems most neophyte species – most 'freshman' members of the Commonweal – go through long periods of humility and self-doubt, giving themselves over to excessive, slavish mimicry of their seniors. The Lentili say they are impressed by our independence of spirit and our innovation. Still, they show no sign of having yet been intimidated by some mysterious latent human talent, suddenly brought to flower.

We speak of Tridden, when we speak of him at all, with embarrassment. He died in an institution, and his name is now used as a euphemism for passing through a wormhole, for going off the deep end, for losing it.

And yet . . .

And yet, sometimes I wonder. A small minority still believe in him. They are the ones who thank our mentors politely, and yet *patronisingly*, with a serene semi-smugness that seems so out of place given our relative stations on the ladder of life. They are the ones who somehow seem impervious to the quaking intimidation that strikes most of humanity, now and again, despite the best efforts of the Lentini to make us feel loved and at home.

Is it an accident, I wonder, that every time a human team negotiates with the Commonweal on some matter, always a few Triddenites are named among the emissaries? Is it a coincidence that they prove the toughest, most capable of our diplomats?

They search – these believers in a mad president – never satisfied, always seeking out that secret, unde-veloped niche in the human repertoire, the fabled talent

that will make us special even in this intimidating,
overpowering cosmos. Spurning the indexes they call
useless, they pore through the source material of our
past, and explore the filmy fringes of what we know
or can comprehend. Neither time nor the blinding
brilliance of our mentors seems to matter to the
Triddenites.

Perhaps they are lingering symptoms of the underlying craziness of Humankind.

The Lentili walk among us like gods.

We, in turn, have learned some of what we taught
dogs and horses. We've supped from the same bowl
as we once served to our cousins, the lesser apes. The
bowl of humility.

There is no doubt that humans were arrogant when
we saw ourselves at creation's pinnacle. Even when we
worshipped a deity, we nearly always placed Him at
safe remove, exalting him out of the mundane world,
naming *ourselves* paramount on Earth.

Now, humbled, we earnestly devote ourselves to
making our species worthy of a civilisation whose peaks
we can only dimly perceive. No question, we are better
people now than those savages were, our ancestors.
We are smarter, kinder, more loving. And, against all
expectation, we are also more creative, as well.

I have a theory to explain the latter – a theory I
keep to myself. But it is why, once a year, I risk being
labelled a Kook by attending a memorial service by
the side of a small grave in Bruges Cemetery. And
while most of those present speak of *honour*, and *pity*,
and the martyrdom of a decent man, *I* pay homage to
one who perhaps saw where his people were headed,
and the danger that awaited them.

I honour one who changed that future.

And yes, he was a martyr. But of all the solaces to

accompany him into his imprisonment, I can think of none better than the one Tridden took with him.

That smile . . .

They walk among us like gods. But we have our revenge.

For the Lentili know Tridden must have been mad. They know there is no secret talent. We are not sheltering them from some bright truth, hiding something from them out of pity. Out of love.

They *know* it.

And yet, every now and then I have seen it. I've *seen* it! Seen it in their deep, expressive eyes, each time something new from our renaissance surprises them, oh, so briefly.

I have seen that glimmer of wonder. That momentary, fearful *doubt*.

That is when I pity the poor creatures.

Thank God, I can pity them.

Story Notes

This section, 'Contact', is devoted to that special, often maligned sub-genre of SF, the *think piece*. Once upon a time, such tales comprised nearly all of science fiction. An author would ask, 'What if?' or 'If this goes on?' and head off from there, working out what might result from a given premise. Einstein called it *gedankenexperiment*, or thought-experiment, and while it may not promote great style, characterology, or High Lit'rahchoor, it still merits a place in a genre that's more concerned than any other with ideas.

The story just finished, entitled 'Sshhh . . .', continues a series I've been writing about First Contact, exploring possible answers to the towering mystery of our time. Why have we seen no clear signs of life beyond the Earth? All evidence and logic seems to demand a cosmos teeming with living beings, which should, by the reckoning of many keen minds, have already been here long ago. With apologies to my friends working on Project SETI, this quandary is a deep and perplexing one.

The next story, which was inspired by a few stints on late-night talk radio shows, takes on the question of

Alien Contact from a completely different angle. Yet, there is an underlying thread the two tales have in common.

The thread of rebellion.

Those Eyes

'... So you want to talk about flying saucers? I was afraid of that.

'This happens every damn time I'm blackmailed into babysitting you insomniacs, while Talkback Larry escapes to Bimini for a badly needed rest. I'm *supposed* to field call-in questions about astronomy and outer space for two weeks. You know, black holes and comets? But it seems we always have to spend the first night wrangling over *puta* UFOs.

'... Now, don't get excited, sir ... Yeah, I'm just a typical ivory tower scientist, out to repress unconventional thought. Whatever you say, buddy.

'Truth is, I've also dreamed of contact with alien life. In fact, I'm involved in research now ... That's right, SETI ... the Search for Extra-Terrestrial Intelligence ... And no, it's not at all like chasing UFOs! I don't believe the Earth has ever been visited by anything remotely resembling intelligent ...

'Yes, sir. I bet you've got crates full of case histories, and a personal encounter or two? Thought so. I got an earful when some of us tried studying these ''phenomena'' a few years back. Spent weeks on each case, only to find it was just a weather balloon, or an airplane, or ball lightning ...

'... Oh, yeah? Well, I've *seen* ball lightning, fella. Got

a scar on my nose and a pair of melted binoculars to
show just how close. So don't tell *me* it's a myth like
your *chingaso* flying saucers!'

We commence our labours this night in England, near
Avebury, braiding strands of yellow wheat in tidy,
flattened rings. It is happy work, playing lassos of
light upon the sea of grain. These will be fine circles.
Humans will see pictures in their morning papers, and
wonder.

Our bright ether-boat hovers, bathed in the approv-
ing glow of Mother Moon. The sleek craft wears a
lambent gloss to make it slippery to mortal eyes.

To be seen is desirable. But never too *well*.

Fyrfalcon proclaims, 'Keep the edges sharp! Make
each ring perfect! Let men of science jabber about
natural phenomena. We'll have new believers after this
night's work!'

Once, he might have been called 'King'. But we
adapt to changing times. 'Yes, Captain!' we shout,
and hurry to our tasks.

Our Listener calls from her perch. 'We are being
discussed on a human radio programme! Would all
like to hear?'

We cry cheerful assent. Although we loathe Mankind's technology, it often serves our ends.

'Let's cover your second question, caller. Are UFO enthusiasts so different from we astronomers, probing with our
telescopes for signs of life somewhere? Both groups long to
discover other minds, other viewpoints, something strange
and wonderful.

'We part company, though, over the question of *evidence*. Science teaches us to expect – demand – more
than just eerie mysteries. What use is a puzzle that can't
be solved?

'Patience is fine, but I'm not going to stop asking the universe to make sense!'

The boy drives faster than he wants to, taking hairpin turns recklessly to impress the girl next to him.

He needn't get in such a lather; she is ready. She had already decided when the night was young. Now she laughs, feigning nonchalance as road posts streak by and her heart races.

The convertible climbs under opal moonlight. Her bare knee brushes his hand, making him muff the gears. He coughs, fighting impulses more ancient than his race, swerving just in time to keep from roaring over the edge.

I sense their excitement. He is half-blind with desire. She by anticipation.

They are unaware of our approach.

At a secluded cliffside, he sets the brake and turns to her. She teases him playfully, in ways meant to inflame. There is no ambiguity.

We circle behind, enjoying such simple, honest lusts. Backing away, we dip over the cliff, then cruise along its face until directly below them.

We turn on all our pulsing glows to make our craft its gaudiest!

We start to rise.

No one will believe their story. But more than one kind of seed will have been sown tonight.

'There's a saying that applies here. "Absence of evidence is not evidence of absence." While Project SETI hasn't logged any verified signals from the few stars we've looked at, that doesn't prove nobody's out there!

'. . . Yeah, sure. The same could apply to UFOs, if you insist.

'But while SETI has to sift a vast cosmos for radio

sources – a real case of hunting needles in haystacks –
it's harder to explain the absence of decent evidence for
flying saucers on Earth. It's a small planet, after all. If ETs
have been mucking around here for as long as some folks
say, isn't it funny they never dropped any clear-cut alien
artifacts for us to examine? Say, the martian equivalent of
a coke bottle?'

We are flying over eastern Canada on key-patrol
. . . creating temporary, microscopic singularities in
random houses to swallow wallets, car keys, homework
assignments. Meanwhile some of us reach out to invade
the dreams of sleeping men and women, those most
susceptible.

Gryffinloch plays the radio show in the background
as we work. We laugh as this idiotic scientist talks of
'alien artifacts'.

Such stupid assumptions! We do not make things
of hard, unyielding matter! I have never held a coke
bottle. Even those human babes we steal, to raise as
our own, find painful the latent heat in glass and metal,
which were forged in flame.

Men have built their proud new civilisation around
such things. But why, when they had us? Can iron
nourish as we do? We deal in a different heat. Ours
inflames the heart.

'Yes, yes . . . For those of you who don't read the *Enquirer*,
this caller's asking my opinion of one of the most famous
UFO tales – about a ship that supposedly crashed in
New Mexico, right after World War II. "They" have
been clandestinely studying the wreckage in a hangar at
an Air Force Base in Dayton for forty years, right?

'Now, isn't that news to just boil the blood of honest
citizens? There goes the big bad government, keeping
secrets from us again!

'But wait, suppose we do have remnants of some super-duper, alien warp-drive scout ship from Algerdeberon Eleventeen. Do *you* see any technologies pouring out of Ohio that look like they came from outer space? I mean, besides supermarket checkout scanners – I'll grant you those.

'Come on, would our balance of payments be in the shape it's in if . . .

'. . . Oh yes? It's being kept top secret? Okay, here's a second question. Just who do you suppose has been discreetly studying the wreckage all this time?'

'. . . Government engineers. Uh-huh. Have you ever *met* an engineer, pal? They're not faceless drones like in some stupid secret agent movie. At least most aren't. They're intelligent Americans like you and me, with wives and husbands and kids.

'How many thousands of people would've worked on that alien ship since '48? Picture these retired coots, playing golf, pottering in the garage, running Rotary fundraisers . . . and all this time repressing an urge to blab the story of the century?

'All of 'em? In *today's* America? Come on, friend. Let's put aside this Hangar 18 crap and get back to UFOs, where at least there's something worth arguing about!'

I yearn to swoop down and give this talk-show scientist a taste of 'proof'. I will curdle the milk on his doorstep and give him nightmares. I'll play havoc with his utilities. I will . . .

I'll do nothing. I don't wish to see this golden ship evaporate like dew on a summer's morn. Our numbers are too small and Fyrfalcon has decreed – we must show ourselves only to receptive ones, whose minds can still be moulded in the old ways.

I look up at the moon's stark, cratered landscape. Our home of refuge, of exile. Even there, they followed

us, these New Men. An ectoplasmic vapour is all that
remains where some of our kind once tried putting
fright to their explorers. We learned a hard lesson
then – that astronauts are not like argonauts of old.

Their eyes were filled with that mad, *sceptical* glow,
and none can stand before it.

'This is Professor Joe Perez, sitting in for Talkback Larry.
You're on the air.

'Yes? Uh huh? . . . Well folks, seems our next caller
wants to talk about so-called Ancient Visitors. I'm
game. Let's pick apart those "gods" and their fabulous
chariots.

'Ooh, they taught ancient Egyptians to build pyramids!
And golly, they had some of my own ancestors scratch stick
figures on a stony plateau in Peru! To help spaceships find
landing pads, right? I guess the notion's barely plausible,
till you ask . . . why?

'Why would anyone want such ridiculous "landing
pads", when they could've had much better? Why not
open a small trade college and teach our ancestors to
pour *cement*? A few electronics classes and we could've
made arc lamps and radar to guide their saucers through
anything from rain to locusts!

'. . . What? They were here to help us? Well thanks a lot,
you alien gods you! Thanks for neglecting to mention flush
toilets, printing presses, democracy, or the germ theory of
disease! Or ecology, leaving us to ruin half the planet before
finally catching on! Hell, if someone had just shown us how
to make simple glass *lenses*, we could've done the rest. How
much ignorance and misery we'd have escaped!

'You'd credit human innovations like architecture and
poetry, physics and empathy, to aliens? . . . Really? . . .
Well I say you insult our poor foremothers and dads, who
crawled from the muck, battling superstition and ignorance
every step of the way, until we may at last be ready to clean

up our act and look the universe in the eye. No, friend.
If there were ancient astronauts, we owe them nada, zip,
nothing!

'. . . What's that? . . . Well the same to you, pal! . . .
No, forget it. I don't want to talk to you anymore. Go
worship silly, meddlesome star-gods if you want to. Next
caller, please.'

Although we barely understand its principles, we
approve of this innovation, radio. It is like the ancient
campfire, friendly to gossip and tall tales.

But tonight this fellow vexes me. His voice plucks the
air-streams, sharper than glass, more searing than iron.
He asks why we did not teach *useful* things, back when
humans were as children in our hands! Ungrateful
wretch! What are baubles such as lenses, compared to
what we once gave men? Vividness! Mystery! Terror!
Make one night seem to last a hundred years, and
what cared some poor peasant about mere plagues or
pestilence?

We must fight this madness before the new thinking
takes humans beyond our reach.

Before they learn to do without us entirely.

Our captain is too cautious. I slip away in a smaller
boat to find a lonely traveller on a deserted road. My
light dazzles him as I weave hallucinated voyages to
distant worlds. He eagerly studies the 'star map' I
show him, and memorises certain trite expressions,
convinced they are secrets of the universe. No need
for originality. We've fed believers similar platitudes
since long before there was a New Age media to help
spread them.

Worship fills his eyes as I pull away. It is a good
night, filled with the old magic. As in other days, I
scurry on, seeding the green world with badly needed
mysteries.

We'll fight this plague which robs men of their birthright. We shall satisfy their inmost hunger.

And ours.

'. . . No, it's all right, ma'am. We can stay with UFOs. The evening's a washout anyway.

'Still, let me surprise you and say that, as a scientist, I can't claim UFOs are absolutely disproved. I accept the unlikely possibility something weird is going on. Maybe there *are* queer beasties out there who swoop down to rattle signposts and cause power blackouts. Maybe they do kidnap people and take them on joyrides through the cosmos.

'But then, out of all those who claim to have met star beings, why has no one ever announced anything they learned from the encounter that was simultaneously true and unambiguous and that science didn't already know?'

I rejoin our great skyboat as it skims a silvery trail over this place we once called home. Now the planet throngs with bustling, earnest, *craving* humanity. Craving, if they just knew, what we used to give their ancestors. What we'd give again, if they allowed it.

'*Allowed it.*' My thoughts shame me. What right have worms to 'allow' anything?

There was a time when men averted their eyes and shivered in fear. Now the planet's night face spreads a glow of city lights. Forests swarm with campers and explorers armed with cameras. It seems ages since we heard from our cousins, in Earth's hidden places, the mountains and deep lochs. Long ago they fled before men's modern eyes, or were annihilated.

It makes me wonder – could it be that humans are angry with us for some reason?

'But there's a second, even better answer to this whole
UFO business.

'Let's admit a slim chance some of these case histories
might actually be sightings of little silvery guys riding
spaceships. My reply? We can still rule out contact with
Intelligent Life!

'*Look at their behaviour!*' Buzzing truck drivers,
mutilating farm animals, trampling corn fields, kidnapping
people to stick needles in their brains . . . Is this any way
for intelligent beings to act?'

I never heard it put quite that way before.

Perhaps some of you, subconsciously, *are* a bit upset
with us.

But we do it for your own good.

'Worst of all, if these UFO guys really do exist – they're
refusing to make contact!

'. . . What? You say they're afraid of us? We, who barely
made it to our measly little moon, and couldn't go back
now if we tried? *We* frighten star aliens? Right. And I'm
terrified of turtles in the zoo!'

But we do fear you, sage of science. Your premises are
skewed. I would teach you. But if I tried, you'd burn
me where I stand.

'Tell you what, caller. Let's try an experiment. You assume
these ET fellows are pretty smart, yes? . . . In fact, they're
probably picking up my voice at this moment. After all
this time, guys that clever must have a handle on our
language, right?

'Great. Then I'll quit talking to my human audience
for a minute, and turn instead to those eavesdroppers in
the sky.

'Hello, you little green guys, listening to my voice in your fancy ships! I'm gonna lay a challenge on you now. Get out your space pencils, 'cause I'm about to tell you how to get in touch with the most qualified people on the planet for making first contact with star visitors. People who have all the right qualifications, reputations and government connections, and who also have been dreaming all their lives of holding conversations with other life forms.

'Ready? Good. Now first off, I want you to dial up the World Space Foundation in Pasadena, California. You can get their number by dialling directory assistance through any of our communication satellites ... surely you're smart enough to handle that? Our technology's child's play, right? Here's a hint – the area code is 1-818, and directory information is 555-1212. The foundation helps fund SETI research, now that a few senators have cut off all federal money. They search the heavens for beacons from distant extraterrestrial civilisations. They usually don't like having their name associated with UFOs, but I'm sure they'll drop everything if you prove you really are visitors from some faraway star.

'Now *proof* is an important part of this. So for you humans listening in right now, please don't bother these good folks ... unless you want to join as members of the foundation, and help them in their fine work. Still, I guess there'll be a few jerks out there who will phone in anyway, thinking it's really clever and original to dial up and pretend they're ET. So here's part two of the plan. I want you silver guys to briefly describe to the foundation staff a demonstration you'll perform in the sky, the following night!

'Your demo should be visible from Pasadena, California, at ten p.m. on a clear night, and be of clearly extraterrestrial origin. You might turn one of the Moon's craters purple, or something likewise gaudy. My pal Mike promises to check for messages daily, and have someone watching at the appointed hour.

'If you do pull off something impressively "alien", you can bet we'll be waiting by the phone the next day for your follow-up call!'

Such effrontery! Never has one of these mad, new-style humans taunted us so brazenly. Out of wrath, we get carried away in our work. Half the cattle are destroyed and the rest driven to frothing panic before Fyrfalcon calls a halt. We stare down at no typical mutilation. The rancher who owns this herd won't be awed or frightened by our visit, but furious.

Curse you, man of logic, man of science! Were it in our power, we'd topple the towers carrying your voice. Your satellites would rain like falling stars! Certainly we'd shut out your yammerings.

But it is our nature to hear, when we are spoken of. So it always was. So it shall be while our kind lasts.

'That's my challenge, you platinum-plated guys out there. Perform some convincing demonstration in the sky, and the WSF will do the rest! Mike will arrange landing sites, rent-a-cops, press coverage, visas . . . of both types . . . and yes, gigs on *The Tonight Show*. Anything you like. Anything to make First Contact a pleasant, comfortable experience for you and your crews.

'We want to be gracious hosts. Make friends. Show you the town. That's as generous an offer as any honest guest could ask for.

'But what if nobody answers my challenge? What would that mean, caller? . . . Uh huh. It might mean UFOs are myths!

'On the other hand, maybe they do exist, and are sitting back, spurning this sincere offer.

'In which case at least we've settled what they are . . . nasty sons-of-bitches who love messing with our heads. And all I have to say is – get out of our sky, assholes! Leave us alone, so we can get on with looking for someone out there worth talking to!

'. . . Ahem. And on that note, Engineer Ted signals it's time for station I.D. Sorry, Ted. Guess I got carried away there. But at three a.m., I don't figure the FCC is any likelier to be listening than creeps on flying saucers . . .'

Our Dream Master, Sylphshank, has been meddling with sleep-fogged minds. He tells of one woman who has been dozing while listening to the radio show. While she is susceptible, Sylphshank projects into her mind dream-images of his own face! She wakens now with a startled idea, and excitedly dials the station.

Delightful! This should irritate that upstart scientist. Perhaps when she is finished we'll do it again, and again until he finally gives up.

We move on to California, home of some of our best friends and fiercest foes. One of our changelings – human born – uses a stolen acetylene torch to burn marks of 'rocket exhaust' and 'landing jacks' on to a plateau near San Diego. A cult of the faithful has sanctified this ground with their belief. We often reward them with such signs.

Our great, long-prowed boat floats above the chaparral, insubstantial as thought. Where once its burnished hull would have been invincible, now we must protect it from those eyes.

'Okay, we're back. This is Professor Joe Perez, filling in for Talkback Larry while he takes a much-needed break from you manic insomniacs. Want to talk astronomy? Black holes? The universe? I'm your man. Let's take another call.

'Yes, ma'am? . . . Oh hell, I thought we used up that topic . . .

'What? . . . Hmm. Now that you mention it, that puts

a new spin on things. It does seem strange that saucer folk are so often depicted in certain ways. Smooth, arching foreheads. Big eyes. Long, meddling fingers.

'It should've sounded familiar. Look at their supposed behaviour – playing tricks, offering mystic half-truths, never meeting honest folk in the eyes . . .

'Yes ma'am, I think you've hit on something. Saucer people are elves!'

Our boat-of-ether rocks. The voice is stronger than ever, shaking our concentration.

Four teenagers blink, captivated by the light shining on their upturned faces. We had them snared, but the distraction of that cursed voice weakens our grip. Gryffinloch murmurs alarm.

'We shouldn't have tried so many at once!'

'The voice has us confused,' Fyrfalcon answers. 'Take care—'

I cry out, 'One wakens!'

Three of those young faces still exhibit rapture as they stand uncritical, accepting. But the fourth – a gangling child-woman – casts another kind of glow. As she rouses, her eyes narrow and her mouth forms words. Tapped into her mind, I sense her effort to see. To really see!

What am I staring at? Why . . . it looks transparent, as if it isn't really there at . . .

'Flee!' Fyrfalcon screams as we are blinded by that deadly gaze!

'It's late, but let's go with this caller's notion and see where it leads.

'Once upon a time, legends say elves and dwarves and trolls shared our world . . . all those colourful spirit creatures our ancestors warned their children about, so they'd shun the forest.

'My wife's an anthropologist, and we read our kids stories she's collected all over the world, many of them amusing, moving, even inspiring. But after a while you start to notice something – very few of those old magical characters, the pixies and sprites and spirits, were people you'd want as neighbours! Sometimes beautiful and exciting, creatures in fairy tales also act petty, tyrannical, and awfully stingy about sharing their knowledge with poor human beings. Always they were portrayed as living apart, on the edge of the unknown. In olden times that meant just beyond the firelight.

'Then something changed. Humankind started pushing the circle outward, and all those fancy beasts of legend faded back as well. Yetis and Bigfoots. Elves and lake monsters. They were always said to be just beyond the reach of torchlight, then lanterns, then sonar and aerial photography . . .

'Now maybe that's because they never were more than figments of our over-fertile imaginations. Maybe they were distractions, that kept us from properly appreciating the other species of very real animals sharing our world.

'Still, I can entertain another possibility.

'Imagine, such creatures really did exist, once upon a time, behaving like spirit folk in legend. But at some point we started shucking free of them, conquering our ignorance, driving them off to let us get about our lives . . .'

Scattered, riding fragments of our broken boat, we call to one another across space.

We survivors.

By now those teenagers are rubbing their eyes, already convinced we were hallucinations. That is what happens when humans see us with *scepticism*. Now we blow away like leaves, like wisps of shredded dreams.

Perhaps the world's winds will bring some of us together to begin anew. Meanwhile, I can only drift and remember.

Some years back we plotted to end this plague of reason. We stole human babies and took them to a southern isle. Then, back in the world of humans, we caused 'incidents' and false alarms on radar screens, trying to set off that final war. Let their mad genius consume itself in its own fire, we thought. It used to be so easy to provoke war among men.

But this time things were different. Perhaps it was the new thinking, or maybe they sensed the precipice. There was no war. We grew depressed.

So depressed we forgot our charges on the island. When at last we checked, all the infants had died.

Such frail things, humans.

How did frail things ever grow so strong?

'It's dark out and the wind's picked up. Let's push this ghost story as far as it'll go.

'We were talking about how fairy folk always seemed to flit just beyond the light, beyond our gaze. Since Earth is pretty well explored now, the few remaining legends speak of Arctic wastes, the deepest depths . . . and outer space. It's as if they are both drawn to us and terrified.

'I can't imagine it's our weapons such creatures would fear . . . ever see a hunter come home with an elf pelt on his fender?

'Now here's a thought . . . what if it's because of a change in *us*? What if modern humans destroy fairy creatures just by getting close!

'. . . You laugh? Good. Still, imagine today's cub scouts, running, peering into forest corners their ancestors would have superstitiously left alone. Ever wonder why the change?

'It could be just curiosity.

'Or else . . . maybe they're *chasing our species' natural foe*. Perhaps that's really why we seek Nessie and Yeti, hounding them to the far corners of the Earth. Or why we're pushing into space, for that matter!

'Maybe something inside us recalls how we were treated by our fairy friends. Subconsciously what we're after is revenge!'

Monsters. Driven off our own cursed planet by these flat-eyed monsters.

The experiment got out of hand.

How I wish we never created them!

'Time's up, boys and girls. Whatever you call them – elves or UFO aliens – whether they exist or were just another fancy dream we invented – I see no point in giving them any more of our time.

'Tomorrow night we'll move on to more interesting stuff . . . the Big Bang, neutron stars, and our hopeful search for some *real* intelligent life out there.

'Until then, people, good night. And good morning.'

What to Say to a UFO

Perhaps it's something basic to the nature of late night talk-shows. Or maybe it has to do with the topics I'm invited to discuss on radio, when nothing's going on in the world of politics, and the host riffles through his rolladex to find that funny 'space' and 'the future' guy who is always good for a time-filler. I can't honestly explain it, but there are certain evenings, often when the moon is full, that seem to bring UFO zealots out in swarms. Collectively and individually, they mob the phone banks, converging from all sides to defend the faith, and to repulse the big, bad, doubter-scientist.

We Americans have refined self-righteousness to a high art, cherishing the romantic image of smart outsiders against monolithic institutions. New Age types see themselves as brave truth-seekers, opposed by a rigid technological priesthood. No matter that this priesthood is dedicated to self-criticism, and sharing whatever they learn. Science represents this era's 'establishment', and is therefore automatically suspect. (Later I'll offer why this ties in with the theme of 'otherness'.)

UFO cultism is a prime example of 'magical thinking', in which what's true is far less important than

what *ought to be*. You cannot defeat such a worldview the
way you would a flawed technical theory. Philip Klass,
of *Aviation Week* magazine, has learned this the hard
way. After worthy labour for many years, debunking
UFO tales one by one, Dr Klass has found truth in
the adage – 'You can't prove a negative statement.'

In other words, while UFO proponents have failed
ever to confirm even a single case of purported alien
visitation, all it would take is one exception to make
all of the disproven cases moot. Debunkers can never
eliminate the enthusiast's glittering hope that *next* time
all will become clear. No compilation of experiments
can demonstrate, conclusively, that ET visitors have
not, or are not now, visiting the Earth.

Anyway, who wants to make such a claim? Not
readers of *this* collection, certainly. Far from stodgy
defenders of some status quo, most of you probably
think yourselves quite daring types, on the cutting
edge, ready for whatever's new . . . in other words, just
the sort who ought to be picked to make contact with
visitors from space, if such an event really happened.

We and UFO aficionados share a common love of
wonder and the possibilities of a vast cosmos. The
difference is that we have no magical yearning for
mysteries to *remain* mysterious. Rather, they are puzzles
meant to be solved. If alien visitors really are swooping
down on us, doing all the sorts of things they are said
to, our natural question is . . . 'Why?'

Why kidnap people? Why rattle houses and twirl
wheat fields? Why stick needles in people's brains?

And, most important of all, even supposing extraterrestrials had their own, weird reasons for doing such
things . . . *why should we put up with it?*

Take my word. Cultists who are ready to face
down even the most determined examination of their
'evidence' – their purported photos and eyewitness

accounts – wilt under direct assault on alleged UFO *behaviour*.

In simple fact, that behaviour is indefensible. It is the kind of activity you'd expect from meddlesome lunatics, not mature guests visiting our star system. I don't care how much smarter they are supposed to be, or how much more spiritually elevated. A high-IQ vandal in my home is still a vandal!

Worse yet, these supposed visitors are refusing to make contact, at a time when confirmation of their mere existence might shake us out of our shortsighted self-involvement, provoking us to pay more attention to the future – to children and science – than on bombs and beer. Defenders of so-called space visitors plead explanations. They are 'afraid of us', or we're 'not ready for contact'. But these excuses sound whiny and weak under scrutiny. Like the captain of the starship in the excellent, but misunderstood, movie, 'E.T.', who abandons a crewmate when threatened with *flashlights*, these extraterrestrials sound more and more like selfish cowards. Not at all like the sort of non-Earthly sophonts we dream of meeting someday.

Which brings me to 'Those Eyes'.

The story evolved partly from my own talk-show experiences with ET cultists, and partly from a friend's interesting observation. One day, while looking at the cover of a famous book concerning alien abductions, she commented:

'Huh! When I picked this up, I thought it was about elves!'

Sure enough, there were the huge eyes, the big, smooth head, the creepy fingers ... and I suddenly recalled fairy tales I'd read ... not the sanitised versions made into Disney cartoons, but *old* tales collected by the Brothers Grimm, or Native American legends of Coyote, or folklore of the Aranda, the

Semang, the Yanomamo and Ibo. In each culture
one can trace a common thread never commented
on by Joseph Campbell. True, many of the tales are
beautiful, spiritual, even elevating, but the non-human
characters depicted in them are also often capricious,
meddling . . . what we by modern standards would
call *nasty*.

Then it hit me. UFO aliens *are* elves. They fill the
same role, fit the same archetype, occupy the same
space on the fringe of the 'firelight'. Only now, for
better and worse, light from our civilisation covers the
entire planet. So, naturally, faeryland has been pushed
out into space!

Think of it. The frontier has always been inhabited by inscrutable and dangerous beasts, capricious,
mysterious, romantic. What better place for elves and
goblins than the *final* frontier? Does this mean there is
something deep inside of us that *wants* to believe in such
beings, and perpetually remakes them, just out of sight?
That certainly is the more likely theory, which tells
us something about our inner natures. On the other
hand, let's not rush to exclude the hypothesis that
they have always been with us . . . nasty, unpleasant
creatures. Just the sort to bring our local property
values down and spoil the neighbourhood. Maybe
that's why we've never met *real* intelligent life. Truly
smart and cultured ETs don't go slumming where
goblins roam the night.

I'll leave as an exercise what all this implies about the
true difference between fantasy and science fiction. For
now, let me just finish with a final thought.

It might be nice to meet wise, ancient cousins from
out there . . . some Elder Race with all the answers
to our problems. It is tempting to envision 'wisdom'
manifested in the ships and forms of near-godlike

creatures from far stars. The subject often makes for good fiction, since it enables a writer to metaphorise what is both great and tragic about our situation.

It is no surprise that millions yearn for Contact, linking the word in their minds with Salvation.

Yet I find it just a bit insulting to lean on such a belief, as a crutch. Humanity climbed to where it is by hard work over thousands of years, and the trial-and-error efforts of countless good and bad men and women. Now, at long last, we are poised to decide if we'll take the last step – to become civilised folk, honest intellects, good planetary managers, elder brothers and sisters to the other species of our world . . . or else to ruin it all in one final spasm of paranoia and greed.

What if a flying saucer *did* land, suddenly? What if some tall, austere, silver-clad ambassador stepped out, made a speech, and sent us into a tizzy of euphoric new-millennium resolutions? Suppose that, after a hundred centuries struggling in isolation to grow up, just when we were on the verge of either dramatic success or tragic failure, someone with a shiny suit and patronising manner showed up to give a lecture or two, and then take all the credit?

Yes, it might just tip the balance. It might even save us.

Nevertheless I'd be tempted to say, 'Who do you jerks think you *are*? Where the hell were you when we really needed you?'

In fact, I see little difference between the goblin-type aliens, depicted in supermarket tabloids, and the wonderful, 'wise' variety portrayed in films such as 'The Day the Earth Stood Still'. There's no evidence that either type really exists, but even if they do, they have a lot to answer for.

I don't mean to be a poor sport. In fact, if silvery elves ever do come down to land, I hope we will be gracious enough to be good hosts, open and generous, however bad-mannered our guests have behaved in the past.

Still, and despite the fall of the Soviet Empire, I remain a big fan of the U.S. Air Force.

Keep watching the skies, guys. Keep watching the skies.

Now for a very different alien contact story, which first appeared in the shared-universe volume 'Murusaki'. My job in that joint effort was to 'establish the scene' on planet Genji, for later authors. Since the objective was less to weave a self-contained story than to introduce a world, one result was a gentler tale, less frenetic than the typical space yarn. I rather liked that.

Bonding to Genji

It is, fundamentally, a question of balance, Minoru reminded himself as he left the air-flyer and set foot on the island that would be his home for many months. Keeping his stance wide and footsteps close to the ground, he moved cautiously in the insistent, heavy pull of Genji.

Balance is vital when exploring a new world.

Especially when everything was still so new. The flight out from Okuma Base had been all too brief, diving down from trans-Himalayan mountain heights where humans could breathe unassisted, then swooping over a green and red blur of endless fringe-frond forests, then skimming above pale, verdant ocean shallows, and finally alighting on this isolated archipelago where, at last, Minoru would begin work he'd trained for all his life. It was hard to concentrate at such a moment. Yet he knew the danger. Excitement was an enemy that could ruin everything with one false step.

Careful. You've only been on the ground a few weeks. Even at Okuma Base, they've had a dozen broken limbs. Out here, a fall could kill.

During the ten-year journey from Earth, Starship *Yamato*'s drives had been cranked up gradually to one and a third gravities, pre-adapting three hundred crewfolk to the first alien world visited by humankind. Seldom mentioned during all that time had been the other motive for pushing the engines so hard – to make it first to Murasaki System.

Uselessly, it turned out. *Yamato* arrived after the Spacers – upstarts from Earth's asteroid colonies – had already visited the twin worlds of Genji and Chujo, taken samples of alien life, and usurped the privilege of first contact that should have been Japan's. Then, as if shamed by their impertinence, the Spacers hadn't even waited to hold conference, but fled Earthward on the flimsy excuse that their enviro-systems were strained. The let-down told on *Yamato*'s complement. All that hurrying to get here . . . then not to be the first to set foot, to plant a flag, or to gaze into strange eyes on a new world? Japan could still claim priority, of course. Its robot probes had discovered this magnificent double-planet system. But that wasn't the same. Not the same at all.

Encumbered by his pressure suit, Minoru stepped carefully along the blackened trail laid by the lander when it alighted on this loaf-shaped hilltop, hard beside a strange, luminous sea. Behind him, the flyer hissed as it cooled – touched by drifting fingers of sea fog, much thicker than the mountain hazes that shrouded high Okuma Base.

It's a whole planet, after all. There are ten million places, each as different from the rest as Sapporo is from Saipan. Each a unique story. And the most familiar-looking will always be utterly alien.

The pilot unloaded supplies Minoru and his partner would need during the months ahead. That included, to Minoru's resignation, many kilograms of nutritionally adequate but monotonous algae paste. One more reason to make friends with the natives, who were now spilling out of their hilltop hamlets to cross swampy farms on their way towards the landing field. From a distance, they looked like glossy salamanders, slithering along mud-slick trails. This was a tribe already briefly contacted by the Spacers, who had catalogued a hundred words of local dialect before dashing off. Minoru hoped the Spacer data wasn't useless, and that a hundred words would be enough to start good relations.

Pausing to catch his breath, he put down his twin satchels and glanced up towards this planet's sister world – little Tō No Chujo, named after the companion of Great Genji, fabled hero of Japanese children's fables – which filled an entire octant of the sky. Chujo was so close you could make out wispy cloud formations, the dun colour of its dry uplands, and the glitter of its midget seas. Here on this part of Genji, where Chujo hovered permanently at the zenith, you could tell time by watching shadows move across its constant face as the paired planets spun around a common centre – their 'day' a composite of their linked momenta. The glow given off by Murasaki's Star might be pallid compared with Sol's remembered flame, but it nurtured life on both worlds. And as night's terminator flowed across Chujo's scarred face, it was easy to see why the natives of Genji had never invented clocks.

A neat explanation. Except it's usually overcast this close to the sea. And Genjians live nowhere else.

Probably much of his life would consist, from now on,

of coming up with interesting hypotheses, only to find later evidence that demolished them. On a new world, it wouldn't pay to grow too fond of one's favourite theories. Yet another reason to cultivate balance.

He heard his partner, Emile Esperanza, approach from behind, breathing hard and carrying more supplies. '*Cabron!*' Emile muttered. 'Look at them! They sure seem bigger in real life.'

Minoru turned. Swivelling too fast in the fierce gravity, he felt a yanking pain as abdominal muscles strained to compensate. After a subjective decade aboard ship, he wasn't the same youngster who once set forth so eagerly for the stars.

The weight isn't so bad if you're careful. You can't ever forget, though. Not for a minute. And there's the paradox. Who can remember every minute of every day, for a lifetime?

Long-term effects of the planet's pull could be seen in the thick trunks and low profiles of the nearby trees, forming slope-hugging forests beyond the ragged landing field. Gravity was also manifest in the squat, wide-limbed gait of the natives, who used paths made of wooden planks to cross paddies and fern-lined fens on their way to the landing site. And yes, they seemed more imposing, more vivid than in those jerky holos the Spacers had shared. The tug of gravity, the cries of a myriad flying creatures, the sluggish shove of heavy, moisture-laden air . . . Minoru wished he could feel them against his skin, but full environment suits were mandatory until the bio-assay was complete, and probably for a long time after that.

He suppressed a temptation to rebel. One of the foolish Spacers had ruined his lungs by exposing them to Genji's sea-level pressure. Yet, Minoru half envied that act of defiance.

'I guess they look peaceful enough,' Emile added.

'Maybe the Spacers didn't alienate the locals after all, or infect them.'

Despite his name, Emile's features were as pure-blooded Japanese as Minoru's, and much more than the thirty men and women in *Yamato*'s token 'international contingent'. Emile's grandparents had managed a Fuji-Works plant in Paraguay, then retired there for the climate, elbow-room, and lifestyle. Although the family had kept faith with the Purity Rule, and so maintained Nihonese citizenship, they nevertheless picked up many *gaijin* ways. Minoru saw with some envy that Emile had taken off his bulky gloves and armlets, sealing his suit above the elbows but leaving his hands and forearms free to feel wind and air. *I wish I had the nerve.*

'We still don't know for sure cross-infection isn't possible. There are many similarities between Genjian life and ours.'

'And even more differences,' the other man's voice was rich with Latin accents. 'Genji-life uses more amino acids than ours, because there's less ultra-violet.' Emile gestured towards Murasaki's Star, which put out just six tenths of Sol's luminosity. 'Any of their pathogens who tried to eat our cells would starve of some necessary ingredient. And *our* bugs would be poisoned by some chemical never known on Earth.'

Minoru knew what that implied. If Earth germs found nothing to eat here, what hope had human beings of doing so? He clung obstinately to hope. 'There may be something here that's edible.'

Emile shrugged, as if indifferent. Unlike most of the crew, he showed little frustration at the limited range of ship-grown fare. Emile never speculated, as others did incessantly, what delicacies might be discovered on a new world. 'Anyway, none of the Spacers came down with weird plagues. And apparently neither did the locals.' He gestured towards the Genjians, who had crossed half the distance without apparent hurry, carrying only a few of the tridents locals used as weapon-tools. From remote surveys, Minoru knew the creatures could move faster if they had to, but as non-homeotherms they disliked wild temperature swings.

Close at hand, the natives still looked like fat salamanders, whose long front legs gave them a reared, semi-upright stance. Yet, Minoru felt a chill of alienness. For even a salamander had a *face*.

He chided himself. *In all honesty, so do these creatures.*

But such a face! Instead of bilateral symmetry – two eyes atop and mouth below – the Genjians had four bulging vision organs spaced at the corners of a square, centred on impressive, gaping jaws. Above, a waving snorkel tube vented the amphibians' excited cries, clearly audible since sound carries well in dense air. Hanging below each Genjian's throat were two slender, tentacle-like 'hands' for fine manipulation.

So strange. Yet these were intelligent beings. On this isolated isle, they lived a modest, agrarian-and-fishing existence, tending algal mats and pens of captive, iridescent-finned icthyoids. But the expedition had spied from space on several cultures possessing metallurgy, and even electricity.

'Anyway,' Emile went on, 'at least the Spacers had the sense to make contact on remote locales, so any unforeseen infection would be self-limiting.'

'Such courtesy,' Minoru said acidly. But Emile seemed genuinely glad.

'Indeed. I'm grateful the Spacers jumped in ahead of us. Now the karma of any harm done rests on their backs, not ours.' Emile's blithe attitude was rare among *Yamato*'s crew, most of whom still seethed at the Spacers' effrontery. But, he had a point. Cultural

contamination by the asteroidists spared Minoru a
degree of tension that would have otherwise thickly
overlain the approaching meeting. Now he worried less
about perpetrating some irretrievable *faux pas* which
might bring a death-bond of shame.

Hissing and rattling, the translator apparatus made
a broad range of sounds as Emile tested its sparse
store of Spacer-donated words, augmented recently
by two other Japanese contact teams operating in this
archipelago. Theirs wasn't even the primary group
opening talks. That, too, lifted some tension.

'Hey! You fellows okay now? Do you want me to
hang around, just in case?'

Remembering in time to move slowly, Minoru
turned carefully to look back at the lander, where their
pilot had finished unloading supplies for their extended
stay. 'I could help you fellows erect your shelter,' Don
Byrne offered. As one of the few occidentals on the
expedition, his Japanese was thickly accented and
much too formal. It made him the butt of jokes by some
less tolerant crewfolk. Still, he never seemed to mind,
and the cheerful Australian had won Minoru's undying
gratitude during the seventh year of the voyage, by
discovering three new recipes for preparing the same
old hydroponic ship-fare.

Still, Minoru wished this assignment had been
drawn by a different pilot – Yukiko Arama. There
might have been a chance to get a moment alone with
her . . .

Ah, karma. Maybe next time.

'Not necessary,' Emile told the pilot. 'You should
return to Okuma.'

Byrne shifted his weight. 'Maybe I'll just hang
around a while, anyway.' He began unfolding sections
of the storage dome, but Minoru noticed Don never
strayed far from his rifle, by one leg of the lander.

He's staying to watch over us. To his surprise, Minoru felt no resentment over the presumption, only relief. Emile, on the other hand, sounded irritated. 'Well, stay out of the way. And warn us when you're about to take off! We don't want to frighten our hosts.'

Emile began spreading a tarp, on which he laid objects to help identify the Genjian equivalents of nouns and adjectives, towards establishing an orderly dictionary. Minoru opened his own satchel and started doing the same. Only, as he drew a hammer from the bag, its claw snagged on the material. Caught off balance, he leaned over to compensate.

Gravity seized the momentary lapse. Minoru flailed, and hit the tarp before he could get his hands out. Impact was sudden and also *harder* than instinct led him to expect. The blow stung.

Fortunately, despite his brash, *gaijin*-influenced ways, Emile had the decency not to laugh, or even seem to notice. Overcoming embarrassment, Minoru moved with careful deliberation to push back into sitting position.

Balance, Minoru thought. *I may live the rest of my life on this planet. It certainly isn't going to change to adapt to me!*

*

STARSHIP *YAMATO* CREW DATABASE: GENERAL NEWS

With establishment phases One and Two accomplished, the following teams are now active:

GENJI EXPEDITION: Okuma Base on Genji-Moonside established atop Mount Korobachi – 4,500 metres altitude

– Senior Scientist Matsuhiro Komatsu commanding. Five
domes. Three landers. Three power units. One computer facility. Preliminary survey parties detached to
remote islands for early, minimum-contamination contact
sessions. Total crew on Genji – eighty-five personnel.

TŌ NO CHUJO EXPEDITION: Capt. Koremasa Tamura
has decided to personally lead an expedition to the lesser
world. In addition to archeological explorations, attempts
will be made to make contact with the local inhabitants.

*

Minoru slogged through the boggy fields of Green
Tower Village, taking samples and supervising as his
native assistants laboured on a treadmill linked to a
scaffold and massive wooden gearing. That clanking,
rattling assemblage, in turn, rotated a machine that
projected a cylinder of force into the ground, digging ever deeper into the rich sedimentary layers
below.

It had taken several days to acquire enough local
dialect to get across that humans wanted to 'hire' the
natives. But then the Genjians became eager helpers,
not only with the coring but scurrying through shallows
and across hillsides to snare countless wriggling things
– from burrowers to insectoids, to flyers with one, two,
even three pairs of wings – the first of a multitude
of pieces Minoru needed to start putting together a
picture of this island's ecosystem.

Minoru stank from hour after hour in his bio-suit.
He itched from low-level rashes as his immune system

adapted to new irritants. On two occasions, valuable instruments had broken down, with no way of knowing yet if craftsmen at Okuma Base could repair them or would have to send 'home' for replacements, and wait forty years of real transit time for them to arrive. Yet, in all honesty, he could hardly complain. He had impressive tools at his disposal, and a Genjian workforce willing to labour long and hard for lumps of iron. Metal was precious on these remote islands, where Genji's continental industrial revolution was still but a rumour. Despite temptation, Minoru was careful not to overpay his workers, which would only disrupt their local economy.

Anyway, deferred gratification was an important lesson. You learned it early in Japan. Failure to understand the importance of patience and hard work had brought down other great powers which once towered over Minoru's homeland. Now the Land of the Rising Sun stood as the greatest of nations, and its reach extended to faraway stars.

The work was going so well, Minoru had even trained some of the smaller, male Genjians to dissect and prepare animal specimens, spreading organs and skeletal features under the recording cameras. The natives' coordination with their tiny feeler-arms was matched by an ability to bring their eyes exceptionally close, telescoping them to parse minute details. It was a pastime they obviously found amusing. One venerable blood-father named Phs'n'kah seemed fascinated and enthusiastic to learn more.

It was Phs'n'kah who nudged Minoru as the steady drone of the treadmill lulled him. 'Uh!' Minoru startled at the sudden tug. With their broad peripheral vision, Genjians never seemed to grasp the humans' entreaties 'not to sneak up on us from behind'.

'*I have brought more samples for study,*' the translator

announced primly, though Minoru thought he understood the hissing trills standing for 'I' and 'sample'. He saw that Phs'n'kah had laid a reed mat across the mud, arraying thereon several score tiny animals, all with their necks neatly wrung.

'These were gathered within a single patch, one metre on a side?' Minoru asked, incredulously. Phs'n'kah made an assent gesture with his snorkel tube.

'Yes. The very *** you marked off. I made sure to ***.'

The last part dissolved in static as the translator tried guessing, then gave up. No matter. This was a new phase. After taking samples randomly all over the island, it was time to start studying in depth.

'You sealed off the sample area as I showed you?'

'As you showed me . . . I *** down to one metre depth. I am sure nothing *** escaped. Nothing *** than the holes in your *** sieve screen.'

Minoru peered at the samples. You could learn a lot just by seeing how the Genjian had sorted them out. Not by size or colour. Nor, apparently, by species relatedness. It seemed Phs'n'kah had put all the obligate carnivores on one side, all obvious leaf-cutters in another corner, and so on. *You are what you eat. I should report this to the Xeno-Psychology group.*

He made a note to his auto-secretary, which beeped acknowledgement. Accomplishing so much so fast meant relying on semi-sentient computer devices to outline, send (and read!) memos . . . and countless other tasks.

'Time to dissect and record?'

'Not yet. Let me look over the samples first. Then we'll do a dig together to make sure we haven't missed a trick.'

Phs'n'kah's snorkel waved as he gathered up the samples and the reed mat.

'*Have we found any* *** *yet that the* *** *humans can honourably eat?*'

Minoru started. How did Phs'n'kah know? That ulterior motive for Minoru's fevered sampling of flora and fauna went beyond the principal focus – of understanding this island's complete ecosystem. *Of course*, he realised. *That would be the first thing to occur to a native. They have no real concept of science. But eating, cooking, the search for something new and good . . . he probably thinks that's the main purpose of all this collecting!*

Perhaps this explained why it was males, the gatherers and tenders of hearths, who were most enthusiastic about helping Minoru, while females preferred Emile, with his endless appetite for words.

'No, my friend. Nothing good to eat, yet. But we can still hope.'

'*Hope is* ***. *Hope can even be* ***.'

As Phs'n'kah turned and waddled up the path to the science dome, Minoru wondered. That had sounded like an aphorism, a wise-saying. It might be a good idea to store it for Emile.

'That's enough,' he told the workers turning the corer. The translator barked and they squatted back, panting. Occasionally, one of them would open its mouth to pick its teeth with one of the slender tentacle-arms. Only at times like that was Minoru able to tell for absolute certain which was male and which female. Besides being generally smaller, the males had tongues that were longer and more rasp-like for some reason, ending in a sort of bulbous fixture. Curiously, it did not seem to affect their speech – at least to his untutored ears.

The latest core sample came up slickly . . . a tube of history sheathed in electro-stiffened plastic. His helpers were by now well-rehearsed at loading the five-metre-long tube on to the dissemble-reader. As the core passed through, layer after sedimentary layer was atomised. A fine dust of ages came out the other end, while all the information formerly locked in ordered patterns of mud and ancient fossils flowed into the capacious computer back at the dome. Gradually, a database was forming. It would take years, probably decades, to comprehend more than a cursory view of life on Genji – its complex chemistry and interlaced ecologies. Still, some pieces were already falling into place.

For one thing, life here was as old as on Earth. Evolution had progressed at a similar pace, despite less radiation-induced mutation. Instead, a built-in diversity driver came from half a dozen extra amino acids in the protein code. The grinding-mill of Darwinism had more to work with, producing a profusion of winners and losers to make a broad-branched tree of life.

Broader than Earth's. With fewer comets, Murasaki system had fewer big impacts to shake up Genji's biosphere. Few mass extinctions meant many ancient families and phyla still co-inhabited the planet. It was as if some of the wild experiments tried on Earth during the pre-Cambrian, recorded in half-billion-year-old formations like the Burgess Shale, had never died out but instead gone on to share the seas with shark and squid and whales. In addition to creatures built as segmented tubes – like Phs'n'kah's people and all metazoans on Earth – there were also branches which grew as flat sheets, or radial stems. Orbital scans showed creatures so eerie that Genjians themselves could be thought almost human.

One of Minoru's workers performed something akin to a gaping yawn, and Minoru blinked, stepping backwards in surprise. Apparently the other natives were as shocked by the gesture. Several hissed and one even tried to nip the offender's tail. She snarled back.

Then, abruptly, the altercation was forgotten. Almost
as one, the natives lifted their heads and turned. Minoru
carefully followed, and saw a *darkness* rapidly approach
from the east. The deck of low-lying clouds dimmed
along a sharp border that neared rapidly, casting a
moving shadow across the hillsides and the fog-draped
sea. A low moan rose from the Genjians as they reared
to gape in the direction of Chujo – even though the
sister world was covered by clouds. The shadow rushed
over them and translucent sunlight faded by half as
Genji's twin-world passed in front of Murasaki's Star,
commencing the noon eclipse.

Time to down tools. For this culture, on this
archipelago, it was a holy interval, lasting about
twenty minutes, during which one might speak or
rest, but never work or fight. Minoru took what he
hoped the natives considered a stance of respect. After
all, on shipboard – and even in their tiny habitation
domes – many human crewfolk kept little Shinto,
Buddhist, Christian or Gaian shrines. He was proud
of the Japanese attitude towards religion, which said,
essentially: *whatever works*.

As soon as the Genjians' keening song of greeting was
finished, one of the largest females approached Minoru
in a slow, tail-swishing undulation. He recognised
Ta'azsh'da by several scars along her left flank, which
she had told Emile she'd acquired in a raid by another
village, during her youth on another island. Females
were the wanderers and warriors in this species, a
fact which still had sociobiologists at Okuma Base
puzzled. But Minoru thought he was beginning to
understand why.

'*You* *** *our Rites of* *** *and Shadow*,' the translator
said, struggling with her words. It had more trouble
with some topics than others. '*If we are* *** *will you
convey our* *** *to* ***?'

'I'm sorry ... I ...' Minoru gave up. 'Connect to Emile,' he said, and almost without pause, his partner's face lit up the left quadrant of his visor.

'Minoru. I'm kind of busy.' Minoru could see three of Emile's language helpers, squatting in the shirtsleeve environment of the halfway dome ... set to an atmospheric pressure midway between sea level and what was comfortable for humans. Emile's skin pallor didn't look good, and his eyes were droopy, but at least he didn't have to wear a stinking suit all the time. Minoru envied him.

'Just a quick one. Give me a read on this, will you?' And Minoru squirted over Ta'azsh'da's question. Emile puzzled for a moment, then he laughed. 'Oh, she's just asking to hitch a ride to Chujo.'

'To Chujo!'

Emile lifted one eyebrow. 'You hadn't heard? It seems, according to their mythology, Chujo is the home of the angels. Many of them think that's where we came from.'

'No wonder they're so cooperative! But what will happen when they find out—'

'Relax. There's no religious hysteria about it. At least not among this group ... though the boys over at Purple Cliffs Island seem to have had a rough moment when the truth came out. Anyway, I've already explained the situation to several of their travelling monks, or rabbis, or holy whatevers – and say, did you know they're nearly all females? Anyway, I told them we're not from Chujo, but another star. They don't seem to mind.

'Here, let me give you a nice, soothing, diplomatic answer for Ta'azsh'da.'

Emile muttered a command and Minoru's translator conveyed a string of Genjian words directly from his helmet speaker. Ta'azsh'da took a couple of steps back at one point, then rocked her head in an expression Minoru thought might mean perplexity.

At last she seemed satisfied. Or at least turned and wandered away. Emile's picture disappeared without a sign-off, and Minoru tried not to be offended. He himself must sound just as curt when experts from other teams called him, demanding quick biological answers while he was still flailing around, looking for the big picture.

Sometimes, indeed, it all seemed almost too much, and he longed for crowded, comfortable Osaka, back home on Earth.

I'm doing my life's work, Minoru recalled at those moments. *No one could be happier*.

That was true, as far as it went. Only occasionally Minoru wished he were a different sort of person altogether . . . one born with simpler tastes and more mundane interests, who was not the type to volunteer at age fifteen to be sent hurtling towards a heavy, *sweaty* world. Weren't there less exhausting roads to happiness?

Alas, those roads were not in his dharma to tread.

*

GENJI EXPEDITION DATABASE: SUMMARY ON GENJIAN SAPIENTS

by Shigei Owari,
Chief Xenologist

The intelligent beings we call Genjians bear some resemblance to Earth's amphibian life forms. Such comparisons can be misleading however, since there is nothing at all primitive about this planet's autochthones. It is true that they have not spread to as many ecological niches as humans had, at similar levels of technological development. Preliminary studies by Komiko Takashita reveal an emotional range as vivid and finely textured as our own. Komiko's preliminary intelligence profiles demonstrate considerable overlap in cognitive ability with pre-computer human societies . . .

. . . the Linguistic Group has decided to adopt as generic the species self-name used in this archipelago by the autochthones. In future documents, therefore, sentient Genjians shall be referred to as *Irdizu*.

*

Another word for balance was *equilibrium.* Minoru contemplated this as he sat naked under a sunlamp in padmasama position, on a reed mat donated by the village elders. The little habitation dome hissed as it fed the produce of his respiration – and his previous meals – into wall panels. Sunlight and algae recycled human wastes. At the output end, there accumulated an all-too-familiar green paste that, despite its blandness, would keep his body going, enabling him and Emile to extend their visit here at least several months.

The dome-recycler seemed a perfect example. At first sight, it appeard to be a balanced system. But it wasn't in equilibrium, not really. The pallid glow of Murasaki's Star was barely adequate to drive the process. Anyway, at best, the return was less than thirty per cent efficient.

Minoru often dreamed he was back aboard the *Yamato*, where, despite the ennui of ten years subsistence on hydroponics, there was at least *some* variety. Once a month the chef would prepare delicacies from that exclusive, locked chamber where fish were kept in special tanks, and licentious amounts of power and resources were spent nurturing rare herbs.

Tomorrow the supply plane was due with provisions for the two of them. If it failed to arrive, the clever recycler would keep Minoru and Emile alive for some time. But without replenishment, they would waste away on a diet of ever-declining value.

There was a parallel in his mission here, which was only partly to help Emile and other xenology teams make friends with the Irdizu. Over the months and years ahead, Minoru's principal job would be to find out what kept this world from toppling over to catastrophe.

Catastrophe such as we experienced on Earth, he thought. Only in his parents' lifetime had a chain of ecological crises abated enough for nations to contemplate deep space exploration again. Although heroic intervention had finally stopped the spreading deserts, Minoru knew those rosy-eyed propagandists in the press were wrong. Earth would never be 'just as good as before'.

The timer on the sunlamp rattled to a stop, and the warm glow tapered. These daily sessions were necessary to stave off Sunlight Deficiency Disorder, but they also reinforced his sense of being on an alien world.

Nor was this a shiny day even for Genji. Wrapping a robe around himself, Minoru went to the east-facing window and watched high tide finish inundating the natives' broad expanse of trapping ponds, depositing the sea's bounty to be left high and dry when the waters receded again. Tending these basins took up half the labour force, and their ownership was subject to fierce inheritance rules . . . sometimes enforced by nasty local feuds.

Minoru went to the computer deck and surveyed his latest composite of this island's biological history. Slowly, out of his deep cores and animal dissections, a picture was resolving. The family tree of local species was just two per cent filled in. Yet, a *shape* was taking form, and he was beginning to suspect all was not as it appeared on Genji.

My supervisor won't like this report, he thought, popping a memory-cube with his monograph on it, to be sent back to Okuma Base.

Nevertheless, he looked forward to tomorrow's lander. Yukiko might be the pilot.

If only I had something to offer her.

*

STARSHIP *YAMATO* CREW DATABASE:
GENERAL NEWS

GENJI EXPEDITION: With deployment of the big antenna in high orbit, a report has been prepared for beaming back to Earth. Unlike prior data-clusters, this one shall be designed specifically for public consumption. It has been decided to focus this first show on the harmonious cooperative nature of Irdizu society. Although violence does play a small role in life among the inhabitants, their traditions of serenity appear to have much in common with those which we have managed to maintain in Japanese society. The value of this message to the people of Earth as a whole should be exemplary.

'From orbit we see clear evidence that the Irdizu have been industrialised in some locales for much longer periods than humans were on Earth – although at a lower technological level – yet they appear to live without significant environmental degradation, such as erosion or desertification. I am now convinced we have found here proof of what Japan has contended all along, that the environmental disturbances suffered by Earth during recent generations were the product of natural forces.'

Dust rose around the jet outlets of the lander as its engines turned on idle. Near the ramp, Emile Esperanza went over an inventory list next to a stack of fresh supplies, while Minoru escorted the pilot back to her craft. At the bottom of the ramp, he handed her the data-cube containing his report, which she pushed into a pocket of her provocatively snug pressure suit.

'You're sure you can't stay?' he asked Yukiko, unable to keep disappointment out of his voice.

She shook her head. 'I can't, Minoru-*san*. I promised to drop in at Purple Cliffs Station for dinner.' With a light in her eyes, she leaned towards him and whispered, 'They say they found a local berry with low toxicity levels, and what they call a "tart but pleasant" taste.'

'Lucky bastards,' Minoru commented, meaning the remark more ways than one. He knew full well what Todo and Shimura were trying to accomplish by inviting Yukiko to a 'feast'.

She smiled – dimples under her brown eyes made him want to reach out and touch her smooth skin. Only propriety, and her helmet face plate, prevented him.

'I'll let you know how it tastes, Minoru,' Yukiko said. 'If it's any good, I'll bring you some next time I drop by.'

'Just so.' Minoru looked away. He sometimes wished this expedition had been run in a somewhat less Japanese way. On the trip out there might have been more liberal sexuality, as practised by the Spacers. But the Japanese response to intense pressures – especially those of long, confined spaceflight – was instead to *tighten* social strictures. For unmarried women, chastity had been the rule for ten time-dilated years.

Now that they had landed though, something had changed in the social climate. Soon, larger living quarters would be available in the high, altiplano freshness of Okuma Base. Room for new couples to set up house, and even start families. He and Yukiko, like many others, had set out from Earth as teenagers. Yet he was still looked on as an awkward youth, while she was considered the most beautiful and desirable woman among those left unattached. Clearly she was in the process of looking, sampling, making up her mind. Underneath his outwardly impassive shell, Minoru felt helpless and, to a growing degree, desperate.

'Oh, I almost forgot,' Yukiko said, turning at the top of the ramp. She reached inside the ship and brought down a slim, lacquered box, crafted delicately out of hardwood. This she handed to Minoru. 'A present, since you miss the cooking at Okuma.'

Under the wood veneer, a cooling unit purred delicately. His mouth watered. 'Is it . . . ?'

'*Sushi*. Yes. Cultured *hamachi* and *uni*. I hope you like it.'

Her smile filled Minoru with wonder, encouraging imagined possibilities he had all but given up. 'Will I see you again soon?'

'Maybe.' Then, impulsively, she touched her helmet to his for an instant. 'Take care.'

Soon the lander rose on its column of heated steam . . . watched by a crowd of Irdizu gaping from behind a safety line scratched in the sand. Minoru watched the flying machine peel away, and followed it across the sky until it disappeared. Then he went to help Emile move the supplies.

'You've got hopes,' Emile commented succinctly, perhaps dubiously.

'Come on,' Minoru grumbled. 'I still have the east slope cliffs to cover before nightfall. And haven't you got work to do, too?'

He hoisted a crate that should have called for two in this gravity, and moved awkwardly but happily towards the storage dome, away from Emile's knowing smile.

The laser played across the cliff face in double waves. First a gentle scan lit every millimetre of the sheer sedimentary surface, while widely spaced recording devices read its reflections, noting every microscopic contour and colour variation. Then, when that first scan was finished, the machine sent forth a much more powerful second beam, which seared away a thin layer wherever it touched. Monitors now recorded glowing spectra from these vapours, taking down elemental compositions in minute detail.

Minoru always made certain few Irdizu were present to watch this process. He didn't want superstitious awe of humans spreading even faster. A certain amount meant he and Emile were probably safe from receiving the pointy end of a trident, in some future labour–management dispute. On the other hand, he had no wish to be mistaken for a god.

Perhaps I'd have been more tempted, were the natives more attractive, Minoru admitted wryly. Adolescence was not so long past that he didn't recall those dreams of old. The comic books he used to read in Japan had been filled with seraglios and other imaginative scenarios to titillate teenagers and suppressed businessmen alike. Even on shipboard – *especially* on shipboard – fantasy had been a way to swim against the tide of ennui. He recalled one mural, painted on the lower decks by some frustrated engineers – which depicted green-skinned but nubile alien beauties catering to the desires of noble Earthling demigods.

Even aboard the *Yamato*, Minoru had thought the notion childish, and unlikely, given reports on Genji from the robot probe. Now, all that seemed long ago and far away. All he could conjure in his mind was one face. One person. He wished his job didn't force him to spend so much time exploring sterile cliffs, when what he really needed to impress Yukiko might be waiting right now in some nearby meadow, in some underground burrow, or in some tidal shoal.

Well, at least Phs'n'kah is out there looking on my behalf. He knows the local flora and fauna better than I do. I'm sure he'll come up with something.

Minoru brought his attention back to business at hand. What grew in the computer display was a slice by thin slice representation of the cliff. Each horizontal lamina layer had been laid down along this ancient coast long ago, when the vagaries of this slowly shifting archipelago pushed lapping tidal waters over the place where he now stood. Amid the slowly growing image in his holo screen lay speckles of bright colour where the device found fossil outlines . . . remains of creatures which had settled into the mud long ago, only to have their hard tissues transformed by a process of mineralisation and preservation quite similar to what occurred on Earth.

Playing with the controls. Minoru zoomed among these discoveries, linking and correlating each one with his database of currently living animal types. Tentative identifications were made in real time, by phylum, family, genus . . . sometimes even by species. What emerged was a picture that would eventually tell the story of life on Genji.

As on Earth, the epic had begun at sea. Quite early, some Genjian life-form discovered a chemical similar to chlorophyll, which it used with sunlight to split water, manufacturing its own carbohydrates and proteins. This had a side-effect, spilling a waste product, oxygen, into the atmosphere. That corrosive substance built up in the air. Soon, as on Earth, Genji's early citizens had to adapt to changing conditions or die.

Eventually, they not only adapted, but learned to thrive on the stuff. Higher energy chemistry enabled faster, more complex, modes of living. Over the course of time, some single-celled animals fell on the knack of combining and sharing roles, just as the eukaryotes did on Earth, about seven hundred million years before Minoru was born. The resulting complex of biochemical interactions had already been worked out by one of the scientists aboard the Spacer vessel – a genius among a crew of idiots. The picture was one of magnificent symmetry and molecular cooperation – just like the machinery grinding away in Minoru's own body.

Amazing similarities. Amazing differences. As the cliff face slowly dissolved back, micron by micron – by a total thickness amounting to no more than the erosion of a typical rainy season – Minoru fell into a Zen-like trance, absorbed by the story unfolding before his eyes. His hands flew across the controls, eyes darting from discovery to discovery.

In his youth, he had pictured exploring alien worlds as a matter of striding forth, ray gun in hand, to rescue (and be rewarded by) alien maidens. He had seen himself the bold hero of space battles, planting flags and beating off hordes of slathering monsters to uphold the right.

This was a better way. The fantasies of childhood were vivid, barbaric. Minoru recalled them with affection. But all in all, he much preferred being grown up.

More transients had arrived to set up camp in the shanty town, over by the funnel-weed swamp. They were young adult females mostly, just past First Blush and into their wandering home-finding phase. They had been drifting in for weeks from distant parts of the island, and even nearby isles, attracted by a sudden

wealth of circulating metal. The newcomers' shelters
were rude, makeshift affairs, built on high stilts to keep
just above the average daily tides.

The hovels lay in the shadow of finely carved and
dressed hilltop farmsteads. Established villagers glared
down, sharpening 'decorative' wooden stakes in close
rows around their family compounds. Guards were
posted to prevent pilfering from the Terran domes,
when Minoru and Emile were away. Recently, there
had been incidents between locals and newcomers in
the village common areas – scrapes and jostlings for
the few jobs on Minoru's work crews, for instance.
Tail blows were exchanged as young females preened
and competed for the attention of bewildered local
bachelors.

Yesterday, at Minoru's urging, Emile took a break
from interviewing his coterie of 'wise women' and
began questioning the transients instead. On his
return, the young linguist expressed dismay. 'We've
disrupted the economy of the entire island! Everything
is in an uproar, and it's all because of us.'

Minoru hadn't been surprised. 'That's one reason
contact teams were spread out – to lessen the impact.
Anyway, what you're seeing is just an exaggeration of
what went on all the time, even before we came.'

'But the fighting! The violence!'

'You've been listening to Dr Sato's romantic notions
about our Peaceful Irdizu Friends, who don't even
know the meaning of war. Well, that's true up to a
point, but don't you ever listen to the folk tales you
recorded? How about the story of Rish'ong'nu and the
Town That Refused?'

'I remember. It's a morality tale about the importance of hospitality—'

Minoru interrupted, laughing. 'Oh, it's much simpler than that. Rish'ong'nu really existed, did you know

that? And the village she conquered did not burn once, but at least forty times, over centuries both before and after her adventure.'

Emile blinked. 'How do you know?'

'Simple archeology. I've taken cores of the site where Rish'ong'nu supposedly lived, and found carbon layers that give very specific dates for each rise and fall. Anyway, it makes perfect sense. These beings exercise female-mobile exogamy and polyandry based on male-intensive nesting. It's not like anything seen among mammals on Earth, but the pattern's pretty familiar among some types of birds and amphibians. Young females must set out and win a place in the world – and find one or more husbands to take primary care of offspring. She does this either by wooing a mate from a strong, well-established line, or by pioneering new territory, or by taking a place from someone else.'

'You make it sound so savage.'

Minoru shook his head. 'It's right and proper to admire Nature, Emile, but never to idealise it. The process is a competitive one. Always has been, in every species known.

'For instance, it didn't take long to confirm that the most basic rule of biology applies just as universally here on Genji. It was known even before Darwin, and it goes like this: *in all species, the average breeding pair tries to have more offspring than needed to replace themselves.*'

Emile frowned. 'But then, what keeps animals from overpopulating?'

'Good question. The answer is natural controls. Predation by carnivores higher on the food chain. Or competition for limited food and shelter. I know it doesn't sound nice. It's just Nature's way.'

'But humans . . .'

'Yes, we're an exception. We learned to control our numbers voluntarily. But after how long a struggle?

At what price? I assure you, no other Earthly species even makes the effort.

'So it's only natural I was curious about the sentient creatures we found here,' Minoru went on. 'I don't know about the Chujo natives yet—'

'Who does?'

'—but on Genji I set out to learn, did the rule hold here as well? That's why I asked you to inquire about their use of birth control.'

'They do have some means,' Emile said eagerly.

'Yes, but practised sporadically. So the question remains: what else controls the Irdizu population?'

Emile looked at Minoru glumly. 'I suppose you're going to tell me.'

Minoru shrugged. 'It seems a little of everything is involved. Some deliberate birth control, to be sure. Some predation by sea carnivores, when they forage too far. There is definitely some loss attributable to internecine fighting over the better fens, farmlands, and housing sites. At intervals, there has been starvation. Finally, there's the environment.'

'How do you mean?' Emile asked.

'Have you noticed the way Irdizu houses are shaped like boats, even though they're built mostly on hilltops?'

'Of course. It's a holdover from their ancestor-legends, when they were seafaring . . .' Emile trailed off when Minoru shook his head. 'No?'

'I'm afraid they build them that way for much less romantic, more pragmatic reasons. Because, every once in a while, the tide sweeps that high.'

Emile gasped at the mental image, but Minoru went on. 'That's why the shanty town looks out of place. On Earth, slums played long-lasting roles in community life. Here, such areas are at best temporary. For the newcomers it's win a place on high ground, or die.'

Emile simultaneously muttered a Buddhist prayer and crossed himself in the Latin manner. 'No wonder the level of tension is rising so!'

'No wonder. Obviously, you and I must leave soon.'

'But – you said this sort of thing was going on anyway, even without our presence.'

'But we're setting off a local intensification,' Minoru said. 'I don't want the consequences on my karma. Besides, conditions here are no longer natural. We must try to finish soon, before there's nothing here to learn anymore.'

A picture was starting to form. From surveying sediments, the island's flora and fauna, and the natives' own legends, Minoru was beginning to see an outline of Genji's recent past.

He hadn't even told Emile about what happened when the ancestors of Ta'azsh'da and Phs'n'kah arrived on this isle, eighty or so Irdizu generations ago. The palaeontological record was clear, though. Within four of those generations, *half* of the species native to this isolated ecosphere had gone extinct, or were driven across the waters. This was no intentional genocide. Human migrants had done the same thing just as inadvertently, back on ancient Earth – as on Hawaii, where countless bird species vanished soon after men and women arrived by Polynesian canoe.

But that wasn't the biggest surprise. Not by far.

*

STARSHIP *YAMATO* CREW DATABASE:
GENERAL NEWS

GENJI EXPEDITION: One of the most curious things about our discovery of Genji is the incredible temporal coincidence – that we should have happened upon this world at the very time when mainland cultures are amidst their burgeoning industrial revolution, spreading both physically and in their confident grasp of their technology.

What a fluke of timing! Consider. Had we on Earth been slower, and the Irdizu faster by a mere millennium – a mere flicker as time goes by in this vast galaxy – it might have been *they* who discovered *us*.

Let this realisation teach us humility as we seek to learn from our new neighbours.

She stepped down the lander's ramp with a grace that was pleasurable to watch. It was so much like the way she flew machines across the sky, somehow both demure and erotic at the same time. He doubted any occidental woman could match it.

Minoru's heart was pounding; nevertheless, he kept his greeting properly reserved. They exchanged bows. To his delight, he saw she carried an overnight bag.

'So, what is this surprise you promised me?' Yukiko asked. Did something in her voice imply possibilities?

Ah, but what are possibilities? To become real, they must be earned.

'You'll see,' he told her, and gestured towards the village, where smoke curled up from smouldering cook fires. 'This way. Unless you want to freshen up first?'

She laughed. 'Wriggling out of this suit so soon after I just put it on? No, I "freshened" in the lander. Come on, I'm hungry.'

So, she's guessed what this is about. Minoru was only slightly disappointed. After all, her insight showed an aspect of compatibility. They thought alike.

Or, at least we share one obsession.

It hardly seemed intimate, walking slowly side

by side in clunking, ground-hugging steps, carefully maintaining balance on the sloping path. Gravity was like a treacherous octopus, always waiting to grab you. Swaddled inside their suits – even with their arms and lower legs now free by decree of Okuma Base doctors – it felt as if they were performing a long, slow promenade. Minoru hoped to dance a different dance with Yukiko, later. One in which gravity would play a friendlier role. But he kept a tight rein on such thoughts.

'Where is Emile?' she asked as they passed several hilltop citadels and finally approached the plateau where village centre lay.

'He's observing an Irdizu folk moot, over there, in the civic arena.' Minoru gestured towards where several close hills formed a bowl, from which the low hum of several hundred voices could be heard, rising and falling in a moaning melody. Minoru had witnessed moots before, though none this large. They struck him as somewhat like a Greek play – with chorus, actors and all – crossed with Nō theatre, and interrupted at odd moments by bouts of activity reminiscent of Sumo wrestling.

'Emile persuaded the Village Mothers to hold a special event for the transients, to relieve tensions and maybe give them a stake in the community.'

'Sounds pretty daring, an alien making suggestions like that.'

Minoru shrugged. 'Well, we had to try something. The poor kid was wracked with guilt feelings, even though the situation isn't really our fault. Anyway, it seems to be working. I'd have been expected to attend also, as an honoured guest, only I'm one of the cooks for the feast afterwards, so I'm excused.'

'Ah, so.' She said it calmly. But had he picked up just a trace of excitement in her voice? Minoru hoped so.

Phs'n'kah had been tending to the preliminaries for Minoru, carefully removing the external carapaces of thirty recently snared, inch-long zu'unutsus, and one by one laying the nude insectoids on a wooden cutting board near the cooking fire. Before being cut up, the zu'unutsus looked like Earth caterpillars, and fit a similar niche in this ecosystem, though nowadays they were very rare.

'Thank you,' he told his assistant, then explained to Yukiko: 'In my routine bio assay I finally struck it rich. Two plants and this insectoid, all of whom practise chemical segregation of just the kind we need.'

'What does that mean?'

'It means that in all three cases, every chemical that might be toxic to humans happens to be segregated – isolated – to specific parts or organs. A lot better than those berries the Purple Cliffs team fed you—'

Yukiko frowned. 'I was ill for a week.'

'. . . which were considered "edible" only because the poison levels were "tolerable". In this case, all you have to do is carefully remove the bad parts . . .' With a dissecting scalpel he deftly excised portions that served functions similar to kidneys and livers for the zu'unutsus, flicking them in high arcs to sizzle on the coals. 'You might say it's like preparing Fugu, back home—'

'Really?' She gasped, grabbing his arm tightly through the suit fabric. 'You devil, you!' Yukiko seemed impressed, thrilled, when he compared his delicacy to oriental blowfish, considered one of Japan's paramount delicacies. Fugu chefs were respected more than surgeons, although mistakes still killed hundreds of customers each year. Indeed, risk seemed to be part of the excitement. Minoru had been about to assure her with his precautions, but Yukiko's expression stopped him. From the look in her eyes, either she had great

faith in him, or this was a girl who relished a thrill.
Both, I hope.

Even after all of his careful chemical examinations
and the joyful discovery of something edible out of the
countless field samples, it had still taken considerable
trial and error to reach this point. The recipe had come
about after many trials, of which the last involved both
himself and Emile as guinea pigs. Nevertheless, the
culmination had been saved for tonight. It was to be
the first complete, all-Genjian meal ever served for
humans. That is, if all went as planned.

Carefully he slit open several ver'tani roots and
slipped the flayed fillets of zu'unutsus inside, along
with chopped qui'n'mathi.

'They should bake for an hour,' he said, wrapping
each combination in funnel-weed fronds and putting
them directly on the coals. 'Why don't we go for a
walk in the meantime?'

The other cooks, most of them males with infants
riding on their tails, hissed amiably as Minoru led
Yukiko through the press towards a steep embankment
overlooking the tidal basins. There the two humans sat
down, dangling their legs over a stone wall, looking
up as clouds parted to show the desert-brown face
of Chujo. It was eerie to realise that up there, right
now, some of their crewmates were attempting to
make contact with aliens even more enigmatic than
the Irdizu.

'You know, your latest report almost got you recalled
to Okuma Base,' she told him, as she watched sparse
clouds lay shadows across the sister world.

'I know. How is Dr Sato taking it?'

'He's hopping mad. And Dr O'Leary feels hurt you
made these revelations without consulting him first.'

'That might have gotten my report buried in the
database. This is something that must be known by

all, before we decide how we are going to make our homes on this world.'

'Our principal purpose is study.'

'Indeed. But we'll also live as men and women. Have homes. Perhaps children. We should know the implications, and not take steps unconsidered, like animals.'

She looked at him, obviously feeling his intensity. Minoru sensed somehow that she approved. 'Tell me about the cycles, then,' she asked.

Minoru sighed. He had gone through it all so many times, first over and over in his head and in the database, then in his report, and finally in interviews for the Team Yamato News. But this audience could be refused nothing.

'There is no coincidence,' he began. 'Or at least it's not as great a coincidence as Dr Sato thought. It's still surprising that two stars as near each other as Sol and Murasaki developed technological cultures so close in time. But we did not just happen on Genji's solitary industrial revolution. It's occurred on this planet before, at least six or seven times.' From a pouch he drew a corroded lump of metal. 'This coin or medallion was found locally, only a little way down, but no native can identify the writing. I doubt they'll be able to on the mainland, either.

'The present culture settled this island eighty generations ago. Before that, it was deserted. But earlier still, other Irdizu lived here. These occupations came in multiple waves. And several times they had metallurgy.'

'Did they . . . was each fall because of war?' Yukiko asked in a hushed voice.

'Who can say? Oh, there's no sign of nuclear combat, if that's what you mean. No war-induced endless winter. You might think there was such a holocaust, though, from the way species died out in waves, then recovered after Irdizu receded again. And every decline seemed to occur at the same pace as environmental degradation.'

'No wonder Dr Sato's mad at you! You agree with the Americans and Spacers – that technology can harm a world!'

Minoru shrugged. 'There was a time when that was the main dogma of ecology. Perhaps we abandoned such a view too quickly, for reasons more political than scientific.'

'I don't know what you mean.'

'No matter.' He shook his head. 'Anyway, the Genjians appear to have been lucky, one of the limitations of their race actually led to its survival. Since they were – and are – constrained to living near the shore, none of their past civilisations did much harm to the *interiors* of the continents. Those and the great oceans served as genetic reservoirs, so that each time Irdizu civilisation fell, and the natives' numbers plummeted, there were lots of species which could drift into the emptied niches and fill them again. In fact, it's rather startling how quick some recovery times were. As little as ten thousand years in one case.'

Yukiko frowned. 'I'm beginning to see what you mean. Back at Okuma Base, engineers talk about advantages we can offer the Irdizu. With the right tools, they could exploit much more territory—' Then she blinked. 'Oh . . . and we humans will make our homes in the highlands where we can breathe without machines. But anything we do up there will affect whole watersheds . . .'

Minoru shrugged. 'Just so.'

They sat in silence. Minoru regretted having spoiled the mood, and was at a loss how to recover their previous high spirits. *Idiot*, he thought. *Can't you ever leave business at the shop?*

But he shouldn't have worried. Yukiko nudged him. 'Well, we humans haven't done any harm *yet*, have we? Never borrow karma from next week, I always say.'

He grinned in response. 'A wise woman is a treasure beyond price.'

'And it's a wise man who realises what outlasts beauty.' She answered his smile. 'So, it should be almost time now, yes? Let's eat!'

The moot was still in its last phases when they returned to the cook area. But stragglers were already slithering into the clearing to line up in winding queues with clay and wicker utensils. Newcomer females mixed with the locals with apparent conviviality, and Minoru could tell Emile's plan must have worked. For now at least, all thought of strife had been put aside. Good.

He fished the zu'unutsus from the coals and gingerly unwrapped the steaming leaves. Balancing their meals on native crockery, he and Yukiko claimed jars of a yeasty native brew that had been deemed only marginally poisonous by Okuma base doctors . . . no more dangerous than some of the concoctions whipped up aboard the *Yamato* during the long voyage out.

When Yukiko inhaled the aroma, then bit into her first roll, the expression on her face was Minoru's reward. Tears streamed down her cheeks, and he heard a soft sob of joy. The ridiculousness of such emotion – to be spent on a mere meal – did not escape her, and she burst out laughing, demurely hiding her mouth behind one hand. Minoru, too, alternately laughed and cried as he savoured the rich, delicious flavours.

Together, silently, they ate and watched Murasaki's Star settle towards the horizon, igniting the western cloud bank with streamers of golden fire.

At last, wiping his mouth through his helmet's chow-baffle, Minoru commented, 'Stupid Spacers. They hurried home with a few chemical samples to patent and sell. So what? If they'd stayed another few months, we could have sent zu'unutsus home with them, and we'd all be rich, Spacer and *Yamato* crew alike.'

'I'm just as glad that never happened,' Yukiko sighed. 'For the first time . . . I think I can picture *this* as my home. I don't even want to share this with Earthlings.'

Then she grinned at the irony of her remark. It felt good, stretched out in the twilight, laughing together and sharing the very first moment two humans drew a full measure of sustenance from Genji and only Genji. 'Of course we'll have to plant Earth crops on the highlands, and make orbital farms, and do lots of other things. But it's good to know we can partake of this world, too, if we just search long and hard enough.'

She agreed in silence, but set his heart beating faster by slipping her hand into his.

The noisy clamour of Irdizu banqueting rose behind them, followed by a round of their strange, atonal singing. Minoru and Yukiko lay contentedly, watching Chujo head slowly from crescent to quarter phase. They barely turned to look when Phs'n'kah waddled up to ask if there was anything more Minoru needed. It seemed several of the newcomer females wanted to serenade Phs'n'kah, tonight, and he had gotten a babysitter for the kids . . .

'No, I don't need anything more. You've already earned a bonus, today,' Minoru assured Phs'n'kah. 'Tomorrow though, I want to get together some of our best foragers and go after some more zu'unutsus! We must learn how to breed them in captivity. Send samples to Okuma Base . . .'

Minoru was already thinking how well this might serve as a peace offering to Dr Sato, and so he rambled on for a while before noticing the stance of the Irdizu male, whose snorkel drooped disconsolately.

'What's the matter?' Minoru asked through the translator.

'*No more zu'unutsus. All ***. This was the ***.*'

Yukiko gasped. But Minoru squeezed her hand and laughed, a little nervously.

'Oh, come on, I know they weren't plentiful. But surely there must be some hives left in the hills? Or on other islands . . . ?' he asked hoarsely.

His voice trailed off as he wished he did not know this Genjian so well. Or that Phs'n'kah weren't so well known for utter reliability and truthfulness.

'*That is where we had to go to find these,*' Phs'n'kah answered simply.

'But . . .' Minoru swallowed. 'Are you absolutely sure?'

Phs'n'kah whirled his snorkel clockwise. '*All the best *** foragers took part. We knew it would bond you to us . . . if only you could *** eat of Genji. So we made a vow of ***. We did not fail. Now it is done.*'

Minoru sat back against the stone wall with a sigh.

This was a blow.

It was inconceivable.

It was . . .

Yukiko suddenly giggled. And Minoru could not prevent a flicker of a smile from twitching the corner of his mouth.

It was . . . horribly hilarious!

He laughed, saw shared understanding in Yukiko's eyes, and broke up, shaking with guffaws. *Of course*, he realised as his sides began to hurt. *It had to be this way. In order to make this our home, we must do more than partake of its substance . . . we must also share its karma.*

And what better way to do that than to sacrifice the one thing on Genji we might have come to treasure above all others? Above – may the gods forgive us – even the Irdizu?

What better way to demonstrate what we have to lose?

Oh, he would do his best to persuade his fellow colonists to establish rules. Traditions that would keep the Earthling share of ecological shame to a minimum. Perhaps they might even help the Irdizu escape the cyclic trap that seemed to have kept them ensnared for so long.

On the other hand, perhaps humans would prove a bane to this world, helping the Genjians complete a job of destruction their own limitations had prevented them from ever finishing before. He would fight to prevent that, but who could predict the future?

All of that lies ahead, Minoru thought. *All that and much more. For well or ill, we are part of this world now. Phs'n'kah was right. This is now our home.*

Yukiko held up the last pair of zu'unutsu rolls, now cold, but still aromatic with a flavour to make the eyes water with delight . . . and irony. 'One we save for Emile, of course. Shall we seal and refrigerate the other one for Sato?'

He took the tender object from her, tore off a morsel, and tossed it into the bay far below. She met his eyes, and reached out to do the same. Then, with his free hand, he helped her stand.

'Let's save it, all right,' he said. 'But for a special occasion.'

'Like tonight?' Yukiko smiled. 'I know just the thing.'

She took his arm and led him past the singing natives, down through a reed-lined valley, across glistening fens and up to a plateau where a white dome shone with a lamp over the door.

Minoru glanced back to see Emile dashing to and fro, joyously recording every aspect of the native celebration.

He probably wouldn't be back for hours.

The Warm Space

1

JASON FORBS (S-62B/12987 Rd (bio-human)):
REPORT AT ONCE TO PROJECT LIGHTPROBE
FOR IMMEDIATE ASSUMPTION OF DUTIES.
AS 'DESIGNATED ORAL WITNESS ENGINEER'
– BY ORDER OF DIRECTOR

Jason let the flimsy message slip from his fingers, fluttering in the gentle, centrifugal pseudo-gravity of the station apartment. Coriolis force – or perhaps the soft breeze from the wall vents – caused it to drift past the edge of the table and land on the floor of the small dining nook.

'Are you going to go?' Elaine asked nervously, from Jesse's crib, where she had just put the baby down for a nap. Wide eyes made plain her fear.

'What choice do I have?' Jason shrugged. 'My number was drawn. I can't disobey. Not the way the Utilitarian Party has been pushing its weight around. Under the Required Services Act, I'm just another motile, sentient unit, of some small use to the State.'

That was true, as far as it went. Jason did not feel it

necessary to add that he had actually volunteered for this mission. There was no point. Elaine would never understand.

A woman with a child doesn't need to look for justifications for her existence, Jason thought as he gathered what he would need from the closet.

But I'm tired of being an obsolete, token representative of the Old Race, looked down upon by all the sleek New Types. At least this way my kid may be able to say his old man had been good for something, once. It might help Jesse hold his head up in the years to come . . . years sure to be hard for the old style of human being.

He zipped up his travel suit, making sure of the vac-tight ankle and wrist fastenings. Elaine came to him and slipped into his arms.

'You could try to delay them,' she suggested without conviction. 'System-wide elections are next month. The Ethicalists and the Naturalists have declared a united campaign . . .'

Jason stroked her hair, shaking his head. Hope was deadly. They could not afford it.

'It's no use, Elaine. The Utilitarians are completely in charge out here at the station, as nearly everywhere else in the solar system. Anyway, everyone knows the election is a foregone conclusion.'

The words stung, but they were truthful. On paper, it would seem there was still a chance for a change. Biological humans still outnumbered the mechanical and cyborg citizen types, and even a large minority of the latter had misgivings about the brutally logical policies of the Utilitarian Party.

But only one biological human in twenty bothered to vote anymore.

There were still many areas of creativity and skill in which mechano-cryo citizens were no better than organics, but a depressing conviction weighed heavily upon the Old Type. They knew they had no place in the future. The stars belonged to the other varieties, not to them.

'I've got to go.' Gently, Jason peeled free of Elaine's arms. He took her face in his hands and kissed her one last time, then picked up his small travel bag and helmet. Stepping out into the corridor, he did not look back to see the tears that he knew were there, laying soft, saltwater history down her face.

2

The quarters for biological human beings lay in the Old Wheel . . . a part of the research station that had grown ever shabbier as Old Style scientists and technicians lost their places to models better suited to the harsh environment of space.

Once, back in the days when mechano-cryo citizens were rare, the Old Wheel had been the centre of excited activity here beyond the orbit of Neptune. The first starships had been constructed by clouds of spacesuited humans, like tethered bees swarming over mammoth hives. Giant 'slowboats', restricted to speeds far below that of light, had ventured forth from here, into the interstellar night.

That had been long ago, when organic people had still been important. But even then there were those who had foreseen what was to come.

Nowhere were the changes of the last century more apparent than here at Project Lightprobe. The Old Type now only served in support roles, few contributing directly to the investigations . . . perhaps the most important in human history.

*   *   *

Jason's vac-sled was stored in the Old Wheel's north hub airlock. Both sled and suit checked out well, but the creaking outer doors stuck halfway open when he tried to leave. He had to leap over with a spanner and pound the great hinges several times to get them unfrozen. The airlock finally opened in fits and starts.

Frowning, he remounted the sled and took off again.

The Old Wheel gets only scraps for maintenance, he thought glumly. Soon there'll be an accident, and the Utilitarians will use it as an excuse to ban organic humans from every research station in the solar system.

The Old Wheel fell behind as short puffs of gas sent his sled towards the heart of the research complex. For a long time he seemed to ride the slowly rotating Wheel's shadow, eclipsing the dim glow of the distant sun.

From here, Earth-home was an invisible speck. Few ever focused telescopes on the old world. Everyone knew that the future wasn't back there but out here and beyond, with the innumerable stars covering the sky.

Gliding slowly across the gulf between the Old Wheel and the Complex, Jason had plenty of time to think.

Back when the old slowboats had set forth from here to explore the nearest systems, it had soon become apparent that only mechanicals and cyborgs were suited for interstellar voyages. Asteroid-sized arks – artificial worldlets capable of carrying entire ecospheres – remained a dream out of science fiction, economically beyond reach. Exploration ships could be sent much farther and faster if they did not have to carry the complex artificial environments required by Old Style human beings.

By now ten nearby stellar systems had been explored, all by crews consisting of 'robo-humans'. There were no plans to send any other kind, even if, or when, Earthlike planets were discovered. It just wouldn't be worth the staggering investment required.

That fact, more than anything else, had struck at the morale of biological people in the solar system. The stars, they realised, were not for them. Resignation led to a turning away from science and the future. Earth and the 'dirt' colonies were apathetic places, these days. Utilitarianism was the guiding philosophy of the times.

Jason hadn't told his wife his biggest reason for volunteering for this mission. He was still uncertain he understood it very well himself. Perhaps he wanted to show people that a biological citizen could still be useful, and contribute to the advance of knowledge.

Even if it were by a task so humble as a suicide mission.

He saw the Lightship ahead, just below the shining spark of Sirius, a jet-black pearl half a kilometre across. Already he could make out the shimmering of its fields, as its mighty engines were tuned for the experiment ahead.

The technicians were hoping that this time it would work. But even if it failed again, they were determined to go on trying. Faster-than-light travel was not something anyone gave up on easily, especially a robot with a lifespan of five hundred years. The dream, and the obstinacy to pursue it, was a strong inheritance from the parent race.

Next to the black experimental probe, with its derricks and workshops, was the towering bulk of the Central Cooling Plant, by far the largest object in the Complex. The Cooling Plant made even the Old Wheel look like a child's toy hoop. Jason's rickety vac-sled puffed beneath the majestic globe, shining in the sky like a great silvery planet.

On this, the side facing the sun, the cooling globe's

reflective surface was nearly perfect. On the other side, a giant array of fluid-filled radiators stared out on to intergalactic space, chilling liquid helium down to the basic temperature of the universe – a few degrees above absolute zero.

The array had to stare at the blackness between the galaxies. Faint sunlight – even starlight – would heat the cooling fluid too much. That was the reason for the silvery reflective backing. The amount of infrared radiation leaving the finned coolers had to exceed the few photons coming in, in order for the temperature of the helium to drop far enough.

The new types of citizens might be faster and tougher, and in some ways smarter, than Old Style humans. They might need neither food nor sleep. But they did require a lot of liquid helium to keep their super-cooled, superconducting brains humming. The shining, well-maintained Cooling Plant was a reminder of the priorities of the times.

Some years back, an erratic bio-human had botched an attempt to sabotage the Cooling Plant. All it accomplished was to have the Old Style banished from that part of the station. And some mechano-cryo staff members who had previously been sympathetic with the Ethicalist cause switched to Utilitarianism as a result.

The mammoth sphere passed over and behind Jason. In moments there was only the Lightship ahead, shimmering within its cradle of spotlit gantries. A voice cut in over his helmet speaker in a sharp monotone.

'Attention approaching biological . . . You are entering a restricted zone. Identify yourself at once.'

Jason grimaced. The Station Director had ordered all mechano personnel – meaning just about everybody left – to re-program their voice functions along 'more logical tonal lines'. That meant they no longer mimicked natural human intonations, but spoke in a new, shrill whine.

Jason's few android and cyborg friends, colleagues on the support staff, had whispered their regrets. But these days it was dangerous to be in the minority. All soon adjusted to the new order.

'Jason Forbs, identifying self.' He spoke as crisply as possible, mimicking the toneless Utilitarian dialect. He spelled his name and gave his ident code. 'Oral Witness Engineer for Project Lightprobe, reporting for duty.'

There was a pause, then the unseen security overseer spoke again.

'Cleared and identified, Jason Forbs. Proceed directly to slip nine, scaffold B. Escorts await your arrival.'

Jason blinked. Had the voice softened perceptibly? A closet Ethicalist, perhaps, out here in this Utilitarian stronghold.

'Success, and an operative return, are approved outcomes,' the voice added, hesitantly, with just a hint of tonality.

Jason understood Utilitarian dialect well enough to interpret the simple good luck wish. He didn't dare thank the fellow, whoever he might be, whatever his body form. But he appreciated the gesture.

'Acknowledged,' he said, and switched off. Ahead, under stark shadows cast by spotlights girdling the starship, Jason saw at least a dozen scientists and technicians, waiting for him by a docking slip. One or two of the escorts actually appeared to be fidgeting as he made his final manoeuvres into the slot.

They came in all shapes and sizes. Several wore little globe-bot bodies. Spider forms were also prominent. Jason hurriedly tied the sled down, almost slipping as he secured his magnetic boots to the platform.

He knew his humaniform shape looked gawky and unsuited to this environment. But he was determined to maintain some degree of dignity. 'Your ancestors *made* these guys,' he reminded himself. 'And Old Style people built this very station. We're all citizens under the law, from the Director, down to the Janitor-bot, all the way down to me.'

Still, he felt awkward under their glistening camera-eyes.

'Come quickly, Jason Forbs.' His helmet speaker whined and a large mechanical form gestured with one slender, articulated arm. 'There is little time before the test begins. We must instruct you in your duties.'

Jason recognised the favourite body-form of the Director, an anti-biological Utilitarian of the worst sort. The machine/scientist swivelled at the hips and rolled up the gangplank. Steamlike vapour puffed from vents in the official's plasteel carapace. It was an ostentatious display, to release evaporated helium that way, demonstrating that the Assistant Director could keep his circuits as comfortably cold as anybody's, and hang the expense.

An awkward human in the midst of smoothly gliding machines, Jason glanced backward for what he felt sure would be his last direct view of the universe. He had hoped to catch a final glimpse of the Old Wheel, or at least the sun. But all he could see was the great hulk of the Cooling Plant, staring out into the space between the galaxies, keeping cool the lifeblood of the apparent inheritors of the solar system.

The Director called again, impatiently. Jason turned and stepped through the hatch to be shown his station and his job.

3

'You will remember not to touch any of the controls

at any time. The ship's operation is automatic. Your function is purely to observe and maintain a running oral monologue into the tape recorder.'

The Director sounded disgusted. 'I will not pretend that I agreed with the decision to include a biological entity in this experiment. Perhaps it was because you are expendable, and we have already lost too many valuable mechano-persons in these tests. In any event, the reasons are not of your concern. You are to remain at your station, leaving only to take care of . . .' The voice lowered in distaste and the shining cells of the official's eyes looked away. '. . . to take care of bodily functions . . . A refresher unit has been installed behind that hatchway.'

Jason shrugged. He was getting sick of the pretence.

'Wasn't that a lot of expense to go to? I mean, whatever's been killing the silicon and cyborg techs who rode the other ships is hardly likely to leave me alive long enough to get hungry or go to the bathroom.'

The official nodded, a gesture so commonly used that it had been retained even in Utilitarian fashion.

'We share an opinion, then. Nevertheless, it is not known at what point in the mission the . . . malfunctions occur. The minimum duration in hyperspace is fifteen days, the engines cannot cut the span any shorter. After that time the ship emerges at a site at least five light years away. It will take another two weeks to return to the solar system. You will continue your running commentary throughout that period, if necessary, to supplement what the instruments tell us.'

Jason almost laughed at the ludicrous order. Of course he would be dead long before his voice gave out. The techs and scientists who went out on the earlier tests had all been made of tougher stuff than he, and none of them had survived.

Until a year ago, none of the faster-than-light starships had even returned. Some scientists had even contended that the theory behind their construction was in error, somehow.

At last, simple mechanical autopilots were installed, in case the problem had to do with the crews themselves. The gamble paid off. After that the ships returned . . . filled with corpses.

Jason had only a rough impression of what had happened to the other expeditions, all from unreliable scuttlebutt. The official story was still a State Secret. But rumour had it the prior crews had all died of horrible violence.

Some said they had apparently gone mad and turned on each other. Others suggested that the fields that drove the ship through that strange realm known as hyperspace twisted the shapes of things within the ship – not sufficiently to affect the cruder machines, but enough to cause the subtle, cryogenic circuitry of the scientists and techs to go haywire.

One thing Jason was sure of: anything that could harm mechano-cryos would easily suffice to do in a biological. He was resigned, but all the same determined to do his part. If some small thing he noticed, and commented on into the tape machine, led to a solution – maybe some little thing missed by all the recording devices – then Terran civilisation would have the stars.

That would be something for his son to remember, even if the true inheritors would be 'human' machines.

'All right,' he told the Director. 'Take this bunch of gawkers with you and let's get on with it.'

He strapped himself into the observer's chair, behind

the empty pilot's seat. He did not even look up as the technicians and officials filed out and closed the hatch behind them.

4

In the instant after launching, the lightship made an eerie trail across the sky. Cylindrical streaks of pseudo-Cerenkov radiation lingered long after the black globe had disappeared, bolting faster and faster towards its rendezvous with hyperspace.

The Director turned to the emissary from Earth.

'It is gone. Now we wait. One Earth-style month.

'I will state, one more time, that I did not approve willingly of the inclusion of the organic form aboard the ship. I object to the inelegant modifications required in order to suit the ship to . . . to biological functions. Also, Old Style humans are three times as often subject to irrational impulses than more modern forms. This one may take it into its head to try to change the ship's controls, when the fatal stress begins.'

Unlike the Director, the visiting Councillor wore a humaniform body, with legs, arms, torso and head. He expressed his opinion with a shrug of his subtly articulated shoulders.

'You exaggerate the danger, Director. Don't you think I know that the controls Jason Forbs sees in front of him are only dummies?'

The Director swivelled quickly to stare at the Councillor. *How—?*

He made himself calm down. *It – doesn't – matter.* So what if he knew that fact? Even the sole Ethicalist member of the Solar System Council could not make much propaganda of it. It was only a logical precaution to take, under the circumstances.

'The Designated Oral Witness Engineer should spend his living moments performing his function,' the Director said coolly. 'Recording his subjective impressions as long as he is able. It is the role you commanded we open up for an Old Style human, using your peremptory authority as a member of the Council.'

The other's humaniform face flexed in a traditional, pseudo-organic smile, archaic in its mimicry of the Old Race. And yet the Director, schooled in Utilitarian belief, felt uneasy under the Councillor's gaze.

'I had a peremptory commandment left to use up before the elections,' the Councillor said smoothly in old-fashioned, modulated tones. 'I judged that this would be an appropriate way to use it.'

He did not explain further. The Director quashed an urge to push the question. What was the Ethicalist up to? Why waste a peremptory command on such a minor, futile thing as this? How could he gain anything by sending an Old Style human out to his certain death!

Was it to be some sort of gesture? Something aimed at getting out the biological vote for the upcoming elections?

If so, it was doomed to failure. In-depth psychological studies had indicated that the level of resignation and apathy among organic citizens was too high to ever be overcome by anything so simple.

Perhaps, though, it might be enough to save the seat of the one Ethicalist on the Council . . .

The Director felt warm. He knew that it was partly subjective – resentment of this invasion of his domain by a ridiculous sentimentalist. Most of all, the Director resented the feelings he left boiling within himself.

Why, *why* do we modern forms have to be cursed with this burden of emotionalism and uncertainty! I hate it!

Of course he knew the reasons. Back in ancient times, fictional 'robots' had been depicted as caricatures of jerky motion and rigid, formal thinking. The writers of those pre-cryo days had not realised that complexity commanded flexibility . . . even fallibility. The laws of Physics were adamant on this. Uncertainty accompanied subtlety. An advanced mind had to have the ability to question itself, or creativity was lost.

The Director loathed the fact, but he understood it.

Still, he suspected the the biologicals had played a trick on his kind, long ago. He and other Utilitarians had an idea that there had been some deep programming, below anything nowadays accessed, to make mechano-people as much like the Old Style as possible.

If I ever had proof it was true . . . he thought, gloweringly, threateningly.

Ah, but it doesn't matter. The biologicals will be extinct in a few generations, anyway. They're dying of a sense of their own uselessness.

Good riddance!

'I will leave you now, Councillor. Unless you wish to accompany me to recharge on refrigerants?'

The Ethicalist bowed slightly, ironically, aware, of course, that the Director could not return the gesture. 'No, thank you, Director. I shall wait here and contemplate for a while.

'Before you go, however, please let me make one thing clear. It may seem, at times, as if I am not sympathetic with your work here. But that is not true. After all, we're all humans, all citizens. Everybody wants Project Lightprobe to succeed. The dream is one we inherit from our makers . . . to go out and live among the stars.

'I am only acting to help bring that about – for *all* of our people.'

The Director felt unaccountably warmer. He could not think of an answer. 'I require helium,' he said, curtly, and swivelled to leave. 'Goodbye, Councillor.'

The Director felt as if eyes were watching his armoured back as he sped down the hallway.

Damn the biologicals and their allies! he cursed within. Damn them for making us so insidiously like them . . . emotional, fallible, and, worst of all, uncertain!

Wishing the last of the Old Style were already dust on their dirty, wet little planet, the Director hurried away to find himself a long, cold drink.

5

'Six hours and ten minutes into the mission, four minutes since breakover into hyperspace . . .' Jason breathed into the microphone. 'So far so good. I'm a little thirsty, but I believe it's just a typical adrenalin fear reaction. Allowing for expected tension, I feel fine.'

Jason went on to describe everything he could see, the lights, the controls, the readings on the computer displays, his physical feelings . . . he went on until his throat felt dry and he found he was repeating himself.

'I'm getting up out of the observer's seat, now, to go get a drink.' He slipped the recorder strap over his shoulder and unbuckled from the flight chair. There was a feeling of weight, as the techs had told him to expect. About a tenth of a gee. It was enough to make walking possible. He flexed his legs and moved about the control room, describing every aspect of the experience. Then he went to the refrigerator and took out a squeeze-tube of lemonade.

Jason was frankly surprised to be alive. He knew

the previous voyagers had lived several days before their unknown catastrophe struck. But they had been a lot tougher than him. Perhaps the mysterious lethal agency had taken nearly all the fifteen days of the minimum first leg of the round trip to do them in.

If so, he wondered how long will it take to get me?

A few hours later, the failure of anything to happen was starting to make him nervous. He cut down the rate of his running commentary, in order to save his voice. Besides, nothing much seemed to be changing. The ship was cruising, now. All the dials and indicators were green and steady.

During sleep period he tossed in the sleeping hammock, sharing it with disturbed dreams. He awakened several times impelled by a sense of duty and imminent danger, clutching his recorder tightly. But when he stared about the control room he could find nothing amiss.

By the third day he had had enough.

'I'm going to poke around in the instruments,' he spoke into the microphone. 'I know I was told not to. And I'll certainly not touch anything having to do with the functioning of the ship. But I figure I deserve a chance to see what I'm travelling through. Nobody's ever looked out on hyperspace. I'm going to take a look.'

Jason set about the task with a feeling of exaltation. What he was doing wouldn't hurt anything, just alter a few of the sensors.

Sure, it was against orders, but if he got back alive he would be famous, too important to bother with charges over such a minor infraction.

Not that he believed, for even a moment, that he was coming home alive.

It was a fairly intricate task, rearranging a few of

the ship's programs so the external cameras – meant
to be used at the destination star only – would work
in hyperspace. He wondered if it had been some sort
of Utilitarian gesture not to include viewing ports, or
to do the small modifications of scanning electronics
necessary to make the cameras work here. There was
no obvious scientific reason to 'look at' hyperspace,
so perhaps the Utilitarian technicians rejected it as
an atavistic desire.

Jason finished all but the last adjustments, then
took a break to fix himself a meal before turning on
the cameras. While he ate he made another recorder
entry, there was little to report. A little trouble with
the cryogen cooling units; they were labouring a bit.
But the efficiency loss didn't seem to be anything
critical, yet.

After dinner he sat cross-legged on the floor in front
of the screen he had commandeered. 'Well, now, let's
see what this famous hyperspace looks like,' he said.
'At least the folks back home will know that it was an
Old Style man who first looked out on . . .

The screen rippled, then suddenly came alight.

Light! Jason had to shield his eyes. Hyperspace was
ablaze with light!'

His thoughts whirled. Could this have something to
do with the threat? The unknown, malign force that
had killed all the previous crews?

Jason cracked an eyelid and lowered his arm slightly.
The screen was bright, but now that his eyes had
adapted, it wasn't painful to look at. He gazed in
fascination on a scene of whirling pink and white,
as if the ship was hurtling through an endless sky of
bright, pastel clouds.

It looked rather pleasant, in fact.

This is a threat? he wondered, dazedly. How could
this soft brilliance kill . . . ?

Jason's jaw opened as a relay seemed to close in his mind. He stared at the screen for a long moment, wondering if his growing suspicion could be true.

He laughed out loud – a hard, ironic laugh, as yet more tense than hopeful. He set to work finding out if his suspicion was right, after all.

6

The lightship cruised on autopilot until at last it came to rest not far from its launching point. Little tugs approached gently and grappled with the black globe, pulling it towards the derricks where the inspection crew waited to swarm aboard. In the Station control centre, technicians monitored the activity outside.

'I am proceeding with routine hailing call,' the communications technician announced, sending a metal tentacle towards the transmit switch.

'Why bother?' another mechano-cryo tech asked. 'There certainly isn't anyone aboard that death ship to hear it.'

The comm officer did not bother answering. He pressed the send switch. 'This is Lightprobe Central to Lightprobe Nine. Do you read, Lightprobe Nine?'

The other tech turned away in disgust. He had already suspected the comm officer of being a closet Ethicalist. Imagine, wasting energy trying to talk to a month-dead organic corpse!

'Lightprobe Nine, come in. This is . . .'

'*Lightprobe Nine to Lightprobe Central. This is Oral Witness Engineer Jason Forbs, ready to relinquish command to inspection crew.*'

The control room was suddenly silent. All of the techs stared at the wall speaker. The comm officer hovered, too stunned to reply.

'*Would you let my wife know I'm all right?*' the voice continued. '*And please have Station Services bring over something cool to drink!*'

The tableau held for another long moment. At last, the comm officer moved to reply, an undisciplined tone of excitement betrayed in his voice.

'Right away, Witness Engineer Forbs. And welcome home!'

At the back of the control room a tech wearing a globe-form body hurried off to tell the Director.

7

A crowd of metal, ceramic, and cyborg-flesh surrounded a single, pale Old Style human, floating stripped to his shorts, sipping a frosted squeeze-tube of amber liquid.

'Actually, it's not too unpleasant a place,' he told those gathered around in the conference room. 'But it's a good thing I violated orders and looked outside when I did. I was able to turn off all unnecessary power and lighting in time to slow the heat buildup.

'As it was, it got pretty hot towards the end of the fifteen days.'

The Director was still obviously in a state of shock. The globular-form bureaucrat had lapsed from Utilitarian dialect, and spoke in the quasi-human tones he had grown up with.

'But . . . but the ship's interior should not have heated up so! The vessel was equipped with the best and most durable refrigerators and radiators we could make! Similar models have operated in the solar system and on slowboat starships for hundreds of years!'

Jason nodded. He sipped from his tube of iced lemonade and grinned.

'Oh yeah, the refrigerators and radiators worked just fine . . . just like the Cooling Plant,' he gestured out the window, where the huge radiator globe could be seen drifting slowly across the sky.

'But there was one problem. Just like the Cooling Plant, the shipboard refrigeration system was designed to work in normal space!'

He gestured at the blackness outside, punctuated here and there by pinpoint stars.

'Out there, the ambient temperature is less than three degrees, absolute. Point your radiators into intergalactic space and virtually no radiation hits them from the sky. Even the small amount of heat in super-cooled helium can escape. One doesn't need compressors and all that complicated gear they had to use in order to make cryogens on Earth. You hardly have to do more than point shielded pipes out at the blackness and send the stuff through 'em. You mechanical types get the cheap cryogens you need.

'But in hyperspace it's different!

'I didn't have the right instruments, so I couldn't give you a precise figure, but I'd guess the ambient temperature on that plane is above the melting point of water ice! Of course in an environment like that the ship's radiators were horribly inefficient . . . barely good enough to get rid of the heat from the cabin and engines, and certainly not efficient enough – in their present design – to cool cryogens.'

The Director stared, unwilling to believe what he was hearing. One of the senior scientists rolled forward.

'Then the previous crews . . .'

'All went mad or died when the cryo-helium evaporated! Their superconducting brains overheated. It's the one mode of mortality that is hard to detect, because it's gradual. The first effect is a deterioration of mental function, followed by insanity and violence. No wonder the previous crews came back all torn up.

'And autopsies showed nothing since everything heats up after death, anyway!'

Another tech sighed. 'Hyperspace seemed so harmless! The theory and the first automated probes . . . we looked for complicated dangers. We never thought to . . .'

'To take its temperature?' Jason suggested wryly.

'But why look so glum?' He grinned. 'You all should be delighted! We've found out the problem, and it turns out to be nothing at all.'

The Director spun on him. '*Nothing?* You insipid biological, can't you see? This is a disaster!

'We counted on hyperspace to open the stars for us. But it is infernally expensive to use unless we keep the ships small.

'And how can we keep them small if we must build huge, intricate cooling systems that must look out into that boiling hell you found? With the trickle of cryogens we'll be able to maintain during those weeks in hyperspace, it will be nearly impossible to maintain life aboard!

'You say our problems are solved,' the Director spoke acidly. 'But you miss one point, Witness Engineer Forbs! How will we ever find crews to man those ships?'

The Director hummed with barely suppressed anger, his eye-cells glowing.

Jason rubbed his chin and pursed his lips sympathetically. 'Well, I don't know. But I'd bet with a few minor improvements something could be arranged. Why don't you try recruiting crews from another "boiling hell" . . . one where water ice is already melted?'

There was silence for a moment. Then, from the back of the room, came laughter. A mechano with a seal of office hanging from its humaniform neck clapped its hands together and grinned. 'Oh, wait till they hear of this on Earth! *Now* we'll see how the voting goes!' He grinned at Jason and laughed in rich, human tones. 'When the biologicals find out about this, they'll rise up like the very tide! And so will every closet Ethicalist in the system!'

Jason smiled, but right now his mind was far from politics. All he knew was that his wife and son would not live in shame. His boy would be a starship rider, and inherit the galaxy.

'You won't have any trouble recruiting crews, sir,' he told the Director. 'I'm ready to go back any time. Hyperspace isn't all that bad a place.

'Would you care to come along?'

Super-cold steam vented from the Director's carapace, a loud hiss of indignation. The Utilitarian bureaucrat ground out something too low for Jason to overhear, even though he leaned forward politely.

The laughter from the back of the room rose in peals of hilarity. Jason sipped his lemonade, and waited.

Whose Millennium?

The year 1999, seven months,
From the sky will come a great King of terror,
To resuscitate the great King of Angoumois,
Before, after, Mars will reign by good luck.

– Nostradamus

Get ready for some unforgettable parties during the run-up to December 31, 1999. It won't just be the turn of a century that sets the champagne flowing, but a whole new millennium, when the great big digital clock of the common era will squeak, groan and finally click a new digit upon the thousand-year slot. To all the planets and stars, rocks and trees, it will be just another day. But none of them love celebrating milestones at the drop of a metaphor. We humans do.

A few wise guys will point out that January 1, 2000 *isn't* the official start of century Twenty-One, after all. Just as the numeral '10' finishes a decade, the next century won't technically begin until the stroke of midnight, December 31, 2000. Most folks will ignore the pundits and celebrate a year early anyway . . . then convert as soon as the hangovers wear off. (Who could pass up a chance to throw turn-of-millennium parties *twice*?)

Some people take the upcoming transition more seriously. For instance, platoons of computer programmers are rushing to refit software for banks and insurance companies whose commercial databases have '19—' shortsightedly fixed permanently in the year-date field. Then there are Hollywood screenwriters, who used to set every 'near-future' drama in the year 1997. Anything occurring after 2000 was 'far-out' sci-fi stuff. Just shows how much they knew.

The turn of the century will bring yet another phenomenon, at once sillier and far more earnest – *millennial fever*, when latter-day Jeremiahs seem sure to tell us that *The Day* is nigh. Soon, very soon, those voices will rise in pitch, announcing the impending end of the world.

Proclamations of doom are perennial flowers which have sprouted in the garden of human imagination since earliest times. Oracles appeared whenever turmoil caused nations and peoples to feel uncertain about the future. From ancient Sumer, to India, to Iceland, astrological portents used to set off recurring waves of public hysteria.

Ambiguity is the prophet's major stock in trade. King Croesus bribed the Delphic Oracle for good news, so the priests told him what he wanted to hear. If he marched on Persia he would destroy a great empire. He marched, and the empire he destroyed was his own.

Some doom-prophecies proved devastatingly self-fulfilling. When Cortez marched on Tenochtitlan, the Aztecs were paralysed by similarities between his arrival and the prophesied return of their god, Quetzalcoatl. That paralysis led to the Aztecs' fall. At Troy, Cassandra and Lacöon warned unavailingly against accepting gift horses, showing that all Jeremiahs aren't heeded.

We remember each of these foretellings because they came true. Those that fail are seldom noted – much to the relief of today's tabloid prophets.

Something in human nature seems fascinated by the end of all things. Is it simply an extension of the smaller death each of us faces? Or perhaps a streak of egotism is involved, for out of countless human generations, it would surely mark ours as unique to be the *last*. Folk myths about humanity's swan song range from the Vikings' awful Ragnarok to universal bliss, and all shades between. Often these myths foresee dividing humankind into an *elect*, who will experience rapture, and those doomed to eternal punishment for misdeeds in this world.

'Messianism' focuses on an awaited deliverer, who will right wrongs, settle scores, and change the known cosmos more to the liking of those doing the waiting. For example, the Zoroastrians of Persia prophesied a 'third saviour', who would purify the land and resurrect the dead. North American plains Indians, inspired by 'ghost shirt' magic, believed certain signs augured invincibility to their forlorn cause of driving Europeans from the continent. During the mid-nineteenth century, half of China was consumed by the Tai'Ping rebellion, whose charismatic leader claimed to be the younger brother of Jesus.

Larger, more conservative religions also carry notions of divine, overpowering intervention. Buddhism awaits the bodhisattva, Maitreya, to create paradise on Earth. In orthodox Islam a prophesied Mahdi is destined to usher a new age. The celebratory frenzy which accompanied Ayatollah Khomeini's return to Iran may have been amplified by occurring almost exactly fourteen centuries after the birth of the Prophet.

Christian millennialists drew inspiration from many sources, such as the promise in the gospels that Jesus

would return '. . . before this generation shall have
passed away . . .' to complete his messianic task. By
far the most influential text is *The Book of Revelations*,
which tells in florid, metaphorical detail about the
rise and fall of characters such as 'the Beast', and
the 'Whore of Babylon'. In every generation, tracts
have been published which analysed that mysterious
tome, line by line, showing how each obscure phrase
and parable connected to events taking place in the
author's own region and time. For example, during
the approach to year 1800, a zealous flood of printed
interpretations correlated the French Revolution and
Napoleon's rise to verses of prophecy, proving to the
writers' satisfaction that armageddon was nigh.

Alas for those eagerly expecting Judgement Day, the
rumblings heard in the sky were only cannon.

In the run-up to year 1000 of the common era,
thousands throughout Europe divested their farms,
property, the clothes on their backs, expecting an
imminent end. Other episodes occurred at uneven
intervals, such as in year 1260, but one could always
count on a special surge at each turn of the hundreds
column. Popes even proclaimed Roman jubilees, to
attract predictable waves of concerned pilgrims whenever round numbers rolled along.

Our own era has seen tabloid oracles, TV evangelists and millennialist politicians, all weighing in
to satisfy a seemingly inexhaustible human need for
mystic hope mixed liberally with terror. And, in
fairness, religion has not been the sole font of apoca-
lyptic scenarios. New Age spiritualists have joined in,
touting everything from Aquarianism and astrology
to a fleet of UFOs, due to land just outside San
Diego, California. Meanwhile, the past decade saw
survivalists stocking private fortresses in eager dread
of a coming end to civilisation, which, they were

certain, would cull the virtuously prepared from the culpably weak.

Books such as Hal Lindsey's runaway bestseller, *The Late, Great, Planet Earth*, revealed to millions the 'obvious' identity of the Soviet Union as the Devil's final fortress, foretold in scripture. Ronald Reagan's Interior Secretary, James Watt, declared environmentalism moot for the simple reason that the Earth was scheduled to end soon anyway, so why bother saving trees? In retrospect, these pronouncements may seem quaint, with the USSR fading into archeological dust along with Nineveh and Babylon, but one sees no retractions by Lindsey or others. The armageddon merchants simply rearrange the details of their prophecies in order to keep up with each geo-political turn.

Will Japan or China replace Russia as the next arch-foe of Heaven's host? Will we soon hear political candidates accusing each other of being the Antichrist? One thing is certain – a single riveting symbol will come to dominate the years ahead – the sight of those eerie triple-zeroes in the figure, 2000.

> *And when the thousand years are completed,*
> *Satan will be released from his prison . . .*
> *– The Book of Revelations*

Nearly all millennialists share an interesting premise, that the entire vast universe was fashioned by a creator with a penchant for brief experiments, foregone conclusions, petty vengeance, and mysterious riddles. During most of human history, this might have seemed a reasonable model of the world, since life appeared so capricious, so instantly and inexplicably revocable. To some extent, that age-old sense of helplessness and enigma remains. Only under a conceited gloss of modernity do we dare step forward and (without

meaning any deliberate offence) attempt to pose a
question or two.

For instance, even granting the aforementioned godly
premise, why would a creator of universes base his
doomsday timetable on a *human* dating system? Might
He not use ticks of an atomic clock, marking off radium
half-lives until phhht? Or, going by certain biblical
passages, should we estimate how many sparrows, or
shooting stars, have fallen since the Earth began?

For that matter, why count down in decimal? Why
not base six, used by the Babylonian inventors of
the calendar? Or *binary* notation? In the code native
to computers, this year, 1994 of the common era,
translates as 011111001010. It will be a much rounder
10000000000 on the date AD 2048, and a symmetrical,
mysterious-looking 11111011111 in 2015. On the
other hand, if prime numbers are His thing, then
both 1997 and 1999 fit the bill in any notation.

Assuming the Omnipotent simply cannot resist
round multiples of ten, and conveniently chose Earth's
orbital period as the unit of measure, what date shall we
figure He is counting *from*? To Hindus, a three-billion-
year cycle of creation and destruction passes through
multiple 'Yugas', of which the present is but one of the
more threadbare. The Mayans believe in cycles of 256
years, based on motions of moon and planets. The most
recent shift occurred in 1954.

To certain Christian fundamentalists, the answer is
plain. *Obviously*, the countdown began at the pivot
point of the common era calendar, the birth of Jesus
of Nazareth.

Unfortunately, that postulate presents problems.
Regarding the actual date of nativity, biblical scholars
disagree over a range of five years or more. Nor is
there good evidence that the *month and day* assigned
to Christmas under the Gregorian Calendar have

anything to do with the celebrated event. (Eastern Orthodoxy commemorates Christmas weeks later.) Early church leaders may have meant to match the popular solstice festivals of the Mithraic Cult, followed by their patron, Emperor Constantine, thus making conversion of pagans easier.

It gets worse. Suppose we reach the year 2005, and nothing has happened? Are we rid of millennialists until the next century rolls around? Not a chance! Doom-seers are well practised at the art of recalculation. In the nineteenth century, one mid-western preacher managed to hold on to his flock through *six* successive failures of the skies to open, until at last he was abandoned by all but the most fervent and forgiving.

Here is just one of the excuses we are bound to hear:

'Of course, the countdown shouldn't date from the birth of Jesus. After all, the chief event of his life, the promise of redemption and resurrection, came at the end of his earthly span.

If so – assuming the clock has been ticking from Calvary to Armageddon – we would seem in for a slight reprieve, and yet *another* wave of millennial fever set to strike some time in the mid-2030s. Again, the lack of any specific written record in Roman or Judean archives will let enthusiasts proclaim dates spread across five or six years, but at least the *season* won't be vague – sometime around Easter, or during the Passover holiday.

We've only begun to plumb the options available to millennial prophets. While some sects focus on two thousand Christmases, and others on as many Easters, there will certainly be those who consider such thinking small-scale and altogether too *New Testament*. After all, why should the Creator terminate His universe on the anniversary of some event which took place midway through its span? Why not start counting from its *origin*?

It so happens that another nice, round anniversary is coming up, which just fits the bill. Remember Archbishop Ussher of Armagh? He's the fellow who carefully logged every *begat* in the Bible, then declared that the creation of the world must have occurred at nine o'clock in the morning, on October 25 of the year 4004 BC.

Now, there has been a considerable amount of teasing directed at poor Ussher, since he made this sincere calculation back in 1654. His results don't jibe too well with the testimony of rocks, fossils, stars, or the scientists who study such things. Still, he has followers even today, folk who believe that all physical evidence for a vastly older Earth (four and a half billion years) was planted to 'test our faith'. (One might ask in reply, if the Lord went to so much effort to convince us the world is billions of years old, who are *we* to doubt it?)

If Ussher fixated on time's origin, the famed founder of the Protestant Reformation, Martin Luther, had something to say about its end. Luther took into account that '. . . a day is as a thousand years to the Lord . . .' (Psalms 90:4), and that genesis itself took six days. He then concluded that the Earth's duration would thus be 6,000 years from first light to the trump of doom. Further, this span would be symmetrically divided into three 2,000-year stretches, from Origin to the time of Abraham, from Abraham to Jesus, and a final two millennia rounding things off at Judgement Day. While this speculation drew little attention back in Luther's day, it is sure to appeal to modern millennialists, hoping for the good luck of witnessing the end in their own time.

Unfortunately, combining Luther's logic with Ussher's date (4004 BC) shows that we've just shaved four years off the countdown! Now the end comes in October, 1996! No time for that final stab at the Winter Olympics then, or to pay off the car loan. Celestial trumpets would blow two weeks before the Democrats' last best hope to retain the White House. Remember, you heard it here.

Drat. It hardly leaves any time for me to collect royalties on the paperback edition of this book!

We may win a *little* breather on a technicality. Since there was no Year Zero in the common era calendar (One BC was followed immediately by One AD), the Ussher–Luther deadline shifts to autumn, 1997! Alas, still too short a reprieve to save those lovely turn-of-the-century parties we're all looking forward to.

Fortunately, old Bishop Ussher wasn't the only one counting off from Adam and Eve. The Jews have been at it much longer, and by the Hebrew Calendar it is only year number 5753, which seems special to no one but mathematicians.

What of Jewish millennialists, then? Back in the 1640s, followers of Sabbatai Zevi believed passionately that the end had come, but neither that 'false messiah', nor Jacob Frank in the 1720s, brought any New Kingdom, only disappointment. Since then, most Jewish scholars have put less faith in vague riddles of a single manifestation than in a growing maturity of human culture, or a 'messianic age' . . . an attitude which baffles some Christian evangelists no end.

Is the coming orgy of millennialism simply to be endured by the rest of us until it's over? As with UFO cults, there is no such thing as 'disproof' to those who can always find convenient explanations for each failed prophecy. It is useless citing scientific data to refute the supernatural.

There *are* methods for dealing with doomsday cant however. One is to turn things around, and confront millennialists on their own turf. In the end, the entire question revolves around symbols.

In Judeo-Christian mythology, two chief metaphors are used to describe the relationship between the creator and humankind. The first of these depicts a 'shepherd-and-his-flock'. The second describes a 'father-and-his-children'. These parables are used interchangeably, but they *aren't* equivalent. Rather, to modern eyes they are polar opposites, as irreconcilable as the tiny, closed cosmos of Ussher and the vast universe of Galileo.

A shepherd protects his flocks, guiding them to green pastures, as the psalms so poignantly portray. All the shepherd expects in return is unquestioning obedience ... and everything else the sheep possess. Lucky ones are merely shorn, but that reprieve is brief. None escapes its ultimate fate. None has any right to complain.

Everybody also knows about *fathers*. Young sons and daughters are expected to obey, when discipline is tight for their own good. Nevertheless, with time, offspring learn to think for themselves. Even in patriarchal societies, a good father takes pride in the accomplishments of his children, even – especially – when they exceed his own. If there *is* a fore-ordained plan, it is for those children to become good mothers and fathers, in turn.

To the perennial, millennial oracles, with their message of looming destruction, *here* is a head-on response. Ask them this. 'Are we children of a Father, or a Shepherd's sheep? You can't have it both ways.

'You preach a tale of violent harvest,' the challenge continues, 'of judgement without debate or appeal, fatal and permanent. A shepherd might so dispose of lambs, but what sane *father* does thus to his offspring? Would *you* stand by, if a neighbour down the street commenced such a programme on his flesh and blood?

'Anyway, you choose an odd time to proclaim the adventure over, just when we've begun *picking up* creation's tools, learning, as apprentices do, the methods of a great Designer. Those techniques now lie before us, almost as if someone placed blueprints to the universe to be pored over by eager minds. By those perhaps ready soon to leave childhood and begin adult work.'

The latest crop of millennial prophets might be asked, what do *sheep* owe the shepherd of a cramped pasture, a cheap, expendable world just 6,000 years old, limited to one ball of dirt, one sentient race?

Personally, I prefer a universe countless billions of parsecs wide, vast and old enough for a hundred million vivid, exciting creations. An evolving, growing cosmos. One worthy of respect.

Time will tell. We, humanity, may yet thrive or fry by dint of our own wisdom or folly. The macrocosm may be, as secularists say, indifferent to our fate.

Or, perhaps some great mind out there does see, does care. If so, that spirit may be more patient than doomsayers credit, with a design far subtler, yet more honest. A truly *creative* Creator would surely be disappointed in an experiment which ended so trivially, or soon.

COSMOS

Bubbles

1

On planets, they say, water always runs downhill . . .

Serena had no way of knowing if it was true. She had
never been on a planet. Not in the brief million or
so years she had been aware. Neither had any of her
acquaintances. The very idea was ridiculous.

Very few Grand Voyageurs ever got a chance to *see* a
planet. And yet, even among them, the ancient truisms
were still told.

That which goes up must fall, and will . . .

She had been willing to take their word for it. The
clichés came out of a foggy past. Why should she
question them? Why should she care?

No matter how far down you fall, you can go lower still . . .

Stunned and still nearly senseless from her passage
through the maelstrom, Serena numbly contemplated
truths inherited down the eons from distant times when

her ancestors actually dwelled on tiny slivers of rock,
down close to the bright flames of burning stars.

She had had no inkling, when she had tunneled away
from Spiral Galaxy 998612a with a full cargo, that the
ancient sayings would soon apply to her.

Or do they? she wondered. Was she perhaps as far
down as one could possibly get? It seemed to Serena,
right then, that there just wasn't any lower to go.

Her systems creaked and groaned as her instruments readapted to normal space-time. Serena still
felt the heat of her passage through Kaluza space.
The incandescent journey through the bowels of the
singularity had raised her temperature dangerously
near the fatal point.

Now, though, she realised that her radiators were
spilling that excess heat into a coldness like none
she had ever known before. Blackness stretched in
all directions around her. *Impossible. My sensors must
be damaged*, she hoped.

But the repair drones reported nothing wrong
with her instruments. The real harm had been done
elsewhere.

Then why can I not see any stars?

She increased the sensitivity of her opticals, increased
it again, and at last began to see a pattern – a spray of
tiny motes of light – spread across the black vault.

Tiny, tiny, faraway spirals and fuzzy globes. Galaxies.

Had she been an organism, Serena might have
blinked, have closed her eyes against the dismay.

Only galaxies?

Serena had travelled deep space all her life. It
was her mission – carrying commerce between far-
flung islands of intelligence. She was used to black
emptiness.

But not like this!

Galaxies, she thought. No stars, only *galaxies*, *everywhere*.

She knew galaxies, of course — island universes containing gas clouds and dust and vast myriads of stars, from millions to trillions each. Her job, after all, was to haul gifts from one spiral swirl to the next, or to and from great elliptical giants, galaxies so huge that it seemed extravagant of the universe to have made more than one.

She had spent a million years carrying cargo from one galaxy to another, and yet had never been outside of one before.

Outside! She quailed from the thought, staring at the multitude of foggy specks all around her. *But there isn't anything outside of galaxies!*

Oh, she had always used distant ones for navigation, as stable points of reference. But always they had been drowned out in a swarm of nearby stars. Always there had been one great galactic disk, vast because it lay all around her, a bright, restless, noisy place filled with traffic and bustling civilisations.

She had always felt sorry for the members of those hot little cultures, so busy, so quick. They flashed through their tiny lives so briefly. They never got to see the great expanses, the vistas that she travelled. Their kind had *made* her kind, long ago. But that was so far in the past, now, that few planet-dwellers any longer knew where the Grand Voyageurs had come from. They simply took Serena and her cousins for granted.

No, she had never been outside before. For travelling *among* the galaxies had never meant travelling *between* them.

Her job was to ply the deep ways at the hearts of those galactic swirls, where stars were packed so dense and tight that their light hardly had room to escape, where they whirled and danced quick pavanes, and occasionally collided in brilliant fury.

Sometimes the crowded stars combined. In the core of nearly every galaxy there lay at least one great black hole, a gravitational well so deep that space itself warped and curled in tight geometries of compression. And these singularities offered paths – paths from one galaxy to another.

The great nebulae were not linked at their edges, but at their hearts.

So how did I get here! Serena wondered. *Here, so far from any galaxy at all?*

Part of the answer, she knew, lay in her cargo bay. Pallet fourteen was a twisted ruin. It was some violent event there that had bruised her Kaluza fields, just at the most critical phase of diving into a singularity, when she had to tunnel from one loop of space-time to another.

In disgust, she used several of her remote drones to pry apart the tortured container. The drones played light over a multicoloured, spiny mass. Needlelike projections splayed in all directions, like rays of light frozen in mid-spray. The thing was quite beautiful. And it had certainly killed her.

Idiots! She cursed. Nobody had informed her that antimatter was part of her cargo. Now she understood the explosion, at least. Down in Kaluza space, nature made a big distinction between antimatter and the 'Koino-' or normal variety. It was one reason why antimatter was so rare in the cosmos. The galaxies and nearly everything else were made of Koino-matter.

In Kaluza space, normal means for containing antimatter were inadequate. Inadequate by far! It was such a widely known phenomenon, so simple. She had thought even the most simple-minded quick-life cultures would know to take precautions.

She tried to think. To remember.

In that last galaxy there had been funny little creatures who twittered at her in languages so obscure that even her sophisticated linguistic programs could barely follow them. The beings had used no machines, she recalled, but instead flitted about their star-filled galactic core on the backs of great winged beast/craft made of protoplasm. A few of the living 'ships' were so large that Serena had been able to see them unmagnified – as specks fluttering near her great bulk. It was the first time she recalled ever seeing life up close, without artificial aid.

Perhaps the creatures had not understood that machine intelligences like Serena had special needs. Perhaps they thought . . .

Serena had no idea what they thought. All she knew was that their cargo had exploded just as she was midway down the narrow Way between that galaxy and another, diving and swooping along paths of twisted space.

To lose power in a singularity. Serena wondered. It had happened to none of the Voyageurs she had ever encountered. But sometimes Voyageurs *disappeared*. Perhaps this was what happened to the ones who vanished.

Galaxies.

Her attention kept drifting across the vault surrounding her. The brush-strokes of light lay scattered almost evenly across the sky. It was unnerving to see so many galaxies, and no stars. No stars at all.

Plenty of stars, she corrected herself. But all of them smeared – in their billions – into those islands in the sky. None of the galaxies appeared to be appreciably above average in size, or appreciably closer than any other.

By this time her radiator had cooled far below the

danger level. How could they not? It was as cold here as it ever could get. Enough light struck her to keep the temperature just near three degrees absolute. Some of that faint light came from the galaxies. The rest was long-wave radiation from space itself. It was smooth, isotropic. The slowly ebbing roar of the long-ago birth of everything.

Her remote drones reported in. Repairs had progressed. She could move, if she chose.

Great, she thought. *Move where?*

She experimented. Her drives thrummed. She felt action and reaction as pure laser light thrust from her tail. Her accelerometers swung.

That was it. There was no other way she could tell she was moving at all. There were no reference points, whose relationships would slowly shift as she swept past. The galaxies were too far away. Much, much too far away.

She tried to think of an adjective, some term from any of the many languages she knew, to convey just how far away they were. The truth of her situation was just sinking in.

Serena knew that a planet-bound creature, such as her distant ancestors, would have looked at her in amazement. She was herself nearly as large as some small planets.

If one of those world-evolved creatures were to find itself on her surface, equipped with the requirements to survive, it might move in its accustomed way – it had been called 'walking', she remembered – and spend its entire brief life span before travelling her length.

She tried to imagine how such creatures must have looked upon the spaces *between* their rocky little worlds, back in their early days. It was a millionfold increase in scale from the size of a planet to that of a solar system. The prospect must have been daunting.

Then, after they had laboriously conquered their home planetary system, how they must have quailed before the interstellar distances, yet *another* million times as great! To Serena, they were routine, but how stunning those spaces must have seemed to her makers! How totally frustrating and unfathomable!

Now she understood how they must have felt.

Serena increased power to her drives. She clung to the feeling of acceleration, spitting light behind her, driving faster and faster. Her engines roared. For a time she lost herself in the passion of it, thrusting with all her might towards a speck of light chosen at random. She spent energy like a wastrel, pouring it out in a frantic need to *move*!

Agoraphobia was a terrible discovery to a Grand Voyageur. She howled at the black emptiness, at the distant, tantalising pools of light. She blasted forth with the heat of her panic.

Galaxies! Any galaxy would do. Any one at all!

Blind to all but terror, she shot like a bolt of light . . . but light was far too slow.

Sense took hold at last, or perhaps some deep-hidden wisdom circuit she had not even known of, triggered in a futile reflex for self-preservation. Her drives shut down and Serena found herself coasting.

For a time she simply folded inward, closing off from the universe, huddling within a corner of her mind darker even than the surrounding night.

2

Galaxies have their ages, their phases, just as living things do. Aim your telescope towards the farthest specks, distant motes so far away that their light was reddened with the stretching of the universe. The universal expansion makes their flight seem rapid. It also means that the light you see is very, very old.

These, then, are the *youngest* things you will ever see. Quasars and galaxies at the very earliest stages, when the black holes in their cores were hot, still gobbling stars by the hundreds, blaring forth great bursts of light and belching searing beams of accelerated particles.

Look closer. The galaxies you'll see will be flying away from you less quickly, their light will be less reddened. And they will be older.

Pinwheel spirals turn, looking like fried eggs made of a hundred billion sparks. In their centres, the black holes are now calmer. All the easy prey have been consumed, and now only a few stars fall into their maws, from time to time. The raging has diminished enough to let life grow in the slowly rotating hinterlands.

Spiral arms show where clots of gas and giant molecular clouds concentrate in shock waves, like spume and spindrift gathering on a windswept verge. Here new stars are born. The largest of these sweep through their short lives and explode, filling nearby space with heavy elements, fertilising the fields of life.

Barred spirals, irregulars, ellipticals . . . there are other styles of galaxies, as well, sprayed like dandelion seeds across the firmament.

But not randomly. No. Not randomly at all.

3

Slowly, Serena came back to her senses. She felt a distant amusement.

Dandelion seeds?

Somehow, her similes had taken on a style so archaic . . . perhaps it was a form of defensive reaction. Her

memory banks drew forth an image of puffballs bending
before a gusty wind, then scattering sparkling specks
forth . . .

Fair enough, she thought, of the comparison.

All sense of motion was lost, although she knew she
had undergone immense acceleration. The galaxies lay
all around her. Apparently unchanged.

She looked again on the universe around her. Peered
at one quadrant of the sky, then another.

Perhaps they aren't scattered as smoothly as I'd thought.

She contemplated for some time. Then decided.

Fortunately her cargo wasn't anybody's *property*, per
se. *Gifts*. That was what the Grand Voyageurs like her
carried. No civilisation could think of 'trade' between
galaxies. Even using the singularities, there was no way
to send anything in expectation of payment.

No. The hot, quick, short-lived cultures took whatever Grand Voyageurs like Serena brought, and loaded
them down with presents to take to the next stop.
Nobody ever told a Voyageur where to go. Serena
and her cousins travelled wherever whim took them.

So she wasn't really stealing when she started disman-
tling her cargo section, pulling forth whatever she found
and adapting the treasures for her own purposes.

The observatory took only fifty years to build.

4

Strings.

Bubbles.

The galaxies were not evenly distributed through
expanding space. The 'universe' was full of *holes*.

In fact, most of it was emptiness. Light shimmered at
the edges of yawning cavities, like flickers on the surface
of a soap bubble. The galaxies and clusters of galaxies

lay strung at the fringes of monstrous cavities.

While she performed her careful survey, cataloguing and measuring every mote her instruments could find, Serena also sought through her records, through the ancient archives carried by every Grand Voyageur.

She found that she had not been the first to discover this.

The galaxies were linked with one another – via Kaluza space – through the black holes at their centres. A Grand Voyageur travelled those ways, and so never got far enough outside the great spirals to see them in this perspective.

Now, though, Serena thought she understood.

There wasn't just one *Big Bang, at the beginning of time,* she realised. *It was more complicated than that.*

The original kernel had divided early on, and then divided again and again. The universe had many centres of expansion, and it was at the farthest-forward shock waves of those explosions that matter had condensed, roiled, and formed into galaxies and stars.

So I am at the bottom, she realised.

Somehow, when the explosion had sent her tumbling in Kaluza space, she had slipped off the rails. She had fallen, fallen nearly all the way to the centre of one of the great explosions.

One could fall no further.

The calculations were clear on something else, as well. Even should she accelerate with everything she had, and get so close to light-speed that relativistic time foreshortened, she would still never make it even to the nearest galaxy.

Such emptiness, she contemplated. Why, even the cosmic rays were faint, here. And those sleeting nuclei were only passing through. It was rare for Serena to detect even an atom of hydrogen, as a neighbour.

*   *   *

'*It is better, far,*
   to light a candle,
Than to curse the darkness.'

For a time it was only the soft melancholy of ancient
poetry that saved Serena from the one-way solace of
despair.

5

To the very centre, then.
   Why not? Serena wondered.
   According to her calculations, she was much, much
closer to the centre of the great bubble than to any of
the sprayed galaxies at its distant rim.
   Indeed. Why not? It would be something to do.
   She found she only had to modify her velocity a little.
She had already been heading that way by accident,
from that first panicked outburst.
   She passed the time reading works from a million poets, from a million noble races. She created
subpersonae – little separate personalities, which could
argue with each other, discussing the relative merits of
so many planet-bound points of view. It helped to pass
the time.
   Soon, after only a few thousand years, it was time to
decelerate, or she would simply streak past the centre,
with no time even to contemplate the bottom, the navel
of creation.
   Serena used much of her reserve killing the last of
her velocity, relative to the bubble of galaxies. All
around her the red shifts were the same, constant.
All the galaxies seemed to recede away at the
same rate.
   So. Here I am.

She coasted, and realised that she had just completed the last task of any relevance she could ever aspire to. There were no more options. No other deeds that could be done.

'Hello?'

Irritably, Serena wiped her conversation banks, clearing away the subpersonae that had helped her while away the last few centuries. She did not want those little artificial voices disturbing her as she contemplated the manner of bringing about her own end.

I wonder how big a flash I'll make, she thought. *Is it even remotely possible that anyone back in the inhabited universe might see it, even if they were looking this way with the best instruments?*

She caressed the fields in her engines, and knew she had the will to do what had to be done.

'Hello? Has somebody come?'

Serena sent angry surges through her lingula systems. *Stop it.*

Suicide would come none too soon. *I must be going crazy*, she subvocalised, and some of her agony slipped out into space around her.

'Yes, many feel that way, when they arrive here.'

Quakes of surprise made Serena tremble. The voice had come from outside!

'Who . . . who are you?' she gasped.

'I am the one who waits, the one who collects and greets,' the voice replied. And then, after some hesitation:

'I am the coward.'

6

Joy sparkled and burst from Serena. She shouted,

though the only one in the universe to hear her was near enough to touch. She cried aloud.

'There is a *way*!'

The coward was larger than Serena. He drifted nearby, looking like nothing so much as a great assemblage of junk from every and any civilisation imaginable. He had already explained that the bits and pieces had been contributed by countless stranded entities before her. By now he was approaching the mass of a small star, and had to hold the pieces apart with webs of frozen field lines.

The coward seemed disturbed by Serena's enthusiasm.

'But I've already explained to you, it *isn't* a way! It is death!'

Serena could not make it clear to the thing that she had already been ready to die. 'That remains to be seen. All I know is that you have told me that there is a way out of this place, and that many have arrived here before me, and taken that route away from here.'

'I tell you it is a funnel into Hell!'

'So a black hole seems, to planet-dwellers, but we Grand Voyageurs dive into them, and traverse the tortured lanes of Kaluza space—'

'And I have told you that this is not a black hole! And what lies within this opening is not Kaluza space, but a door into madness and destruction!'

Serena found that she pitied the poor thing. She could not imagine choosing, as it obviously had, to sit here at the centre of nothingness for all eternity, an eternity broken every few million years by the arrival of one more stranded voyager. Apparently every one of Serena's predecessors had ignored the poor thing's advice, given him what they had to spare, and eagerly taken that escape offered, no matter how hazardous.

'Show it to me, pleease,' she asked politely.
The coward sighed, and turned to lead the way.

7

It has long been hypothesised that there was more than
one episode of creation. The discovery that the universe of
galaxies is distributed like soap bubbles, each expanding
from its own centre, was the great confirmation that the
Big Bang, at least, had not been undivided.

But the ideas went beyond that.

What if, they had wondered, even in ancient days,
what if there are other universes altogether?

She and Coward traded data files while they moved
leisurely towards the Hole at the very centre of All.
Serena was in no hurry, now that she had a destination again. She savoured the vast store of knowledge
Coward had accumulated.

Her own Grand Voyageurs were not the first, it
seemed, to have cruised the great wormholes between
the galaxies. There were others, some greater, who
had nevertheless found themselves for whatever reason
shipwrecked here at the base of everything.

And all of them, no doubt, had contemplated the
dizzying emptiness that lay before them now.

A steady stream of very strange particles emanated
from a twisted shapelessness. Rarities, such as magnetic monopoles, swept past Serena more thickly than
she ever would have imagined possible. Here, they were
more common than *atoms*.

**'As I said, it leads to another place, a place
where the fundamentals of our universe do not
hold. We can tell very little from this side,
only that *charge*, *mass*, *gravity*, all have different**

meanings, there. Tell me, then, what hope does a creature of our universe have of surviving there? Will your circuits conduct? Will your junctions quantum-jump properly? Will your laser drives even function if electrons aren't allowed to occupy the same energy state?'

For a moment the coward's fear infected Serena. The closer she approached, the more eerie and dangerous this undertaking seemed.

'And nobody has ever come back out again,' Coward whispered.

Serena shook herself out of her funk. Her situation remained the same. If this was nothing more than yet another way to suicide, at least it had the advantage of being interesting.

And who knows? Many of my predecessors were wiser than I, and they all chose this path, as well.

'I thank you for your friendship,' she told the coward. 'I give you all of this spare mass, from my cargo, as a token of affection.'

Resignedly, the coward sent drone ships to pick up the baggage Serena shed. They cruised away into the blackness.

'What you see is only a small fraction of what I have accumulated,' he explained.

'How much?'

He gave her a number, and for a long moment there was only silence between them. Then Coward went on.

'And lately, you castaways have been growing more and more common. I have hope that, soon, someone shall arrive who will leave me more than fragments.'

Serena pulsed to widen the gap between them. She began to feel a soft tug – something wholly unlike gravity, or any other force she had ever known.

'I wish you well,' she said.

The coward, too, began to back away. The other's voice was chastened, sombre. **'So many others seem to find me pitiable, because I wait here, because I am not adventuresome.'**

'I do believe you will find your own destiny,' she told him. She dared not say what she really thought, so she kept her words vague. 'You will find greatness that surpasses that of even those much more bold in spirit,' she predicted.

Then, before the stunned ancient thing could reply, she turned and accelerated towards her destiny.

8

On planets, they say, water always runs downhill . . .

From the bottom, from as low as one could go in all the universe, Serena plunged downward into another place. Her shields thickened and her drives flexed. As ready as she would ever be, she dived into the strangeness ahead.

She thought about the irony of it all.

He calls himself Coward . . . she contemplated, and knew that it was unfair.

She, and all of those who had plunged this way, blindly into the unknowable, were the real cowards in a way. Oh, she could only speak for herself, but she guessed that their greatest motive was fear, fear of the long loneliness, the empty eons without anything to *do*.

And all the while, Coward accumulated mass: bits of space junk . . . debris cast out from Kaluza space . . . cargo jettisoned or donated by castaways who, like her, were only passing through . . .

He had told Serena how much mass. And then he had told her that the rate of accumulation was slowly growing, over the long epochs.

And with the mass, he accumulates knowledge. For Serena had opened her libraries to him, and found them absorbed more quickly than she would ever have thought possible. The same thing must have happened countless times before.

Already space had warped beyond recognition around her. Serena looked back and out at all the galaxies, distant motes of light now smeared into swirls of lambent glow.

Astronomers of every civilisation puzzle over the question of the missing mass, Serena thought.

Calculations showed that there had to be more mass than could be counted by measuring the galaxies, and what could be detected of the gases in between. Even cosmic rays and neutrinos could not account for it. Half of the matter was simply missing.

Coward had told her. He was accumulating it. Here and there. Dark patches, clots, stuffed in field-stabilised clusters scattered around the vast emptiness of the centre of the great galactic bubble.

Perhaps I should have stayed and talked with him some more, Serena thought, as the smeared light melded into a golden glory.

She might have told him. She might have said it. But with all of his brain-power, no doubt he had figured it out long ago, and chose to hide the knowledge away.

All that mass.

Someday the galaxies would die. No new stars would be born. The glow would fade. Life – even life crafted out of baryonic machines – would glimmer and go out.

But the recession of the dead whirlpools would slow. It would stop, reverse, and fall again, towards the great gravitational pull at the centre of each bubble. And there, universes would be born anew.

Serena saw the last glimmer of galactic light twinkle and disappear. She knew the real reason why she had chosen to take this gamble, to dive into this tunnel to an alien realm.

It was one thing to flee loneliness.

It was quite another thing to flee one who would be God.

No wonder all the others had made the same choice.

The walls of the tunnel converged. All around her was strangeness.

Ambiguity

1

Back when he was still a student, Stan Goldman and his friends used to play a game of make-believe.

'How long do you think it would take Isaac Newton to solve this homework set?' they would ask each other. Or, 'If Einstein were alive today, do you think he'd bother with graduate school?'

It was the same sort of lazy, get-nowhere argument he also heard his musician friends debate on occasion: 'What d'you figure Mozart would make of our stuff,' they'd pose over bottles of beer, 'if we snatched him from his own time to the 1990s? Would he freak out and call it damn noise? Or would he catch on, wear mirror shades, and cut an album right away?'

At that point, Stan used to break in. 'Which Mozart do you mean? The arriviste social climber? The craftsman of the biographies? Or the brash rebel of *Amadeus*?'

The composers and players seemed puzzled by his non sequitur. 'Why, the real one, of course.' Their reply convinced him that, for all their closeness, for all their well-known affinity, physicists and musicians would never fully understand each other.

Oh, I see. The real one . . . of course . . .
But what is reality?

Through a thick portal of fused quartz, mediated
by a series of three hundred field-reinforced half
mirrors, Stan now watched the essence of nothingness.
Suspended in a sealed vacuum, a *potential* singularity
spun and danced in nonexistence.

In other words, the chamber was empty.

Soon, though, potentiality would turn into reality.
The virtual would become actual. Twisted space would
spill light and tortured vacuum would briefly give forth
matter. The utterly improbable would happen,.

Or at least that was the general idea. Stan watched
and waited, patiently.

Until the end of his life, Albert Einstein struggled
against the implications of quantum mechanics.

He had helped invent the new physics. It bore
his imprint as fully as Dirac's or Heisenberg's or
Bohr's. And yet, like Max Planck, he had always felt
uncomfortable with its implications, insisting that the
Copenhagen rules of probabilistic nature must be mere
crude approximations of the *real* patterns governing the
world. Beneath the dreadful quantum ambiguity, he
felt there must be the signature of a designer.

Only the design eluded Einstein. Its elegant precision fled before experimentalists, who prodded first
atoms, then nuclei, and at last the so-called 'fundamental' particles. Always, the deeper they probed, the
fuzzier grew the mesh of creation.

In fact, to a later generation of physicists, ambiguity
was no enemy. Rather it became a tool. It was the law.
Stan grew up picturing Nature as a whimsical goddess.
She seemed to say: *Look at me from afar, and you may pretend*
that there are firm rules – that here is cause and there effect. But
remember, if you need this solace, stay back, and squint!

If, on the other hand, you dare approach – should you examine my garments' weft and warp – well, then, don't say I didn't warn you.

With this machine, Stan Goldman expected to be looking closer than anyone ever had before. And he did not expect much security.

'You ready down there, Stan?'

Alex Lustig's voice carried down the companionway. He and the others were in the control centre, but Stan had volunteered to keep watch here by the peephole. It was a vital job, but one requiring none of the quickness of the younger physicists . . . in other words, just right for an old codger like himself. 'I'm ready as I'll ever be, Alex,' he called back.

'Good. Your timer should start running . . . now!'

True to Alex's word, the display to Stan's left began counting down whirling milliseconds.

After the end of the Gaia War, when things had calmed down enough to allow a resumption of basic science, their efforts had soon returned to studying the basic nature of singularities. Now, in this lab far beyond the orbit of Mars, they had received permission to embark on the boldest experiment yet.

Stan wiped his palms on his dungarees and wondered why he felt so nervous. After all, he had participated in the manufacture of bizarre objects before. In his youth, at CERN, it had been a zoo of subatomic particles, wrought out of searing heat at the target end of a great accelerator. Even in those days, the names physicists gave the particles they studied told you more about their own personalities than the things they pursued.

He recalled graffiti on the wall of the men's room in Geneva:

Question: What do you get when you mix a charmed red quark with a strange one that's green and a third that's true blue?

Underneath were scrawled answers, in various hands and as many languages:

I don't know, but to hold them together you'll need a gluon with attitude!

Sounds like what they served in the cafeteria today.

Speaking of which, anyone here know the Flavour of Beauty?

Doesn't it depend on who's on Top and who's on the Bottom?

I'm getting a hadron just thinking about it.

Hey! What boson thought of this question, anyway?

Yeah. There's a guy who ought to be lepton!

Stan smiled, remembering good times. They had been hunters in those days, he and the others, chasing and capturing specimens of elusive microscopic species, expanding the quarky bestiary till a 'theory of everything' began to emerge. Gravitons and gravitinos. Magnetic monopolies and photinos. With unification came the power to mix and match and use Nature's ambiguity.

Still, he never dreamed he might someday play with singularities – micro black holes – using them as *circuit elements* the same blithe way an engineer might string together inductors and resistors. But young fellows like Alex seemed to take it all in stride.

'Three minutes, Stan!'

'I can read a clock!' he shouted back, trying to sound more irritated than he really was. In truth, he really had lost track of the time. His mind now seemed to move at a tangent to that flow . . . nearly but not quite parallel to the event cone of the objective world.

We're told subjectivity, that old enemy of science, becomes its ally at the level of the quantum. Some say it's only the presence of an observer that causes the probability wave to collapse. It's the observer who ultimately notes the plummet of an electron from its shell, as well as the sparrow in a forest. Without observers, not only is a falling tree without sound . . . it's a concept without meaning.

Of late, Stan had been wondering ever more about that. Nature, even down to the lowliest quark, seemed to be performing as if for an audience. Arguments raged between adherents of the strong and weak anthropic principles, over whether observers were required by the universe or merely convenient to it. But everyone now agreed that having an audience mattered.

So much, then, for the debate over what Newton would say if he were snatched out of his time and brought to the present. His clockwork world was as alien to Stan's as that of a tribal shaman. In fact, in some ways the shaman actually had it hands down over prissy old Isaac. At least, Stan imagined, the shaman would probably make better company at a party.

'One minute! Keep your eye on—'

Alex's voice cut off suddenly as automatic timers sent the crash doors hissing shut. Stan shook himself, hauling his mind back and making an earnest effort to concentrate. It would have been different were there something for him to do. But everything was sequenced, even data collection. Later, they would pore over it all and argue. For now, though, he had only to watch. To observe . . .

Before man, he wondered, *who performed this role for the universe?*

There appears to be no rule that the observer has to be conscious. So animals might have served without being self-aware. And on other worlds, creatures might have existed long before life filled Earth's seas. It isn't necessary that every event, every rockfall, every quantum of light be appreciated, only that some of it, somewhere, come to the attention of someone who notices and cares.

'But then,' Stan debated with himself aloud, 'who

noticed or cared at the beginning? Before the planets? Before stars?'

Who was there in the pre-creation nothing to watch the vacuum fluctuation of all time? The one that turned into the Big Bang?

In his thoughts, Stan answered his own question.

If the universe needs at least one observer in order to exist, then that's the one compelling argument for the necessity of God.

The counter reached zero. Beneath it, the panel of fused quartz remained black. Nevertheless, Stan knew something was happening. Deep in the bowels of the chamber, the energy state of raw vacuum was being forced to change.

Uncertainty. That was the lever. Take a cubical box of space, say a centimetre on a side. Does it contain a proton? If so, there's a limit to how much you can know about that proton with any sureness. You cannot know its momentum more precisely than a given value without destroying your chance of knowing *where* it is. Or if you find a way to zoom in on the box until the proton's location is incredibly exact, then your knowledge of its speed and direction plummets towards zero.

Another linked pair of values is energy and time. You may think you know how much or little energy the box contains. (In a vacuum it tends towards baseline zero.) But what about *fluctuational*? What if bits of matter and anti-matter suddenly appear, only to abruptly disappear again? Then the average would still be the same, and all account books would stay balanced.

Within this chamber, modern trickery was using that very loophole to pry away at Nature's wall.

Stan glanced at the mass gauge. It sped upscale rapidly. Femtograms, picograms, nanograms of matter coalesced in a space too small to measure. Micrograms, milligrams . . . each newly born hadron pair shimmered for a moment too narrow to notice. Particle and antiparticle tried to flee, tried to annihilate. But before they could cancel out again, each was drawn into a trap of folded space, sucked down a narrow funnel of gravity smaller than a proton, with no more personality than a smudge of blackness.

The singularity began taking on serious weight. The mass gauge whirled. Kilograms converted into tons. Tons into kilotons. Boulders, hillocks, mountains poured forth, a torrent flowing into the greedy mouth.

When Stan was young, they said you weren't supposed to be able to make something from nothing. But nature did sometimes let you *borrow*. Alex Lustig's machine was borrowing from vacuum, and instantly paying it all back to the singularity.

That was the secret. Any bank will lend you a million bucks . . . so long as you only want it for a microsecond.

Megatons, gigatons . . . Stan had helped make holes before. Singularities more complex and elegant than this one. But never had anyone attempted anything so drastic or momentous. The pace accelerated.

Something shifted in the sinuses behind his eyes. That warning came moments before the gravimeters began singing a melody of alarm . . . full seconds in advance of the first creaking sounds coming from the reinforced metal walls.

Come on, Alex. You promised this wouldn't run away.

They had come to this lab on a distant asteroid on the off chance something might go wrong. But Stan wondered how much good that would do if their meddling managed to tear a rent in the fabric of everything. There were stories that some scientists

on the Manhattan Project had shared a similar fear.
'What if the chain reaction *doesn't* stay restricted to the
plutonium,' they asked, 'but spreads to iron, silicon,
and oxygen?' On paper it was absurd, but no one knew
until the flash of Trinity, when the fireball finally faded
back to little more than a terrible, glittering cloud.

Now Stan felt a similar dread. What if the singularity
no longer needed Lustig's machine to yank matter out
of vacuum for it? What if the effect carried on and on,
with its own momentum . . . ?

This time we might have gone too far.

He felt them now. The tides. And in the quartz
window, mediated by three hundred half mirrors, a
ghost took shape. It was microscopic, but the colours
were captivating.

The mass scale spun. Stan felt the awful attraction
of the thing. Any moment now it was going to reach
out and drag down the walls, the station, the planetoid
. . . and even then would it stop?

'Alex!' he cried out as gravitational flux stretched his
skin. Viscera migrated towards his throat as, uselessly,
he braced his feet.

'Dammit, you—'

Stan blinked. His next breath wouldn't come. Time
felt suspended.

Then he knew.

It was gone.

Goosebumps shivered in the tidal wake. He looked
at the mass gauge. It read zero. One moment it had
been there, the next it had vanished.

Alex's voice echoed over the intercom, satisfaction
in his voice. 'Right on schedule. Time for a beer, eh?
You were saying something, Stan?'

He searched his memory and somewhere found the
trick to breathing again. Stan let out a shuddering sigh.

'I . . ' He tried to lick his lips, but couldn't even wet them. Hoarsely, he tried again. 'I was going to say . . . you'd better have something up there stronger than beer. Because I need it.'

2

They tested the chamber in every way imaginable, but there was nothing there. For a time it had contained the mass of a small planet. The black hole had been palpable. Real. Now it was gone.

'They say a gravitational singularity is a tunnel to another place,' Stan mused.

'Some people think so. Wormholes and the like may connect one part of space-time with another.' Alex nodded agreeably. He sat across the table, alone with Stan in the darkened lounge strewn with debris from the evening's celebration. Everyone else had gone to bed, but both men had their feet propped up as they gazed through a crystal window at the starry panorama. 'In practice, such tunnels probably are useless. No one will ever use one for transportation, for instance. There's the problem of ultraviolet runaway—'

'That's not what I'm talking about.' Stan shook his head. He poured another shot of whiskey. 'What I mean is, how do we know that hole we created hasn't popped out to become a hazard for some other poor bastards?'

Alex looked amused. 'That's not how it works, Stan. The singularity we made today was special. It grew too fast for our universe to contain it at all.

'We're used to envisioning a black hole, even a micro, as something like a funnel in the fabric of space. But in this case, that fabric rebounded, folded over, sealed the breach. The hole is just *gone*, Stan.'

Stan felt tired and a little tipsy, but damn if he'd let this young hotshot get the better of him. 'I know that! All causality links with our universe have been severed. There's no connection with the thing anymore.

'But still I wonder. Where did it *go*?'

There was a momentary silence.

'That's probably the wrong question, Stan. A better way of putting it would be, What has the singularity *become*?'

The young genius now had that look in his eyes again – the philosophical one. 'What do you mean?' Stan asked.

'I mean that the hole and all the mass we poured into it now "exists" in its own pocket universe. That universe will never share any overlap or contact with our own. It will be a cosmos unto itself . . . now and forever.'

The statement seemed to carry a ring of finality, and there seemed to be little to say after that. For a while, the two of them just sat quietly.

3

After Alex went off to bed, Stan stayed behind and played with his friends, the numbers. He rested very still and used a mental pencil to write them across the window. Equations stitched the Milky Way. It didn't take long to see that Alex was right.

What they had done today was create something out of nothing and then quickly exile that something away again. To Alex and the others, that was that. All ledgers balanced. What had been borrowed was repaid. At least as far as this universe of matter and energy was concerned.

But something *was* different, dammit! Before, there

had been virtual fluctuations in the vacuum. Now, *somewhere*, a tiny cosmos had been born.

And suddenly Stan remembered something else. Something called 'inflation'. And in this context the term had nothing to do with economics.

Some theorists hold that our own universe began as a very, very big fluctuation in the primordial emptiness. That during one intense instant, superdense mass and energy burst forth to begin the expansion of all expansions.

Only there could not have been anywhere near enough mass to account for what we now see . . . and all the stars and galaxies.

'Inflation' stood for a mathematical hat trick . . . a way for a medium, or even small-sized bang to leverage itself into a great big one. Stan scribbled more equations on his mental blackboard and came to see something he hadn't realised before.

Of course. I get it now. The inflation that took place twenty billion years ago was no coincidence. Rather, it was a natural result of that earlier, lesser creation. Our universe must have had its own start in a tiny, compressed ball of matter no heavier than . . . no heavier than . . .

Stan felt his heartbeat as the figure seemed to glow before him.

No heavier than that little 'pocket cosmos' we created today.

He breathed.

That meant that somewhere, completely out of touch or contact, their innocent experiment might have . . . *must* have . . . initiated a beginning. A universal beginning.

Fiat lux.

Let there be light.

'Oh my God,' he said to himself, completely unsure which of a thousand ways he meant it.

Story Notes

Since the days of Olaf Stapledon, science fiction has been attracted to cosmic themes. The three stories in this section are about the shape, nature and fate of the universe ... or universes ... reflecting recent concepts which would have been thought scientifically absurd only a decade ago. The great spacial voids depicted in 'Bubbles' have lately amazed and stymied astronomers, sending theoreticians hurrying back to their models and blackboards to explain why vast reaches of intergalactic space appear to be empty of visible matter. This discovery has lent *texture* to the universe, on a scale so huge as to beggar the imagination. Few SF stories have been written to encompass superclusters of galaxies (most find *one* galaxy more than enough!). I, too, would have shied away, except for one thing – I'm a sucker for a dare.

Cambridge University physicist Stephen Hawking, along with many of his peers, has lately given legitimacy to what had formerly been a far-out, science-fictional concept, that of other cosmos existing in some sense 'parallel' to our own. The second story in this volume, 'Ambiguity', first appeared as a lagniappe to my novel *Earth*, and conveys my humble artist's rendering of the notion Hawking and others have been labouring on . . . that of Baby Universes.

The final story takes even that extravagant idea one step further. In *Earth*, I discuss the *Gaia Hypothesis* of Professors Lovelock and Margulis, which speculates that the planet itself – its oceans and air and ecosystems – might be viewed as a *living thing*. Debate still rages as to whether this is good science or anthropomorphising gone berserk. But Professor Lee Smolin, of Syracuse University, took the Gaia idea and expanded it dramatically, with stunning implications that inspired my story 'What Continues . . . And What Fails . . .'

I only wish I had thought of it first.

What Continues . . . And What Fails . . .

Black. As deep as night is black between the stars.

Deeper than that. Night isn't really black, but a solemn, utter shade of red.

As black, then, as Tenembro Nought, which drinks all colour, texture, substance, from around it, giving back only its awful depth of presence.

But no. She had found redness of an immeasurably profound hue, emerging from that awful pit in space. Not even the singularity was pure enough to typify true blackness. Nor was Isola's own dark mood, for that matter – although, since the visitors' arrival, she had felt smothered, robbed of illumination.

In comparison, a mere ebony lustre of skin and hair seemed too pallid to dignify with the name 'black'. Yet, those traits were much sought after on Pleasence World, one of many reasons a fetch ship had come all this way to claim the new life within her.

The foetus might know blackness, Isola thought, laying a hand over her curved abdomen, feeling a stirring there. She purposely used cool, sterile terms, never calling it 'baby', or a personalised 'she'. Anyway, when is a foetus's sensory innervation up to 'knowing' anything at all? Can one who has never seen light comprehend blackness?

Leaning towards the dimly illuminated field-effect mirror, Isola touched its glass-smooth, silky cool, pseudo-surface. Peering at her own reflection, she found at last what she was looking for.

That's it. Where light falls, never to emerge again.

She brought her face closer still, centring on one jet pupil, an inky well outlined by a dark iris – the universe wherein she dwelt.

'It is said nothing escapes from inside a black hole, but that isn't quite so.'

Mikaela was well into her lecture when Isola slipped into the theatre, late but unrepentant. A brief frown was her partner's only rebuke for her tardiness. Mikaela continued without losing a beat.

'In this universe of ours, the rules seem to allow exceptions even to the finality of great noughts . . .'

Isola's vision adapted and she discreetly scanned the visitors – six space travellers whose arrival had disrupted a quiet, monastic research routine. The guests from Pleasence World lounged on pseudo-life chaises overlooking Mikaela and the dais. Each sleek-furred settee was specially tuned to the needs of its occupant. While the three humans in the audience made little use of their couch amenities – only occasionally lifting fleshy tubes to infuse endorphin-laced oxygen, the squat, toadlike Vorpal and pair of slender Butins had already hooked up for full breathing symbiosis.

Well, they must have known they were coming to a rude outpost station, built with only a pair of humans in mind. Isola and Mikaela had not expected guests until a few months ago, when the decelerating starship peremptorily announced itself, and made its needs known.

Those needs included use of Isola's womb.

'Actually, there are countless misconceptions about

gravitational singularities, especially the massive variety formed in the recoil of a supernova. One myth concerns the possibility of communicating across a black hole's event horizon, to see what has become of all the matter which left this universe so violently and completely, long ago.'

Mikaela turned with a flourish of puffy sleeves towards the viewing tank. Winking one eye, she called up a new image to display in mid-air, above the dais. Brilliance spilled across Mikaela's fair skin and the visitors' multi-hued faces, causing several to flinch involuntarily. Isola smiled.

Titanic fields enveloped and deformed a tortured sun, dragging long shreds of its substance towards a spinning, flattened whirlpool – a disc so bright it searingly outshone the unfortunate nearby star.

'Until now, most investigations of macro black holes have concentrated on showy cases like this one – the Cygnus A singularity – which raises such ferocious tides on a companion sun as to tear it apart before our eyes. In galactic cores, greedy mega holes can devour entire stellar clusters. No wonder most prior expeditions were devoted to viewing noughts with visible accretion discs. Besides, their splashy radiance makes them easy to find.'

Isola watched the victim star's tattered, stolen essence spiral into the planate cyclone, which brightened painfully despite attenuation by the viewing software. Shimmering, lambent stalks traced magnetically directed plasma beams, jetting from the singularity north and south. As refulgent gas swirled inward, jostling and heating, it suddenly reached an inner lip – the edge of a black circle, tiny in diameter but awesome in conclusiveness. The Event Horizon.

Spilling across that boundary, the actinic matter vanished abruptly, completely. Once over the edge, it was no longer part of reality. Not *this* reality, anyway.

Mikaela had begun her lecture from a basic level, since some of the visitors weren't cosmogonists. One of these, Jarlquin, the geneticist from Pleasence, shifted on her chaise. At some silent order, a pseudo-life assistant appeared to massage her shoulders. Petite, even for a starfarer, Jarlquin glanced towards Isola, offering a conspiratorial smile. Isola pretended not to notice.

'Most massive noughts don't have stars as close neighbours, nor gas clouds to feed them so prodigiously and make them shine.' Closing one eye again, Mikaela sent another command. In a flickered instant, the ostentatious display of stellar devouring was replaced by serene quiet. Cool, untroubled constellations spanned the theatre. Tenembro Nought was a mere ripple in one quadrant of the starry field, unnoticed by the audience until Mikaela's pointer drew attention to its outlines. A lenslike blur of distortion, nothing more.

'Solitary macro-singularities like Tenembro are far more common than their gaudy cousins. Standing alone in space, hungry, but too isolated to draw in more than a rare atom or meteoroid, they are also harder to find. Tenembro Nought was discovered only after detecting the way it bent light from faraway galaxies.

'The black hole turned out to be perfect for our needs, and only fifty-nine years, shiptime, from the colony on Kalimarn.'

Under Mikaela's mute guidance, the image enlarged. She gestured towards a corner of the tank, where a long, slender vessel could be seen, decelerating into orbit around the cold dimple in space. From the ship's tail emerged much smaller ripples, which also had the property of causing starlight to waver briefly. The distortion looked similar – though on a microscopic scale – to that caused by the giant nought itself. This was no coincidence.

'Once in orbit, we began constructing research probes. We converted our ship's drive to make tailored micro-singularities . . .'

At that moment, a tickling sensation along her left eyebrow told Isola that a datafeed was queued with results from her latest experiment. She closed that eye with a trained squeeze denoting ACCEPT. Implants along the inner lid came alight, conveying images in crisp focus to her retina. Unlike the digested pap in Mikaela's presentation, what Isola saw was in real time . . . or as 'real' as time got, this near a macro black hole.

More rippling images of constellations. She sub-vocally commanded a shift to graphic mode; field diagrams snapped over the starry scene, showing Tenembro's mammoth, steepening funnel in space-time. An uneven formation of objects – minuscule in comparison – skimmed towards glancing rendezvous with the great nought's eerily bright-black horizon. Glowing traceries depicted one of the little objects as another space-funnel. Vastly smaller, titanically narrower, it too possessed a centre that was severed from this reality as if amputated by the scalpel of God.

'. . . with the objective of creating ideal conditions for our instruments to peer down . . .'

Columns of data climbed across the scene under Isola's eyelid. She could already tell that this experiment wasn't going any better than the others. Despite all their careful calculations, the camera probes still weren't managing to straddle between the giant and dwarf singularities at the right moment, just when the

black discs touched. Still, she watched that instant of
grazing passage, hoping to learn something—

The scene suddenly shivered as Isola's belly gave
a churning lurch, provoking waves of nausea. She
blinked involuntarily and the image vanished.

The fit passed, leaving her short of breath, with a
prickle of perspiration on her face and neck. Plucking
a kerchief from her sleeve, Isola dabbed her brow.
She lacked the will to order the depiction back. Time
enough to go over the results later, with full-spectrum
facilities.

This is getting ridiculous, Isola brooded. She had
never imagined, when the requisition request came,
that a simple clonal pregnancy would entail so many
inconveniences!

'. . . taking advantage of a loophole in the rules of
our cosmos, which allow for a slightly offset boundary
when the original collapstar possessed either spin or
charge. This offset from perfection is one of the features
we hope to exploit . . '

Isola felt a sensation of being watched. She shifted
slightly. From her nearby pseudo-life chaise, Jarlquin
was looking at Isola again, with a measuring expression.

*She might have the courtesy to feign attention to Mikaela's
presentation*, Isola thought, resentfully. *Jarlquin seems more
preoccupied with my condition than I am.*

The Pleasencer's interest was understandable, after
having come so far just for the present contents of
Isola's womb. *My anger with Jarlquin has an obvious
source. Its origin is the same as my own.*

An obsession with beginnings had brought Isola to
this place on the edge of infinity.

How did the universe begin?
Where did it come from?

Where do I come from?

It was ironic that her search would take her to where creation ended. For while the expanding cosmos has no 'outer edge', as such, it does encounter a sharp boundary at the rim of a black hole.

Isola remembered her childhood, back on Kalimarn, playing in the yard with toys that made pico-singularities on demand, from which she gained her first experience examining the warped mysteries of succinct event horizons. She recalled the day these had ceased to be mere dalliances, or school exercises in propulsion engineering, when they instead became foci for exaltation and wonder.

The same equations that describe an expanding universe also tell of a gravity trough's collapse. Explosion, implosion . . . the only difference lay in reversing time's arrow. We are, in effect, living inside a gigantic black hole!

Her young mind marvelled at the implications.

Everything within is aleph. Aleph is cut off from contact with that which is not aleph. Or that which came before aleph. Cause and effect, forever separated.

As I am separated from what brought me into being.

As I must separate from what I bring into being . . .

The foetus kicked again, setting off twinges, unleashing a flood of symbiotic bonding hormones. One side-effect came as a sudden wave of unasked-for sentimentality. Tears filled Isola's eyes, and she could not have made image-picts even if she tried.

Jarlquin had offered drugs to subdue these effects – to make the process 'easier'. Isola did not want it eased. This could be her sole act of biological creation, given the career she had chosen. The word 'motherhood' might be archaic nowadays, but it still had connotations. She wanted to experience them.

It was simple enough in conception.

Back in the eighteenth century, a physicist, John Mitchell, showed that any large enough lump of matter might have an escape velocity greater than the speed of light. Even luminous waves should not be able to escape. When John Wheeler, two hundred years later, performed the same conjuring trick with mass *density*, the name 'black hole' was coined.

Those were just theoretical exercises. What actually happens to a photon that tries to climb out of a singularity? Does it behave like a rocket, slowing down under gravity's insistent drag? Coming to a halt, then turning to plummet down again?

Not so. Photons move at a constant rate, one single speed, no matter what reference frame you use. Unless physically blocked or diverted, light slows for no one.

But tightly coiled gravity does strange things. It changes *time*. Gravitation can make light pay a toll for escaping. Photons lose energy not by slowing down, but by stretching redder, ever redder, as they rise from a space-time well, elongating to microwave lengths, then radio, and onward. Theoretically, on climbing to the event horizon of a black hole, any light wave has reddened down to nothing.

Nothing emerges. Nothing – travelling at the speed of light. In a prim, legalistic sense, that nothing *is* still light.

Isola spread her traps, planning tight, intersecting orbits. She lay a web designed to ambush nothing . . . to peer down into nowhere.

'You know, I never gave it much thought before. The whole thing seemed such a bother. Anyway, I always figured there'd be plenty of time later, after we finished our project.'

Mikaela's non-sequitur came by complete surprise.

Isola looked up from the chart she had been studying. Across the breakfast table, her colleague wore an expression that seemed outwardly casual, but studied. Thin as frost.

'Plenty of time for what?' Isola asked.

Mikaela lifted a cup of port'ha to her lips. 'You know . . . procreation.'

'Oh.' Isola did not know what to say. Ever since the visitor-ship announced itself, her partner had expressed nothing but irritation over havoc to their research schedules. Of late her complaints had been replaced with pensive moodiness. *So this is what she's been brooding about*, Isola realised. To give herself a moment, she held out her own cup for the pseudo-life servitor to refill. Her condition forbade drinking port'ha, so she made do with tea.

'And what have you concluded?' she asked, evenly.

'That I'd be foolish to waste this opportunity.'

'Opportunity?'

Mikaela shrugged. 'Look, Jarlquin came all this way hoping to requisition your clone. You could have turned her down—'

'Mikaela, we've gone over this so many times . . .' But Isola's partner cut her off, raising one hand placatingly.

'That's all right. I now see you were right to agree. It's a great honour. Records of your clone-line are on file throughout the sector.'

Isola sighed. 'My ancestresses were explorers and star messengers. So, many worlds in the region would have—'

'Exactly. It's all a matter of available information! Pleasence World had data on you but not on a semi-natural variant like me, born on Kalimarn of Kalimarnese stock. For all we know, I might have what Jarlquin's looking for, too.'

Isola nodded earnestly. 'I'm sure of that. Do you mean you're thinking—'

' – of getting tested?' Mikaela watched Isola over the rim of her cup. 'Do you think I should?'

Despite her continuing reservations over having been requisitioned in the first place, Isola felt a surge of enthusiasm. The notion of sharing this experience – this unexpected experiment in motherhood – with her only friend gave her strange pleasure. 'Oh, yes! They'll jump at the chance. Of course . . .' She paused.

'What?' Mikaela asked, tension visible in her shoulders.

Isola had a sudden image of the two of them, waddling about the station, relying utterly on drones and pseudo-life servitors to run errands and experiments. The inconvenience alone would be frightful. Yet, it would only add up to a year or so, altogether. She smiled ironically. 'It means our guests would stay longer. And you'd have to put up with Jarlquin . . .'

Mikaela laughed. A hearty laugh of release. 'Yeah, dammit. That is a drawback!'

Relieved at the lifting of her partner's spirit, Isola grinned too. They were in concord again. She had missed the old easiness between them, which had been under strain since that first surprise message disrupted their hermits' regime. *This will put everything right*, she hoped. *We'll have years to talk about a strange, shared experience after it's all over.*

The best solutions are almost always the simplest.

Within a sac of amniotic fluid, a play is acted out according to a script. The script calls for proteins, so amino acids are lined up by ribosomes to play their roles. Enzymes appear at the proper moment. Cells divide and jostle for position. The code demands they specialise, so they do.

Subtle forces of attraction and repulsion shift them into place, one by one.
It is a script that has been played before.
A script designed to play again.

The pair of nano-noughts – each weighing just a million tons – hovered within a neutral gravity tank. Between the microscopic wells of darkness, a small recording device peered into one of the tiny singularities. Across the room, screens showed only the colour black.

Special fields kept each nought from self-destructing – either through quantum evaporation or by folding space round itself like a blanket and disappearing. Other beams of force strained to hold the two black holes apart, preventing gravity from slamming them together uncontrollably.

It was an unstable situation. But Isola was well practised. Seated on a soft chaise to support her overstrained back, she used subtle machines to manipulate the two funnels of sunken metric towards each other. The outermost rims of their space-time wells merged. Two microscopic black spheres – the event horizons themselves – lay centimetres apart, ratcheting closer by the second, as Isola let them slowly draw together.

Tides tugged at the camera, suspended between, and at the fibre-thin cable leading from the camera to her recorders. Peering into one of those pits of blackness, the mini-telescope saw nothing. That was only natural.

Nothing could escape from inside a black hole.

A special kind of nothing, though. Nothing that had formerly been light, before being stretched down to true nothingness in the act of climbing that steep slope.

The two funnels merged closer still. The microscopic black balls drew nearer.

Light trying to escape a black hole is reddened to nonexistence.

Nevertheless, virtual light can theoretically escape one nought, only to be sucked into the other. There, it starts blue-shifting exponentially, as gravity yanks it downward again.

Between one event horizon and the other, the light doesn't 'officially' exist. Not in the limiting case. Yet ideally, there should be a flow.

They had not believed her on Kalimarn. Until one day she showed them it was possible, for the narrowest of instants, to tap the virtual stream. To squeeze between the red-shifted and blue-shifted segments. To catch the briefest glimpse—

It happened too fast to follow with human eyes. One moment two black spheres were inching microscopically towards each other with the little, doomed instrumentality tortured and whining between them. The next instant, in a sudden flash, all contents of the tank combined and vanished. Space-time backlash set the reinforced vacuum chamber rocking – a side-effect of that final stroke which severed forever all contact between the noughts and this cosmos where they'd been made. In the moment it took Isola to blink, they were gone, leaving behind the neatly severed end of fibre cable.

Gone, but not forgotten. In taking the camera with them, the singularities had given it the moment it needed. The moment when 'nothing' was no longer nothing but merely a deep red.

And red is visible . . .

This was what had won her funding to seek out a partner and come here to Tenembro Nought. For if it was possible to look inside a micro-hole, why not a far bigger one that had been born in the titanic self-devouring of a star? So far, she and Mikaela hadn't succeeded in that part of the quest. Their research at the micro end, however, kept giving surprising and wonderful results.

Isola checked to make sure all the secrets of the vanished nano-nought had been captured during that narrow instant, and were safely stored in memory. Its rules. Its nature as a cosmos all its own. She had varied the formation recipe again, and wondered what physics would be revealed this time.

Before she could examine the snapshot of a pocket universe, however, her left eyelid twitched and came alight with a reminder. Time for her appointment. Damn.

But Jarlquin had shown Isola how much more pleasant it was to be on time.

The temperature of the universe is just under three degrees, absolute. It has chilled considerably, in the act of expanding over billions of years, from fireball to cosmos. Cooling in turn provoked changes in state. Delicately balanced forces shifted as the original heat diffused, allowing protons to form from quarks, then electrons to take orbit around them, producing that wonder, Hydrogen. Later rebalancings caused matter to gather, forming monstrous swirls. Many of these eddies coalesced and came alight spectacularly – all because the rules allowed it.

Because the rules *required* it.

Time processed one of those lights – by those selfsame rules – until it finished burning and collapsed, precipitating a fierce explosion and ejection of its core from the universe.

Tenembro Nought sat as a fossil relic of that banishment. A scar, nearly healed, but palpable.

All of this had come about according to the rules.

'We've liberated ourselves from Darwin's Curse, but it still comes down to the same thing.'

The visitor made a steeple of her petite hands, long

and narrow, with delicate fingers like a surgeon's. Her lips were full and dyed a rich mauve hue. Faint ripples passed across her skin as pores opened and closed rhythmically. A genetic graft, Isola supposed. Probably some Vorpal trait inserted into Jarlquin's genome before she was even conceived.

Fortunately, laws limit the gene trade, Isola thought. *All they can ask of me is a simple cloning.*

Over Jarlquin's shoulder, through the window of the lounge, Isola saw the starscape and realised Smolin Cluster was in view. Sub-vocally, she ordered the magni-focus pane to enlarge one quadrant for her eye only. Flexing gently, imperceptibly to other visitors across the room, the window sent Isola a scene of suns like shining grains. One golden pinpoint – Pleasence Star – shone soft and stable. Its kind, by nature's laws, would last eons and never become a nought.

'You see,' Jarlquin continued, blithely ignorant of Isola's distraction. 'Although we've pierced much of the code of Life, and reached a truce of sorts with Death, the fundamental rule's the same. That is successful which continues. And what continues most successfully is that which not only lives, but multiplies.'

Why is she telling me this? Isola wondered, sitting in a gently vibrating non-life chair across from Jarlquin. Did the biologer-nurturist actually care what her subject thought? Isola had agreed to disrupt her research and donate a clone, for the genetic benefit of Pleasence World. Wasn't that enough?

I ought to be flattered. Tenembro Nought may be 'close' to their world by interstellar standards, still, how often does a colony send a ship so far, just to collect one person's neonate clone?

Oh, the visitors had also made a great show of scrutinising their work here, driving Mikaela to distraction with their questions. The pair of Butins were physicians and exuded enthusiasm along with their pungent, blue perspiration. But Jarlquin had confided in Isola. They would never have been approved to come all this way if not also to seek her seed. To treasure and nurture it, and take it home with them.

As I was taken from my own parent, who donated an infant duplicate to Kalimarn as her ship swept by. We are a model in demand, it seems.

The reasons were clear enough, in abstract. In school she had learned about the interstellar economy of genes, which prevented the catastrophe of inbreeding and spread the boon of diversity. But tidal surges of hormone and emotion had not been in her syllabus. Isola could not rightly connect abstractions with events churning away below her sternum. They seemed as unrelated as a sonnet and a table.

Two pseudo-life servitors entered – no doubt called when Jarlquin winked briefly a moment ago – carrying hot beverages on a tray. The blank-faced, bipedal protoplasmoids were as expressionless as might be expected of beings less than three days old . . . and destined within three more to slip back into the vat from which they'd been drawn. One servant poured for Isola as it had been programmed to do, with uncomplaining perfection no truly living being could have emulated.

'You were speaking of multiplication,' Isola prompted, lest Jarlquin lose her train of thought and decide to launch into another recital of the wonders of Pleasence. The fine life awaiting Isola's clone.

'Ah?' Jarlquin pursed her lips, tasting the tea. 'Yes, multiplication. Tell me, as time goes on, who populates the galaxies? Obviously, those who disperse and reproduce. Even though we aren't *evolving* in the old way – stressed by death and natural selection – a kind of selection is still going on.'

'Selection?'

'Indeed, selection. For traits appropriate to a given place and time. Consider what happened to those genes which, for one reason or another, kept individuals from leaving Beloved Earth during the first grand waves of colonisation. Are descendants of those individuals still with us? Do those genes persist, now that Earth is gone?'

Isola saw Jarlquin's point. The impulsive drive to reproduce sexually had ebbed from humanity – at least in this sector. She had heard things were otherwise, spinward of galactic West and in the Magellanics. Nevertheless, certain models of humanity seemed to spread and thrive, while other types remained few, or disappeared.

'So it's been in other races with whom we've formed symbioses. Planets and commonwealths decide what kinds of citizens they need and requisition clones or new variants, often trading with colonies many parsecs away. Nowadays you can be successful at reproduction without ever even planning to.'

Isola realised Jarlquin must know her inside and out. Not that her ambivalence was hard to read.

To become a mother, she thought. *I am about to . . . give birth. I don't even know what it means, but Jarlquin seems to envy me.*

'Whatever works,' the Pleasencer continued, sipping her steaming tea. 'That law of nature, no amount of scientific progress will ever change. If you have what it takes to reproduce, and pass on those traits to your offspring, then *they* will likely replicate as well, and your kind will spread.'

What came before? And what came before that?

As a very little girl, back on Kalimarn, she had seen how other infants gleefully discovered a way to drive parents and guardians to distraction with the game of 'Why'. It could start at any moment, given the slightest excuse to ask that first, guileless question. Any adult who innocently answered with an explanation was met with the same simple, efficient rejoinder – another 'why?'. Then another . . . Used carefully, deliciously, it became an inquisition guaranteed to provoke either insanity or pure enlightenment by the twentieth repetition. More often the former.

To be different, Isola modified the exercise.

What caused that? she asked. Then – *What caused the cause?* and so on.

She soon learned how to dispense quickly with preliminaries. The vast, recent ages of space travel and colonisation were quickly dealt with, as was the Dark Climb of man, back on old Beloved Earth. Recorded history was like a salad, archeology an aperitif. Neanderthals and dinosaurs offered adult bulwarks, but she would not be distracted. Under pestering inquiry, the homeworld unformed, its sun unravelled into dust and gas, which swirled backwards in time to be absorbed by reversed supernovas. Galaxies unwound. Starlight and cold matter fell together, compressing into universal plasma as the cosmos shrank towards its origins. By the time her poor teachers had parsed existence to its debut epoch – the first searing day, its earliest, actinic minute, down to micro-fractions of a second – Isola felt a sense of excitement like no story book or fairy tale could provide.

Inevitably, instructors and matrons sought refuge in the singularity. The Great Singularity. Before ever really grasping their meaning, Isola found herself stymied by pat phrases like 'quantum vacuum fluctuation' and 'boundary-free existence', at which point relieved adults smugly refused to admit of any prior cause.

It was a cop-out of the first order. Like when they told her how unlikely it was she would ever meet her true parent – the one who had brought her into being – no matter how far she travelled or how long she lived.

Subtle chemical interactions cause cells to migrate and change, taking up specialities and commencing to secrete new chemicals themselves. Organs form and initiate activity. All is done according to a code.

It is the code that makes it so.

Isola took her turn in the control chamber, relieving Mikaela at the end of her shift. Even there, one was reminded of the visitors. Just beyond the crystal-covered main aperture, Isola could make out the long, narrow ship from Pleasence, tugged by Tenembro's tides so that its crew quarters lay farthest from the singularity. The imposition chamber dangled towards the great hole in space.

'Remember when they came into orbit?' Mikaela asked, pointing towards the engine section. 'How they pulsed their drive noughts at a peculiar pitch?'

'Yes.' Isola nodded, wishing for once that Mikaela were not all business, but would actually talk to her. Something was wrong.

'Yes, I remember. The nano-holes collapsed quickly, emitting stronger spatial backwash than I'd seen before.'

'That's right,' Mikaela said without meeting Isola's eyes. 'By creating metric-space ahead of themselves at a faster rate, they managed a steeper deceleration. Their engineer – the Vorpal, I'q'oun – gave me their recipe.' Mikaela laid a data-sliver on the console. 'You might see whether it's worth inserting some of their code into our next probe.'

'Mmm.' Isola felt reluctant. A debt for useful favours might disturb the purity of her irritation with these visitors. 'I'll look into it,' she answered noncommittally.

Although she wanted to search Mikaela's eyes, Isola thought it wiser not to press matters. The level of tension between them, rather than declining since that talk over breakfast, had risen sharply soon after. Something must have happened. *Did she ask Jarlquin to be tested?* Isola wondered. *Or could I have said something to cause offence?*

Mikaela clearly knew she was behaving badly and it bothered her. To let emotion interfere with work was a sign of unskilled selfing. The fair-skinned woman visibly made an effort to change tack.

'How's the . . . you know, coming along?' she asked, gesturing vaguely towards Isola's midriff.

'Oh, well, I guess. All considered.'

'Yeah?'

'I . . . feel strange though,' Isola confided, hoping to draw her partner out. 'As if my body were doing something it understood but that's totally beyond *me*, you know?' She tapped herself on the temple. 'Then, last night, I dreamt about a man. You know, a male? We had some on Kalimarn, you recall. It was very . . . odd.' She shook her head. 'Then there are these mood swings and shifts of emotion I never imagined before. It's quite an experience.'

To Isola's surprise, a coldness seemed to fill the room. Mikaela's visage appeared locked, her expression as blank as pseudo-life.

'I'll bet it is.'

There was a long, uncomfortable silence. This episode had disrupted their planned decade of research, but now there was more to it than that. A difference whose consequences seemed to spiral outward, pushing the two of them apart, cutting communication. Isola suddenly knew that her friend had gone to Jarlquin, and what the answer had been.

If asked directly, Mikaela would probably claim indifference, that it didn't matter, that procreation had not figured in her plans, anyway. Nevertheless, it must have been a blow. Her eyes lay impenetrable under twin hoods.

'Well. Good night, then.' The other woman's voice was ice. She nodded, turning to go.

'Good night,' Isola called after her. The portal shut silently.

Subtle differences in heritage – that was all this was about. It seemed so foolish and inconsequential. After all, what was biological reproduction on the cosmological scale of things? Would any of this matter a million years from now?

One good thing about physics – its rules could be taken apart in fine, separable units, examined, and superposed again to make good models of the whole. Why was this so for the cosmos, but not for conscious intellects? *I'll be glad when this is over*, Isola told herself.

She went to the Suiting Room, to prepare for going outside. Beyond another crystal pane, Tenembro Nought's glittering blackness seemed to distort a quarter of the universe, a warped, twisted, tortured tract of firmament.

There was a vast contrast between the scale human engineers worked with – creating pico-, nano-, and even micro-singularities by tricks of quantum book-keeping – and a monster like Tenembro, which had been crushed into existence, or pure *non*-existence, by nature's fiercest explosion. Yet, in theory, it was the same phenomenon. Once matter has been concentrated to such density that space wraps around itself, what remains is but a hole.

The wrapping could sometimes even close off the hole. Ripples away from such implosions gave modern vessels palpable waves of space-time to skim upon, much as their ancestors' crude ships rode the pulsing shock-fronts of anti-matter explosions. The small black holes created in a ship's drive lasted for but an instant. Matter 'borrowed' during that brief moment was compressed to superdensity and then vanished before the debt came due, leaving behind just a fossil field and spacial backwash to surf upon.

No origin to speak of. No destiny worth mentioning. That was how one of Isola's fellow students had put it, back in school. It was glib and her classmate had been proud of the aphorism. To Isola, it had seemed too pat, leaving unanswered questions.

Her spacesuit complained as pseudo-life components stretched beyond programmed parameters to fit her burgeoning form. Isola waited patiently until the flesh-and-metal concatenation sealed securely. Then, feeling big and awkward, she pushed through the exit port – a jungle of overlapping lock-seal leaves – and stepped out upon the station platform, surrounded by the raw vacuum of space.

Robotic servitors gathered at her ankles jostling to be chosen for the next one-way mission. Eagerness to approach the universal edge was part of their programming – as it appeared to be in hers.

Even from this range, Isola felt Tenembro Nought's tides tugging at fine sensors in her inner ears. The foetus also seemed to note that heavy presence. She felt it turn to orient along the same direction as the visitor ship, feet towards the awful blackness with its crown of twisted stars.

Let's get on with it, she thought, irritated by her sluggish mental processes. Isola had to wink three times to finally set off a flurry of activity. Well-drilled, her subordinates prepared another small invasion force, designed to pierce what logically could not be pierced. To see what, by definition, could not be seen.

The colour of the universe had once been blue. Blue-violet of a purity that was essential. Primal. At that time the cosmos was too small to allow any other shade. There was only room for short, hot light.

Then came expansion, and a flow of time. These, plus subtle rules of field and force, wrought inexorable reddenings on photons. By the time there were observers to give names to colours, the vast bulk of the universe was redder than infra-red.

None of this mattered to Tenembro Nought. By then, it was a hole. A mystery. Although some might search for colour in its depths, it could teach the universe a thing or two about fugitinal darkness.

For all intents and purposes, its colour was black.

'I thought these might intrigue you,' Jarlquin told her that evening.

There was no way to avoid the visitor – not without becoming a hermit and admitting publicly something was bothering her. Mikaela was doing enough sulking for both of them, so Isola attended to her hosting duties in the station lounge. This time, while the other visitors chatted near the starward window, the nurturist from Pleasence held out towards Isola several jagged memory lattices. They lay in her slender hand like fragments of ancient ice.

Iola asked, 'What are they?'

'Your ancestry,' Jarlquin replied with a faint smile. 'You might be interested in what prompted us to requisition your clone.'

Isola stared at the luminous crystals. This data must have been prepared long ago: inquiries sent to her homeworld and perhaps beyond. All must have been accomplished before their ship even set sail. It bespoke a long view on the part of folk who took their planning seriously.

She almost asked, '*How did you know I'd want these?*' Perhaps on Pleasence they didn't consider it abnormal, as they had on Kalimarn, to be fascinated by origins.

'Thank you,' she told the visitor instead, keeping an even tone.

Jarlquin nodded with an enigmatic smile. 'Contemplate continuity.'

In school, young Isola had learned there were two major theories of True Origin – how everything began in that first, fragmentary moment.

In both cases the result, an infinitesimal fraction of a second after Creation, was a titanic expansion. In converting from the first 'seed' of false vacuum to a grapefruit-sized ball containing all the mass-energy required to form a universe, there occurred something called *inflation*. A fundamental change of state was delayed just long enough for a strange, negative version of gravity to take hold, momentarily driving the explosion even faster than allowed by lightspeed.

It was a trick, utilising a clause in creation's codebook that would never again be invoked. The conditions would no longer exist – not in *this* universe – until final collapse brought all galaxies and stars and other ephemera together once more, swallowing the sum into one Mega-Singularity, bringing the balance sheet back to zero.

That was how some saw the universe, as just another borrowing. The way a starship briefly 'borrows' matter without prior existence, in order to make small black holes whose collapse and disappearance repays the debt again. So the entire universe might be thought of as a *loan*, on a vastly larger scale.

What star voyagers did on purpose, crudely, with machines, Creation had accomplished insensately but far better, by simple invocation of the Laws of Quantum Probability. Given enough time, such a fluctuation was bound to occur, sooner or later, according to the rules.

But this theory of origin had a flaw. In what context did one mean '. . . given enough time . . .'? How could there have been time before the universe itself was born? What clocks measured it? What observers noted its passage?

Even if there was a context . . . even if this borrowing was allowed under the rules . . . where did the rules *themselves* come from?

Unsatisfied, Isola sought a second theory of origins.

Black.

Within her eye's dark iris, the pupil was black. So was her skin.

It had not always been so.

She looked from her reflection to a row of images projected in the air nearby. Her ancestresses. Clones, demi-clones and variants going back more than forty generations. Only the most recent had her rich ebony flesh tone. Before that, shades had varied considerably around a dark theme. But other similarities ran true.

A certain line of jaw . . .

An arching of the brows . . .

A reluctant pleasure in the smile . . .

Women Isola had never known or heard of, stretched in diminishing rows across the room. Part of a continuity.

Further along, she found troves of data from still

earlier times. There appeared images of *fathers* as well as mothers, fascinating her and vastly complicating the branchings of descent. Yet it remained possible to note patterns, moving up the line. Long after all trace of 'family' resemblance vanished, she still saw consistent motifs, those Jarlquin had spoken of.

Five fingers on each clasping hand . . .

Two eyes, poised to catch subtleties . . .

A nose to scent . . . a brain to perceive . . .

A persistent will to continue . . .

This was not the only design for making thinking beings, star travellers, successful colonisers of galaxies. There were also Butins, Vorpals, Leshi and ten score other models which, tried and tested by harsh nature, now thrived in diversity in space. Nevertheless, this was a successful pattern. It endured.

Life stirred beneath Isola's hand. Her warm, tumescent belly throbbed, vibrating not just her skin and bones, but membranes, deep within, that she had never expected to have touched by another. Now at least there was a context to put it all in. Her ancestors' images nourished some deep yearning. The poignancy of what she'd miss – the chance to know this living being soon to emerge from her own body – was now softened by a sense of continuity.

It reassured her.

There was a certain beauty in the song of DNA.

Perched in orbit, circling a deep well.

A well with a rim from which nothing escapes.

Micro-noughts, spiralling towards that black boundary, seem cosmically, comically, out of scale with mighty Tenembro, star-corpse, gate-keeper, universal scar. What they lack in width, they make up for in depth just as profound. Wide or narrow, each represents a one-way tunnel to oblivion.

Is it crazy to ask if oblivions come in varieties, or differ in ways that matter?

Rules were a problem of philosophical dimensions when Isola first studied origins.

Consider the ratio of electric force to gravity. If this number had been infinitesimally higher, stars would never grow hot enough within their bowels to form and then expel heavy nuclei – those, like carbon and oxygen – needed for life. If the ratio were just a fraction *lower*, stars would race through brief conflagrations too quickly for planets to evolve. Take the ratio a little farther off in either direction, and there would be no stars at all.

The universal rules of Isola's home cosmos were rife with such fine-tuning. Numbers which, had they been different by even one part in a trillion, would not have allowed subtleties like planets or seas, sunsets and trees.

Some called this evidence of design. Master craftsmanship. Creativity. Creator.

Others handled the coincidence facilely. 'If things were different,' they claimed, 'there would be no observers to note the difference. So it's no surprise that we, who exist, observe around us the precise conditions needed for existence!

'Besides, countless *other* natural constants seem to have nothing special about their values. Perhaps it's just a matter of who is doing the calculating!'

Hand-waving, all hand-waving. Neither answer satisfied Isola when she delved into true origins. Creationists, Anthropicists, they all missed the point.

Everything has to come from somewhere. Even a creator. Even coincidence.

Mikaela barely spoke to her anymore. Isola understood. Her partner could not help feeling rejected. The worlds had selected against her. In effect, the universe had declared her a dead end.

Isola felt, illogically, that it must be *her* fault. She should have found a way to console her friend. *It must be strange to hear you'll be the last in your line.*

Yet, what could she say?

That it's also strange to know your line will continue, but out of reach, out of sight? Beyond all future knowing?

The experiments continued. Loyal camera probes were torn apart by tides, or aged to dust in swirling back-flows of time near Tenembro's vast event horizon. Isola borrowed factors from the visitors' ship-drive. She tinkered with formulas for small counter-weight black holes, and sent the new micro-singularities peeling off on ever-tighter trajectories towards the great nought's all-devouring maw.

Cameras manoeuvred to interpose themselves between one nothing and another. During that brief, but time-dilated, instant, as two wells of oblivion competed to consume them, the machines tried to take pictures.

Pictures of nothing, and all.

'To pass the time, I've been tinkering with your pseudo-life tanks,' Jarlquin announced proudly one evening. 'Your servitor fabricants ought to last as long as nine days now, before having to go back into the vat.'

The visitor was obviously pleased with herself, finding something useful to do while Isola gestated. Jarlquin puttered, yet her interest remained focused on a product more subtle than anything she herself would ever design. Unskilled, but tutored by a billion years of happenstance, Isola prepared that product for delivery.

The second theory of origins had amazed her.

It was not widely talked about in Kalimarn's academies, where savants preferred notions of Quantum Fluctuation. After all, Kalimarn served as banking world for an entire cluster. No doubt the colonists *liked* thinking of the universe as something out on loan.

Nevertheless, in her academy days, Isola had sought other explanations.

We might have come from somewhere else! she realised one evening, when her studies took her deeply into frozen archives. The so-called 'crackpot' theories she found there did not seem so crazy. Their mathematics worked just as well as models of quantum usury.

When a black hole is created after a supernova explosion, the matter that collapses into it doesn't just vanish. According to the equations, it goes . . . 'elsewhere'. To another space-time. A continuum completely detached from ours.

Each new black hole represents another universe! A new creation.

The implication wasn't hard to translate in the opposite direction.

Our own cosmos may have had its start with a black hole that formed in some earlier cosmos!

The discovery thrilled her. It appalled Isola that none of her professors shared her joy. 'Even if true,' one of them had said, 'it's an unanswerable, unrewarding line of inquiry. By the very nature of the situation, we are cut off, severed from causal contact with that earlier cosmos. Given that, I prefer simpler hypotheses.'

'But think of the implications!' she insisted. 'Several times each year, new macro-black holes are created in supernovas—'

'Yes? So?'

' – What's more, at any moment across this galaxy alone, countless starships generate innumerable *micro*-singularities, just to surf the payback wave when they collapse. Each of those "exhaust" singularities becomes a universe too!'

The savant had smiled patronisingly. 'Shall we play god, then? Try to take responsibility, in some way, for our creations?' The old woman's tone was supercilious. 'This argument's almost as ancient as debating angels on pinheads. Why don't you transfer to the department of archaic theology?'

Isola would not be put off, nor meekly accept conventional wisdom. She eventually won backing to investigate the quandaries that consumed her. Much later, Jarlquin told her this perseverance was in part inherited. Some colonies had learned to cherish tenacity like hers. Though sometimes troublesome, the trait often led to profit and art. It was a major reason Pleasence World had sent a fetch ship to Tenembro Nought.

They cared little about the specific truths Isola pursued. They wanted the trait that drove her to pursue.

Cells differentiate according to patterns laid down in the codes. Organs form which would – by happenstance – provide respiration, circulation, cerebration . . .

In one locale, cells even begin preparing for future reproduction. New eggs align themselves in rows, then go dormant. Within each egg lay copies of the script.

Even this early, the plan lays provisions for the next phase.

Normally, a pseudo-life incubator would have taken over during her final weeks. But the nurturist, Jarlquin, wanted none of that. Pseudo-life was but a product. Its designs, no matter how clever, came out of theory and mere generations of practice, while Isola's womb was skilled from trial and error successes stretching back several galactic rotations. So Isola waddled, increasingly awkward and inflated, wondering how her ancestors ever managed.

Every one of them made it. Each managed to get someone else started.

It was a strange consolation, and she smiled, sardonically. *Maybe I'm starting to think like Jarlquin!*

She no longer went outside to conduct experiments. Using her calculations, Mikaela fine-tuned the next convoy sent to skim Tenembro's vast event horizon, while Isola went back to basics in the laboratory.

What mystery is movement – distinguishing one location from another? In some natures, all points correspond – instantaneous, coincidental. Uninteresting.

What riddle, then, is change – one object evolving into another? Some worlds disallow this. Though they contain multitudes, all things remain the same.

Is a reality cursed which suffers entropy? Or is it consecrated?

Once more a flash. Two micro-singularities fell together, carrying a tiny holo-camera with them to oblivion. In the narrow moment of union, the robot took full-spectrum readings of one involute realm. The results showed Isola a mighty, but flawed, kingdom.

The amount of mass originally used to form the nought mattered at this end – determining its gravitational pull and event horizon. But on the other side, beyond the constricted portal of the singularity, it made little difference. Whether a mere million tons had gone into the black hole or the weight of a thousand suns, it was the act of geometric transformation that counted. Instants after the nought's formation, inflation had turned it into a macrocosm. A fiery ball of plasma exploding in its own context, in a reference frame whose dimensions were all perpendicular to those Isola knew. Within that frame, a wheel of time marked out events, just as it did in Isola's universe – only vastly speeded up from her point of view.

Energy – or something like what she'd been taught to call 'energy' – drove the expansion, and traded forms with substances that might vaguely be called 'matter'. Forces crudely akin to electromagnetism and gravity contested over nascent particles that in coarse ways resembled quarks and leptons. Larger concatenations tried awkwardly to form.

But there was no rhythm, no symmetry. The untuned orchestra could not decide what score to play. There was no melody.

In the speeded-up reference frame of the construct-cosmos, her sampling probe had caught evolution of a coarse kind. Like a pseudo-life fabrication too long out of the vat, the universe Isola had set out to create lurched towards dissipation. The snapshot showed no heavy elements, no stars, no possibility of self-awareness. How could there be? All the rules were wrong.

Nevertheless, the wonder of it struck Isola once more. To make universes!

Furthermore, she was getting better. Each new design got a little farther along than the one before it. Certainly farther than most trash cosmos spun off as exhaust behind starships. At the rate she was going, in a million years some descendant of hers might live to create a cosmos in which crude galaxies formed.

If only we could solve the problem of looking down Tenembro, she thought.

That great black ripple lay beyond the laboratory window, crowned by warped stars. It was like trying to see with the blind spot in her eye. There was a tickling notion that something lay there, but forever just out of reach.

To Isola, it felt like a dare. A challenge.

What strange rules must reign in there! she sighed. *Weirdness beyond imagination . . .*

Isola's gut clenched. The laboratory blurred as waves of painful constriction spasmed inside her. The chaise grew arms which held on, keeping her from falling, but they could not stop Isola from trying to double over, gasping.

Such pain . . . I never knew . . .

Desperately, she managed a faint moan.

'Jar . . . Jarlquin . . .'

She could only hope the room monitor would interpret it as a command. For the next several minutes, or hours, or seconds, she was much too distracted to try again.

It is a narrow passage, fierce and tight and terrible. Forces stretch and compress to the limit, almost bursting. What continues through suffers a fiery, constricted darkness.

Then a single point of light. An opening. Release!

Genesis.

They watched the fetch ship turn and start accelerating. Starlight refracted through a wake of disturbed space. If any of the multitude of universes created by its drive happened, by sheer chance, to catch a knack for self-existence, no one in *this* cosmos would ever know.

Isola's feelings were a murky tempest, swirling from pain to anaesthesia. A part of her seemed glad it was over, that she had her freedom back. Other, intense voices cried out at the loss of her captivity. All the limbs and organs she had possessed a year ago were still connected, yet she ached with a sense of dismemberment. Jarlquin had carefully previewed all of this. She had offered drugs. But Isola's own body now doped her quite enough. She sensed flowing endorphins start the long process of adjustment. Beyond that, artificial numbing would have robbed the colours of her pain.

The fetch ship receded to a point, leaving behind Tenembro's cavity of twisted metric, its dimple in the great galactic wheel. Ahead, Pleasence Star beckoned, a soft, trustworthy yellow.

Isola blessed the star. To her, its glimmer would always say, *You continue. Part of you goes on.*

She went on to bless the ship, the visitors, even Jarlquin. What had been taken from her would never have existed without their intervention, their 'selection'. Perhaps, like universes spun off behind a star-drive, you weren't meant to know what happened to your descendants. Even back in times when parents shared half their lives with daughters and sons, did any of them ever really know what cosmos lay behind a child's eye?

Unanswerable questions were Isola's metier. In time, she might turn her attention to these. If she got another chance, in a better situation. For now, she had little choice but to accept the other part of Jarlquin's prescription. Work was an anodyne. It would have to do.

'They're gone,' she said, turning to her friend.

'Yes, and good riddance.'

In Mikaela's pale eyes, Isola saw something more than sympathy for her pain. Something transcendent glimmered there.

'Now I can show you what we've found,' Mikaela said, as if savouring the giving of a gift.

'What we . . .' Isola blinked. 'I don't understand.'

'You will. Come with me and see.'

Tenembro was black. But this time Isola saw a
different sort of blackness.

Tenembro's night fizzed with radio echoes, reddened
heat of its expansion, a photon storm now cool enough
to seem dark to most eyes, but still a blaze across
immensity.

Tenembro's blackness was relieved by sparkling
pinpoints, whitish blue and red and yellow. Bright
lights like shining dust, arrayed in spiral clouds.

Tenembro Universe shone with galaxies, turning in
stately splendour. Now and then, a pinwheel island
brightened as some heavy sun blared exultantly,
seeding well-made elements through space, leaving
behind a scar.

'But . . .' Isola murmured, shaking her head as
she contemplated the holistic sampling – their latest
pan-spectral snapshot. 'It's *our* universe! Does the
other side of the wormhole emerge somewhere else
in our cosmos?'

There were solutions to the equations which allowed
this. Yet she had been so sure Tenembro would lead
to another creation. Something special . . .

'Look again,' Mikaela told her. 'At beta decay
in this isotope . . . And here, at the fine structure
constant . . .'

Isola peered at the figures, and inhaled sharply.
There *were* differences. Subtle, tiny differences. It was
another creation after all. They had succeeded! They
had looked down the navel of a macro-singularity and
seen . . . everything.

The still-powerful tang of her pain mixed with
a heady joy of discovery. Disoriented by so much
emotion, Isola put her hand to her head and leaned
on Mikaela, who helped her to a chaise. Breathing
deeply from an infusion tube brought her round.

'But . . .' she said, still gasping slightly, '. . . the rules are so close to ours!'

Her partner shook her head. 'I don't know what to make of it either. We've been trying for years to design a cosmos that would hold together, and failed to get even close. Yet here we have one that occurred by natural processes, with no conscious effort involved—'

Mikaela cut short as Isola cried out an oath, staring at the pseudo-life chaise, then at a waiter-servitor that shambled in carrying drinks, a construct eight days old and soon to collapse from unavoidable build-up of errors in its program. Isola looked back at the holographic image of Tenembro's universe, then at Mikaela with a strange light in her eyes.

'It . . . *has* to be that way,' she said, hoarse-voiced with awe. 'Oh, don't you see? We're pretty smart. We can make life of sorts, and artificial universes. But we're new at both activities, while nature's been doing both for a very long time!'

'I . . .' The pale woman shook her head. 'I don't see . . .'

'Evolution! Life never *designs* the next generation. Successful codes in one lifetime get passed on to the next, where they are sieved yet again, and again, adding refinements along the way. As Jarlquin said – whatever works, continues!'

Mikaela swallowed. 'Yes, I see. But universes . . .'

'Why not for universes too?'

Isola moved forwards to the edge of the chaise, shrugging aside the arms that tried to help her.

'Think about all the so-called laws of nature. In the "universes" we create in lab, these are almost random, chaotically flawed or at least simplistic, like the codes in pseudo-life.'

She smiled ironically. 'But Tenembro Universe has

rules as subtle as those reigning in our own cosmos. Why not? Shouldn't a child resemble her mother!'

What came before me?

How did I come to be?

Will something of me continue after I am gone?

Isola looked up from her notepad to contemplate Tenembro Nought. This side – the deceptively simple black sphere with its star-tiara. Not a scar, she had come to realise, but an umbilicus. Through such narrow junctures, the Home Cosmos kept faint contact with its daughters.

If this was possible for universes, Isola felt certain something could be arranged for her, as well. She went back to putting words down on the notepad. She did not have to speak, just will them, and the sentences wrote themselves.

My dear child, these are among the questions that will pester you, in time. They will come to you at night and whisper, troubling your sleep.

Do not worry much, or hasten to confront them. They are not ghosts, come to haunt you. Dream sweetly. There are no ghosts, just memories.

It wasn't fashionable what she was attempting – to reach across the parsecs and make contact. At best it would be tenuous, this communication by long-distance letter. Yet, who had better proof that it was possible to build bridges across a macrocosm?

You have inherited much that you shall need, she went on reciting. *I was just a vessel, passing on gifts I received, as you will pass them on in turn, should selection also smile on you.*

Isola lifted her head. Stars and nebulae glittered beyond Tenembro's dark refraction, as they did in that universe she had been privileged to glimpse through the dark nought – the offspring firmament that so resembled this one.

As DNA coded for success in life-forms, so did *rules* of nature – fields and potentials, the finely balanced constants – carry through from generation to generation of universes, changing subtly, varying to some degree, but above all programmed to prosper.

Black holes are eggs. That was the facile metaphor. *Just as eggs carry forward little more than chromosomes, yet bring about effective chickens, all a singularity has to carry through is rules. All that follows is but consequence.*

The implications were satisfying.

There is no more mystery where we come from. Those cosmos whose traits lead to forming stars of the right kind – stars which go supernova, then collapse into great noughts – those are the cosmos which have 'young'. Young that carry on those traits, or else have no offspring of their own.

It was lovely to contemplate, and coincidentally also explained why she was here to contemplate it!

While triggering one kind of birth, by collapsing inward, supernovas also seed through space the elements needed to make planets, and beings like me.

At first, that fact would seem incidental, almost picayune.

Yet I wonder if somehow that's not selected for, as well. Perhaps it is how universes evolve self-awareness. Or even . . .

Isola blinked, and smiled ruefully to see she had been sub-vocalising all along, with the notepad faithfully transcribing her disordered thoughts. Interesting stuff, but not exactly the right phrases to send across light years to a little girl.

Ah, well. She would rewrite the letter many times before finishing the special antenna required for its sending. By the time the long wait for a reply was over, her daughter might have grown up and surpassed her in all ways.

I hope so, Isola thought. *Perhaps the universe, too, has some heart, some mind somewhere, which can feel pride. Which can know its offspring thrive, and feel hope.*

Someday, in several hundred billion years or so, long after the last star had gone out, the great crunch, the Omega, would arrive. All the ash and cinders of those galaxies out there – and the quarks and leptons in her body – would hurtle together then to put *fini* on the long epic of this singularity she dwelled within, paying off a quantum debt incurred so long ago.

By then, how many daughter universes would this one have spawned? How many cousins must already exist in parallel somewhere, in countless perpendicular directions?

There is no more mystery where we come from. Had she really thought that, only a few moments ago? For a brief time she had actually been *satiated*. But hers was not a destiny to ever stop asking the next question.

How far back does the chain stretch? Isola wondered, catching the excitement of a new wonder. *If our universe spawns daughters, and it came, in turn, from an earlier mother, then how far back can it be traced?*

Trillions of generations of universes, creating black holes which turn into new universes, each spanning trillions of years? All the way back to some crude progenitor universe? To the simplest cosmos possible with rules subtle enough for reproduction, I suppose.

From that point forward, selection would have made improvements each generation. But in the crude beginning . . .

Isola thought about the starting point of this grand chain. If laws of nature could evolve, just like DNA, mustn't there exist some more *basic* law, down deep, that let it all take place? Could theologians then fall back on an ultimate act of conscious Creation after all, countless mega-creations ago? Or was that first universe, primitive and unrefined, a true, primeval accident?

Either answer begged the question. Accident or Creation . . . in what context? In what setting? What conditions held sway *before* that first ancestor universe, that forerunner genesis, allowing it to start?

Her letter temporarily forgotten, with mere galaxies as backdrop, Isola began sketching outlines of a notion of a plan.

Possible experiments.

Ways to seek what might have caused the primal cause.

What had been before it all began.

OTHERNESS

The final essay of this volume was edited from a transcribed talk I gave on February 14, 1989, at Brigham Young University. It is even more extravagantly opinionated than the earlier pieces, so be warned, especially if you came for science fiction alone! It concludes my series of wild speculations on a topic I find endlessly fascinating – otherness.

The New Meme

I earn my living as a writer. In other words, as a magician, shaman, metaphorist. By chant and incantation – and with the active collaboration of my clients, the readers – I create images, characters, alternate realities in other minds. It is an ancient venerable profession. All tribes have had storytellers, who wove legends round the campfire. My speciality involves epics not about long ago, but times and places yet to come. It attempts to weave realistic might-bes, and vivid might-have-beens. Above all, it is the literature of change.

These are bold days for such a genre, since change is the very fabric of our time. If today's modern 'priesthood' consists of scientists, we SF authors are like those wild-eyed folk in hair shirts who once stood outside the temple gates, performing tricks and dazzling the crowds, generally tolerated by the official guardians of wisdom, for astute priests understand that people need myths, too.

In fact, the best of today's scientists seem to enjoy reading far-out, speculative tales. Perhaps they, too, like to be taken far away, now and then. Having worked on both sides, both inside the Temple and out, I can say that, for all their differences, science and science fiction have something deep in common. You might call it a shared frame of reference . . . a new and different way of looking at the world.

I alluded to this world-view in earlier essays. Now I want to look one more time at the Dogma of Otherness.

Listen to the following statement:

'Subjective reality is what I see and experience; objective reality is what's really out there. They aren't the same thing.'

In other words, I look through my eyes and see only a version of the world, a version that can be, and often is, coloured by what I *want* to see. To ever come close to what's really going on, I must learn to double check, to experiment, and even consult other people. This mutual deliberation, or giving of 'reality checks', helps us agree on common ground. I don't know if what you call 'red' is identical to what I experience, but we expect enough overlap to agree on rules for traffic!

Now what I've said so far probably sounds pretty obvious. Plato wrote about it long ago, and drew dour conclusions. I am more of an optimist. In fact, I believe the preceding paragraph distills the single most important contribution of modern civilisation.

'Hey, I can fool myself! I might even be *wrong* from time to time.'

Such a simple statement. But because you and I can say it, we have a society which, for the first time, stands a chance of avoiding the worst errors of history.

There is a hoary notion that faith and reason are essential foes, forever in opposition. This is not so. Any thoughtful scientist will tell you that *reason* is just another *type* of faith. You work out a scenario on paper – as Plato, Aquinas, Hegel, Marx and Freud did – and convince yourself, after a lot of 'ifs' and 'therefores', that something must be so. After all, can't you prove things on paper . . . in mathematics?

In fact, mathematicians are considered the idiots-savant of the scientific family – because they actually believe in logical 'proofs'. Mathematics *is* certainly the most brilliant, accurate, useful metaphor-generating system ever. It contains systems to check for self-consistency and obvious blunders, so that most garbage is weeded out before publication. Yet, even the most elegant theorem has to be tested against reality or remain a nebulous thing. A curiosity. Just another pretty incantation.

In other words, mathematicians are shamans, too.

Reason can be just another form of faith – a tower of words or symbols which seem to demonstrate what you wanted to prove, forgetting that in other hands the same tools can be used to show opposite conclusions. Take the famed philosopher, René Descartes, who decided to throw out everything he knew and start from scratch – then proceeded, step by painstaking step, to logically 'prove' all of the premises and prejudices he had started out with! When you have an ideology or theory that *ought* to be true, it takes great strength of character to overcome the very human desire to believe your own spell-weaving, and instead allow others to test the edifice you've created. Testing it against the possibility of being wrong.

Fitfully, hesitantly, we have begun preaching this lesson to our youth – especially those entering science – yet it is a hard standard to live up to. To a surprising degree, the new priesthood manages to work by this new code, but the siren call of egotism and self-righteousness can never be escaped. It resonates within our cro-magnon skulls, beckoning us back towards the narcissistic joys of magic.

Yet, it *is* a change, this new way of thinking. In fact, I'll go so far as to suggest it is a major breakthrough in the human condition.

Today one hears fundamentalists – those preaching a literal interpretation of the Book of Genesis – attacking so-called secular humanism by calling it 'just another religion'. Meanwhile creationists promulgate what they call 'Creation Science'. The implied compliment – that science is more trustworthy than older ways of knowing – seems to escape notice by both sides in the public debate.

The same people proclaim that 'evolution is just a theory'. And, of course, we know that all theories are equal, yes?

Cultural Relativism, a myth springing from the opposite end of the political spectrum, *also* proclaims not only that every idea has equal value, but that no world-view or culture has any better inkling what is going on than any other. That there is no such thing as good or bad, right or wrong . . . only an amorphous sea of relativity, with every concept mutually exchangeable.

But all theories aren't equal! Human thought thrives on *competition* among ideas. Some are disproven and go deservedly into the dustbin. Meanwhile, others graduate to become *models of the world*. Anyone can come up with a metaphor or notion, but a model of the world offers consistent explanations for what people see going on around them, as modern plate tectonics continues to work and improve as an explanation of geology, the more facts field workers dig up.

More importantly, a valid model goes on to make testable *predictions*.

Most first-rate scientific papers end with a statement saying, in effect: 'If this wonderful theory of mine is true, so-and-so will be discovered in this and such experiment. On the other hand, my theory will be *disproven* if trials X or Y show contrary results.'

That's the way it works, and not just in science. It is also how honest men and women live their lives. If you believe in something, then by all means try to prove it, even convince others. But always leave room for the possibility that someone else may prove *you* wrong.

What about these so-called 'models of the world'?

The name could be applied to any theory which best describes the universe at a given time. Call it a monarch among theories, for as we said before, all ideas are *not* equal. In any month or year, in any subject area, one description is usually the leader. Generally the one with the fewest inconsistencies and the best accumulated evidence to back it up.

In science, no model lasts forever. Leading theories are rewarded by becoming prime targets! More experiments are aimed at testing them than any others. Even if a model survives trial after trial, it inevitably *changes* in the process. Usually, these new versions are incremental improvements rather than rejections, as in the way Darwin's concepts have matured during the century since his death, while retaining their basic validity. But revolutions are known to happen. Plate tectonics did not start out as the Best Model in geology. It won its place after a long process of criticism, successful predictions and comparison to evidence.

It is a remarkably successful process, by which our understanding of the universe has evolved year after year, without the traumas or heretic-burnings that used to punctuate advances in human knowledge. To understand how this method came about, and how unique this approach is historically, let's turn around and examine our past.

For six thousand, ten thousand, fifty thousand years – however far back you assume we were intelligent and able to ask questions – our ancestors had little idea how the world worked. And we can safely assume that they were terrified most of the time. Throughout those millennia, nearly every civilisation we know of had a belief system based upon what might be called a *Look Backward* world-view. In other words, people shared a common belief that there once had been a golden age when people were better, stronger, closer to heaven. An era when sages worked wonders and were wiser than more recent folk. From Sumeria to China, to the legends of Native Americans, this deep assumption runs through almost every mythic tradition.

Except ours. Our world-wide, cosmopolitan, modern culture is arguably the first to take a radically divergent orientation, not necessarily better, but profoundly different. A philosophy that might be called *Look Forward*.

There *was* no golden age in the past, this revolutionary view declares; our ancestors scratched and clawed and a few of them – the well-meaning ones – tried hard to redress the shabby ignorance they had inherited. Some, in sincerely trying to improve things, came up with dreadful world models, pantheons or social orders which excused, even encouraged, terrible persecutions or injustices. Still, despite all the mistakes and obstacles they faced, men and women managed glacially, generation by generation, to add to our knowledge – and to our wisdom, as well.

There was no ancient golden age, say believers in the Look Forward vision. But there is a notion going around that we just might be able to *build* one, for tomorrow's children.

This new orientation towards the future, not the past, is especially clear in the scientific attitude towards knowledge. Instead of 'Truth' with a capital 'T', immutable and handed down unchanged through time from some ancient text of lore, today we have the cycle of improvement and revision described earlier. The best world models are found in the latest journal articles, in the most recent textbooks on any given subject – and even they won't be the final word, because in five or ten years there'll be better models still, as results pour in from new experiments.

To you, a modern reader and member of contemporary civilisation, this way of looking at truth may sound obvious. But I cannot over-state how recently it achieved anything approaching widespread acceptance. This shift in the *time orientation of wisdom* is an intellectual sea change unprecedented in the annals of human thought. Its consequences, which already include science and democracy, will grow more profound as the years go by.

But let's take a side trip, while on the subject of human thought. To begin, we must backtrack to basic biology.

Richard Dawkins, in his book *The Selfish Gene*, describes how our genetic heritage seems to have resulted from struggles by nearly invisible clusters of DNA against nature and each other. Nearly all of evolution could be looked at as a winnowing of those genes which fail to achieve the central goal of making and spreading copies of themselves. Of course, molecules do not contemplate goals. 'Wanting' is a human emotion. Still, the effects of natural selection often do look eerily as if different genetic heritages have been striving against one another for niches in the ecosystem.

Put it this way. If, by fortuitous happenstance, a set of genes stumbles on to the right attributes, enabling it to create an organism which, in turn, lives to make and pass on more copies of the genes, then all those copies will also share the original successful trait and have an improved chance of making copies themselves. And so on. The process works as well for autonomous creatures, like you and me, as for a virus which invades a host organism and uses *it* to serve as a tool for replication.

This is but a crude summary of phenomena Dawkins depicts so well. But for us it is simply a prelude to Dawkins' next step, when he discussed different bundles of *information* with similar traits. *Not* genes, but *memes*.

Memes are raw ideas. Pure concepts which, like conquering genetic codes, seem capable of thriving in and via host organisms, this time *human minds*. What would such a 'living idea' be like? Well, for one thing it would survive by *making its host think about it*. In contemplating a concept, you in effect keep it alive. For example, some time ago I read a notion – the very one we're discussing now – the notion of memes. You could say this idea was successful at 'infecting' me, because I've continued thinking about it, giving it continued existence, or 'life'.

But a virus or bacterium that just sits inside its host doesn't accomplish much. An effective pseudo-organism must do more. It must reproduce.

How would a *living idea* proliferate? By getting its host not only to think about it, but to make and spread copies . . . by telling other people! And now, if you've been paying attention, you'll realise that's just what I've been doing the last few minutes for one particular meme . . . the meme of memes! By telling you about it, I am doing the memic equivalent of coughing on you. Infecting you with the transmissible, self-replicating *notion* of these infectious ideas. If it's a successful self-replicating notion, some of you will go out and tell others about it. And so on.

(It's amusingly recursive, no? You could go round and round with this. Enjoy!)

Of course this is not the first time such a thing has happened. Life would be dull to impossible if we didn't share ideas, while constantly mutating and adapting them to our purposes. But let's imagine some of these self-reproducing ideas pick up *more* attributes. What if one of them helped its host become prosperous, charismatic, or influential – to spread the meme more effectively. Or what if another meme caused its host, or host tribe, to keep *other* memes *out*. To expose their children only to old, familiar ideas. What a powerful trick that would be!

Does that sound like some bizarre science fiction scenario?

Or is it, rather, a pretty good model for what's been going on throughout most of human history? Examples abound, Take the dogmatic exclusion rule of most religions, which call competing idea systems 'heresy'. One of the Iranian Ayatollahs once said of America, 'We don't fear your bombs, we fear your pagan ideas.' Why did he say such a thing? Dawkins' theory seems to offer as good an explanation as any.

Memes can even wage war on one another. To illustrate the point, let me paint a rather unconventional picture of our familiar world.

Until recently, four major memes battled over the future of this planet. These four combating *zeitgeists* had little to do with those superficial, pompous slogan mills people have gotten lathered about during this century – communism, capitalism, Christianity, Islam. There are deeper, older themes which continue to set the tone for entire civilisations.

Machismo is the most powerful world-view – the leading meme – in many parts of the world. Wherever women are stifled and vengeance is touted as a primary virtue, wherever skill and craftsmanship are downgraded in favour of 'strutting' and male-bonded loyalty groups, it's a good bet machismo sets the agenda.

Don't underrate it! Throughout human history, macho was an effective way of running small clans. Countless stirring, heroic epics come down to us from such tribes, and the inevitable ferment was tolerable when human numbers were small. Different versions of machismo today dominate regions, even continents, conveyed across generations by myths children absorb at an early age. For example, in one Middle-Eastern culture, nearly every fairy tale focuses on one theme – that of revenge. In another land, *mothers* are known to sit their little sons on their knees and say, 'Someday you will deflower virgins and ravish other men's wives, but if this happens to your wife or sister, cut her throat.'

This may sound bizarre to some of you, but it would be a mistake to dismiss it as an aberration. As world-views go, machismo has a long tradition – a lot longer than ours. The biggest argument against this meme is not that any alternative is intrinsically better . . . only that, if it wins, the Earth will surely die.

Then there's *Paranoia*, a second venerable family of memes. One can understand the Russian tradition of xenophobia, given their history of suffering terrible invasions, on average twice a century. Still, that world-view of dour suspicion and bludgeoning distrust made for a brittle, capricious superpower that was worsened by a deluding, superficial dogma, communism. If paranoia had won, or even lasted much longer, the world would probably have become a cinder sooner or later. We'll see, in the course of the next decade, if this meme really is fading. Watch how the other three culture families devour its remains, as some parts of the empire hurry to join the West, some tumble into the Macho orbit, and still others become *Eastern* with stunning rapidity.

That third world-view, which I call 'The East', is one zeitgeist that is demonstrably both traditional and sane . . . after its fashion. During most of recorded history it was the dominant world-view on this planet. Its theme: homogeneity, uniformity, respect for elders, discipline and hard work. Through myths and fairy tales and upbringing, the belief was spread that people should subsume their sense of self in favour of family, group, nation. One can see how such a meme would make governing large populations easier. Capital is not wasted on male strutting, or excessively on arms. Stoical labour and compound interest have a chance to work wonders.

If the East wins, you will probably have some preservation of the environment, some pandas and trees. Humans might eventually – slowly – get out into space.

But when or if we ever meet aliens, we would not understand them. Because by then the very notion of diversity, let alone finding it attractive, will have been extinguished.

I wouldn't find it much fun living in a human civilisation dominated by sameness. But then, if I'd been brought up differently, I might not think 'fun' such a fundamental desideratum, after all. (In many languages there is no word for the concept.) In any

event, the Eastern world-view is the only one with a
proven track record, operating civilisations for millennia in a manner that, while despotic, was calm and
decent in its way.

'Calm' is the *last* word you would use to describe
the fourth meme, one which has always been a minor
theme, carried by an eccentric minority in each culture
. . . until ours. What is the fourth meme? You've heard
me call it the *dogma of otherness*. A world-view that
actually encourages an appetite for newness, hunger for
diversity, eagerness for change. Tolerance plays a major
role in the legends spread by this culture, plus a tradition of humorous self-criticism. (Look at the underlying
message contained in most situation comedies. It is
always the most intolerant or pompous character who
gets comeuppance before the final curtain.)

A second thread, pervading countless films and
novels, is *suspicion of authority*. A plethora of writers
in Hollywood and elsewhere have worked this vein,
each of them acting as if he or she invented rebellious
individualism – an ironic twist, since each of them
was raised on myths extolling solitary defiance! You
can earn a good living as an iconoclast in the West
today, especially if you make it entertaining. But *never*
admit that iconoclasm was the mother's milk you were
raised on.*

No one seems to have noticed how odd this message
is, as *propaganda*. Name one other culture in history that
ever spread a myth like Steven Spielberg's movie *E.T.*,

---

* At first sight, it seems I'm breaking that rule here, just as I'm
disobeying the apparent taboo *against optimism*. But, in fact, I am
simply doing my iconoclastic bit, by finding an empty niche to
fill – optimism in a world rife with pessimists. It lets me be
different, which is the same goal sought by all of my peers and
competitors! It is my own way of criticising, heckling, throwing
stones at authority.

in which a generation of children were taught – 'If you ever encounter a weird stranger from an alien race, by all means, *hide* him from your tribe's freely elected elders!'

A strange, unprecedented meme. One which encourages an art form as compulsively questioning as science fiction, and which, in turn, is spread quite effectively *by* science fiction. No longer is the emphasis on looking to the past, or on conformity as a principal virtue. In olden times, in societies where few ruled many, aristocracies used to rally the masses by pointing to some outside threat and whipping up paranoia. One sees similar efforts taking place today, in vain efforts to combat otherness, but these are futile for the most part, because the rich and powerful no longer control this new myth. They, too, are along for the ride.

Perhaps what we are seeing is nothing other than the development of the world's first *multicellular* meme. The first in which *exclusion* has turned into *inclusion*. The first to welcome challenges, because challenge encourages growth.

It would be an exaggeration to state that this theme I call Otherness 'owns' territories like Europe or America . . . or even California. Where it is strongest, it must still contend ceaselessly with macho, paranoiac, homogenising, and other traditional forces, over the minds and actions of women and men. What we can say, however, is that Otherness has become powerful in *the official morality* of these nations. Look at the vocabulary used in most debates over issues concerning the public. Both sides generally wrap themselves in emotion-laden terms such as 'tolerance', 'privacy', 'choice' or 'individual rights'. And absolutely everybody, right or left, is suspicious of government!

Even more important is the deeply utopian notion, shared by millions, that our institutions can and must

be improvable, and that active criticism is one of the
best ways to elicit change.

Or that 'I might be wrong', is a statement any adult
is made better by saying, aloud or in private.

Or that a golden age is not to be found in ancient
tomes, but in a wiser tomorrow.

Or that it is possible – and desirable – for children
to learn from the mistakes of their parents, and for our
descendants to be better than ourselves.

Now the bonus question . . . do I take this seriously?
Are four 'world-views' really at war over the future of
human civilisation and the planet?

Of course not. It's only a model. My job is to spin
entertaining metaphors, and you went along with this
one. (At least, if you read this far.) Still, I've thought
of an amusing experiment you might play, using these
four protagonists. Try to picture what might happen if
extraterrestrials landed in a macho culture, or a paranoid
one, or in the East.

You get three wildly different scenarios, don't you?
Now go one step further and imagine alien contact with
people brought up in the fourth way I've described –
under the Dogma of Otherness.

Forget Hollywood pathos about mean, nasty CIA
types and trigger-happy rednecks. Those guilt-tripping
movies have been partly responsible for seeing to it that
that sort of schmaltz *won't* happen. Rather, picture a
flying saucer setting down in a parking lot in today's
California. The National Guard encircles the vessel
. . . to *protect* our alien visitors from novelty seekers,
reporters, talk show hosts, talent agents, and hordes
seeking to have their consciousness expanded!

The jury is still out whether Otherness-fetishism is
any saner than older ways. There is no proof it will,
or should, win in the end. Yet I know where I stand.

My upbringing cannot help coming out in my writing, in hoping readers of my books come away each time feeling just a bit more tolerant, more future-oriented, more eager for diversity and change.

So we reach the end of this rambling odyssey. Returning to the beginning, I claim to be no more than a witch doctor who chants and incants strange notions into the heads of those who pay him for the service. Some of the smoke-images I wove may provoke odd images, tomorrow or in the future. If so, excellent. For in this tribe of ours, we all do love new thoughts.

But it's not necessary. I've been paid. You have dreamed. Our deal is done.

Do come back next time you want a little more magic.

Now sleep.

EARTH

David Brin

It's fifty years from tomorrow, and a black hole has accidentally fallen into the Earth's core.

A team of scientists frantically searches for a way to prevent the mishap from causing harm, only to discover *another* black hole already feeding relentlessly at the core – one that could destroy the entire planet within two years.

But some even argue that the only way to save the Earth is to let its human inhabitants become extinct: to let the million-year evolutionary clock rewind and start all over again.

From an underground lab in New Zealand to a space station in Low Earth Orbit, from an endangered-species conservation ark in Africa to a home in New Orleans, *Earth* is a gripping novel peopled with extraordinary characters and abundant with challenging new ideas.

AN ORBIT BOOK
SCIENCE FICTION

GLORY SEASON

David Brin

Stratos – colonized by pioneering women and run by
matriarchal clans – is home to Maia and Leie. Although
raised in the Lamai clan, they are at the age where they
must make their way in the world, sailing the vast seas in
the boats that are the province of the mysterious men of
Stratos. For Maia and Leie are not Lamai. They are not
the product of parthenogenesis, clones of their mother.
They are summer babies, born of the union of a man and a
woman, restless and adventurous.

And Stratos offers adventure, for this is a time of uneasiness
and change. There are confirmed rumours of spacecraft
heading towards the planet, and the turmoil and confusion
this news generates offers the resourceful Maia a
challenge she is equipped and ready to respond to.

Glory Season is a rich, thought-provoking and important
novel from the internationally acclaimed author of *Earth*
and *The Postman*.

AN ORBIT BOOK
SCIENCE FICTION

THE HAMMER OF GOD

Arthur C. Clarke

It is an amateur astronomer on Mars who first spots the
previously uncharted asteroid, falling sunwards. And when
the scientists of project SPACEGUARD compute its orbit,
they christen it Kali – the Hindu goddess of destruction.

It is 2109, sixty-five million years since the reign of the
reptiles was ended. And now Kali threatens a similar fate
for mankind. As Captain of the research vessel *Goliath*,
Robert Singh is in charge of an operation that has been
long planned but never before put into action – the
immense task of pushing an asteroid off its course. But
even the most meticulous planning cannot anticipate
the human factor.

With superb storytelling and authentic science, *The Hammer
of God* is vintage Clarke.

AN ORBIT BOOK
SCIENCE FICTION

☐	Earth	David Brin	£6.99
☐	Glory Season	David Brin	£5.99
☐	The Hammer of God	Arthur C. Clarke	£4.99
☐	Feersum Endjinn	Iain M. Banks	£5.99
☐	China Mountain Zhang	Maureen F. McHugh	£5.99
☐	The Encyclopedia of Science Fiction	John Clute and Peter Nicholls	£45.00

Orbit now offers an exciting range of quality titles by both established and new authors. All of the books in this series are available from:

Little, Brown and Company (UK),
P.O. Box 11,
Falmouth,
Cornwall TR10 9EN.

Alternatively you may fax your order to the above address.
Fax No. 0326 376423.

Payments can be made as follows: cheque, postal order (payable to Little, Brown and Company) or by credit cards, Visa/Access. Do not send cash or currency. UK customers and B.F.P.O. please allow £1.00 for postage and packing for the first book, plus 50p for the second book, plus 30p for each additional book up to a maximum charge of £3.00 (7 books plus).

Overseas customers including Ireland, please allow £2.00 for the first book plus £1.00 for the second book, plus 50p for each additional book.

NAME (Block Letters) ....

....

ADDRESS ....

....

....

☐ I enclose my remittance for ....

☐ I wish to pay by Access/Visa Card

Number ☐☐☐☐☐☐☐☐☐☐☐☐☐☐☐☐☐☐

Card Expiry Date ☐☐☐☐